'A crime thriller with the lot: murder, deceit, corruption and a hint of romance . . . Ayliffe takes you deep inside the worlds of politics and the media, with a heavy dose of international intrigue thrown in.'
Michael Rowland

'A thriller ripped straight from the headlines.'
Sydney Morning Herald

'Bailey proves nothing is more dangerous than a man who can fall no further. An absolute cracker of a thriller.'
Chris Uhlmann

'Action-packed scenes . . . as tight as any novel from the likes of David Baldacci or Lee Child.'
Glam Adelaide

'Who needs Jason Bourne when you can have John Bailey?'
Chris Bath

'If Rake were a journalist, with a talent that equals his capacity to survive being beaten up, Bailey would be him.'
Julia Baird

Praise for *The Enemy Within*

'A cracking yarn told at breakneck speed. I couldn't put it down.'
Chris Hammer

'Sharp, gritty, sophisticated. Ayliffe's criminal world is terrifyingly real.'
Candice Fox

'A breathlessly written book, ripped from today's headlines, this is a cracking read that blurs the line between fact and fiction. More please.'
Michael Robotham

Also by Tim Ayliffe
The Greater Good
The Enemy Within
Killer Traitor Spy

TIM AYLIFFE

STATE OF FEAR

SIMON &
SCHUSTER

London · New York · Sydney · Toronto · New Delhi

STATE OF FEAR
First published in Australia in 2019 by
Simon & Schuster (Australia) Pty Limited
Level 4, 32 York St, Sydney NSW 2000
This edition published in 2023

10 9 8 7 6 5 4

New York Amsterdam/Antwerp London Toronto Sydney New Delhi
Visit our website at www.simonandschuster.com.au

© Tim Ayliffe 2019

A catalogue record for this
book is available from the
National Library of Australia

ISBN: 9781925640960

Cover design: Luke Causby/Blue Cork
Cover image: Evelina Kremsdorf/Trevillion Images
Typeset by Midland Typesetters, Australia
Printed and bound in Australia by Griffin Press

The paper this book is printed on is certified against the
Forest Stewardship Council® Standards. Griffin Press holds
chain of custody certification SCS-COC-001185. FSC®
promotes environmentally responsible, socially beneficial
and economically viable management of the world's forests.

This book is dedicated to my Mum and Dad

You can't reach good ends through evil means,
because the means represent the seed
and the end represents the tree.

Martin Luther King Jr, 1967

CHAPTER 1

LONDON

'Any questions?'

John Bailey was standing behind a podium looking out warily over the packed conference room.

'Anyone?'

Bailey had been invited to Chatham House to give a speech about Islamic terrorism because his experiences as a former Middle East Correspondent were unique. He had been kidnapped and tortured by extremists in Iraq.

Some of the people in the crowd looked even more relieved than he was that the speech was over. Most were already on their feet, heading for the exit where his editor from *The Journal*, Gerald Summers, was schmoozing with a woman from British intelligence.

He stepped down from the podium and started weaving his way towards the back of the room. By the time he got there it was clear that something was wrong.

'What're you doing? Move!' A man rammed his shoulder into Bailey's chest. 'Don't go outside, it's not safe!'

'Take it easy, fella.' Bailey patted the guy on the shoulder, trying to calm him down. 'What's happened?'

The guy was already gone, pushing his way towards the other side of the room.

Bailey turned his attention towards the commotion at the door. The people who'd left Chatham House were streaming back inside. Panicked, running from something, or someone.

Bailey went against the tide, heading for the big blue door. Old habit.

'Excuse me. Excuse me, please.'

He made it to the entrance and hugged the doorframe until he spotted a gap, slipping outside into the dim afternoon light. A misty rain was falling, bathing the ground in a shiny slick, reflecting the grey sky above.

'Get back! Get back!'

A policeman was standing on the edge of the footpath, his hands outstretched, ordering people to move away.

'Everybody, get back! Get back, now!'

The cop was barking orders at the crowd while keeping one eye on the cause of the commotion on the edge of St James's Square.

A man dressed in a black hoodie and jeans, a woman kneeling at his feet.

The man was holding her by the hair, yanking it backwards, and waving a large knife at the people who had decided not to run. His audience. Some of them had mobile phones, filming the violent scene unfolding in front of them. Others stood with mouths wide-open, feet frozen to the concrete, their fear sailing through the crowd like a rampant ghost.

'Please . . . please. No.'

The woman was desperately pleading for her life.

'Shut up!' The man screamed at her, before turning his attention back to the crowd. 'For the bombs, the bullets and the occupation of our lands!'

He had a thick North London accent. Bailey couldn't quite make out the colour of his skin because of the shadow of the hoodie on his face.

'Put down the knife.' The policeman stepped towards him. 'It doesn't need to be this way. You don't want to do anything stupid.'

'You're the criminal, not me!'

Bailey recognised the woman on her knees. She had been at the conference, one of the earnest faces that had watched him deliver his speech. She looked like she was aged around forty. Black overcoat, navy suit, scarf torn away, lying on the road beside her.

'Please, don't do this. Please! I have children. I have –'

'Shut up!'

'Don't!' The policeman edged closer. 'Don't do it.'

The man raised the knife again, pointing it at the sky. 'The war is here! Allahu Akbar!'

He plunged the knife into the woman's throat, sending a spray of blood onto the road, cutting deep, until the blood was rushing down her chest, transforming the colour of her dress from blue to purple. She slumped to the ground, a large pool of blood gathering around her head and shoulders in a dark, contorted halo. Bailey studied her face, her vacant stare, as the dark pool expanded, slowly, on the bitumen – the life flowing out of her – eventually touching the foot of her killer.

The policeman turned back to the crowd of horrified onlookers, his face the colour of ash.

'Get back, all of you!'

He looked like he was fresh out of the academy. The poor bastard didn't even carry a gun. Hardly any British police did. His only weapon was the heavy baton that he was clutching, tightly, in his right hand.

He turned back to the man in the hoodie. 'Put down the knife! This is your last chance. Put down the knife!'

The man in the hoodie pointed at the small gathering of people on the steps at Chatham House. 'You want to know about terrorism? Look at yourselves!'

A grey BMW four-wheel drive skidded to a stop on the northern corner of St James's Square. The doors flew open, four men jumped out, dressed in black with helmets, ballistic vests and semi-automatic rifles. Members of the London Metropolitan Police's Counter Terrorism Command known as SO15. The rapid response team whose sole purpose was stopping terrorists. Bailey knew these guys. He'd seen them take down a cell in London back in 2005. Within seconds, they were fanning out across the street, the butts of their rifles locked on their shoulders, fingers on triggers, muzzles pointed at the man in the hoodie.

'Put down the weapon!' one of them yelled.

The bloke with the knife turned his head towards the guns now trained on him, then back at the people on the footpath.

'You will all see! You will pay for what you do!'

He was waving his knife at the people watching, some of them still filming. Videos that would later be used as cheap, effective propaganda by terrorist recruiters online.

'For the last time, put down the knife!'

The man lowered the blade, stepping over the woman's body, moving towards the crowd.

'You're all slaves!'

The armed police edged closer, their hundreds of hours of training ensuring that they moved as one.

The man took another step towards the footpath, pulling his hoodie back off his head. Bailey was less than ten metres away. He had a clear view of his face. Young. Anglo. Red hair. Freckles. Barely a man. A crazed look in his bloodshot eyes. Bailey had seen eyes like that before. Militia fighters pumped up on amphetamines. Another place. Another time. The same hateful ideology.

'Don't do it, mate,' the policeman with the baton in his hand said. 'Just put down the knife.'

4

'Don't do it!' Bailey heard himself call out.

The young man looked at Bailey, like he knew him, holding his stare. Smiling.

'Don't,' Bailey tried again. 'It's not worth it.'

The man turned away, surveying the crowd until he found what he was looking for – a kid holding a smartphone, filming the show. He lifted the knife again, shoulder height, and ran directly towards him.

POP! POP! POP! POP! POP! POP! POP! POP!

The police opened fire, their bullets pounding into his chest, the impact slamming him to the ground. They moved in quickly, one of them kicking away the knife from his hand, sending it scuttling across the road. There was no resistance. He was already dead.

The policeman with the baton ran over to the woman on the ground. She still hadn't moved. Down on one knee, he touched her neck, desperate for a way to bring her back to life. It was useless. Both carotid arteries had been severed. She was gone.

'Bailey!' A hand landed on Bailey's shoulder and he spun around, startled.

Gerald.

'What on earth just happened?'

Bailey said nothing, turning back to the two bodies on the road.

The crowd started building again. People were coming back outside from Chatham House, the East India Club, the London Library and the other buildings that surrounded the square. He could hear the sounds of sirens in the distance. Getting louder. Closer.

A policeman was talking to the kid with the smartphone, asking him about the video and if he had broadcast it live. The kid was nodding his head. He had. He didn't know why.

A teenage punter with a smartphone, the unwitting producer of a terrorist snuff film.

'Bailey?' Gerald tried again. 'Bailey, are you okay?'

'Another one.'

'What?'

'Another lost kid, brainwashed by these bastards.'

'It's a bloody –'

'And that woman.' Bailey pointed at the body a few metres from where the young man was lying, riddled with bullets, on the road. 'She was here for the conference. I remember seeing her inside.'

'Bloody hell,' Gerald said. 'You're kidding.'

'No. I'm not.'

Poor woman, thought Bailey. One of her last experiences was having to sit through his crappy speech on one of those uncomfortable red chairs.

'I've got this covered, guys.' Candice Simmons appeared beside them.

Simmons was the young reporter Gerald had sent to London to replace Bailey after his breakdown. He knew her type and he didn't like her.

'I've already fired off a tweet and spoken to the desk.'

'Thanks, Candice,' Gerald said.

'What'd you see?' Bailey said.

'Enough.'

Simmons was ambitious. Bailey didn't have a problem with that, as long as it didn't get in the way of the truth. Not everyone was looking for the truth these days.

'Like I said, I've got this,' she said.

'You can take the aftermath. The investigation. I'm going to tell people what happened.'

'Now, hang on!'

Bailey stared at her. 'Where were you?'

'Inside.'

'Then you didn't see what happened.'

'No, but videos will be online within seconds.' She pointed at the crowd of people, many of them with heads bowed, staring into their phones. 'I'm the correspondent and –'

'And what?' Bailey looked at Gerald, waiting for him to intervene.

Gerald Summers was *The Journal*'s editor. It was his call.

'What did you see, Bailey?'

Too much.

'Everything.'

Bailey looked Gerald in the eyes, taking a moment to reassure his old friend that he had this.

'Candice,' Gerald turned to Simmons, 'Bailey does the lead. The blow by blow on the ground. The first-person about the shit show that he saw.'

'But –'

'Decision's made. Get moving.'

Simmons nodded her head and shot Bailey a fuck-you glare. There wasn't time to argue. A policeman was preparing to say something to a small gathering of reporters who were already yelling questions from the footpath. Candice headed in their direction.

'You sure you're okay with this, Bailey?'

'Why wouldn't I be?' Bailey didn't like what Gerald was suggesting. 'What do you want? A thousand words?'

'Whatever you need. Quick as you can.' Gerald looked at his watch. 'It's the middle of the night in Sydney. I'm going to organise another print run for metros.'

CHAPTER 2

John Bailey never missed a deadline. Not when it mattered.

Within an hour, Bailey's eyewitness account had gone global. Job done.

The bodies of the killer and his victim had already been removed from the road and the crowds were starting to disperse.

It was time to go.

'The only thing left is the identity of the attacker,' Candice said. 'I've got a source at the Yard on that front.'

'Thanks, Candice. Give me a call if you need me.' Gerald turned to Bailey. 'Hungry?'

'I just want to get out of here.' Bailey stepped closer to Gerald so that Simmons was out of earshot. 'And a friendly warning: I'm not up for the long debrief, okay?'

Bailey had seen a lot of bad shit over the years as a war reporter bouncing in and out of places like Beirut, Jerusalem, Afghanistan and Iraq, and his post-traumatic stress disorder had a habit of rearing its ugly head. He may have been back doing the job that made him tick, but violence was his trigger. He knew it. Gerald knew it too.

'Okay, mate,' Gerald said. 'Fine by me.'

Bailey had also done enough talking for one day. An hour standing on his own in front of an audience at Chatham House was plenty. He'd been invited to talk to Britain's security services about the world's most wanted terrorist, Mustafa al-Baghdadi, the leader of the Islamic Nation group. Gerald had said it'd be good PR for the paper and a good way for Bailey to debrief. Or, so he'd thought.

Bailey was also the only western journalist to have talked face to face with Mustafa al-Baghdadi. It had been almost fifteen years since Bailey had woken up, tied to a chair, somewhere in Northern Iraq. The people sitting on the red chairs at Chatham House hadn't come to listen to Bailey tell stories about how he'd been bashed and tortured. They were only interested in everything he could tell them about Islamic Nation and its leader.

Mustafa al-Baghdadi's violent militia was getting hammered by the United States and its allies in Syria and Iraq, where Islamic Nation's so-called 'caliphate' was shrinking by the day. Mustafa had responded by taking his war to the cities and suburbs of the western world, orchestrating dozens of terrorist attacks – suicide bombings, gun massacres, stabbings – killing thousands of innocent people. Authorities everywhere were desperate to stop him.

Bailey had told the audience that Mustafa would never stop. That despite all the killing, he believed that God was on his side. For Mustafa, the world was at the beginning of a centuries-long war. A battle for ideas. And his sickness was spreading.

Gerald followed Bailey into the Piccadilly Circus Underground and onto the long escalator that took them under the city. At the bottom, they veered left into a dust-smeared tunnel and onto the first train that turned up on the Piccadilly Line platform, heading west.

By the time they got off the tube at Hammersmith, Bailey was on edge. He hadn't had a drink in ninety-two days and a whisky was all he could think about. The warm brown liquid used to calm him. Help him forget. Until he'd lost control.

Bailey had barely spoken to Gerald since they'd left St James's Square. His mind had been elsewhere, thinking back over what had happened at Chatham House. Something wasn't right. It wasn't just that a woman had been murdered, or even that Islamic Nation had already claimed responsibility for the attack. It was the look that the killer had given Bailey before he charged into a hail of police gunfire. Their eyes had met. A moment of familiarity. That smile. The killer had recognised Bailey. But how?

'You did a good job back there,' Gerald said. 'With the speech, I mean. You did well with the speech.'

Bailey turned left towards the river. It would be light for another hour or so, and the streets were bustling with people, many of them in a hurry to order that first pint at one of the pubs along the Thames. Drink away the sadness of another senseless killing on the streets of London. The story would have been plastered all over the internet by now, along with amateur videos of violence to shock and share. It's all they'd be talking about. Again.

'Bailey?'

'Did I, Gerald?' Bailey said, without breaking his stride. 'Wouldn't say it was the most memorable part of the afternoon, though. Would you?'

Bailey was keeping a steady pace, without once looking at Gerald.

'Okay, Bailey. I give up. Where're we headed, then?'

'A pub.'

'You sure that's a good idea?'

Gerald had teamed up with Bailey's partner, Sharon Dexter, to confront him about his drinking. It was mainly Dexter's idea. Her ultimatum. Whisky had become the third wheel in their relationship. It had to go. Bailey knew that his life was better with Dexter in it, so he hadn't put up a fight. He had been doing well these past few months. He'd even been to a few Alcoholics Anonymous meetings and got himself a sponsor.

'Bailey?'

Bailey stopped walking and grabbed Gerald by the coat, pulling him close. 'Who gives a fuck about my speech!'

'Bailey, I didn't mean –'

'I just saw a woman bleed-out on the street and a brainwashed kid gunned down! You want to talk about a fucking speech?'

'I'm sorry.' Gerald stepped back, palms in the air. 'I was just trying to –'

'Trying to what? What were you trying to do?'

'I don't know, Bailey. Maybe, get you to talk like a normal person? Get inside that closed mind of yours, check that you're okay?' Gerald paused, his voice softening. 'We've been here before, mate.'

Bailey let go of Gerald's coat, patting the creases with his hands. 'Yeah, well. Consider me checked.'

'Really?'

Gerald was one of the few people that Bailey listened to. He owed him more.

'Really, I'm good.'

'It's all fine, Bailey.' Gerald straightened his collar. 'We don't need to talk about it. Our flight's at six o'clock in the morning. Let's just get something to eat and have an early night.'

'That's exactly what I had in mind,' Bailey said. 'I know a place.'

'Welcome to my favourite watering hole,' Bailey said when they arrived at an old brick building with a sign out front: 'The Dove: The home of London's best bangers and mash.'

He led them down the side of the pub, away from the river, and through the back door.

'Chester.' Bailey nodded at the guy with flushed cheeks behind the bar and sat down on one of the three wooden stools that filled the tiny room.

'John Bailey.' Chester looked surprised as he reached across the beer taps, shaking Bailey's hand. 'Been a while. How the bloody hell are you?'

'Good, mate.' Bailey slapped Gerald on the chest with the back of his hand. 'This is Gerald Summers. The most powerful newspaper editor in Australia.'

Chester laughed and extended his hand to Gerald, who was shaking his head, embarrassed and slightly irritated.

'So, lads. What're we having, then?'

'Lemonade for me. Gerald?'

'Make that two.'

Chester chortled through his nose and dropped two tumblers on the bar.

'I was serious about the lemonade, mate,' Bailey said.

'Really?'

'Really.'

'Off the drink, then?'

'Nothing gets past you, Chester.' Bailey said. 'Meet the new me.'

'Nice place you've got here,' Gerald said, trying to steer the subject away from Bailey's old habit.

'Smallest bar in the world, right, Chester?'

Seeing the bartender had lifted Bailey's mood.

'You got it, Bailey.' Chester was beaming. 'Or, so says the Guinness Book of Records.'

'Hemingway drank here too.'

'Really?' Gerald couldn't tell if they were joking.

'As sure as the sun also rises,' Chester said.

'Clever.' Bailey took a sip of his lemonade. 'This tastes like shit, thanks Ernest. Back in a minute. Boys' room.'

Chester's eyes followed Bailey until he disappeared around the corner.

'He really off the drink, then?' Chester said.

'Yeah.'

'Probably not a bad idea. The last time Bailey was here, I found him asleep on the floor of the gents when I was cleaning up. Wasn't pretty.'

'I've been around the block with Bailey a few times,' Gerald said. 'He wasn't lying. He's off it.'

Two minutes later, Bailey sat back on his stool. 'Stop talking about me. And Chester? Get us a menu, would you? You know what I'm having, but Gerald might want something fancy.'

Chester slid a menu across the bar for Gerald.

'Give it a break, Bailey,' Gerald said.

'Sorry, mate. Drinking and giving you a hard time have been my two favourite pastimes. You can't expect me to give both of them away.' Bailey winked at Chester. 'Why don't you pour yourself one of those expensive whiskies you've got hidden under the bar. One of us needs to enjoy a drink tonight. Gerald, give Chester your card.'

'You're a pain in the arse sometimes, you know that?'

'So they say.'

CHAPTER 3

Spending too much time at a place like The Dove was dangerous. It reminded Bailey of the bad old days when he would drink his way through the day, from the moment he got up in the morning until he was so wasted that he could almost forget all the shocking things he'd seen. Now he had two more for the pile. The kid with the knife and that poor woman in the blue dress who had died in a pool of her own blood.

Bailey knew that Gerald would want to stay close to him tonight. They'd been through three wars in three decades of friendship. Iraq, Afghanistan and then Iraq again. Gerald had been on assignment with Bailey in Fallujah when he was kidnapped by Mustafa al-Baghdadi's Islamic fundamentalists back in 2004.

The only other battle they'd experienced together was the one they never talked about. Gerald was the person who'd found Bailey, passed out, drunk and defeated, in London. When Bailey was at rock bottom. When being alive didn't matter so much anymore.

But right now Bailey needed to get out of The Dove. Get some fresh air. A walk to process the day. Alone. Gerald would forgive him for skipping out. He always did.

'Hey Chester,' Bailey said to the bartender when Gerald went to the toilet. 'Tell Gerald I'll meet him in the hotel lobby at three-thirty in the morning.'

Chester raised an eyebrow. 'Three-thirty?'

'On the six am back to Sydney, mate. I didn't book it.'

'All right, then,' Chester said. 'And Bailey?'

'Yeah?'

'If you don't mind me saying, it's good to see you back on your feet.'

'Never stopped walking, old boy.' Bailey slipped off his stool. 'Thanks for the bangers.'

After crossing to the other side of the Thames via Hammersmith Bridge, Bailey hit an old dirt track that he knew ran along the river for miles. Apart from the odd evening jogger, he would have the path all to himself. He could think, collect himself, remember how far the rehabilitation of John Bailey had come and all the things he stood to lose if he gave up.

Top of that list were his 28-year-old daughter, Miranda, and Bailey's girlfriend, the police detective, Sharon Dexter. The two women that he'd once left behind so that he could chase the adrenalin of war. Bailey and Miranda were in a good place and although things had been a little rocky with Dexter in the past, he wasn't about to risk going off the rails because of what he'd seen at St James's Square. Rock bottom was a lonely place and he wasn't going back there. Not again.

There wasn't much of a moon and the path was growing darker with every step. Despite the afternoon drizzle, the canopy of trees that lined the path had kept the track relatively dry, and the dirt was crunching, loudly, against the soles of Bailey's boots.

On the other side of the river, huddles of people were chatting under clouds of cigarette smoke outside the pubs, the hum of their conversations floating across the water. The only other sounds were the occasional splashes from fish, or birds, in the water, and small animals – rats or squirrels, most likely – rustling in the leaves.

Bailey had been walking for almost half an hour when he noticed someone on the track behind him. By the sound of their feet, he guessed they were at least thirty metres back. They didn't appear to be getting any closer. He didn't bother turning around. It was probably just someone out enjoying a walk. Barnes Bridge, where he'd planned to cross the river and circle back to Chiswick, was just up ahead.

He climbed the steps onto the bridge and was midway across when he noticed the footsteps following him. Now he wanted to know who was back there. Get a glimpse of their face. Reassure his already rattled mind. He stopped, leaning on the rail, pretending to take in the view up the river.

The shadow at the other end of the bridge paused, before starting again towards him. Bailey could see that it was a man, dressed in an overcoat, wearing a hat that looked like a fedora, carrying a cane. By his steady stride, the cane looked like it was for another purpose.

Bailey felt his heart start racing, a tingle in his spine.

He called out, trying to ease the tension, when the man was within earshot. 'Nice night for a walk.'

'Indeed. Good evening.'

The man tapped the brim of his hat and paused, briefly, before continuing along the bridge.

Bailey watched the man disappear into the trees. He stared at the water for another minute so that his heart could return to its standard beat, before resuming his walk. The paranoia had left him feeling stupid.

He made it to the other side of the bridge, stepping carefully down the large rocks that had been positioned as stairs, and headed north-east along the riverbank. In about ten minutes, he'd make a left turn into the underpass at Hogarth Roundabout towards Chiswick High Road, where he'd get a train back to his hotel in

Paddington. He could already smell the hops burning at the old Fuller's brewery on the edge of the A4.

The pathway was more difficult to navigate on this side of the river. More like a dirt track beaten into the riverbank by the random flow of footprints. He was taking it slow, careful not to trip on the uneven ground in the darkness.

A stick cracked on the path behind him.

Bailey stopped, turning around. Another shadow was heading his way. He could tell it was a man by the way that he moved. Athletic, strong build, jogging skilfully along the track.

Bailey's heart sped up, his skittishness returning, wondering whether it was just another local enjoying an evening jaunt, like the guy in the fedora.

Something didn't feel right.

There was no way that Bailey could traverse the track as quickly as the bloke behind him, so he stepped to the side to let him pass.

Only, he didn't pass.

'Are you John Bailey?'

The words almost caused Bailey to fall over.

'Are *you* John Bailey?' He repeated the question, more forcefully, stepping closer.

'Yeah.'

'I have a message for you.'

Bailey couldn't see the guy's face clearly in the darkness, but he could tell that he was young. Early twenties, at most, wearing a tracksuit and trainers, dressed for a run.

'Have you been following me?' Bailey said, trying to sound composed. 'Who are you?'

The man was fumbling around in the front pocket of his hoodie. Bailey stepped back, his heart racing so fast he could feel the pounding in his ears.

The guy pulled out a piece of paper and handed it to Bailey.

'Mustafa wants to speak to you.'

The name caused Bailey to shudder. 'What?'

'Mustafa al-Baghdadi would like to speak to you.'

Mustafa al-Baghdadi.

'What the hell are you talking about?'

The man looked down at his watch. 'He'll be on that number for exactly forty-nine hours. Then he'll be gone.'

'What does he want?'

He ignored Bailey's question and turned around, jogging back towards Barnes Bridge.

'Hey!' Bailey called after him. 'What does he want?'

The guy was already gone. Blended into the darkness. The track went quiet and all Bailey could hear was the rapid sound of his own breathing.

It was 7.35 pm. He had forty-nine hours to make the call. Or not.

Any normal person would struggle to come up with one good reason why they'd want to speak to a violent terrorist. The journalist in John Bailey had plenty.

CHAPTER 4

MOSUL, 2005

'Get up!'

Bailey could feel a foot digging into his ribs.

'Dog! Get up!'

Lying on the cold stone floor, Bailey had finally managed to get some sleep. He had no idea how long he'd been out, or whether it was night or day.

Slap!

He was awake now, thanks to the sweaty palm of his captor.

Slap!

The man hit him again with his open hand. Harder. At least he was done using his fists. Yesterday's beating was one of the worst. Bailey had no idea what had prompted the violent assault. Not that these guys ever needed a reason.

His hands were tied behind his back, his shoulders were aching, and his lips were lacerated like a well-used breadboard. The swelling pressuring his rib cage was making it difficult to breathe. It was impossible to move without sharp pain.

'Get up!'

Disorientated by the days and nights of beatings, he opened his eyes. All he could see was black. A blindfold was tightly wrapped around his head. He rolled his body towards the voice, trying to sit up. Trying to avoid another beating by men who seemed to enjoy it.

'Give me a –'

'Up!'

A rough hand grabbed him under his armpit, fingers digging into his damaged ribs, pulling him to his feet.

Bailey coughed, trying to clear the dust from his throat. 'Where are we going?'

He knew enough Arabic to ask basic questions and follow orders.

Bailey had been moved so many times during the past few months that he had no idea where he was anymore, and he'd given up trying to learn. The sounds of Iraq were always the same. Sporadic gunfire. Explosions. Car horns. And the voices of the men who had kidnapped him.

'Min huna!'

This way.

The man was leading Bailey across the room, dragging him by the shoulder. He counted ten paces before a door creaked open. The man was behind him now, pushing him forward. Bailey tripped, his knee bashing into a hard stone edge. Stairs.

'Go!'

Struggling back to his feet, Bailey started climbing. Slowly. Even with the blindfold restricting his vision, he could tell that the staircase was narrow. Step by step, spiralling upwards, his shoulders brushing the walls. The man prodded him in the back, keeping him moving. Bailey counted his steps. Thirty-five. Thirty-six. Thirty-seven. After the forty-first step he felt a warm rush of air. Outside.

Engines. Traffic. Birds. A helicopter's rotor blades spinning in the distance.

'Hello, my friend.'

That voice. Posh. Educated. English. The sound of a killer.

The guy who had brought Bailey upstairs untied the restraints on his hands and they flopped by his side, easing the pain in his shoulders. The blindfold was yanked down the back of his head until it came loose, falling around his neck. A wash of white light sent a piercing pain into the back of his eyes, momentarily blinding him. He blinked, rapidly, trying to focus.

Mustafa's head came first. The smiling face of the madman who had orchestrated his kidnapping in Fallujah. The same intense eyes, black robe and beard that Bailey remembered from the first time they'd met.

He looked past Mustafa at the rooftops of the city. It was a place that Bailey knew well.

Mosul.

'How are you feeling?'

Bailey ignored him. He hadn't been outside for weeks, and he was revelling in the fresh air, away from the stink of Mustafa's goons. From where they were standing in Mosul's right bank, the view was mesmerising. Date palms along the mighty Tigris. A barge packed with produce for the market, drifting slowly on the water. Blocks of white and yellow apartments. Clotheslines pegged with symbols of ordinary life. Fields of sun-kissed grass. And the Grand Mosque, its beautiful golden domes glistening in the sun.

There was a long line of cars on the bridge below, where American humvees were blocking the traffic. Bailey could see marines manning some kind of security checkpoint, stopping and searching vehicles before waving them through.

Up here! Here!

Bailey felt like screaming at the soldiers to come rescue him.

They were too far away.

'The Americans will give up soon.' Mustafa had followed

21

Bailey's eyes to the bridge. 'As soon as they realise they can't win. When American mothers grow tired of losing their sons.'

'What do you know about American mothers?'

'A mother's love is the same, wherever you are, John Bailey.'

Mustafa had an annoying habit of addressing Bailey by his full name.

'What the fuck do you want from me?'

'Such anger –'

'Of course I'm fucking angry. What'd you expect? How long's this going to go on?'

After all the beatings, after being forced to watch one of Mustafa's men cut the throat of an American marine, Bailey had been spiralling into a depressive state. He wasn't a journalist anymore. He was someone's prisoner. A prisoner to his own thoughts. Part of him wanted it all to be over. For his life to end. To make it all stop.

But there was still that little voice inside his head, telling him to hang on. The voice of his daughter, almost a woman now. He barely knew her. He needed to stay alive. He needed to make up for lost time because every child needed a father. Even a hopeless one like Bailey.

'What do you want from me?'

'It's good to see you again.'

'Can't say I feel the same. Answer my fucking question.'

'There's so much anger in you, John Bailey. Why?'

'Why don't you go ask the bloke who ripped out my fingernails?'

Mustafa ignored the question and looked down at his watch.

'Come. There's something that I want you to see.' He put his hand around the back of Bailey's neck and walked him to the edge of the rooftop, pointing at the US army checkpoint on the bridge. 'Ask yourself, why are the Americans still here?'

Bailey was confused. 'I'm an Australian journalist, as I keep telling you. I'm not part of this war.'

'Nation building, they say.' Mustafa clearly wasn't interested in anything that Bailey had to say. 'We don't need their nation. Bush, Blair, even your John Howard. They're all crusaders for a decadent way of life that we don't want.'

'What does that have to do with me?'

Mustafa looked at the clock on his wrist again, tightening his grip on the back of Bailey's neck. 'Watch.'

Down on the bridge a marine was pointing his rifle at the window of a car, yelling at the driver, his voice carried by the wind. Moments later, the car was surrounded by more Americans with assault rifles.

A light flashed on the bridge.

Boom!

Bailey could feel the explosion vibrate through his feet.

The car was reduced to a burning shell, flames leaping into a cloud of black and grey. As the smoke cleared, Bailey started counting bodies. Seven. Eight. Maybe more. The bodies of marines lying on the blackened road around the car. The dark silhouette of the suicide bomber sitting upright in the front seat, eerily peaceful. Mission complete.

'A warrior, now seated with God.'

'You did that?'

'This is only the beginning.' Mustafa still had hold of Bailey's neck, whispering in his ear. 'I have an army of men and women ready to give their lives.'

Bailey stared at the ruins on the bridge, trying to make sense of Mustafa's forever war.

The mangled car. The dead. The injured, writhing in agony, their screams bouncing off the stone buildings in a torturous echo.

'What do you want?' Bailey tried again.

Mustafa was so close that Bailey could feel each word on his skin. 'Piece by piece, I want to take back our lands from the infidels. From Mosul to Baghdad, to Damascus. The caliphate is coming.'

CHAPTER 5

SYDNEY

'Mate, wake up.'

Bailey felt a tap on the shoulder.

'We just landed. Time to go.'

Bailey didn't move.

'Come on.'

Gerald was shaking him now, trying to get him to open his eyes.

'All right. All right.'

Bailey sat upright, wiping the drool from his bottom lip with the back of his hand.

'Give me a bloody minute.'

He had only fallen asleep a few hours out from Sydney. He was also unnerved by the fact that Mustafa al-Baghdadi had returned to his dreams. Maybe it was because of his speech. Maybe it was because of what had happened out the front of Chatham House. Or maybe it was because that sadistic prick had told Bailey to call him.

Bailey wasn't game to tell Gerald. He didn't want his friend – and boss – to feel compelled to book him an appointment with another bloody shrink. He'd done his time lying on leather couches, staring at ceilings, spilling his guts to clever doctors with soothing voices.

It had been an unusually long journey home to Sydney. After taking off late from Heathrow, their flight had been delayed for eleven hours in Singapore. Gerald hadn't managed to get much more sleep than Bailey, and the two men were barely talking to each other by the time they were collecting their bags from the carousel in the arrivals hall.

And there was something else bothering Bailey.

'This is bullshit.' Bailey lifted his duffel bag into the back of the taxi. 'What could be so bloody important that we need to go into work?'

'Penelope says it's urgent,' Gerald said. 'That's all I know.'

Penelope. Gerald's personal assistant.

'If it's so urgent why couldn't she tell you more on the phone?'

'I don't know, Bailey! We were trying to get through immigration when she called. Why don't you damn well ask her when you see her in thirty bloody minutes' time!'

Bailey knew he was behaving like a child, but he was so exhausted that he didn't care. They'd only been on the ground in London for around four days and his body clock was all over the shop. He just wanted to get home and fall asleep to the sound of a Rolling Stones record.

Penelope was standing out the front of *The Journal* waiting for them when their taxi pulled up on Sussex Street.

'Okay, out with it.' Bailey started before he had even one foot out of the car. 'As much as I love you, Penelope, it'd better be good.'

The look on Penelope's face made Bailey regret his bluntness.

'There's a man inside asking for you. Says he knew you from Baghdad,' she said. 'I told him that you were due back last night. He's been sitting inside ever since. He won't leave!'

Bailey had spent so much time in Iraq, the man inside could have been anybody. Military. Politician. Kurdish separatist. Journalist. Intelligence agent. Civilian. Security contractor. The list was endless.

'Give a name?'

'Omar someone.'

Bailey knew exactly who was waiting.

'Where is he?'

'Same place he's been all night,' Penelope said, pointing at the big glass doors behind her. 'Foyer.'

Bailey was already on the move before Penelope had finished answering.

A dishevelled man, unshaven, dressed in old jeans and a linen shirt, was sitting on the edge of a sofa near the front desk. His eyes were closed and he was resting his head in the palm of his right hand, his elbow keeping him propped upright as he slept.

'Omar.' Bailey patted him, gently, on the shoulder. 'Omar, wake up. It's Bailey.'

Omar shuddered, briefly, and opened his eyes. He stumbled to his feet, shaking Bailey's hand and leaning in to kiss him on the cheek.

'It has been a while, my friend,' Omar said. 'Too long.'

They'd barely seen each other in twenty years. Omar had lost most of his hair but his dark olive skin had preserved his handsome face. Unlike Bailey, he'd somehow managed to maintain his slim physique. He looked tired and his forehead was creased with worry.

'It's good to see you, old buddy. Is everything okay?'

'No, Bailey.' Omar's voice was trembling. 'Everything's not okay.'

'What is it?'

Omar looked over Bailey's shoulder. There was only Mick, the security guard, sitting at the front desk, out of earshot, and Gerald, who was walking towards them.

'Omar, is that you?'

'Hello, Mr Summers.'

They shook hands.

'Please, it's Gerald.'

Bailey ignored Gerald and studied Omar's face, his dark-ringed eyes and the foot that was tapping on the tiles in a nervous staccato. Something was wrong, all right. They needed to move somewhere they could talk. 'Let's go upstairs to Gerald's office.'

Gerald's assistant was waiting for them at the elevator.

'Pen,' Gerald said, 'can you please organise some tea and breakfast. We're going to need some privacy with our old friend. And hold my calls.'

Back in Baghdad, Omar Haneef was the guy who knew how to keep western reporters safe. His official occupation was that of a driver. For John Bailey he was a 'fixer', which meant that he did a lot of things. The kind of tasks that didn't appear in job advertisements. Omar had a good contact book and he knew how to get around Iraq without crossing Saddam's security forces, or the gangsters who made money out of robbing and kidnapping westerners.

After the first Gulf War, Iraq became a no-go zone for reporters like Bailey. It was too dangerous. Saddam Hussein had lost the war in Kuwait and he was tightening his grip on his country, brutally quashing any sign of dissent. Omar's connection to western journalists, like Bailey, made him a target for the Republican Guard. Bailey knew they had to get him out. Luckily, the Australian Government agreed. Omar was granted a refugee visa and, after making it to Turkey, he boarded a plane bound for Sydney.

Like most refugees, he was buoyed by the chance at a new life. He got a job as a taxi driver and bought a house in Sydney's western suburbs, where he met his wife and started a family.

Bailey had caught up with Omar a couple of times during his visits back to Australia. But he couldn't remember the last time they'd seen each other.

'Have a seat, Omar.' Gerald pointed to the sofa in the corner of his office, which overlooked the growing cluster of buildings on the foreshore at Cockle Bay.

'Are you okay, mate?' Bailey said, noticing the beads of sweat on Omar's brow.

'No.' Omar slumped forward with his head in his hands. 'I'm far from okay.' He was talking into his open hands, shaking his head.

Finally, he sat up. 'You said to me, many years ago, that if I ever got into trouble, then you would be there for me.'

'I did. And I meant it.'

They were interrupted by a gentle knock at the door.

Penelope appeared holding a tray with a teapot, jug of milk, three mugs and a plate of croissants. She placed the tray on the coffee table and left.

Omar stared at the door, waiting for it to close again.

'It's my son, Tariq.' Omar took a deep breath. 'He's missing.'

Gerald looked across at Bailey, waiting for him to respond.

'Are you sure?' Bailey said.

'Yes. He's only fifteen years old.' Omar handed Bailey a postcard-sized picture of a young, handsome boy in a blue school uniform. 'When he doesn't come home, I know.'

'How long's he been gone?'

'One week. His friends don't even know where he is. At least, that's what they tell me.'

'Have you gone to the police?'

Omar shook his head. He went to say something, then paused and took a sip of his tea. His hand was shaking and the cup bounced around on the saucer when he put it down.

'Omar?' Bailey said. 'Why haven't you gone to the police?'

'Has he done something?' Gerald joined the conversation, looking for a straight answer. 'Something that might get him into trouble?'

Omar leaned forward and put his head in his hands again, sobbing, quietly.

'Take your time, Omar. We're in no hurry here.'

Gerald placed a box of tissues on the table in front of him.

Bailey didn't know what to say, what to do. They just sat there, waiting for Omar to calm down and start talking again. Bailey's eyes drifted from Omar to a crane that was hovering above a building covered in scaffolding at Barangaroo. The high-roller casino complex with the untouchable views. Like Sydney needed another bloody place for people to do their dough.

'Omar?' Gerald said.

Omar sat up again, using the tissues to wipe his eyes, blow his nose. His chest was flexing, in and out, with each stuttering breath.

'Tariq has been talking to people. People we don't know, people we couldn't know.'

'What people?' Bailey said.

'After he went missing, my wife found conversations on our family computer, conversations he was having with people on the internet.'

'What conversations, Omar? For us to help, you need to tell us everything.'

'People, I don't know, bad people.' Omar was stuttering, struggling to get it out. 'Tariq could be about to do something very stupid.'

Gerald looked across at Bailey, alarmed.

'Omar,' Bailey said, 'do you think Tariq has been talking to Islamic extremists over the internet?'

Omar leaned back on the sofa, covering his eyes with the palms of his hands. He was sobbing loudly now, his body jolting with his tears.

'Omar?' Gerald leaned forward, patting him on the knee.

'We need you to answer the question,' Bailey said. 'Has Tariq been communicating with extremists over the internet?'

'Yes.'

'You said that he was planning something stupid, something bad. What is it, Omar? We need you to tell us exactly what you know.'

'I think he's preparing for something.' Omar was stuttering again. 'Helping them to do something, something bad.'

Gerald went to say something, but Bailey cut him off. 'This next bit's important, Omar.' Bailey reached across the table, placing his hand on Omar's shoulder. 'I need you to sit up. Sit up and look at me.'

Omar did as he was told, letting out a long, sighing breath, wiping his bloodshot eyes.

'Who's he been talking to, Omar? I need a name.'

Bailey already knew the name. He just needed to hear Omar say it.

'The man's name . . . his name . . . is Mustafa.'

Bailey felt the bile rising from his stomach, burning the back of his throat. What the hell had he just walked into?

31

CHAPTER 6

So much for going home.

It was just after seven-thirty in the morning when Bailey climbed out of a taxi in Leichhardt. He opened the white picket gate, pausing to rummage through his bag for his keys, and walked up the steps onto Dexter's front porch.

The sensor light came on even though the sun had been up for more than an hour. It must have been timed for the winter. A small detail that Bailey found interesting.

The light went off by the time Bailey had gathered his thoughts, contemplating what he'd say to the woman inside. He knew that Dexter was home because he'd spoken to her on the phone a quarter of an hour ago. The conversation had not gone well.

'Where are you? London?'

'Got back this morning. I need to see you, we've got a bit of a problem here.'

'We?'

Bailey knew that she was being facetious.

'Let's not talk on the phone. Are you at work, or at home?'

'Home. Better be quick, just got out of the shower.'

'Sounds like I –'

'Don't even go there, Bailey.' She sounded tired. 'And I'm busy. If you're not here in fifteen, I'm gone.'

Dexter hung up without giving Bailey a chance to respond. She was usually off to work before the sun came up. The late start probably meant a late finish the night before, if she'd even been to bed at all. All-nighters had become a feature of Sharon Dexter's job. The crazy hours were the price of being promoted from her old job in Homicide to be the new head of the Joint Counter Terrorism Team, a sprawling taskforce of state and federal cops that had been thrown together to stop extremists from killing people.

Standing on Dexter's front porch, Bailey decided against using the key that she'd cut for him. Judging by the tone of their conversation, she might ask for him to give it back.

He knocked instead.

Bailey heard footsteps inside before Dexter opened the door, ruffling her hair with a towel. She barely even looked at him as she turned around and walked back down the hall.

'Why didn't you use your key?' she said with her back to him.

He couldn't win.

They hadn't seen each other for a week and Dexter was pissed at him for not telling her about his trip to London until he was boarding the plane at Sydney International. Ordinarily, she wouldn't have cared. They both had jobs that required unconventional hours and days. The only problem was that when Bailey's plane was refuelling in Singapore, he was supposed to have been sitting beside Dexter at their favourite restaurant, which happened to be an old gastro pub in Balmain that had once belonged to her parents. A night out together to stop and smell the roses.

'Sorry, Sharon. Been a rough few days.'

'So I hear,' she said, tying her damp brown hair into a ponytail.

Already dressed in a pair of jeans and a jacket, Dexter looked like she was ready to leave.

'Sharon, I'm sorry.' Bailey walked over to where she was

standing in the kitchen, reaching out for her arm. 'Gerald sprung the trip on me. I couldn't say no.'

'Communication, Bailey. I know you're in this, I am too. But we need to talk to each other.'

'I'm sorry. I know I'm not perfect.'

Dexter laughed. 'No one's suggesting you're perfect.'

Remembering that he'd bought her something, Bailey reached into his pocket. 'A little piece of England.' He held out a miniature English bobby's helmet. 'It's a pencil sharpener for your desk.'

'Who uses pencils?' She took it anyway, trying not to smile. 'You're bloody hopeless, you know that?'

Bailey took a chance and wrapped his arms around her. 'So, you missed me, then?'

'Maybe, a little bit.' She pulled back, interrogating the red in his eyes, her hands cupping his cheeks. 'You don't look great, if you don't mind me saying.'

'Just tired,' he said. 'Barely got a wink on the plane.'

'Are you okay?'

He knew what she was really asking him. She wanted to know if the attack out the front of Chatham House was weighing on him, bringing him down. It was.

'I'm good,' he lied.

Talking about that dead woman lying on the road would just make him think about her more. How she died. The knife. The blood. Bailey just wanted to forget. Standing in the kitchen in front of one of the good things he had going in his life was the best fix he knew.

His hand wandered, cheekily, up the side of her back and under her jacket, catching the curve of her breast.

'Get out of it.' She pushed his hand away, playfully. 'No time for that.'

Bailey tried again. 'I'll be quick.'

'That's not selling it to me.' She stepped back, picking up a steaming mug of instant coffee from the island bench, taking a sip. 'I need to get to work.'

Work. Dexter could blame Bailey all she liked for the small problems in their relationship – and she'd mostly be right – but she was also so desperate to prove herself in counter-terrorism that she barely had time for anything else. Including Bailey.

'Yeah, about work . . .'

Dexter took another long drag of her coffee. 'What about it?'

Bailey didn't know how to begin telling her about the fifteen-year-old kid who might be planning a terrorist attack. 'I need to tell you something.'

She looked at her watch. 'You've got exactly one minute.'

'I'll give you the abridged version,' Bailey said. 'A kid from Wiley Park's gone missing. His dad just told me he's been talking to jihadists over the net. He's worried his son's planning some kind of attack.'

She put down her mug on the kitchen table. 'You're shitting me.'

'No,' Bailey said, 'I'm not.'

'Where'd this come from?'

'The kid's father is my old fixer from Baghdad. He's been here for more than twenty-five years. Good man. Good family. Scared shitless for his boy. He's just a kid.'

'I've seen some kids do some bad shit, Bailey.'

Dexter was right. Terrorist recruiters were targeting kids because they asked fewer questions and were more inclined to believe all that crap about the afterlife. The softest targets for recruiters were the kids from migrant communities because they often felt like outcasts. They needed friends, someone to tell them that they belonged. Most of them didn't understand what they were getting into until it was too late.

'What else do you know? And I want to know everything,' Dexter said, sharply. 'I mean it, Bailey. Everything.'

'Not sure I can do that.'

'Don't.' Dexter's neck lined with tension. 'You know you can trust me, and this isn't a game, or a bloody newspaper story. These things can go sideways very fast.'

Bailey didn't want to betray Omar's trust, but he knew that he couldn't find the kid on his own. Tariq had already been missing for a week and, if Dexter was right, he didn't want to be on the wrong side of this if it went bad.

'Okay.' Bailey readied himself for another argument. 'Here's the caveat. We're going to need to share information. If you find out anything, I want to know.'

'We'll see about that.'

'I won't get in your way. I'm looking for a happy ending here. He's just a kid.'

'Just a kid? Just a kid shot dead a police accountant in Parramatta. Stabbed a cop in Melbourne. I've lost count of the number of *kids* fighting in Syria right now. Let's not underplay this thing before we even know what it is we're looking at, okay?'

'All I'm asking for is some intel coming back. He's fifteen. From what I can gather, this has caught his family by surprise.'

'Always does.' Dexter drained the rest of her coffee, placing her mug in the sink. 'I'll do what I can, Bailey. But if I find something that leads me to think that an attack might be imminent, all bets are off.'

Bailey didn't bother arguing with her on that point because she was right. If Tariq had succumbed to the ideology and believed that God wanted him to be a killer, there might be no pulling him back from the brink. So he shared what Omar had told him and Gerald less than an hour ago.

But he didn't tell her everything.

He didn't tell her that he had a phone number in his pocket that might belong to Mustafa al-Baghdadi. That the FBI's Most Wanted Terrorist might be calling the shots on this from wherever he was hiding in Iraq. Or Syria. That information was for later, after Bailey had a better handle on exactly what the hell was going on. Time to find out if he really was a player in all this, and why.

'What're you going to do now?' Dexter said.

Bailey grabbed a banana from the fruit bowl. 'I'm off to visit a guy I know.'

'Helpful. Very helpful,' Dexter said. 'And Bailey?'

'Yep?' He was already moving towards the door.

'Don't go getting any stupid ideas.'

'Yeah, well.' Bailey opened the door, turning back around. 'You know what they say about that.'

'Enlighten me.'

'There's no such thing as stupid ideas, only stupid people.'

He closed the door before she had a chance to respond.

CHAPTER 7

Coffee.

If Bailey couldn't go home to recharge his batteries with the sounds of the Rolling Stones spinning on his turntable, then he needed something to perk him up.

These days, that meant coffee.

The Italian café near the Town Hall on Norton Street would fix him. With coffee thicker than double-whip cream, it packed a punch. The café was just up the hill from Dexter's house and the walk would be good for him. Help clear his head.

One of the perks with laying off the booze was that Bailey had dropped a few kilograms and his fitness was coming back. The fitness he'd lost way back in the 1980s after he'd quit the gym, packing away his boxing gloves and rugby boots, so that he could chase stories in the seedier suburbs of Sydney. When his obsession with journalism began. It was also about the same time that Bailey had first met Sharon Dexter. He was *The Journal*'s young gun crime reporter who had been breaking stories about corrupt cops running drugs and prostitutes in Kings Cross, and she was the young police constable tipping him off.

It had been a difficult time to be a woman in uniform, especially someone who looked like Dexter. The few other women in the service had warned her that sexual harassment was just part of the job. Dexter had never accepted it, telling Bailey during one of their secret meetings how she'd broken the finger of a detective for pinching her on the backside.

They were just friends, back then. Kindred spirits with the same drive for justice. They only became romantically involved when Bailey returned to Australia after his first stint in the Middle East. His marriage had long broken down, and after more than a decade as a war reporter, he had too. Dexter had helped him get back on his feet.

Bailey had a bad habit of putting his job before everything and everyone. So when America's war machine started purring after the September 11 attacks, he headed back to the Middle East. This time he almost didn't make it home.

More than a dozen years later and Dexter and Bailey were back together again. This time she was the one obsessed with the job, determined to prove that she'd earned her place at the leadership table because she was the best candidate for the job, not because she was filling some quota. The daughter of a Balmain publican, Dexter was driven by the same bold integrity that had drawn Bailey to her decades earlier. She was tough. She was stubborn. She had a big heart inside. Bailey wouldn't change a thing about her.

Bailey turned onto Norton Street and the café was just up ahead. He looked down at the old G-Shock watch on his wrist: 8.54 am.

The watch had been a gift from his father, given to him before he boarded his first flight to Beirut as a 25-year-old.

'You'll need something that can take a few knocks,' Jack Bailey had said.

That was more than a quarter century ago and Jack was dead. A heart attack at the age of seventy-one. Bailey's mother, Ros, hadn't lasted much longer. His parents had outlived Bailey's younger brother, Mike, who had died in a car accident after finishing high school. The brothers had been tight. Losing Mike was something that Bailey would never get over. Not that he'd wanted to. The pain helped him to remember.

The watch had been through a lot. The highs, the lows and the blows. But it was still ticking.

'Ciao, Bailey!'

Marco reached his hand through the café's takeaway window and Bailey shook it.

'You good, mate?'

'Always!'

Marco knew that Bailey wasn't going to sit down with all the young mums and prams inside. The barista pumped the coffee grounds into his portafilter, latching it to the machine, and waited for the thick brown liquid to spill into a takeaway cup on the steel tray below.

'You know, Bailey, the Azzurri are going to beat your boys in October.'

Marco was the only Italian that Bailey knew who liked rugby and Marco loved giving it to him about the Wallabies, who'd been struggling to win a game lately.

'Italians can't play rugby, Marco. You know that. Ball's the wrong shape and you don't get points for diving.'

Marco laughed, holding out Bailey's double espresso through the window. 'Your coffee just went up.'

Bailey took his double espresso and headed back down Norton Street to the park. He found a bench away from the playground, sat down, and withdrew the crumpled slip of paper from his pocket, opening it so that he could read the numbers scribbled in ink. It had been almost two days since it had been handed to him on the banks of the Thames. Bailey's window to call Mustafa al-Baghdadi was closing.

He didn't want to make the call. He didn't want to listen to the jihadist's justification for murder. He was thinking about Douglas McKenzie, the US marine beheaded by one of Mustafa's men. Bailey had watched it happen. He was there, in the room, tied to a chair.

For Mustafa, Bailey wasn't the enemy back then. He was the messenger. The man who would tell his story, explain to the world that he was merely a warrior fighting the evils of the western world. The protector of the future. Mustafa's posh accent and eloquent speech set him apart from the other extremists. The even tone of his voice was frightening. It was the thing Bailey remembered more clearly than anything. The voice he heard in his sleep.

Bailey took a swig of his coffee, wishing it was something stronger. He stared up at the sky, catching an Airbus A380 flying overhead. A loud humming noise followed, louder than usual because of the clouds. Every few minutes, another plane vibrated through the air on its way to Mascot. So loud that parents watching their kids at the playground paused their conversations and looked up. The planes were part of everyday life around here under the flight path, where it still cost two million bucks for a house. It was madness.

9.12 am.

It was the middle of the night in Iraq and Syria. Bailey had spent so many years traversing the Middle East that he was good at calculating time zones in his head.

Placing the paper cup on the bench beside him, he used his free hand to dig his phone from his pocket. Unlocking it, he held down the zero key until it turned into a plus sign, and dialled the number.

After five long beeps there was a clicking sound followed by more beeps, like he was being put on hold, or redirected. Then more clicks before, finally, someone answered. Bailey knew they were there because of the heavy breathing down the line.

'John Bailey here.'

He didn't know what else to say.

The words were met with more breathing. Sighing in, and out.
He waited.

'It's been a long time, John Bailey.'

The unmistakable voice sent a chill through Bailey's spine,
making him shudder.

'I listened to your speech,' Mustafa said. 'The one you gave in
London.'

Bailey wondered how the hell that was possible. No recordings
were permitted at Chatham House. Off the record; Chatham House
rules. It was where the bloody rule came from.

He decided not to go there. 'And?'

'You have your views, I have mine.'

'You didn't like it, then?'

Mustafa took a while to respond. 'You think you know me, but
you don't.'

Hearing Mustafa's voice made him feel sick. Bailey had been
on the phone for less than thirty seconds and, already, he wanted
to hang up.

'Never said I did. Then, or now. I can only go off what you told
me, what I saw,' Bailey said. 'Anyway, you wanted me to call you.
Why?'

'What did you think of the brave martyr's statement at St James's
Square?'

'The brainwashed kid? Your work? Another wasted life.'

'You were always so quick to judge, John Bailey.'

'My nature.'

'There are plenty more like him, you know. Good soldiers are
not hard to find.'

'Is that why we're talking?'

42

Another plane was flying overhead, smaller than the A380, but just as loud.

'I think you know why.'

'No, really, I don't. Enlighten me.' Bailey wasn't about to tell Mustafa that he knew about Tariq. He didn't want to say anything that might expedite the plan.

'Working for the CIA,' Mustafa said, his voice more like a growl. 'Your betrayal has brought us back together.'

'I don't work for the CIA. I'm a journalist.'

'What you saw in London was nothing. In a few days, you'll know.'

'Killing more innocent people?'

'We'll talk again, soon.'

'Betrayal? What the hell are you talking about, Mustafa?'

'I know what you did.'

Click.

He was gone.

I know what you did.

What the hell was he talking about? What betrayal?

Bailey's hand was shaking.

He folded the piece of paper, catching a glimpse of his three missing fingernails, the skin red and wrinkled. Mustafa's men had done that to him. The nails had never grown back.

CHAPTER 8

Talkback radio hosts only ever discussed three things in Sydney: terrorism, house prices and how much people were paying for their power bills. Usually, in that order.

The topic of the day today was the soaring prices of electricity and gas.

'You tell me, dear listeners, why our politicians think it's okay for Australians to pay more for our own gas than the Japanese?'

Bailey hated opinionated journalism and he'd made no secret of his special dislike for Keith Roberts, whose yapping voice was raging from the speakers in the taxi.

'The energy minister is here with me in the studio. Her name is Jennifer Owens. She's completely incompetent, I tell you. I'll say it again, she's completely incompetent! It's the only way to describe a member of a government that makes its own citizens pay more for gas than the spot price overseas –'

'Keith, if you'll let me get a word in here.'

'No, Jennifer. I won't. Why would I? It's your incompetence that's sending this nation to ruin. What do you say to the poor old dear who won't put her heater on this winter because she can't afford it? There's a question I'll let you answer. Jennifer? Jennifer?'

After more than two decades on the radio, Roberts was king of the airwaves. He loved the power of his opinions and often boasted

44

that he'd brought down prime ministers and premiers. The sad thing was that he was right.

'I'd say we're doing the best we can, Keith. And, and –'

'And what, Jennifer? What? You've got no idea. You're all at sea like our last prime minister. Your old boss. Lost at sea, no idea.'

'Steady on there, Keith.'

It had taken the taxi almost an hour to make it across the city in the busy morning traffic, not helped by the streets that had been shut down because of the mysterious light rail project that seemed to be more about cutting down historic trees than laying tracks. They were only a few streets away from Bailey's home in Paddington but he couldn't take Roberts' incessant yapping any longer.

'Mate, mind giving the radio a rest?'

The driver shook his head. 'This is good stuff, important! Keith Roberts speaks for all of us. Not just you rich people in Paddington.'

This bloke had earned the chip on his shoulder. The wealth divide was growing by the month in Sydney and taxi drivers were the new working poor, especially after Uber had been given a free pass to take half of their business.

'Okay, mate.' Bailey would put up with Roberts, but he wasn't going to cop being bundled in with all the eastern suburbs yuppies. 'Do I look like some rich prick to you?'

The taxi driver turned around, sizing up Bailey's worn jeans, flannelette shirt and five o'clock shadow. 'Guess not. But you get my point.'

'I get it.'

Bailey wound down his window to get some air. He had bigger things on his mind than worrying about Keith Roberts. Like why the world's most wanted terrorist was accusing him of betrayal, and why a fifteen-year-old kid from a good family was about to ruin his life and possibly many others.

He needed to find Tariq and, at this precise moment, he had no idea how. Bailey needed help from someone who knew how to find people who didn't want to be found. It just so happened that that someone had been sleeping in his spare room for the past three months.

'Ronnie!'

Bailey called out as soon as he opened the front door.

'Ronnie! Are you here, mate?'

Bailey checked the bedroom, the kitchen and the lounge. There was no sign of him.

He opened the fridge and had a sniff of a plastic takeaway box half-filled with pad thai. It smelled good, fresh. He put the box in the microwave and had one more scour of the house. The only things missing were the fishing rods from the courtyard.

Bailey grabbed his car keys, a fork and the steaming box of noodles and headed out the door. He knew exactly where Ronnie Johnson would be.

'Hello stranger.'

He didn't get far. There was a woman standing on his front porch when he opened the door. She almost wore the pad thai.

'Hi Annie. Sorry, now's not a great time.'

Annie Brooks. His AA sponsor. She lived around the corner and had a habit of dropping by, unannounced.

'Read your story in the paper.' She flashed him a concerned smile, knowing it'd get him. 'Made me worried about you.'

'I'm good, Annie. No slip-ups.'

The steam from the pad thai was burning his fingers. He stepped around her, resting the takeaway container in a pot plant. The dead fern wouldn't mind.

'Sorry, too bloody hot.' With his hands free, he gave her a hug. 'How are you?'

'I'm good. Could do with a coffee, though. Got time for a quick one?'

'This about me, or you?'

Their conversations were always a two-way street. It was the way things rolled for people battling the booze. Bailey didn't want to let her down.

'You.'

She was just checking in. Her usual trick. A casual pop-in for a chat. Talking with Annie wasn't like a session with a shrink. She had her own head full of demons and she understood Bailey's world better than most.

They also had a history together.

The first time Bailey had met Annie Brooks wasn't in the Alcoholics Anonymous meeting at the church hall around the corner from his house. It was in Beirut. Annie had been a television reporter back in the day when commercial networks cared about international news. Lebanon was a tiny country; all the foreign correspondents knew each other. They shared information. Travelled together. Drank together. And from time to time, they even slept together. Aid workers liked to call it 'emergency sex'. It was basically the same thing for correspondents. Sex on the fly. A moment of intimacy. Something that connected them to an ordinary life.

Annie had only lasted a year in Beirut before she was called back to Sydney to present the six o'clock nightly news. She held the job for almost fifteen years, became a household name, until some all-too-clever TV executive decided that she wasn't 'fuckable' enough anymore and replaced her with a younger version of herself. Commercial television was like that. Brutal. And sexist.

Unlike Bailey, it wasn't the job that drove Annie to the bottle. She'd always been a drinker. Bailey had seen it firsthand in Beirut. He used to marvel at how she could put away the best part of a bottle of vodka and get up for an early flight the next morning, raring to go. He found out later that she used to start the day with bloody Marys at breakfast.

Bailey liked his conversations with Annie because, in their own way, they'd both been knocked down onto the canvas and made it back to their feet. They had lived experiences. Wolves to keep outside the door.

'Can I give you a bell later?' Bailey said. 'Got a bit on my plate.'

Annie squinted her eyes, sizing up whether he was trying to blow her off.

'You look tired.'

'So people keep telling me. I can never sleep on planes.'

'You haven't been to a meeting in a while.'

'Been in London, remember?'

'For two months?'

'Not really my thing, those meetings. You know that.'

Bailey hated sitting in a room full of strangers. Listening to a room full of problems. He hated how everybody in the circle had to have their say. Even the ones who didn't want to be there. Like the rich kid whose parents kept bailing him out of prison and threatening to cut off his trust fund if he didn't attend AA. And the bloke who said that he didn't have a problem and that he was only coming because his wife had threatened to divorce him.

The twelve steps also irritated Bailey, especially the religious stuff. How could a guy who had turned water into wine at a piss-up two thousand years ago end up being the patron saint of Alcoholics Anonymous?

He'd told that joke at his first AA meeting and Annie had been the only person who'd laughed. It was enough for Bailey. They might not have seen each other for the best part of twenty years, but anyone who got his humour would probably understand the rest of him. Once Annie and Bailey started catching up, he had no more use for the meetings.

'And I've got you now, Annie,' Bailey said. 'No need for the church hall anymore.'

She smiled. 'Yes, you do.'

'And I'm not blowing you off. I just don't have time today.'

'Tonight?'

'I'll give you a ring.'

CHAPTER 9

The road leading to Bronte Beach was so steep that it was like dropping out of the sky. The brakes on Bailey's old Corolla squealed all the way to the bottom.

He found a parking spot opposite the short strip of restaurants and cafés, then fed the meter an exorbitant amount of gold coins. It was stinking hot for April. Knowing that his rusty old piece of junk was in the very low-risk category for car theft, he left the window open so that it wouldn't be a sauna when he got back.

As far as he could tell, he was the only guy at the beach wearing Blundstone boots and a flannelette shirt. Actually, he was one of the only people wearing much in the way of clothing at all.

People were dripping with money around here, and those who didn't have any liked to pretend that they did. The old guy in the linen pants with the young blonde clutching his arm looked like the real deal. So did the middle-aged woman in lycra leggings walking a snow-white pair of poodles. Everybody else looked the same. Tanned twenty-somethings with most of their bodies on show. People who worked the type of jobs that funded a lifestyle, not a life. Good luck to them.

Bailey picked up a couple of coffees and headed across the grass towards the sand. Bronte was less than three hundred metres long, so it was easy to spot the large man standing on the rocks under the northern headland. It was Ronnie Johnson's favourite fishing spot, where he liked to throw in his line at least a few times a week.

Bailey took his time dragging his feet through the sand, giving him longer to check out the morning sunbathers paying homage to the sky; their skin, tight and taut, glistening with oil. It was even slower going on the sand because he hadn't bothered to remove his boots. At least the rubber soles made it easier when he was clambering over the rocks to Ronnie's spot below the cliff.

'Caught anything, old boy?'

Ronnie was crouched over, baiting his hook. Bailey had no idea whether his old friend had seen him coming. He usually did. After almost four decades as an intelligence agent, there wasn't much that Ronnie Johnson didn't see coming.

'Few bites, bubba.' Ronnie was concentrating on the hook and didn't look up. 'The big one's out there. Bream, maybe even whiting, if I get lucky. Dinner for us, tonight.'

'Yeah, sure.' Bailey said. 'I might take a couple of steaks out of the freezer, just in case.'

Ronnie stood up. Six foot four, with a barrel chest and arms like canons, he was an imposing figure. Even if he was pushing sixty.

'You need to have faith, bubba. This is what I do for a living, now. Remember? I'm getting good.'

'So you keep saying. I'll only believe you're retired when I'm looking down on your grave.'

'No offence, but I hope it's the other way round.' Ronnie winked at him. 'By the way, that AA girl came around asking about you last night.'

'She found me.'

'Easy on the eye, that one.' Ronnie smiled. 'What does Detective Dexter think about her?'

Alcoholics Anonymous may have been Sharon's idea, but Bailey hadn't told her about Annie Brooks. He didn't see the point.

'No issues there, mate.'

Ronnie shrugged his big shoulders and turned back towards the water, squinting at the sun, his shadow stretching across the rocks to the scorched grass at the base of the cliff.

'Bought you a coffee.'

Ronnie took a sip and then handed the cup back to Bailey. 'Hold it for me, bubba, while I work the magic.'

He stepped closer to the edge of the water, dangling the rod back over his shoulder to his right. He checked Bailey, then swung his arm around, letting the hook sail into the sky above the waves until it plopped into the water around forty metres out.

'Not bad. Maybe there's a future for you outside the agency, after all?'

'Thanks, bubba.' Ronnie reached into his pocket and grabbed a cigar, wedging it in the corner of his mouth so that he could use his spare hand to spark it.

'Light-up day, is it?'

Ronnie was always giving up smoking. After a few puffs, he turned around with a big grin on his face. 'Fish like the smell, my second lure.' Turning back towards the water, he jiggled his rod. 'How was London? Saw what happened on the news. How many attacks over there now? Eight? Ten?'

'Who's counting?' Bailey said. 'Lot of fear, though. It's getting to the place.'

'That's what they want.'

'Don't have to tell me that,' Bailey said. 'Anyway, we need to talk.'

'So, talk. I've got all the listening time in the world.'

Bailey's head darted from left to right to see if there was anyone else within earshot. There wasn't. Unless you counted the guy on the paddle board fifty metres out, or the sand flies nipping at his neck.

'It's about Mustafa al-Baghdadi,' Bailey said, eventually. 'I spoke to him, on the phone.'

Ronnie laughed and turned around with a pair of eyebrows that said stop bullshitting me.

'I'm serious.'

'Come on, bubba. What'd you really want to talk about?'

Bailey stepped closer to where Ronnie had cast his line from the rock ledge, the waves crashing below.

'I think he was behind what happened in London.'

'This isn't a joke, then?'

'No, Ronnie. It's not.'

'London attacks? Doesn't surprise me.' Ronnie bent down and planted the rod between the rocks. He didn't seem to care about his catch, anymore. 'What's it got to do with you?'

'A lot, it seems.'

'Like what? Apart from your unscheduled vacation with that mad son of a bitch.'

Bailey let Ronnie's last words float away in the salty air.

'Did you really speak to him?' Ronnie checked one last time.

'Why would I make up a story like that?'

'When?'

Bailey looked at his watch. 'About two hours ago, give or take.'

'What'd he want?'

Ronnie was sounding very interested for someone who was supposed to have been retired.

'He told me he didn't like my speech at Chatham House.'

'Probably means you did a good job, bubba.' Ronnie blew a cloud of smoke at the water. 'Can't be the reason he called, though. Doesn't add up.'

'It wasn't,' Bailey said. 'He was warning me.'

'About what?' Ronnie put his cigar back in his mouth. 'He tell you he was planning something?'

'That's exactly what I'm telling you.'

'Sorry, bubba. Not buying that one.'

'I'm not asking you to buy anything.' Bailey didn't like being patronised. 'Whatever it is he's got cooking, it's connected to me.'

'Enlighten me.'

'Remember Omar from Baghdad? The fixer that Gerald and I used in those early days?'

Ronnie had been the CIA's station chief in Baghdad when Bailey and Gerald were sent to cover the first Gulf War.

'Yeah, I remember him.'

'Well, he got refugee status and he's an Australian citizen now. Lives in Sydney. His fifteen-year-old son's gone missing. Omar thinks he's been communicating with Islamic Nation over the net. Maybe even Mustafa himself.'

Ronnie stubbed his cigar into the rocks and picked up his fishing rod, slowly reeling it in.

'And there's something else,' Bailey said. 'Mustafa said something on the phone that's been bothering me.'

'Which is?'

'He accused me of betraying him, said I've been working for you lot. What the hell could he mean by that?'

Ronnie stopped reeling in his line. 'There's something that I haven't told you, bubba.'

Bailey's heart skipped a beat, wondering where Ronnie was going.

'Earlier this year, there was a security breach at the State Department. Thousands of secret files were stolen by Russian hackers and published by Wikileaks. Your name was mentioned in those files, bubba – as an intelligence source.'

'A what?' Bailey was angry. He was a journalist, not a spook. Or a source.

'There's a file on you, bubba. The information you gave us straight after your release. It's out there.'

Bailey had a vague memory of sitting in a room recounting to Ronnie and the other CIA people everything he could remember about his time in captivity. The people. Places. Conversations. Sounds. Smells. Anything that offered an insight into Mustafa al-Baghdadi and his terrorist outfit. Their motivations. How organised they were. What weapons they had. Anything. Everything.

'What the fuck, Ronnie?' Bailey tossed the dregs of his coffee on the rocks, crushing the paper cup in his hand. 'What's in the file?'

'It was so long ago, I can't even remember.'

'Bullshit! You're the one who interviewed me back in Baghdad. You know exactly what's in that file!'

Ronnie drained the rest of his coffee in one long gulp, throwing the empty cup into his tackle box.

'I'm not bullshitting you, bubba. It's been so long since I've seen that file, I've forgotten. Remember, we didn't know much about Mustafa back then. He was just another fanatic.'

Bailey didn't know what to believe. Ronnie might be his friend, but the old spy had also mastered the art of lying. He always had an ulterior motive. Guys like Ronnie never 'left' the CIA, even when they were gone.

'Yeah, well,' Bailey spat out, 'now he's top of your government's list of wanted terrorists, and for some bloody reason, he's got it in for me.'

'Guess you're going to need my help, then, hey bubba?'

Ronnie could be very useful. The tricky bastard had even saved Bailey's life. More than once.

TIM AYLIFFE

'Are you offering?'

'I'm offering.'

Bailey knew the offer wasn't being proffered out of the goodness of his heart. The chance to snare the world's most wanted terrorist was exactly the type of catch that Ronnie was after.

'We need to find the kid.' Bailey was calming down. 'And Ronnie?'

'Yeah?'

'Save me the trouble searching the Wikileaks dump. I want to see my file.'

'I think I can manage that,' Ronnie said. 'What's your plan with the kid?'

'School's out at three. Thought I might introduce myself to some of Tariq's friends. Omar's meeting me there.'

'Hold on!' Ronnie was distracted by a sudden weight on his line. 'Here we go!'

Moments later, something was bobbing in the waves in front of them. Unfortunately for Ronnie, it wasn't a fish.

He dangled the line over to Bailey, who took delight in unhooking the sodden shoe.

'It's a ten,' Bailey said. 'My size. Shame we don't have more time; now you're getting good you could catch me the other one.'

CHAPTER 10

DEXTER

All over the city, hulking concrete blocks had been dropped onto the pavement outside buildings and busy pedestrian areas. The government had put them there to stop terrorists from using vehicles as weapons against people. Berlin. London. Nice. Melbourne. It was a cheap way to kill people and the number of attacks was growing.

Some footpaths had more bollards than others, like the one out the front of a grey, featureless building in the heart of the city on Goulburn Street. The home of the Australian Federal Police. Five concrete blocks had been put there to protect the hundreds of cops walking in and out of the foyer each day, including Detective Chief Inspector Sharon Dexter.

Dexter had left work just after two o'clock that morning and she was about to walk back through the door six and a half hours later. She lived for the job. It gave her purpose, a reason to get moving each day. It was why she and Bailey were so good and bad for each other. Two sides of the same coin.

Dexter had been in her late thirties the first time they'd gotten together. Bailey had just moved home from the Middle East when he approached her in a bar. She hadn't seen him in more than a decade but she recognised him instantly. Shaggy haircut. Unironed shirt. That gravelly voice wrapped inside a cheeky grin.

'Buy you a drink, officer?'

'It's detective, now.'

'How many fingers did you break to get that title?'

Bailey had a good memory and an uncanny ability to get under her skin. In a good way.

'Several,' she said. 'I've made it my thing. I can show you, if you like?'

'How about I just get you that drink.'

Dexter smiled as she remembered back over that first night together. And the one after, when Bailey turned up on her doorstep with a bunch of service station flowers in his hand. He was a bit hopeless and there was something about his eyes that told her that he needed fixing. Neither of those things had stopped her from falling in love with him.

After stubbing a half-smoked cigarette into a concrete barrier, Dexter swiped her ID card at the entrance and headed for the elevators. She didn't like that she was smoking again, although she had her reasons. The main one being that it gave her an opportunity to get away from her desk, where she was spending countless hours staring at computer screens, trawling through phone and email logs, monitoring hundreds of terrorist suspects, trying to separate the ones who talked about killing from those who were prepared to do it. Smoking had been keeping her sane.

The Joint Counter Terrorism Team – or JCTT – was a sprawling taskforce made up of the Australian Federal Police, the Australian Security Intelligence Organisation, the New South Wales Crime Commission and state cops like Dexter.

Dexter's new job was just as lonely as her last one. It's what happens when a cop takes down a corrupt police commissioner. *You never finger one of your own.* Corruption had tentacles. You never knew how far they reached. Dexter had been moved for her own safety. It just so happened that Dexter's 'move' had ended up being a promotion. Well overdue, according to the deputy commissioner who had put her there. Whatever the reason, she was desperate to prove that she deserved every stripe on her shoulder. Not least because she was a woman.

The top brass liked to boast that times had changed. But that was bullshit. There were more blokes in charge than ever before. Dexter pretended that it didn't bother her because her work spoke for itself. As long as she got the job done, respect would come. Mostly, she was right. The respect had come. She was the homicide detective who had spent decades locking up bad people. Murderers. Drug dealers. Even corrupt cops.

She knew how to take punches and throw them too. She wasn't interested in politics or climbing the greasy pole. Dexter was an old-fashioned cop, trained on the streets, driven by justice and a desire to stop people from doing bad things. Now her focus was terrorism.

'Anything?'

Dexter rattled the back of Nugget's chair with her hand, causing him to jump. 'Shit, boss!'

'Anything interesting?'

She leaned forward so that she could read the files that Nugget had been scanning on one of the three computer screens that were collectively beaming a big blue light on his face. Mostly transcripts of telephone calls and messages from people on the terrorism watch-list.

'Not yet,' Nugget said, without turning around. 'Just going through the logs, seeing who our favourite nut jobs have been speaking to.'

Detective Don Benson was a short, stocky, straight-talking bloke with a neck almost as wide as his head. It was why everyone called him Nugget.

'Anyone in particular?'

'No, boss,' he said. 'I'm only just getting started.'

Despite being a chauvinistic arsehole, Nugget was good at his job. He was a typical hard-head copper who, like Dexter, had spent most of his career in Homicide and knew the mean streets better than any federal police or intelligence investigator.

'Anything on the kid?' Dexter had already put the word out about Tariq.

'Not yet,' Nugget said.

'How about you guys?' Dexter raised her voice so that the other members of her team could hear. 'Michael? Kate?'

Two young cops looked up from their computer screens, shaking their heads. 'Nothing.'

Dexter's team was tasked with monitoring the terrorism watch-list. The problem was there were four hundred names on it. Police didn't have the resources to track everyone. The 24-hour surveillance of one person would take twenty police officers. To monitor four hundred people would need eight thousand officers. Dexter's team had to be selective, take a punt on people they believed were the most dangerous.

About one hundred and fifty people on the watch-list had returned to Australia after fighting for groups like Islamic Nation in Iraq and Syria. Others had made the list simply because they had friends or relatives still over there and police feared that they might have the same radical tendencies, or could be sending money overseas to buy guns and make bombs for the battlefield. Most of them were connected. Brothers. Sisters. Cousins. Neighbours. Someone from the same mosque, or prayer group. There was always a link, you just needed to dig.

Tariq's name wasn't on the list. He was a complete unknown. 'Lone-wolf terrorists', or 'cleanskins', didn't turn up that often and they were always the hardest to find. Tariq had been missing for approximately a week. He was fifteen years old. Someone out there must be helping him. Someone must know something.

'He can't be working alone. Keep looking.'

Dexter had asked her team to zero in on the people on the list who lived in Western Sydney to see if they could pick up any chatter that might involve the kid.

'Exactly what we're doing, boss.'

Dexter had been in the office for five minutes and she'd already had enough of Nugget's attitude and the stale coffee breath that was hovering above his computer terminal.

'Keep at it,' she said, before tapping Nugget's fat neck. 'And Nugget?'

'Yeah?'

'You might want to get yourself a mint.'

Dexter ignored his huff and walked over to where Kate and Michael were sitting.

'What about our special friends?'

'Pretty quiet,' Kate answered. 'Couple of chats, nothing exciting.'

Dexter watched as Kate clicked on the name of one of the people using encrypted messaging services, which they'd recently been granted permission to track, and up came a conversation from late the night before.

Cuz

Where u?

Darlene's house. Come

Who there?

Usual crew

Got anything?

Bit of gear

Cool. C u soon

Bring your wallet, no free rides
Get fucked
Seriously. No pay no point

'Can you believe these guys?' Kate said. 'One minute they're talking about sharia law, next, they're smoking ice pipes together. Fucking hypocrites.'

Dexter knew the link between drug use and extremism was surprisingly high, with terrorist suspects moving in and out of the party scene and the mosque. Some of them had even admitted to becoming religious fanatics because it helped them kick a drug habit.

'Give me a shout if there's any chatter about the kid. I'll check in with the feds, see what they've got,' Dexter said, pointing to the office up the end of the hall.

Dexter had only made it a few steps before Kate called her back. 'Wait!'

A message was flashing on the screen. An alert about a new conversation involving another guy on the list.

'What've you got?'

'The Salmas.'

The Salma brothers – George, Benji and Alex – were thugs. Muscled-up labourers who all worked for their father's construction business. They had a reputation for intimidating other building contractors and developers, and not always paying their debts. More recently, the brothers had come to the attention of authorities when their cousin, Ahmed Sajed, travelled to Turkey on George Salma's passport, and then turned up in an Islamic Nation video in Iraq. That was enough to get a warrant to access George's phone. Rather than bringing George in for questioning, they'd decided to monitor him. See where it led.

Dexter leaned across Kate's shoulder while she operated the mouse, zooming in on the conversation.

Bro, we gotta make that movie
When?
Now
Camera?
Yep. Meet at the house?
Ok
C u in 20

The conversation ended.

'Nugget!' Dexter called out. 'We need eyes on the Salmas, as many as you can. Now!'

They couldn't know what the brothers were talking about. It could be anything. But this was how they operated in counter-terrorism. Jumping at any lead. They didn't have a choice.

CHAPTER 11

'Is that all you've got?'

The old priest was needling the kid, willing him to hit harder.

'C'mon, I can hit harder than that!'

The kid slugged the heavy bag with a right hook. It swung to the left, sending Father Joe with it. The old man would have fallen over had his feet not been shoulder-width apart. Six decades in the gym had taught him that.

'Now you're getting it!' Father Joe's words were finally getting through, and being belted back at him with force.

The kid followed through with a four-punch combination, two left jabs, right hook and an upper-cut. Simple, effective. Boxing 101.

'Two more minutes, Jake,' Father Joe said. 'Make them count!'

Jake was mixing it up now. Five-punch combos, six, then eight, twelve. The blows on the bag were getting harder as the seconds ticked down. The kid wasn't tiring. Sixty-odd kilograms, all muscle. And he could hit, all right. Hard.

Joe hadn't noticed Bailey standing in the corner, watching the old man at work. 'One minute left, Jake. Go for it!'

The clock in Joe's head was usually spot-on. Bailey remembered it from his university days when the boxing priest was willing him to punch out the pain of losing his brother.

The old man always had a project, a kid to mentor. Someone with spirit who deserved something better than the cards they'd been dealt.

Bailey could see that Jake wasn't just a kid who needed someone to look out for him. Jake had talent.

'Get those legs apart!' Joe yelled at him. 'Don't lean in! You've got it, Jake. Let them know!'

He kept on going, hitting harder. Bailey had known kids like him before.

Whack!

For the parents who didn't want him.

Whack!

The rich kids who looked down on him.

Whack!

The bullies who made fun of him. The girls who ignored him.

Whack! Whack!

The sound of his gloves slamming against the bag echoed throughout the gym.

'Keep it going, kid!'

The minute was done but Jake wasn't. Joe was letting him punch it out.

Some of the others in the gym, a couple of girls, mostly boys, stopped what they were doing and watched him bob and weave around the bag. He had so much energy he looked unstoppable.

'All right, son.' Joe eventually stepped to the side of the bag, easing the weight off his shoulder. 'I think we're done.'

Feeling the pressure go off the bag, Jake finally eased up. Stepping back, he wiped the sweat off his brow with the back of his glove and put his hands on his head, trying to control his breathing.

Joe walked around and slapped him on the shoulder.

'Suck it in, kid. Good session. Time to hit the showers.'

Jake shook his head. 'I've got more, Father Joe. I want to keep going.'

'Enough on the pads. You got something extra? Hit the park. Five laps, fast–slow intervals. Then back here, pronto. You need to get back to school soon.'

Jake looked at him, disappointed.

'If you want to be a boxer, you need to shed a few kilos. Do you want to box, Jake?'

'You know I do.'

'Good. Because you've got it, Jake. I want to book a fight soon.'

Jake was peeling off his gloves and getting ready for his run when Father Joe noticed Bailey standing by the door. He looked away again, ignoring him.

'How'd the new gloves feel, Jake?'

'Red hot, Father Joe. Like a second skin.' Jake had a big smile on his face. The gloves looked brand new. Bailey guessed that Joe had bought them for him. It was probably the only present Jake had ever been given. By the glint in his eye it was clear that he respected them, treasured them. Boxing was going to be Jake's get out of jail card.

Joe watched Jake run out the door, then walked over to Bailey.

'Kid's got talent, mate.'

Bailey held out his hand and Joe shook it.

'Reminds me of you, back when. Full of anger and needing to hit something.'

'Yeah, well. I'm still full of something.'

'Isn't that the truth.'

When Joe laughed his shoulders bounced up and down in a happy rhythm.

'Been a long time, son. What brings you to the mean streets? I take it you're not here for a training session.'

Bailey sucked in his gut. 'Good guess. Other priorities, these days.'

'Like what?'

Bailey ignored the question. 'I'm not here for a conversion, either. By the way, where's the dress?'

'Never was one for uniforms, and rules. Bit like you.'

'Don't blame you. I wouldn't want to associate myself with those clowns in Rome. Big on dresses there, colours for all the seasons.'

'They've given up trying to tell me what to do.'

On any other day, Bailey would have wanted to hear the old Jesuit's take on the Vatican's response to the Royal Commission into the sexual abuse of children, especially considering most of the victims were assaulted in Catholic institutions. You didn't find justice in the confessional, you found it in the courts. Joe knew that. But the cardinals were hell-bent on keeping their dirty secrets – and their cash – for themselves.

'It's them and us, always has been.' It was like the old man was reading Bailey's mind. 'Anyway, this is my church.' He pointed at the kids working out on the exercise equipment in his makeshift gym.

No one could deny him that.

Soup kitchens, domestic violence shelters and the gym he'd set up for troubled kids. Joe's religion was *people*. He'd never been interested in kissing the ring.

'They're lucky to have you, mate.'

'They keep me on my toes.'

The two men spent the next few minutes reminiscing about the days when they were both a little fitter, a little faster and – in Bailey's case – a little thinner, until Joe signalled that he needed to get moving.

'I'd love to stand around talking with you, Bailey,' he said, bending down to pick up a pair of gloves off the floor, 'but I've got to get this place cleaned up before the nuns arrive. If you're not here to glove up, what are you doing here?'

'I'm looking for someone. A kid,' Bailey said. 'He's run away from his parents, a good family. He's caught up in something, something bad.'

'And?'

'Wondering if he's turned up in any of your shelters looking for a feed.'

'Look around, mate,' Joe said, arms outstretched like an eagle. 'Half these kids are runaways.'

'Tariq's different.' Bailey lowered his voice. 'His dad's an old mate from Baghdad. Somehow he's got caught up with some Islamic radicals.'

'Terrorism?'

'He could be about to do something very stupid.'

'I see.' Jake ran back through the door, prompting Joe to look at his watch. 'Good time, kid. You're done.'

Training hours were almost over and the kids needed to shower and get back to school. But first they had to transform the gym into a soup kitchen. The nuns from the convent would start arriving soon and Joe needed to have the place ready, or there'd be hell to pay.

Everyone went to work – stacking mats, placing dumbbells in the corner and unhooking the bags dangling from the roof to clear space for the tables and chairs. If you used the gym, you had to help out. It was part of the deal.

The room wasn't very big. It was an old flower shop in Redfern that Joe had persuaded the state government to lease for him. That was more than twenty years ago. Somehow, he had kept it going. The priest wasn't as good at lifting tables and chairs as he used to be, but he did okay for someone who had just turned eighty-one.

With the boxing ring and the exercise machines taking up half the room, they could only seat about thirty inside, but they'd serve a hundred meals. Easy. Most people only stopped by for a quick feed and left, anyway. Not because they were ungrateful, but because they were ashamed. Hard lives were getting harder. It was the way the city was going. Joe had been watching the poverty divide grow, face by face.

Back when Bailey was a student boxer, it had predominantly been Indigenous Australians who would eat their meals at the gym. These days it was anybody. Anglo, Asian, Middle Eastern. People of all different backgrounds and creeds. A growing number of them were middle-aged women escaping violent or loveless marriages. Bailey knew the statistics. The people of Sydney were changing and so were the battlers who needed help.

There were two rules for the kids who trained at Joe's gym. Firstly, if you wanted to use it, then you needed to work a few shifts serving food and cleaning up. There were six beds in a dormitory that Joe had built in his presbytery around the corner and to get one of those you had to work full-time, around school hours and homework, at the soup kitchen. Most kids only stayed a few weeks or months at a time.

Joe's second rule was that he had to, at least, know first names. Some of the kids got cagey about their surnames, which was understandable, because many of them had been through a lot. But calling someone by their first name was a sign of respect. It was a subtle lesson for young people who had been disrespected their entire, short, lives.

'Here's a photo of Tariq.' Bailey handed a print to Joe. 'That's your copy. Do me a favour and ask around?'

Joe still had half an eye on the kids packing up the gym when he glanced at the photograph in his hand. 'Where's he from?'

'Wiley Park.'

'Right.'

Joe had helped set up food shelters all over Sydney and he knew what was going on in the suburbs better than anyone. Wiley Park was next door to Lakemba, the centre of the city's Muslim community and home to Australia's biggest mosque. It also regularly featured in stories in the news about terrorism.

'I'll put the word out, get in touch if I hear anything.'

'Thanks, Joe.' Bailey headed for the door.

'And Bailey!' Joe called out. 'We should talk, you and me.'

Bailey turned back around. 'About what?'

'Life.'

Bailey was standing in the open doorway, contemplating his answer. 'We can do that.'

CHAPTER 12

The ringing bell jolted Bailey awake and he banged his head on the car window.

He'd parked the car about fifty metres up the road from the set of big black iron gates at Tariq's school. The traffic had been surprisingly good. After throwing down a lamb rogan josh in Glebe, Bailey had made it to Punchbowl with thirty minutes to spare. He'd been using those extra minutes to cash in on part of the sleep debt that had been giving him a heavy head since London.

A stream of boys in blue and grey uniforms were racing across the schoolyard. Thanks to the school bell, he was wide awake, rubbing his eyes, looking for Omar down by the gates where they'd agreed to meet at three o'clock.

The curry had gone down well but he must have got chilli on his fingers back in the restaurant because his eyes were stinging and clouding with water. Distracted by the discomfort, Bailey initially missed the sight of Omar charging past his car towards the school gates.

Bailey used the back of his hands to wipe away the water and with the sting easing to an itch, he climbed out of the car and headed towards the gates, where Omar was now arguing with a couple of school kids. Even from a distance, Bailey could see that he was agitated.

'Tell me what you know! I know you know something!' Omar said, ramming his finger into the chest of one kid, while holding the other by the scruff of his shirt.

The boys were staring at him with clueless, fearful, expressions.

'I don't know what you're on about.'

'Don't lie to me!'

'Omar.' Bailey touched him on the shoulder, trying to get his attention. 'C'mon, mate, settle down.'

'Where's Tariq? Where is he?' Omar's voice was rising with each word. 'Tell me! I know you know something, you must know something!'

Bailey squeezed Omar's shoulder again and he turned around. His blood-red eyes looked how Bailey's felt.

'Let the kid go, mate,' Bailey said.

'But he knows something.' Omar was still holding one of the boys by his shirt. 'He must know something. He must!'

'They're just kids, mate. This isn't the way to get what you need.'

Omar let go, leaning back on the fence, his head shaking with frustration.

'Sorry about that,' Bailey said. 'Omar's just worried about his son.'

The two boys were trying to avoid looking at Bailey, their eyes darting from side to side, unsure whether they should stay, or go.

'No one's in trouble here, fellas. It's just that Tariq hasn't been home for a few days.'

'We don't know anything.' It was the kid who, moments earlier, had Omar's finger poking into his chest. 'We haven't seen Tariq since last week.'

'Thanks for letting us know, mate. That's helpful. Name's John Bailey, what's yours?'

Bailey held out his hand and the kid stared at it for a few seconds before shaking it.

'Hamid, I'm Hamid. This is Geoff.' He pointed to the other kid who was still straightening his shirt around the collar after it had been messed up by Omar.

'Hamid. Geoff. Everyone just calls me Bailey.'

'Well, Bailey, we don't know shit.' Geoff had finished fixing his shirt. 'Who are you, anyway, a cop?'

'Just an old friend of Omar's.'

'How do we know you're not lying?' Geoff was growing in confidence. 'You could be anyone. We don't have to talk to you.'

Omar stepped towards Geoff, grabbing him by the arm. 'You've been in my house, eaten at my family table. Show some respect!'

Geoff pushed his arm away. 'Don't fucking touch me!'

'Geoff! Cool it, bro,' Hamid said. 'He's just trying to find Tariq.'

'Well, he doesn't have to be such a dick about it.'

'You know, Geoff, you're right, mate.' Bailey stepped in front of Omar. 'Everyone just needs to take a breath for a minute.'

'Bailey!'

Bailey turned around at the sound of a familiar voice. Dexter. She didn't look happy.

'Sharon, what're you doing here?'

'No, Bailey.' She was shaking her head. 'That's *my* question. And what you guys are doing right now is not helping anyone.'

'Who's she?' It was Geoff again. 'Are you a cop, lady?'

'Sharon, these are Tariq's friends, Geoff and Hamid.' Bailey pointed at the two boys with scowling faces. 'They were just telling us about the last time they saw Tariq.'

'Bullshit we were –'

'Geoff! Seriously, bro. Keep it cool,' Hamid said. 'Look, Mr Bailey, Mr Haneef, I haven't seen Tariq since school last Tuesday. I'm not sure what's up with him.'

'What d'you mean?' Omar said. 'What d'you mean, you don't know what's up with him?'

Hamid looked over at Geoff, who quickly looked away.

'Fellas,' Bailey said, 'If you know something, you should tell us. A fifteen-year-old boy out on the streets is serious, how would you like being alone and –'

'You know nothing about me, old man,' Geoff said. 'No one would give a shit if I took off. What the fuck do you know?'

'Geoff!' Hamid whacked his friend with the back of his hand, turning to Bailey. 'Look, all I know is that he said he needed to take off for a while, that he was in trouble and that there was something he needed to do.'

'What kind of trouble?' Dexter stepped in front of Bailey so that she could get Hamid's full attention.

'That's all I know, lady.'

'Fuck this.' Geoff turned his back and started walking away.

Hamid looked like he was getting a change of heart too. 'Mr Haneef, I hope you find Tariq soon. I really do. But I don't know what else to tell you.'

'Hamid?' Dexter pulled a card out of her pocket. 'Your mate was right, I am a copper. And it's really important that we find Tariq. If you remember anything else, or you hear anything, give me a call, okay?'

'Yeah, I guess.'

'And don't worry, you're not in any trouble,' she said. 'Your friend just needs our help.'

They watched Hamid run up the street to catch up with Geoff, the pair of them looking back over their shoulders a half dozen times before disappearing around the corner.

'You.' Dexter poked her finger into Bailey's arm. 'Can we have a quiet word?'

Bailey smiled, readying himself for the lecture coming his way. 'Of course.'

Dexter waited until they were far enough away from Omar before she started talking. 'You being here has the potential to seriously jeopardise our chances of finding the kid.'

'How so?' Bailey said.

'I'm not even getting into this with you.'

'Let's avoid the big statements then, shall we?' Bailey didn't like being reprimanded and he especially didn't like the insinuation that he was putting Tariq's life, or anyone else's, in more danger.

'Have you found out anything?' Dexter said.

'I was going to ask you the same question.'

'Here's one thing I can tell you,' Dexter said. 'The deal you thought you had with me about getting twenty-four hours is off. This thing's moving too quickly.'

'Then you do know something,' Bailey said. 'What've you got?'

Dexter grabbed his elbow and walked him further up the street so that her whispering voice wouldn't travel.

'Just chatter, Bailey. Chatter. Along the lines of what you told me. Something's coming. We don't know what, we don't know when. We just know.'

'Sounds like you know bugger all, then.'

'Don't be a smartarse,' Dexter said. 'But here's something I do know. You and I are going back to Omar's house right now. He's going to tell us everything he knows about his son.'

'Is that really necessary?'

Bailey was finding it difficult to separate an old loyalty from his relationship with Dexter and the reality of the dangerous situation in front of them.

'Yes. It is.'

Bailey sighed, knowing she was right. 'I'll talk to Omar.'

'No, you won't. I will. Because within an hour, a car full of AFP investigators will be meeting us there.'

'To what? Search the house?'

Bailey had almost forgotten what Dexter was like on the job. Everything by the book.

'We need to look at any computers they've got. Phones, tablets, whatever.'

'Do what you've got to do,' Bailey said.

'Don't look at me like that, Bailey. I told you these ops can go sideways very quickly. Information doesn't just fall out of the sky, we go looking for it. Just like you're doing right now.'

Bailey knew that she was right. Tariq had been in the suburban wilderness for a week already. If he was involved in something bad, the window for stopping it was closing.

'Let me break the news to Omar.' He tried again, holding up his palms. 'Please.'

Dexter took a moment to answer. 'Okay. But he travels in the car with me. At least it'll be a nicer ride than that pile of junk you drive.'

'The Corolla?' Bailey's face lit up at the mention of his beloved old bomb. 'Why is it that I'm the only one who sees beauty in that car?'

'I think it's time you got your eyes tested.'

He winked at her. 'You know I've got a good eye for all things fine.'

That one drew a half-smile from Dexter. She went to say something, then stopped. 'Let's go.'

They started walking back to break the bad news to Omar about the unscheduled visit to his home.

'And Bailey?' Dexter said before they reached him.

'Yep?'

'Stay out of the way of my investigators. Most of these AFP guys are nerds, they won't mess up Omar's house, they'll do what I say.'

'Don't we all?'

Dexter laughed, knowing there was truth in it. Most federal investigators in counter-terrorism had done their training in university lecture theatres. They dressed a little too sharply and spoke like intellectuals. They pissed off Dexter no end but they'd do exactly what she asked.

CHAPTER 13

Wiley Park was the kind of unremarkable suburb that people passed through without even noticing.

The streets were lined with weatherboard or orange brick houses and concrete driveways that took up half the land. Some families had so many cars that even the big driveways weren't enough, so they parked the vehicles, side by side, on wiry grass lawns.

But the suburb, like the city, was changing.

These days, you wouldn't get much change out of a million dollars for your average house in Wiley Park. And the immigrants who bought cheap houses here in the 1990s were laughing like anyone else that owned a block of land in Sydney. Omar Haneef was one of them.

After arriving from Baghdad, Omar had worked day and night driving his taxi, saving up a deposit for a new home and a new life.

Stepping through the front door, Bailey could see that Omar had done well. The walls inside were freshly painted, the furniture was neat and respectable, and the house was clean and tidy. There was a sense of history here too. Persian rugs on the floor, tapestries on walls and photographs of family and friends in gold-rimmed frames on the sideboard. This was a house where family mattered.

Proud of the life that they'd built, while never forgetting where they came from.

'Please.' Omar gestured to Bailey and Dexter to sit on the sofa in the lounge room.

'Nice house, mate.' Bailey was trying to make conversation while they waited for Noora Haneef to return with the tray she was preparing in the kitchen. 'Good to see you doing well.'

'It's home.'

Noora set down the tray on the table, placing saucers and small cups in front of her husband and their guests. The pear-shaped *dallah* was made of copper and it had been meticulously polished. Noora tilted the pot by its curved handle, pouring the thick black coffee into each cup.

'I'm okay, thanks,' Dexter began, 'I've had –'

Bailey touched Dexter on her knee and gave her a look that told her she was drinking the coffee, whether she wanted it or not. 'This looks lovely, thanks, Noora,' he said.

There were some cultural sensitivities that were worth respecting and refusing a cup of coffee in an Iraqi family's home would be a sign of disrespect. If Bailey and Dexter were going to get Omar and Noora to talk, they first had to respect the rules of the house.

'I was hoping you might be able to join us too, Noora?' Dexter pointed to the three cups on the table.

Noora looked at Omar, who nodded his head. She sat on the sofa beside him.

'So, what can you tell us about Tariq?' Dexter said.

Omar went to speak but Dexter held up her hand.

'If you don't mind, Omar. I'd like to hear from Noora now.'

Noora hesitated until the silence beckoned her to speak.

'My son is a good boy,' she said. 'He's a normal boy. He plays football with his friends, he studies. He's a good Muslim.'

'Pardon my ignorance, Noora. But what do you mean by *good Muslim*?'

Noora gave her husband a hopeful stare.

Bailey cleared his throat and his cup made a loud clinking sound when he placed it back on the saucer. 'Detective Dexter's really just trying to learn everything she can about Tariq. She's just trying to help, Noora. You don't need to worry. We just want to find your son.'

Dexter glared at Bailey, then turned back to Noora. 'John is right, we want to help. Now can you please tell me what you meant?'

'A *good Muslim* is someone who says their prayers, who is gentle and kind, who doesn't drink alcohol, who . . . who knows the importance of family, of community.' Noora was distracted by a sound in the kitchen.

'Is someone else here?' Dexter said.

'Sara? Sara is that you?' Noora called out. 'Come in here, darling. We have guests.'

Bailey remembered that Omar had a daughter too. His firstborn, older than Tariq.

Sara walked into the room. Like her mother, she was wearing a hijab. She had a bag slung over her shoulder, ready to go out.

'John Bailey, Detective Dexter,' Omar said. 'This is our daughter, Sara.'

'Lovely to meet you, Sara,' Bailey said, standing up.

'Is this about Tariq?' Sara walked over and stood next to her mother. 'Please tell me you've found him?'

'Not yet,' Bailey said. 'That's why we're here, to help find him.'

Noora reached for her daughter's hand, holding it tight. The one child that was safe.

'Has he done something wrong?' Sara said.

'We just think he might be in trouble, that's all,' Dexter cut in. 'Have you seen, or heard, from him?'

'Not since last week,' Sara said. 'It doesn't make sense for him to run off.' She sat down on the arm of the sofa. 'As Mum and Dad probably said, he's never done anything like this before.'

'Did you see Tariq hanging around with anyone unusual?' Bailey got back in the conversation. 'Any new friends?'

'No. Tariq's pretty straight.'

'Any of his friends into anything we should be worried about?' Dexter said.

'I don't think so. They just play soccer, video games. Stuff like that. I mean, everyone knows there's plenty of drugs around here – ice, y'know . . . but that isn't Tariq.'

'What do you mean, drugs?' Noora looked up at her daughter, the confusion telling on her face.

'Sorry, Mum.' Sara touched her mother's shoulder. 'I'm not saying that Tariq's into drugs. But plenty of kids are.'

'Tariq does not take drugs,' Noora said, defensively, her eyes trained on Dexter. 'I'm his mother. I can tell you that for certain.'

'Good to know,' Dexter said. 'Sara, exactly when was the last time you saw your brother?'

'A week ago, at dinner. Tuesday night. We all ate together and then I went to university the next morning, early. He went to school.'

'You haven't heard from him? He hasn't called you?'

'No. Nothing.' Sara stood up, slinging her bag over her shoulder. 'I really want to help but I don't know much at all. I've got an important lecture at university, if that's okay?'

They were interrupted by a knock on the door.

'I'll get the door.' Dexter knew exactly who was standing on the Haneefs' front porch. Before she moved to let them in, she pulled a card from her pocket, handing it to Sara. 'Here. Go to class, but I will need to talk to you again. Meantime, if you think of anything, or hear anything, give me a call. Doesn't matter what day, or time. Okay?'

'Of course, thanks.'

After Sara left, Bailey watched in silence as the cavalry moved in. Australian Federal Police, men and women in ill-fitting suits with scowling, serious faces. Dexter took them aside for a quiet chat. The boss.

'What's this?' Omar said to Bailey. 'What's going on?'

'They just need to take a look around.'

'At what?'

'Computers, Tariq's phone, if he has one, stuff like that.'

'We only have one family computer,' Noora said. 'And Tariq took his phone. It's been switched off for days.'

Bailey leaned forward, speaking quietly. 'Omar, when we saw each other this morning, you said that Tariq had been speaking to people over the internet. How do you know that?'

Omar's eyes were darting between the cops at his front door and Bailey.

'Omar?'

'Noora found something on the computer. A strange email account.' Omar looked across at his wife, who nodded for him to continue. 'In the deleted items there was a message.'

Omar was nervous and struggling to get his words out, knowing that they probably wouldn't just be for Bailey.

'Go on, mate. What'd it say?'

'I'll show you.'

Omar handed Bailey a folded piece of paper from his pocket. It was a print-out of an email that had been sent to an account name made up of a series of random letters and numbers.

Young soldier,

Our struggle needs great martyrs like you to show the infidels the power of jihad.

The instructions are coming. Allah is watching. You will be in his arms soon.

Mustafa

'Was this the only message in the account?'

'Yes,' Noora said. 'There may have been more but this was the only one I found.'

'One for the police, then,' Bailey said, eyeing Dexter who was still briefing the Feds at the front door.

Bailey refolded the piece of paper and slipped it into his pocket.

After the AFP officers had collected what they needed, it was time for everyone to go.

'Sharon,' Bailey stopped Dexter on the grass beside Omar's taxi, 'I've got to show you something.'

He reached into his pocket and handed her the piece of paper Omar had just given him. He had to share it now. If Tariq had been dumb enough to exchange messages with Mustafa al-Baghdadi using the family computer, it wouldn't take long for the cops to find out.

'You're kidding me,' Dexter said after reading the message. 'Mustafa?'

'That's what the note says.'

'You think it's Mustafa al-Baghdadi?'

'I know it is.'

She slipped the note into her pocket. 'And what makes you so certain?'

Bailey knew that he had to tell her about the phone call with Mustafa, but he didn't quite know where to start. Withholding information from the police was never a good idea. When the cop concerned was your girlfriend, it was just plain stupid.

'Bailey?'

'I spoke to him.'

'Tariq?'

Bailey shook his head. 'Mustafa.'

'You what?'

Dexter's face was flushed from the surprise. And anger. 'You're fucking kidding me. When? How?'

'This morning, after I left your place.'

'You're unbelievable.' She shook her head and turned her back on him, just for a moment, then she spun back around. 'You realise the position you've put me in?'

Bailey needed to find a way out of this, or he could wind up sitting in a police station all night answering questions he didn't know how to answer.

'Look, I was going to tell you,' he said. 'It was only a few hours ago.'

'A few hours can mean everything.'

'Yeah, well, I'm telling you now.' Bailey didn't like what Dexter was insinuating. 'And I've already got someone looking into the phone number.'

'Ronnie bloody Johnson, no doubt.'

Dexter knew enough about Ronnie to know that he wasn't just anyone.

'How'd you guess?'

Dexter never quite understood the closeness of Bailey's relationship with Ronnie. What had happened in Iraq must have bound them tightly together, because journalists and American intelligence agents were strange bedfellows indeed.

'I'd like Ronnie's number, please. Now.'

There was no point pushing back. Bailey thumbed through his phone and recited his old buddy's digits to Dexter.

'Thank you.' She climbed into her car. 'Ronnie had better answer and he'd better share what he's got, or I'm coming back for you. Then you can meet some of my colleagues down at the station.'

'Don't worry, he will.'

Bailey knew that Ronnie worked fast – faster than any of the cops who worked with Dexter, thanks to the abundant resources of the CIA. It was why he went to him in the first place. But he'd never admit that to Dexter.

'And you're not a cop, Bailey. Remember that.' She started the engine. 'Stay at your place tonight.'

'Shame. I was all up for a cuddle.'

'Then stop pissing me around.'

Bailey watched her speed off down the street, wondering if she was still talking about work and hoping to God that Ronnie would take her call.

He was still holding his phone in his hand when it started to vibrate.

A message from Annie Brooks.

Are you home?

I could do with a chat

How about a walk?

It was the second time she'd been in contact today. Annie was supposed to be Bailey's AA sponsor, but for some reason he was feeling like the strong one.

Sure

Home in 45

He was feeling guilty the moment he hit send. Confiding in a woman like Annie Brooks, someone he'd known in another life, was deeply personal. They were getting close. He felt it.

It was just a walk.

CHAPTER 14

A cloud of smoke was hovering next to the window on Bailey's front porch.

'Been waiting for you, bubba.'

He couldn't see Ronnie, but he could smell his cigar.

'For a second there, I thought my house was on fire,' Bailey said, opening the gate.

'Where would I sleep if I burned the place down?'

'I'm going to start charging you rent soon. You know that, don't you?'

'Now, now. Who's going to water the plants when you're at Sharon's place?' Ronnie stood up, pointing at the dead fern in the pot by the front door.

Bailey laughed. There wasn't a green thumb between them. 'Got anything for me?'

'Matter of fact, I do.'

'Really?'

'Would I lie to you, bubba?'

'Seriously want me to answer that?' Bailey said.

Ronnie took a drag on his cigar, blowing the smoke at the street. 'We ran a trace on that phone number Mustafa was using.'

'And?'

'We couldn't get a location on where the call came from.'

'I thought you –'

'But we traced the SIM card to an address in Al-Qa'im.'

'Northern Iraq?' Bailey had spent enough years in and out of Iraq to know the geography. Al-Qa'im was a small town along the Euphrates that touched the border with Syria. 'Sounds way too simple to me.'

'Cell numbers aren't brought into this world by immaculate reception.'

Ronnie paused for Bailey to acknowledge his bad joke.

'Clever.'

'Thank you.' Ronnie smiled. 'Whoever bought this one did it four years ago, registered to a shopfront in Al-Qa'im. At least, that's what the computer said.'

It made sense, considering what was happening in Iraq. Islamic Nation had been using the Euphrates River Valley in Al-Qa'im to ferry fighters and supplies between Syria and Iraq. It was also one of the group's last known strongholds. On that basis, the intelligence stacked up.

'So, you think it'll help track him down?'

'Doubt it,' Ronnie said. 'You haven't helped us find anything we don't already know.'

We.

'You're pretty plugged in for a guy who spends his days fishing.'

Ronnie ignored the sledge. 'It's no great secret that Mustafa has spent time in Al-Qa'im. Until recently, it was the most solid ground he had. Before the Iraqis took it back, the son of a bitch was living in a hospital.'

'You can't hit a hospital,' Bailey said.

'No. We can't.'

'What happened to the phone?'

'Dead. The SIM card would be a melted blob of plastic by now. But the fact that he had someone give you the number makes me think that Mustafa wants us to believe he's in Al-Qa'im.'

'When he could be anywhere.'

'Exactly.'

Bailey snapped off a twig from his shrivelled fern. 'What happens now?'

'Nothing, bubba.' Ronnie had one last drag on his cigar, then stubbed it into the coffee mug that he'd been using as an ashtray. 'We just wait for him to get in touch again.'

Ronnie knew Mustafa about as well as Bailey did. Maybe better. He also knew that Mustafa should have been dead by now. The fact that he was still alive was clearly getting under Ronnie's skin.

'How long till you get a copy of my file?'

'Still working on that. Won't be long.'

'Anyway, mate.' Bailey could see Annie Brooks walking towards them on the other side of the street. 'I need to go out for a bit.'

Ronnie followed Bailey's gaze, clocking Annie just as she was crossing the road in a pair of bright green tights and a hoodie.

'Hello, boys!' She waved at them.

'Holy hell,' Ronnie whispered. 'You're in a whole world of trouble, bubba.'

'Tell me about it,' Bailey mumbled, quietly, before returning the wave to Annie as she opened the gate. 'Just give me a minute to change.'

The Centennial Park Circuit is exactly 3.8 kilometres. Throw in a kilometre each way from Bailey's house, and he wasn't getting much change from a six-kilometre walk.

A few months ago, Bailey would have been puffing like a chain-smoker and looking for excuses to stop and stretch his hamstrings whenever he could. Now he had some semblance of fitness and an hour on his feet wasn't so daunting.

'Nice sneakers,' Annie said, noticing Bailey's fluorescent blue trainers as they stepped through the gate on Oxford Street and into the park. 'Are they new?'

'My daughter bought them for me. She and my partner have teamed up and formed the "get Bailey fit" brigade. I've told them the gear stops at lycra. No one needs to see that.'

Annie laughed. 'Some girls don't mind a bit of padding.'

'Thanks for the reassurance,' Bailey said, stumbling on a tree root, just managing to stay upright.

They walked down the hill on the sun-tinged grass, passing under the outstretched arms of the Australian figs. The park was usually a feast of green at this time of year but the drought was biting hard, spreading from the bush to the city.

'Sorry, I didn't mean to embarrass you,' Annie said, noticing that Bailey had gone quiet. 'I'm just playing with you.'

'Takes a lot more than that to embarrass me,' Bailey said. 'I've just got a bit on my mind.'

Bailey was feeling guilty. He wanted to get back out there and look for Tariq. But the deal with Annie was important. If she was going to be there for him, then he needed to do the same for her. And he liked her company.

The sun had already disappeared and there wasn't a cloud in the sky. The white beam from the moon was lighting their way.

They hit the circuit down by the café and headed in a clockwise direction around the park.

With the cars locked out at 6 pm, only fitness troupes were left. Running groups. Power walkers. Dog owners out for a stroll, their poo bags dangling from their wrists.

A horse trotted past, its tail raised while it dropped a load on the dirt track. Its rider wasn't stopping to pick that up. They'd need a bloody garbage bag. Horse shit was one of life's great mysteries – how someone who owns a chihuahua cops a fine for failing to pick up a tiny twig of excrement, while a horse owner gets away with leaving a mountain of manure on the pavement. Baffling.

'What are you thinking about?' Annie said.

'I was going to ask you the same question.'

Horse shit wasn't very interesting.

'Am I that transparent?'

'No. You just seem like . . . like there's something bothering you.'

'I had a drink two nights ago.' Annie kept her eyes on the path. 'Half a bottle. Bit more.'

Bailey knew vodka was Annie's poison, so half a bottle couldn't exactly be classed in the 'slip-up' territory. It was a binge.

'Are you okay?'

He wasn't going to admonish her. Alcoholics punished themselves enough, once they'd stopped lying to themselves.

Annie stopped, her torment clear in her watery eyes, glistening in the moonlight. 'Just disappointed. You know the drill.'

'Yeah, well. Doesn't make you weak. Don't overthink this one, Annie. You've been doing so bloody well. Been a saint to me.'

She stopped, their eyes meeting in the night. 'Have I?'

'You know you have. Ninety-four days and counting.'

She stepped closer and Bailey could smell the fruity balm on her lips.

'I just blew up two years of sobriety,' Annie said, shaking her head.

'You know how this works. One day at a time. What's that saying you said to me the first time we caught up?'

'Control the things you can control.'

'Yeah, that's it.'

'Won't work this time.'

'Why? Is there something else?'

She rested her forehead in her hand, looking down at the track. Her shoelace was loose and she bent down to tighten it.

'Annie?'

She stood up again, a tear trickling down her cheek. 'Barron's getting out next month.'

Her ex-husband, Barron Norris. The wealthy property developer who turned out to be a violent drug addict. He was currently serving a two-year sentence for bashing Annie so badly that she'd spent two weeks in a coma and had her jaw reconstructed.

Bailey hated the guy and he'd never even met him. Knowing he'd bashed up Annie was enough. And also because his name was 'Barron'.

'Shit, Annie. I'm sorry,' Bailey said. 'Surely, his parole conditions will be so strict he won't be allowed near you and Louis.'

Louis was Annie's sixteen-year-old son. Bailey had only met him once but Annie talked about him all the time.

'You'd have thought so,' she said, her voice cracking up. 'He can't come near me but somehow he has visitation rights with Louis.'

'Really?'

'Louis doesn't want to see him, of course. Not after what he did to me.'

'What will you do?'

'I'm talking to my lawyer, we'll fight it. Anyway, when I found out I just panicked and hit the bottle.'

'I'm sorry I wasn't around.'

'That's not what I meant; this was my fault.'

'Yeah, well. You know you can call me. Whenever.'

'Thanks, Bailey.'

He squeezed her on the arm and she leaned in, inviting him to put his arms around her. He did and he could feel the curves of her breasts pressing into his stomach. He rested his chin on the top of her head, smelling the shampoo in her hair. Their arms wrapped around each other, neither of them in any hurry to let go. It was Annie who moved first, stepping back, touching the stubble of his chin, giving him a look that most men dreamed about.

'Annie.'

She pulled her hand away, looking embarrassed. 'Sorry. I just needed a hug.'

Bailey pulled her back into his arms, lying to himself that the comforting moment was just for her. He closed his eyes, thinking back to their nights together in Beirut. Watching her walk, naked, from his bed to the shower. Remembering how she used to leave the door open so that he could watch her bathe under the steaming bristles of water, inviting him to join her so they could have one more go for the road. When they were ordinary people. Before they had to be foreign correspondents again.

Sensing the change in him, Annie pulled back again, chin raised until she found his lips with hers. The kiss lasted about five seconds before Bailey remembered where he was, who he was.

'Sorry, Annie. I can't. I –'

'Sharon's a lucky woman.'

'Not sure she'd agree with you,' Bailey said, laughing, awkwardly, at his own joke.

'It's just . . . hard to be alone at the moment.'

'You're not alone.' Bailey touched her shoulder. 'This thing with Sharon, I just can't fuck it up again. We've been to hell and back.'

Annie took a step back on the path. 'Like I said, she's a lucky woman.'

Ding!

A white strobing bicycle light was racing towards them.

'Excuse me!' The guy on the bike called out when he was only metres away.

Bailey and Annie stepped to the side to let him pass. The guy had plastic spears on his helmet to ward off the magpies and a side-mirror strapped to his arm. He was wearing a fluorescent lycra outfit that emphasised the fat gut hanging over his waist like a muffin top.

'That's why I don't wear lycra,' Bailey said, trying to break the tension.

Annie laughed, punching him on the arm. 'You're doing all right.'

'And you're a bloody catch, Annie. You know that, right?' Bailey said.

'Yeah. Yeah.'

'We just need to find you someone who doesn't have a name like Barron.'

CHAPTER 15

Gerald was sitting alone on Bailey's front porch when he arrived home from his walk.

'I'm a popular man tonight,' Bailey said, swinging open the gate. 'I'm surprised you're still talking to me after that plane ride home.'

'I've known you for thirty years, mate. You've been a much bigger pain in the arse than that.'

He had him there.

Gerald took a sip of his whisky. 'How was the park?'

'Nice night for it.' Bailey sat down in the chair next to Gerald. 'I see you've found my stash.'

'I'm doing you a favour.'

Bailey noticed the empty glass on the table. 'Where's Ronnie?'

'He went out. Said something about picking up your file. What's all that about?'

Bailey kept nothing from Gerald. Not after everything they'd been through. So he told him about the CIA file and the phone call from Mustafa al-Baghdadi.

'It's pretty explosive stuff, Bailey. What're you going to do with it?'

Gerald Summers. The editor. Always thinking about his newspaper.

'Nothing, until I know what the hell it's all about. But don't worry, old boy.' Bailey tapped Gerald on the shoulder. 'When there's a story there, I'll write it.'

Gerald undid the top button on his shirt, loosening his tie. He must have gone home for a wardrobe change and to say hello to Nancy. Always the sharp dresser. Even when he was a war correspondent Gerald had worn suits. Including a white one, 'for the heat'. Mr Slick.

'Why are you here, by the way?'

It was unlike Gerald to turn up unannounced. He always had a reason.

'Yes. That.' He shifted, uncomfortably, in his chair. 'I don't quite know how to broach this one with you, mate.'

'The Queen's English will do.'

Gerald took another sip from his glass.

'It's about your job.'

'What about it?'

'The suits are circling, Bailey. This time they're coming after you. I think I'm gone, too.'

More cost-cutting at the newspaper. Bailey could see that Gerald was serious. Only, this conversation should have happened years ago, when Bailey had stopped filing stories because he was a drunken insomniac, torn apart by the things he'd seen. *The Journal* had paid for his rehabilitation and now he was getting fired? It didn't make sense.

'What's brought this on? I've never been more productive, and you know it.'

'The new world, mate. It just isn't for guys like us anymore.'

'What the hell does that mean?'

'Bailey, I'm talking about me too!' Gerald tapped his chest with his fingertips. 'It's both of us. And Judith, Alan, Gavin. We're all being looked at.'

'You've just named *The Journal*'s three best fucking reporters.'

'If you'd just listen to me, Bailey! It's this social media stuff, third party platforms. All this shit about new audiences.' Gerald drained what was left of his whisky. 'Twitter, Facebook, Snapchat, video comments for the web – you guys don't do any of that stuff. And these private equity blokes don't read your articles, mate. They only look at the numbers. The clicks.'

'Let's see the type of stories that get ripped off and shared on social media after guys like me stop breaking them.' Bailey yanked open his front door. 'Fucking suits.'

He slammed the door behind him.

CHAPTER 16

IRAQ

UNKNOWN LOCATION

The restraints were cutting into Bailey's wrists and ankles, creating deep welts that were burning his skin.

The constant pain was making it difficult to sleep.

Not that he was getting much rest with his kidnappers taking it in turns to remind him of his fragility. His worthlessness. Eliminate hope. Teach him about fear.

He was facing a wall, tied to a hardwood chair. Bailey had no idea how long he'd been there.

Hours. Days. A week.

He'd lost track of the time because of the bulb above his head. The bright light illuminating the windowless shithole where he was being held. Always on.

They'd removed his blindfold and gag after strapping him to the chair on the day he'd arrived. He'd been there ever since.

He'd had plenty of time to study every detail of the room. Time to imagine what had gone on here before.

There was a bucket in the corner – Bailey's toilet, when they let him use it.

The floor was layered with sand and pocked with pools of dried blood.

There was a steel wash basin. Old rags piled in the corner. A stack of leather sandals. All sizes.

And the cracked wall.

Rows of bullet holes stretching from one side to the other – two neat lines, one for the adults, the other, slightly lower, for the children.

An entire family lined up and executed. This had probably been their home.

Click.

The door opened behind him.

Footsteps.

More visitors. More pain.

A man appeared in front of him, a gun in his hand.

'Hello, dog!'

He slipped open the chamber of his revolver, offering a toothless smile.

The chamber of the gun was empty.

'What do you want?'

A pointless question but Bailey had to say something, if only to hear himself speak. Remind himself that he was still alive.

The man smiled again, picking a bullet from his pocket, dropping it into one of the six empty holes in the chamber.

'You play game?'

One bullet. A one in six chance of surviving.

'You sick fuck.'

The guy laughed again, holding the pistol to Bailey's temple, spinning the chamber. The loud clinks of metal vibrating through Bailey's skull.

He was breathing in short bursts, heart racing, wondering whether this was it. Whether they'd had enough of him. Whether this game had an ending.

Russian Roulette.

The squeaking tension on the trigger. The cool gun barrel against Bailey's skin.

Clink!

The man erupted into laughter. Bailey could hear someone behind him laughing too.

'Just fun. Just fun.'

The guy with the bad teeth was standing in front of him again, hands in the air.

'Fucking animal.'

The guy didn't seem bothered by Bailey's insults.

'We have another game for you.'

Bailey could hear water sloshing in a bucket behind him. A rag being wrung out.

'No, no more,' Bailey said. 'No more!'

Pleading with these guys was useless.

Bailey knew what was coming.

He started bouncing up and down on his chair. Angry outbursts were his only empowerment. Something to remind himself that he was a person. That he had things worth living for. Miranda. His little girl. Hang on, Bailey. Hang on.

Bailey's chair was yanked backwards. Eyes on the cobwebbed ceiling, a wet cloth shoved onto his face, blocking out the light.

He tried to shake the cloth free. His head swinging from side to side.

A fist pounded his cheekbone, stunning him. He knew what was coming next.

He held his breath as the water splashed onto his face, preventing that first rush of liquid from running through his nostrils and down the back of his throat.

Waterboarding.

The other sick game they played.

The second rush of water went in all the places they wanted it to. The muscles in his throat gagged. A useless reflex with water also streaming through his nose.

And the water kept coming.

Chest burning. Head and muscles aching. The panic of drowning consuming him. The shame of wondering whether he was better off dead.

Another rush. Burning pain. Bailey was dizzy, wondering if this was it.

Then she was there. Right on time. That little voice inside his head. His little girl. Miranda. The kid he'd left to come to this wretched place. The one he owed so much. Telling him that she loved him. Telling him to hang on.

Hang on.

CHAPTER 17

There wasn't much room on the footpath along Oxford Street. The bus stops had queues and so did the cafés serving takeaway coffees. It was 7 am and the street was already bustling.

Bailey's catch-up sleep after London hadn't gone according to plan. The nightmares were back. He'd spent most of the night staring at the ceiling, afraid to close his eyes. Thinking about the bottle. Something to help him forget.

Despite the lack of sleep, Bailey was buoyed by the sunrise. He had an important breakfast engagement. His weekly catch-up with Miranda. He never missed it.

Excited by the prospect of seeing her, Bailey was side-stepping people on the footpath like a rugby player looking for space.

The café where they'd arranged to meet was only a ten-minute walk from his house, giving Bailey ten more minutes to think about whether or not he still had a job. The prospect terrified him.

Telling other people's stories was all that he knew. It gave him meaning, a cause, a reason to get out of bed each day. It wasn't like he didn't have anything else; he had Miranda and Dexter. But they had important jobs, busy lives. After all his brushes with death over the years – and there had been many – he knew that the greatest threat to his mortality was actually himself. The job gave him a routine, kept him going.

If Gerald was right, Bailey could be cleaning out his desk at *The Journal* within days. This private equity mob didn't mess around. When they made a decision, people got marched.

People in boardrooms used to be there to support reporters like Bailey. Now they were just counting clicks, desperate for dollar signs.

Bailey knew he was a technological luddite, but he also knew what made good journalism. And it wasn't the kid cutting clever videos, or the tech entrepreneur making money by stealing articles so that the public could get their stories on their phones for free. No. Journalism cost money. Took time. If only there were more people fighting for it.

Bailey made it to the café and spotted Miranda tapping away on her laptop at the table by the window. The corporate lawyer, always working.

Distracted by the sight of his daughter, Bailey missed the girl walking towards him, thumbing away on her phone, communicating with her virtual friends.

She walked straight into him.

'Shit, mate! Bloody hell!'

Bailey wasn't that tall but, pound for pound, he was much bigger than she was, which meant the coffee she was carrying ended up down her front and on her jeans.

'Watch where you're going, would you!' she said. 'You just spilt coffee all over me. Fuck!'

'Maybe you should watch where you're going?'

'Whatever, old man.'

'There's a whole world out there outside that phone, you know,' Bailey said.

'You're a dickhead.'

'I'm not the one wearing the latte.'

'Yeah?' She pointed at Bailey's stomach. 'Take a look at your shirt.'

He looked down at the brown stain expanding towards his waistline.

'Oh, well.' Bailey gave her a condescending smile. 'One of us worries about how they look, and it isn't me.'

'Dad!' Miranda was standing in the doorway, waving him inside. 'Forget about it. Let's eat.'

Bailey ignored the girl, who was now insisting that he give her some cash for dry cleaning, and joined Miranda inside. Before he even could sit down, his daughter was dabbing at the stain on his shirt with a wet napkin.

'Don't worry about it, sweetheart.' The coffee wasn't the only mark on his shirt. The cuffs were fraying and the collar was a different colour than the rest. 'This one's already on the way out.'

'Shame. It's such a lovely shirt.'

'Now, now.' He waved a finger. 'No need to insult your old man. You know how deeply I care about fashion.'

They ate breakfast talking about the interesting things they'd read, and Miranda updated her father about her mother's travels with Ian the banker. Bailey was always interested. He still had a soft spot for Anthea. They were friends. Or, at least his ex-wife answered his calls.

'Dad?' Miranda's face turned serious. 'I need to talk to you about something.'

Bailey put down his fork even though he'd just speared a strip of bacon. There was something about the tone in her voice that worried him.

'Shoot.'

'It's about me and Peter.'

Doctor Peter Andrews. The live-in boyfriend. The guy who had treated Bailey in hospital after he had been bashed by a sadistic Chinese spy. That felt like a long time ago now. Somehow Doctor Andrews had managed to fix Bailey and hit on his daughter at the same time. Miranda had assured him that she'd been the one who'd made the first move. Not that her admission had made it any better for Bailey.

'Are you guys okay?' Bailey had no idea where this was going.

'Yes. Yes, we're more than . . . okay.' She was sounding nervous, tripping on her words, which was unlike Miranda. 'We're thinking about, you know . . . getting hitched.'

'Hitched?' Bailey frowned. 'That's, that's great, sweetheart.'

'Yeah? You don't look so happy. He's a good guy, Dad.'

Good guy or not, Bailey was feeling like someone had just driven up the back of his car. A moment of shock. These past few years, he'd grown closer to his daughter. He'd won back her trust, no longer the absent father. He didn't want that to change.

'Dad?'

'It's great news, really.' Bailey reached across the table, cupping her hands in his. 'I know the doc's a good guy. I'm happy for you, really. I'm just your dad, that's all. You'll always be my little girl.'

'That won't change.'

She squeezed his hands, looking down at them, touching the fingers where his nails used to be. He'd told her why they weren't there anymore. He'd never meant to, but she had drawn it out of him. Telling his daughter that he'd been kidnapped and tortured was the toughest conversation of his life.

'I don't know why I'm sounding funny about this, Miranda.' Bailey sat back, shaking his head. 'I like the doc. I know he'll look after you. And your mum and I will help you out with the wedding.'

'Thanks, Dad. That means a lot.'

'So, is this official then?'

Miranda looked sheepish. 'Not quite. Peter's going to call you. He wants to do it the right way. Traditional. He wants to ask for your blessing.'

Bailey remembered how he'd done the same with Anthea's father all those years ago. Fathers respected that, however old-fashioned it seemed. He would too.

'I'd take him out for a beer but, you know.'

'Try tea. He's a little nervous, though. So be nice to him.'

'I'm always nice.'

'Dad, don't get me wrong here, but you can be a little grumpy at times.'

'When the doc calls, I'll be on my best behaviour. Promise.'

Bailey raised his hand to let the waiter know they were up for another round of coffees.

'How's Sharon?' Miranda changed the subject. 'Ever considered tying the knot again?'

'Been there, done that. But we're good.' Bailey knocked the table with his knuckles. 'Solid as a rock.' At least, some of the time. He wasn't going there with his daughter.

Miranda had made a big effort with Dexter. They'd first met each other when Sharon and Bailey had gotten together in the late nineties, before he'd walked out on her to cover George W. Bush's wars in Afghanistan and Iraq. Miranda was a kid back then, but she was an adult now. The two women genuinely liked each other and they spoke regularly. Too regularly.

'Can I give you some advice, Dad?'

'No.' Bailey knew what was coming. 'But I think you're about to do it anyway.'

'If you're flying overseas for work, it's a good idea to loop-in the *missus*,' Miranda said, mimicking his voice with a cheeky smile on her face.

'Noted.'

'How was London, by the way?'

The change of subject left Bailey with another question that he didn't want to ponder.

'Nothing too exciting. Speech went okay. Gerald was his usual boring self.'

Miranda understood the underlying affection in her father's insults. What she didn't understand was why he was playing down the murder in St James's Square.

'Dad, you know I read your articles. I've even got a little app that alerts me every time you write something.'

'Yeah, well . . .' A bloke arrived with the coffees. Bailey waited for him to leave before finishing his thought. 'I don't like giving the crazies the satisfaction of being talked about. It's what they want.'

'Another terrorist attack in London. How many in the last twelve months? Three? Four? It must be terrible to be –'

'Miranda, as I said, these nutters want to be talked about.'

He took another sip from his cup, rubbing his eyes. 'You want to know something? The truth is, the world's never been safer.'

'Then why do I feel so afraid?'

Bailey didn't know how to answer that and he was relieved when he felt his phone vibrating in his pocket. Dexter.

'Bailey.' Her voice had a sharp edge to it. 'There's a raid about to go down in Roselands. We think Tariq might be there. You should get here.'

'Got an address?' He was on his feet, phone at his ear, rummaging through his pocket for some cash.

'Just head west and I'll tell you when I can. Raid hasn't happened yet. You'll get a location when we're done.'

Still, it was a hell of a tip-off. Especially given that it was coming from the cop who had given him an earful the night before. Dexter could be a cunning operator. She'd never played him before, but something didn't feel right.

'Appreciate the tip-off, Sharon. What's in it for you?'

Dexter went quiet on the other end of the phone. 'Don't be so cynical. There are areas where we can work together on this.'

This was about the phone call from Mustafa al-Baghdadi. He knew it. Suddenly, Bailey was useful. He didn't like it.

'And Bailey?'

'Yeah?'

'No reporting on this. And don't tell the Haneefs until I give you the word, okay?'

'Got it.'

Bailey hung up and put some money on the table to cover his and Miranda's breakfasts. 'Got to run, sweetheart.'

CHAPTER 18

The benefit of driving west at nine o'clock in the morning was that most of the traffic was heading in the opposite direction towards the city.

Bailey was making good time. Within fifteen minutes, he was driving past the bridal shops, tattooists, massage parlours, tax accountants and charcoal chicken shops lining Parramatta Road. The closer he got to the turn-off at Old Canterbury Road, the grottier the shopfronts. Flaking paint, graffiti-splashed windows. The failing businesses on one of the busiest corridors in Sydney. Another big tick for the politicians who were good at building roads and not much else.

He turned onto Old Canterbury Road and, within five minutes, there was yet more evidence of a generation of political classes who'd fallen asleep at the wheel. Half-built apartment buildings with shopfronts on the ground floor that would probably never be occupied.

The morons running Sydney believed in two things – laying bitumen and letting property developers do whatever the hell they wanted. In this part of the city, new apartment buildings were sprouting out of the ground like weeds. Buildings were approved by council at one height and then, as if by magic, doubled in size. A few extra floors signed off at long lunches where dessert came with a bag of cash. It was happening everywhere and no one was going to jail.

Closing in on Roselands, Bailey still hadn't had any updates from Dexter. He'd been a reporter long enough to know that the police wouldn't hit the house until they knew all that they needed to know about the threat inside. That meant possibly hours of waiting.

He pulled into a service station and picked up a newspaper, a bottle of water and an egg and lettuce sandwich so he that he had something other than the radio in his car to pass the time.

The Police Tactical Operations Unit would already be at a holding area nearby. These were the guys who would conduct the raid. Highly trained tough guys who wore heavy gear, carried heavy weapons, and knew how to clear a house of dangerous criminals within seconds. They would have raced to Roselands minutes after the call went out. The hurry-up and wait.

Bailey turned into a random street off Old Canterbury Road and drove to a spot that the map on his phone told him was the geographical centre of Roselands. It was a small suburb. The house couldn't be more than a few minutes' drive from where he parked his car behind an old box trailer under the shade of a tree.

He looked at his watch. 9.33 am. The waiting game begins.

Bailey switched on the radio, wondering what Keith Roberts was talking about today.

'Okay, my dear listeners, I'm going to tell a few home truths.'

Here we go, thought Bailey. He was just in time for one of Keith Roberts's sermons.

'We've all heard and seen those ghastly pictures from St James's Square in London by now. Another Muslim terrorist who doesn't like our way of life. But you know what he did like, dear listeners? He liked to use the NHS. He liked his publicly funded school. And he also liked the council house that the British Government gave him and his mother to live in.'

Roberts paused to take a breath and shift gears. Bailey knew exactly where he was headed.

'People like that young man with the knife are here too, you know. These jihadis. Living amongst us. Hundreds of them. Maybe thousands. Living off the public tit in some way or form. Collecting cheques while judging our western ways. Apparently, we're the evil ones!

'Now of course, dear listeners, I don't think that all Muslims are bad people. Of course, they're not. But the reality is that the Islamic community isn't doing their bit to help the police to weed out these bad eggs. The people who hate us. Hate our way of life. We've seen it before. Martin Place. Parramatta. Bourke Street in Melbourne. Extremists who reckon that their God – what do they call him? Allah – wants them to kill people like us because of the movies we watch and the fact that we might like a cold beer at the end of the day.'

Roberts was in full flight now and Bailey's hand was hovering in front of the dial, wanting to turn him off. But he kept listening. If only to hear how quickly fear could morph into bigotry.

'The attacks will go on. More people will die. In our cities and our suburbs. This Islamic Nation outfit is like a cancer spreading through our society. And, quite frankly, my dear listeners, Muslims need to do something about it. Where are the clerics standing up and denouncing what happened in London? Where's the leadership? The police need help here and Australia's Muslim community isn't playing ball – they'd rather protect a terrorist than have him face justice.'

Bailey was getting angry now. The way people like Roberts simplified the problem – making it 'us versus them' – only made it worse, adding to people's fears. Should a Catholic bishop apologise for a fundamentalist Christian cult? Or the violent actions of white supremacists who liked to quote the Bible? No. Yet, somehow, all Muslims were responsible for Islamic terrorism.

'So, here's what needs to happen.' Roberts sounded like he was reaching his climax. 'And I say this directly to all Muslims in this country. It's time to dob in a terrorist! Yes, that's right. We can't do it, you need to! Dob. In. A. Terrorist! If you suspect someone of having extremist views, dob them in. If you hear someone saying they like Islamic Nation, dob them in. If you know someone who you think might be sending money to people in the Middle East and that the money could be going to terrorists, dob them in! It's time, people! Let's stop the rot and make our country safe again!'

Click.

Bailey switched off the radio. Guys like Keith Roberts were bad for democracy. The only difference between him and the extremists was that his weapon was a microphone instead of a gun. But it was just as dangerous.

A crack of lightning made Bailey jump in his seat.

He'd fallen asleep in his car again, head up against the window. It was the middle of the day and it was dark outside, big grey clouds dominating the sky.

Raindrops started landing on the car, a patter at first, before the skies opened in a violent storm. The drops of water were quickly replaced by hail, pelting his car like machine-gun fire.

Minutes later, it was over. The clouds had parted and Sydney was covered by blue sky again, the hot sun lifting the water back off the road in a steamy haze.

Sydney's weather was becoming crazy. Almost tropical.

Three hours, and still no call from Dexter. Bailey's impatience got the better of him and he sent her a message. He knew that it would annoy her, but he did it anyway.

Three hours and counting

Roselands isn't exactly a holiday destination

Any updates, detective?

He got the response he was expecting.

No

At least it was a response.

He peeled back the plastic on his egg and lettuce sandwich and prayed that it had been made within the past twenty-four hours. The hard exterior of the bread suggested that it hadn't. He was bored and hungry, so he took the chance. It didn't taste too bad. Although Bailey knew that the measure of a service station lunch wasn't in the taste, it was in what happened later. Fingers crossed.

When the fourth hour ticked over, Bailey rolled back his seat for another siesta. He closed his eyes, and caught a faint hum of an engine. Getting louder. Closer.

He sat up just in time to catch the BearCat in his rear-view mirror, lights flashing, engine roaring. He turned the key in the ignition just as the nine-tonne armoured rescue truck sped past with two guys wearing flash hoods in the front seat.

Bailey swung out onto the street after them, his little Corolla making all kinds of noises that he'd never heard before.

Two turns later and the lights on the roof of the BearCat went dead.

They must have been getting close.

Three more turns and the BearCat skidded to a stop.

Bailey had followed enough cops around over the years to know what was likely to happen next.

The first aim of the Tactical Operations Unit was to stun the target. These guys were used to dealing with dangerous people. Surprise was everything.

Bailey parked a good fifty metres away, trying to avoid being seen.

Seconds later, five police cars blocked off the area around an old weatherboard house with paint peeling off the outside and a shitty old Commodore in the driveway.

The street had multiple entry points, meaning multiple exits.

Sliding down the front seat, ducking his head so that he wouldn't get noticed, Bailey grabbed his notepad from the glove box and started writing down what he saw.

The doors to the BearCat swung open along with the hatch on the roof. The marksman up top was the first to appear. His job was to be the eyes for the team going in. For however long it took, he'd be up there, pointing his M4 carbine rifle at the house, ready to deal with any threat with lethal force.

Bailey counted five others as they poured out of the truck. He'd had enough beers with TOU cops to know all the roles. The team leader would have assigned everyone before they had even left the station. Driver, shield man, marksman, negotiator. They all looked the same. Faces hidden behind flash hoods, goggles and helmets. Each wearing dark navy overalls, ballistic vests, rifles in their right hands and Glock pistols – secondary weapons – strapped to their belts along with a canister of CS spray.

It was all happening so quickly that anyone inside the house would have no idea about the guns pointing in their direction, getting closer. The guy with the ballistic shield was leading them up the concrete driveway towards the front door. Seconds later, he stepped aside to make way for the guy with the ram.

One swing of the metal cylinder and the door was wide open.

'Go! Go! Go!'

The TOU guys moved quickly inside.

If the targets really were terrorists then there was always the chance that they had serious weapons, like bombs. Violent nut jobs could make them using instructions from the internet, with all the ingredients available on the shelf at the hardware store up the road. There was no room for error.

A series of loud bangs echoed from inside, white lights flashing through the windows. Bullets, stun grenades, Bailey didn't know. He just hoped that nobody had put a bullet in Tariq Haneef. This wasn't how it was supposed to end for him. He was only fifteen years old. Young enough to make mistakes. Much too young to die for them.

'Drop your weapon! Drop your weapon!'

The marksman on top of the BearCat was yelling at a guy in a pair of boxer shorts who'd sprinted around from the back of the house with a pistol in his hand.

'Drop it!'

The guy raised the gun at the cop who responded by squeezing the trigger on his rifle, unloading two bullets into his chest.

Bang! Bang!

The gunman fell to his knees. Before his shoulder had even hit the grass the bloke in the hatch squeezed off another two rounds.

The noises from inside the house had stopped and, after a few minutes, the cops walked out the front door with two men, half-dressed, their hands cuffed behind their backs. Covered in tattoos, with bulging muscles and crew cuts, they looked more like drug dealers or standover men than terrorists.

The cops marched them onto the driveway, forcing them to lie face-down, metres from where the guy with the pistol lay dead on the lawn.

There wasn't any sign of Tariq.

By now, another dozen officers, around half of them in uniform, were standing out the front, waiting for the TOU to hand over control to the most senior cop on the scene. Bailey guessed that was Sharon Dexter. She walked over to a stumpy guy in a grey suit and, after a short conversation, she turned around and headed towards Bailey's car.

She didn't look happy.

Dexter tapped on his window, probably wondering why he hadn't already wound it down, considering their eyes had been locked for the past thirty seconds.

'I told you to wait for my message.'

'That was five hours ago. I thought you'd forgotten about me.'

'Do you ever do what anyone tells you?'

'You want the honest answer?'

'I know the honest answer.'

'Boss!' The cop in the grey suit called out from where he was standing on the grass. 'Crime scene's ours!'

She gave him a nod, then turned back to Bailey. 'The kid wasn't in there, but we think he was at some stage.'

'How d'you know?'

'Talk later. We've got a bit to get through.'

'Any IDs for me?'

'Too early, Bailey. But don't feel sorry for the dead guy on the grass. We know these guys. Shit bags, all of them.'

'Suspects known to police, then?'

'I'll give you something. But you're going to have to wait.'

'Mind if I hang around?'

'You're here now.'

Bailey tapped her arm through the window. 'Don't worry, I won't cause any trouble.'

'I know you won't.' Dexter leaned closer. 'Why don't you start up the other end of the street, that little white house with the neat garden.'

Bailey watched Dexter walk back towards the house, where most of the cops were standing around the dead guy on the lawn. He wasn't sold on the tip-off. Of course she'd suggest he start at the house furthest away. There was a crime scene up this end of the street. Police business. Journalists were *persona non grata*.

CHAPTER 19

Bailey hated knocking on doors. It didn't matter how many years he'd been in the game, it still gave him a sick feeling all the way down to his gut.

It was probably because of the death knocks, the worst kind of knock a journalist could make. Always unscheduled. Always unwanted.

As a cub reporter, Bailey had been punched, kicked and even spat on by families and friends of the dead. The vilest behaviour came from relatives of the crooks that society wouldn't miss. Bad eggs taken out of circulation. Good riddance. The families knew it and they figured that journalists only came around to rub it in.

It was different with the innocents. Especially those who'd died in the most awful, heart-wrenching, ways. Those families were often the people who would make you a cup of tea and put out a plate of cookies. The ones who wanted to share their fondest memories, make their case for justice, or at least try to ensure that the obituary was written right.

Today wasn't about death knocks, it was about getting information about the three scumbags whose house had just been raided by the TOU. Even so, Bailey still had that churning feeling in his stomach. Maybe it was the egg and lettuce sandwich that he'd eaten in the car.

Knock. Knock.

'What the fuck do you want?' A young bloke, covered in tattoos, was standing in his doorway, wearing nothing but a pair of old, fraying Y-fronts. 'Who're you, a cop?'

'No, mate. I'm a reporter. I'm wondering if you –'

'All the same to me. Fuck off!'

He slammed the door in Bailey's face. The first knock, over before it had begun.

Bailey could hear the sound of a baby crying next door, hopefully he'd get a better reception there.

A young girl appeared on the other side of a solid metal screen door with a baby clinging to her shoulder. 'Yeah?'

'Your mum around?'

'I am the mum, mate. Got three of them in here.'

She looked like she should have been in school. Short skirt and a singlet. On closer inspection, her white top was covered in snot and food stains.

'John Bailey.' He held out his hand and she just stared at it until he gave up, letting it flop by his side. 'I'm a reporter. Not sure if you heard all that commotion a few houses up?'

'I'm not deaf, mate,' she said. 'Anyone get killed? I heard them gunshots.'

'Not sure.' Bailey didn't want to go into it.

'Mum!' A little voice called out from inside. 'Where's the TV remote?'

'Find it yourself!' She yelled back, then turned to Bailey. 'They think I'm their fucking slave. Bloody kids. Got any?'

'One. She's all grown up.'

'You're lucky. Long way to go here.'

This knock was going better. At least she was talkative.

'What can you tell me about the blokes down the street?' Bailey said.

'Not much. Haven't been there long. I only ever saw them going in and out of Dim's house.'

'Dim?'

She moved the boy to her other hip and popped a dummy in his mouth. 'You're supposed to be a reporter, aren't you? You should know about Dimity Clay?'

Dimity Clay.

The name sounded familiar, but Bailey couldn't remember why.

'Getting old. Remind me.'

'Dim killed herself and her two kids. Her husband was cheating on her. She did it for revenge, apparently. It was in all the papers.'

Bailey avoided reading stuff like that, even when it was in all the papers. But he remembered the case, you couldn't miss it.

'Oh, that one,' he said. 'Horrible story.'

'Mum! Come now, I need you!' The little voice inside was getting louder.

'Wait!' She turned to Bailey. 'Fuck me, it never stops.'

'You need to get in there?' Bailey said.

'No. He's just being a dick. Anyway, about Dim . . . she was my friend. Her bloke was a ratbag, but he didn't deserve that, no one does.'

'Sad . . . for everyone.' Bailey felt stupid stating the obvious. 'About those fellas who moved in, you ever speak to any of them?'

'No. They kept to themselves. Dim's place was vacant for almost a year. Weirdos, if you ask me.'

'What makes you say that?'

'Who'd want to live in that house after what she did? I thought they'd steamroll the place.'

'Mum! Mum! Come on!'

She was about to scream again at the kid inside, so Bailey cut her off. 'Couple more quick questions, before I let you go.'

'Go for it.'

'Did they look like they were religious? And can you remember any strange visitors?'

'Visitors? No. Only ever saw the three blokes that lived there.' She swapped the boy onto her other hip again. He was a pudgy little guy, looked heavy. 'And religious? You mean, did they wear *mooza* dresses, or something?'

'Something like that.'

'No, nothing. Looked like dealers to me, but I don't do that stuff . . . anymore.' She winked at him. 'Unless you're offering.'

Bailey laughed, uncomfortably. 'Thanks for your time.'

Bailey went door to door for the next hour without learning any more than he already knew, which was close to nothing. Nobody seemed to know anything about the men with the BearCat parked on their lawn. Most people would only say that they didn't like the look of them.

His last stop was the neat little house that Dexter had pointed out when she was trying to get rid of him. It was right up the end of the street, a long way from the scene.

There was a chipped wooden handrail next to the three steps at the front door. The rail was a good sign. Older residents were almost always home, and there usually wasn't much that went on in their street that they didn't know about.

He pressed the bell and waited. And waited.

There was a small window by the door and he could just make out the figure of a woman sitting in an armchair with blue television light flickering on her face.

He hit the bell again, rapping his knuckles on the door hoping the vibration might carry.

121

It did.

The woman stood up, slowly making her way to the door. She opened it a few inches, leaving the screen locked as a precaution.

'Hello, my name is John Bailey. I'm a reporter with *The Journal*. I was wondering if I might be able to ask you a few questions?'

'*The Journal*?' she said through the screen. 'Why don't you people ever write about any of the good things that people do around here?'

'Sorry?'

'You said you were from *The Journal*.' She opened the door wider so that she could get a better look at him. 'All you people write about is crime. You'd think I've been living in a ghetto most of my life!'

'I'm sorry about that Mrs?'

'O'Reilly. Carmel O'Reilly. Been living in this house for near on fifty years.'

'Mrs O'Reilly, I'm sorry you think that about the paper. I'll pass on the criticism to the editor, he always likes hearing about how he can do his job better.'

'His fault, is it?' Bailey wasn't getting off the hook that easily. 'I thought you said you were a reporter?'

'I did, and I am.'

Few people managed to flummox John Bailey. Carmel O'Reilly had somehow cornered him inside the first round.

'We may not have all the glamour of the eastern suburbs, Mr Bailey, but there are some good people living here. Good families.'

'I have no doubt, Mrs O'Reilly.'

'Now, what do you want?'

Bailey was feeling relieved that he hadn't been invited inside to hear Mrs O'Reilly's list of other complaints.

'I'm not sure if you heard what happened down the other end of the street a little while ago? There were gunshots.'

'Gunshots? Unfortunately, gunshots don't get me out of my chair anymore, Mr Bailey.'

'Well. About a half hour ago, police raided a house and they –'

'You'd be talking about number forty-six?'

'Number forty-six, that's right.' Finally, Bailey felt like he was getting somewhere. 'Three men were arrested. Actually, one of them has been . . . well . . . he's been –'

'Get it out, Mr Bailey. I'm not a precious wallflower. I've been around. My Alfie served in Vietnam. Fat lot of respect he got for it, mind you. But don't tiptoe around me with details. Especially in my own home.'

'I'm sorry, Mrs O'Reilly. One of them was shot and he's in a bad way.'

She stepped closer to the screen door, her lips almost touching the wire. 'Dead?'

'Looks like it,' Bailey said. 'I'm looking for any information you might be able to tell me about those men.'

Mrs O'Reilly unlocked the latch and stepped past Bailey onto the porch. From where they were standing, they could easily make out the half-dozen police cars blocking the other end of the street and the BearCat on the grass.

'Bad eggs is all I can say.'

She pulled a smoke out of the pocket in her dressing gown and sparked it.

'My doctor told me to give these things away.' She blew the smoke over Bailey's shoulder, like she was doing him a favour. 'What's the point? I'll be eighty-three tomorrow.'

'Fair enough. What else can you tell me?'

'They've only been here a few weeks. Before that the house had been empty for months.'

'I know about Dimity Clay.'

Mrs O'Reilly took another long drag on her cigarette.

'As soon as those men arrived, I knew they were bad news.'

'Why's that?'

'Because I dropped a shopping bag while one of them was standing on the lawn.' Her face scowling with the memory. 'He just stared at me as I got down on one knee and put my oranges away. A woman in her ninth decade. Disgraceful.'

Little things, like good manners, told you a lot about someone. People in their twilight years understood that better than most.

'Sound like arseholes to me.'

'Your word, not mine.'

Mrs O'Reilly clearly didn't like bad language, Bailey could tell by her tone.

'Sorry. It wouldn't take much for someone to help out an older neighbour.'

'But that's not why you knocked on my door, is it, Mr Bailey?'

'No.' Bailey wasn't going to lie to her. 'It's not.'

'You want to know about the boy.'

Dexter wasn't bullshitting him after all. 'What can you tell me?'

She took another drag on her cigarette, looking past Bailey at the flashing lights down the street.

'You're not the police, Mr Bailey. Why should I tell you anything?'

'Because his father's a friend of mine.'

'Then why did you introduce yourself to me as a reporter from *The Journal*?'

From all the doorknocks that Bailey had done over the years, he couldn't remember being interrogated like this.

'I don't know . . . who else would I be?'

Mrs O'Reilly smiled and patted him on the shoulder. 'It's okay, love. I'm just toying with you. I know who you are. You were that war correspondent. I used to read your articles. There must be darkness in there. Just like my Alfie.'

'I wasn't a soldier.'

'If you're doing a job there, that's service.'

Bailey didn't like where the conversation was headed and he needed to get it back on track. 'You were about to tell me about the boy?'

'Alfie didn't like talking about it either.' She paused and stared at him, like she was peering under his hood, inspecting his engine. 'The boy, then. All I can tell you is that yesterday evening I saw him escorted by two men into that house. He looked like he didn't want to be there, like he was afraid.'

'How could you tell?'

'Because the men on either side of him were gripping his arms so tightly that he could barely move.' She grabbed Bailey's arm, reinforcing her point. 'One of the men punched him in the stomach and he fell over, then they dragged him inside. And that's when I called the police.'

'Do you remember what time you made the call, Mrs O'Reilly?'

'Yes, I do. It was about six o'clock because I was just sitting down to watch the news.'

If Carmel O'Reilly had tipped off the cops yesterday, why had it taken them so long to go in? Another question for Dexter.

'Is the boy safe now?

'Not yet, Mrs O'Reilly. He wasn't there.'

'Oh dear.'

'Did you see anything else?'

'No, that's it.'

'Thanks so much for your time, Mrs O'Reilly.'

'You're welcome. I do hope you find him.'

'So do I.' Bailey grabbed hold of the rail and started back down the path.

'And Mrs O'Reilly,' he called back, 'happy birthday for tomorrow.'

She laughed. 'You don't bother celebrating birthdays at my age.'

That was enough doorknocking for one day.

Bailey decided to head back to his car. He needed time to think, because things weren't adding up. One thing in particular. If the men in that house and Tariq were planning an act of terrorism, then why – as Mrs O'Reilly said – did Tariq look like he didn't want to be there? Was he was having second thoughts? Or was he being held against his will?

Back at the house, the dead guy on the lawn was being zipped inside a body bag and carried into the back of an ambulance by two paramedics in blue uniforms. No one would have survived that many bullets. The other two guys were sitting in the back of an unmarked police car. They looked the same, like brothers. Bailey couldn't know that for sure, but it was a good line of inquiry. Another question that Dexter would hopefully answer for him. Later.

Bailey was still the only reporter on the scene. He had watched the raid in person. Even without names he had a good story. He needed to get back to the paper and get it down while it was still fresh in his mind.

He couldn't see Dexter, she must have been inside the house with the forensics team. He wasn't getting anything more from her at the moment, anyway. That was made blatantly obvious by the young cop leaning on Bailey's car.

'Careful with the paintwork, son. I've just had her resprayed.'

'Yeah, right.' The bloke ran his hand across the duco which was covered in a cocktail of dirt and bird shit. 'Time to go, mate. Major crime here. We're shutting down the street.'

Bailey didn't bother arguing with him. He'd got what he came for. He owed it to Dexter not to cause any trouble.

'I was just leaving.'

CHAPTER 20

DEXTER

The Salma brothers lived like pigs.

Clothes were strewn across furniture, along with old newspapers and crumpled pornographic magazines. You couldn't see the coffee table because it was piled so high with fast food containers. The kitchen wasn't any better, rubbish bags dumped in the corner and dirty dishes stacked in the sink.

And the smell. Horrendous. Like someone had sprayed a men's locker room with off milk.

Dexter was smelling her fingers to soften the stench as she walked in and out of the bedrooms searching for any sign of the kid. The rooms weren't any better than the rest of the house. Dirty clothes on the carpet and mattresses slept on without any bed linen. In three bedrooms Dexter counted four beds. One of them was a thin, blue, inflatable mattress in the corner of the room with no windows. She wondered whether that one had been for Tariq.

'Anything interesting, Dave?' Dexter asked the forensic guy who had his head down, dusting the area around the inflatable bed.

'Just starting,' Dave said, without looking up.

'Sorry, dumb question.'

'One thing I can tell you,' he said. 'These blokes were grubby bastards.'

'Not the finest members of society.'

He paused what he was doing and met Dexter's gaze. 'You should go look in the garage.'

'Why's that?'

'Go see for yourself.'

Dexter did as she was told, tracing back past the mess in the lounge, through a door next to the kitchen. Walking down the steps, she almost bumped her head on the large globe that was dangling from the roof in the garage. The globe looked like a fluorescent pear, its bright light bouncing off the shiny concrete floor, illuminating the entrance. The rest of the garage was enveloped in darkness.

'Over here.'

She could just make out Nugget's stumpy silhouette in the corner. Dexter walked towards him, squinting as her eyes adjusted to the dim light. It wasn't a cluttered mess like the rest of the house. No dirty clothes. No rubbish. No porn.

Nugget was standing beside a camera that had been loaded onto a tripod. The camera was pointing at a chair set next to the wall under a black flag with white Arabic writing on it.

'Holy shit.'

Nugget swung around. 'You got that right, boss.'

Dexter couldn't read much Arabic but she recognised the phrase.

Mohammed is the messenger of Allah.

The line was used as a declaration of faith across Islam, known as the *Shahada*. Extremist groups liked to hijack the populist message to legitimise their cause.

Dexter pointed at the camera. 'Is there a card in that?'

'I wasn't planning on touching it till the Feds got here. I'm no good with this tech shit, we need one of the nerds. I'd probably erase what's there, if there is something there.'

'I think we can all guess what's –'

'Speak of the devil!' Nugget interrupted Dexter as Marty Singh from the Australian Federal Police walked through the door. 'No sign of the kid, Marty. But my hunch, he's the star of a movie made right here. A little martyr's message to the world. Grubby little shit.'

Dexter felt a sudden pang of sickness in her gut. Everyone was talking about Tariq as if he was a terrorist. What if the old woman they'd spoken to up the street was right? What if the Salma brothers had been holding Tariq against his will? If that was true, then what they were about to watch could be even more disturbing than a suicide video.

She bent down on one knee and touched the floor, inspecting the dust on her fingertips, trying to imagine what went on here. Other than the flag, chair and the tripod, the garage was empty. No sign of a struggle, or something more sinister.

Singh slipped on a pair of rubber gloves and started gently fiddling with the camera.

'What's there?' Nugget moved closer, trying to get a better look.

'Give me a minute, Nugget. This camera's a relic. I'm surprised it's even digital.'

Dexter stepped around the camera, trying to give Singh more space.

'Bad news, I'm afraid,' Singh said.

Nugget gave him an impatient look. 'What's wrong?'

'Card's gone.'

'Fuck it.' Nugget whacked the wall with his fist. 'We've got to find this kid before he does something stupid.'

'Let's stop and think about this for a minute,' Dexter said. 'What if Tariq was a victim here?'

'Then why hasn't he turned up at a police station?'

Nugget was right. If Tariq had managed to escape and he was innocent, why hadn't he turned himself in?

Dexter stepped back, holding her phone up so that she could get a photograph of the camera pointed at the chair beneath the black flag.

'Chief! You better get out here!'

One of the other cops was calling out from the back of the house.

Dexter walked back through the kitchen and outside onto an undercover patio, where a uniformed policeman was standing beside a woman in a suit, down on her knees, scraping something off a plastic board with a scalpel.

'What is it?' Dexter said.

'These guys were preparing for something, all right.'

It was Bess Langard from the New South Wales Bomb Squad. Langard was a good operator. Thorough. She never talked things up and she certainly never talked things down.

'Trinitrotoluene.'

'Say that again?'

The word sounded familiar to Dexter but she couldn't remember what it was.

'TNT.'

'You've got to be bloody joking.' Nugget had followed Dexter outside and he was standing over her shoulder.

'No, Nugget. I'm not.'

Langard pulled back a tarpaulin, revealing five boxes with images of pressure cookers on them. Two of the pots were sitting on the ground, open, with ball bearings inside. A third one had been dismantled and was lying on its side next to a bunch of loose wires. There was also a bag of black powder and a paint tin that was open with yellow goo inside.

'That one's full of it.' Langard was pointing at the tin. 'There's enough TNT in that to take out half the block.'

131

'Okay,' Dexter said, pointing at the cop in uniform. 'We're going to need to clear half the street. I want homes emptied within a one hundred metre radius of this house. Now.'

The guy in uniform nodded his head and trotted off to do as he was told.

'Hey, Bess?' Dexter said, her eyes back on the bomb-making materials.

'Yeah?'

'Unless I've got this wrong, I'm counting five boxes and only three pressure cookers.'

'That's right.'

'Nugget,' Dexter said. 'I think it's time we introduced ourselves to the two living Salma brothers.'

CHAPTER 21

By the time Bailey made it back to Sussex Street, his body was all but ready to confirm that the egg and lettuce sandwich was a bad idea. Beads of sweat were building on his brow and he needed to get to a toilet. Fast.

'Bailey!'

Word had got around that Bailey had been there for the raid in Roselands, so he was a popular man when he stepped out of the elevator on the newsroom floor.

'Bailey!'

The Journal's Chief of Staff, Rachel Symonds, was so excited that she was almost running across the carpet towards him.

He held up his hand to cut her off. 'In a minute.'

'C'mon Bailey, this is huge. When are we going to –'

Bailey had his hand cupped over his mouth when he shouldered open the door to the men's toilets and went straight for an empty cubicle, emptying his guts into the porcelain.

It took him a few minutes to gather himself. When he walked back outside, Symonds was still waiting for him. She would have heard everything.

'You okay, mate?'

Bailey used a paper towel to wipe away the water he had splashed on his face. 'Service station sandwich. I'll never learn.'

'Here.' She handed him a piece of chewing gum. 'Good for you, even better for me.'

He popped it in his mouth with a wink. 'I wouldn't want you feeling uncomfortable, now, would I?'

'Mate.' Gerald appeared beside them. 'Let's get this thing out there before someone beats us to it.'

The newspaper editor, always thinking about the competition.

'Relax, Gerald. I was the only one there. You've got a story up already, like everyone else. I'll give you the feature. The blow by blow.'

'I know that, Bailey. I want it up. Let's own the traffic on this.'

Gerald was sounding like a guy who wasn't ready to give up his day job. Not yet.

'Got anything new?' Symonds asked the question every chief of staff would ask.

'Not that we can print. Still waiting for IDs. But the cops knew these guys, I'm certain of it.'

Bailey had spoken to Symonds and Gerald on the drive back from Roselands, so they knew most of what he had. Symonds had also been working with Bailey for almost two decades, so she wasn't about to get in his face and tell him how to do his job. It wasn't her style.

'Anything on the scanners?' Bailey said.

'Nothing. We've got the pups watching social, not much there yet, either.' Symonds turned back towards the newsroom. 'Nicki! Got a minute?'

Nicki came bounding up beside them, excitedly. Bailey had only met her once before, when she'd showed him how to set up a twitter account on his phone. Not that he'd ever used it.

'What's up, Rach?'

'Anything more on social about this raid in Roselands?'

'A bit,' Nicki said. 'I'm just writing it up now.'

'What've you got?' Symonds said.

'Local Roselands angle. People worried about heavy-handed cops. Apparently, they stormed in there, guns blazing. Locals are worried about their community being unfairly targeted.'

'Who've you spoken to?' Bailey said.

'I've got heaps off social. Tweets, conversations on Facebook.' She was sounding confident, like the story was in the bag. 'Police minister's just put out a statement too. Not much in it, but it'll help pad out the yarn. The government reassuring people they're keeping them safe.'

'Yeah, but who've you spoken to?' Bailey said again.

'Don't need to. With the social comments and the minister, I can have something up in thirty minutes.'

'I think what Bailey's saying is that you need to make a few follow-ups here, Nicki,' Symonds said.

'Why? The comments are out there. I can build this story now and –'

'I don't want to blunt your enthusiasm,' Symonds said. 'You need to pick up the phone and interview people yourself. The old-fashioned way.'

Bailey couldn't believe the conversation that was unfolding in front of him.

'For starters, how do you know these people are who they say they are?' Bailey said.

'I've got my ways of verifying people online, it's not hard.' Nicki was sounding defensive. 'Cross-checking older conversations, identity checking. I do it all the time. It's why I get my yarns up so quickly and why we own the web traffic.

'And no offence, Bailey, but I'm filing three, sometimes four stories a day, and getting more hits, more shares, than anyone else here.'

'We're a newspaper, not a fucking messaging service.'

'Bailey –'

'Paper? Who reads us on paper, these days?'

'Old guard versus the new, eh?' Gerald laughed, trying to defuse the tension that was building. 'Let's all calm down. You're both right.'

'Can't remember the last time I wrote a story without having spoken to anyone,' Bailey said. He stopped himself from going further. What was the point? He only knew how to do his job one way. Even if Nicki was half-right, he wasn't changing.

Nicki turned to Symonds. 'Do you want me to write the story, or not?'

'Let's take a look at what you've got.'

Nicki made a huffing noise and followed Symonds back to her desk, leaving Bailey and Gerald alone.

'That's the new world, eh, Gerald?'

'The train's already left the station, mate. No point fighting it. How else do we stay competitive?'

'You're sounding like a management dickhead. Even more than usual. Don't defend this crap. Doesn't suit you.'

'Bailey, c'mon –'

'No, seriously, Gerald. What are we doing here? Journalism used to be about chasing the truth, now it's about clicks and shares on platforms that I've never heard of. It's like I woke up one day and some kid who thinks Google's more trustworthy than a doctor has changed the locks on the whole damn news business.

'And what is *Facebook*, anyway? It doesn't make anything. It's like a giant leech that keeps growing, sucking the soul out of media businesses until we're all dead –'

'Bailey.'

'I don't care what people eat for lunch, whether someone on a bus has garlic breath or the things people love about Fridays.'

'Bailey, seriously, can we –'

'This used to be about keeping the public informed, reporting on the good and the bad, holding people accountable! Now, it's only about giving readers whatever will get the most clicks. The world's going to shit!'

If management really was about to clean out the place, maybe it was time to get out. But what would he do?

'Lower your bloody voice, would you?' Gerald grabbed Bailey by the arm, leading him to a corner of the room where no one else could hear them. 'What's wrong with you? This obviously isn't just about the raid in Roselands.'

'No, it's not.'

'Then I don't know what to say, mate. I'm fearing the worst here, for me too. I don't know any more than what I told you last night.'

Bailey let out a long breath, shaking his head. 'I'm not changing.'

'Is that even possible?'

Bailey was so fired up he missed his old friend's joke.

'I'm writing this story the only way I know how. And if that really is the future' – Bailey was pointing at Nicki on the other side of the room – 'I don't want to be a part of it.'

'And I won't judge you for that.'

Gerald was clearly allowing him to talk himself out now, and Bailey didn't like it.

'We're wasting time, anyway. I've got a story to write.'

Bailey walked to his desk and sat down, clearing away the unopened mail from his keyboard. He started tapping away, writing about what he'd seen. A counter-terrorism operation, suspects known to police. One of them shot by a special ops marksman from the roof of a BearCat. The fact that it was Dimity Clay's house gave the story an extra edge and a good headline. No one else had that angle, yet.

In under an hour, he was done. He thought he'd better give Dexter a call before submitting the story for edit, just in case she had something new for him. He dug his mobile out of his jacket pocket and noticed a message waiting on the home screen. He opened it.

Tariq wasn't here

Looks like he made a video

Get on to the family, he might get in touch

Things not adding up

Not for print

Alongside the message was a picture of a camera pointing at a chair beneath a flag commonly used by the Islamic Nation group.

He pressed Dexter's name on his phone, it didn't take long for her to answer.

'I was expecting a call from you half an hour ago. What took you so long?'

'Only just saw the message. Have you watched the video yet?'

'No. The card's missing from the camera. We're still looking for it.'

'I'm going to Omar's house. Meet me there?'

'Yeah,' Dexter said. 'And Bailey?'

'Yeah?'

'The prime minister's office is about to put out a statement. Gardner's fronting the cameras in an hour – they're raising the terror-threat level to *expected*.'

Nicole Gardner had only been prime minister for a few months, but she knew how to play the politics of fear. Look strong, get out in front of a story. Be a leader who knows how to protect the public. Someone who's good in a crisis. A fixer.

'Remind me, how high's *expected* on the chart?'

'One down from *certain*, which is where it'll go if we don't find Tariq inside the next twenty-four hours.'

'Can I print that?'

'I want you to print it. I want it out before the PM's statement to neutralise the politics of this, source it to a senior police officer.'

'Why don't you just write the story?' He regretted the words as soon as they came out.

'Do you want this or don't you?' Dexter said, sharply. 'We're all sick of politicians using incidents like these to create a scare. Politicising security.'

She was right. Although he'd seen the cops do the same thing when they wanted the public to know who was in control. But he bit his tongue. 'Okay. Okay. Give me what you have.'

'You can say the threat level is expected to go up, that there's an ongoing counter-terrorism operation. That police say the threat is real. Hold fire on the rest.'

She meant everything they knew about Tariq.

'Got it,' Bailey said. 'See you soon.'

Bailey re-nosed the top of his story. He hadn't been sure how to write about the fact that police were still dealing with a threat without mentioning Tariq. Now he had a way in.

'Symonds!' Bailey yelled across the room. 'Story's done! I'm on my mobile!'

He knew that Symonds would want to talk about the story when it hit the subs' desk and he didn't have time. He headed straight for the elevator, ignoring the voice calling out for him to hang around for a few minutes. He needed to get back to Wiley Park.

CHAPTER 22

Meandering his Corolla through the poky underground carpark at *The Journal*, Bailey sped up the ramp, driving so fast that he almost missed the hulking figure of Ronnie Johnson standing in the middle of the driveway at the top of the hill. The old spook had a knack for turning up unannounced.

Bailey wound down his window. 'That's one way to get killed.'

'In a hurry, bubba?' Ronnie said, tapping his hand on the roof.

'How could you tell?'

'Got something for you.' Ronnie handed Bailey a large yellow envelope. 'Your file.'

'Thanks.' Bailey took the envelope and threw it on the seat beside him. 'Anything interesting in there?'

'Forgot how much of a nobody Mustafa was back then, compared to Al Qaeda and the others,' Ronnie said. 'But there's a lot in there about what happened to you. Too much, maybe.'

That was Ronnie's way of warning Bailey about whether he needed to go over all that old ground again.

'I want to read it.' Not surprisingly, Bailey was going to ignore the warning. 'Something in there has pissed off Mustafa. Somehow it's personal. I want to know.'

'Okay, bubba. I'll keep asking questions.' Ronnie tapped the roof again. 'Just thought I'd warn you.'

'Thanks.'

Bailey headed up Sussex Street towards the turn-off for Anzac Bridge and the City West Link. Traffic permitting, he'd make it to Wiley Park inside forty minutes.

There was no sign of Dexter's blue unmarked Holden when he arrived outside the Haneefs' house. He had promised to meet her out the front before they went inside. He'd wait.

Bailey cut the engine and picked up the envelope, slicing it open with his finger. It was a slim document. Four pages. No, five. Single-sided. Written in an old-fashioned type.

CIA

CLASSIFIED

Date: 28 January 2005

Location: Baghdad

Subject: Interview with former hostage John Bailey (Australian citizen)

Bailey flipped over the page, skipping past the agency jargon on the coversheet.

Subject kidnapped while on embed with 1st Marine Division US Army in Fallujah on 5 April 2004. Journalist Gerald Summers – Australian – also present. Truck seen driving away. Marines engaged in heavy combat at the time. Two Marines killed. Five injured.

Bailey stopped reading and looked out the window. US soldiers killed because of him? The document wasn't clear. He remembered a lot of noise before he was taken. Heavy gunfire. Bombs. Him and Gerald being separated. Bravo Company had been engaged in a heavy battle with insurgents. He remembered it like yesterday. He kept reading.

Subject estimates that he met Mustafa al-Baghdadi for the first time later that day, or the following day (6 April) in a room, location unknown. Subject believes that he may have been drugged. Subject says he was tied to a chair and forced to watch the execution of Douglas McKenzie, a US Marine who had been kidnapped by an insurgent group in Mosul six months earlier. Video later released of McKenzie beheading. Subject recalls Mustafa al-Baghdadi's anger about US occupation of Iraq and the growing support for his 'movement'. Subject cannot recall name of group.

He skimmed down the page.

Subject moved several times during ten months of captivity. Transported in the trunk of a car, always restrained. Gagged. Blindfolded. Subject recalls the first time he was tortured was in a house that he later discovered to be in Mosul.

It was the only location he could be sure about, other than Baghdad. Bailey had spent most of his time in captivity locked in rooms without windows.

Subject says that his captors were all men. Torture sessions often lasted many hours during consecutive days. Subject confirms subjected to waterboarding but cannot recall how many times (estimates more than ten). Garden tools used to extract finger-nails. Russian Roulette (weapon described as old pistol). Subject regularly beaten. Subject became emotional. Break requested. Interview terminated 28 January at 1905hrs.

Arseholes, thought Bailey. Of course the 'subject became emotional'. Try spending ten months with those animals and then being asked to recount what had happened in detail. Of course he was fucking emotional.

Interview resumed 29 January at 0800hrs.

He skipped past the rest of the torture stuff, flipping a sheet, scanning the document until a sentence caught his eye.

Subject recalls the second time he met Mustafa al-Baghdadi was several months later in Mosul. Subject recalls date palms. Bridge over Tigris River. Grand Mosque in the distance. Subject believes he was standing on a rooftop in the city's right bank. Location confirmed by key landmarks. Subject believes he was allowed outside to witness a car bombing at a US Army checkpoint on the bridge. Confirmed casualties. Presumed dead. Subject recalls Mustafa al-Baghdadi boasting about his growing army. Subject recalls first hearing Mustafa al-Baghdadi mention the word 'caliphate' in Iraq and Syria.

Bailey kept going down the page.

Interview turns to day of rescue. Baghdad, 27 January, 1000hrs. Release negotiated by CIA Station Chief, Ronald B. Johnson. $US1m cash exchange confirmed. Provided by Australian citizen, Gerald Summers. (Australian Government refused ransom request.)

Bailey stopped reading. Ronnie had never told him where the money had come from. Gerald. The guy who backed him, helped rebuild him when he was a drunken, dysfunctional mess. His closest friend. Gerald had money, no doubt. But a million dollars? No one had that much to spare. Bailey could never have repaid that debt. It was probably why Gerald had never told him.

He wiped the moisture that was building in his eyes and kept reading.

Subject recalls final conversation with Mustafa al-Baghdadi about the insurgent leader's past. Following detail unverified. Mustafa al-Baghdadi born in Baghdad suburb of al-A'miriyah. Father was an influential Sunni businessman with ties to Saddam Hussein regime. Father became informant for CIA. Father, mother and three older brothers killed by Saddam forces either late 1991, or start 1992. Unclear. Mustafa al-Baghdadi a small child at the time. Escaped and smuggled out of Iraq by family. Lived with wealthy uncle in London, educated at good schools (unnamed). Became a doctor. Radicalisation of Mustafa al-Baghdadi happened during unspecified time. Subject says following 2003 war, Mustafa al-Baghdadi began spending more time at Finsbury Park Mosque (North London). Returned to home country soon after and began working in hospitals treating wounded Iraqis.

Bailey tossed the file onto the seat beside him. He'd read enough. There was nothing there that he couldn't remember. Nothing he could pinpoint that would give Mustafa al-Baghdadi a reason to reach out and call him.

I know what you did.

He leaned up against the window, closing his eyes. Mustafa's words sounding, over and over in his head. Bailey had no idea what they meant. He was desperate to find out.

CHAPTER 23

Tap, tap, tap.

The ring on Dexter's finger amplified the knock on the window, making Bailey jump in his seat.

'Gave me a fright there, detective,' he said, one foot out the door.

'Not like you to scare so easily.'

Bailey stepped onto the grass beside her, closing the car door.

'I'm getting soft.'

'Yeah, you are,' she said, patting his stomach with her hand.

He sucked in his gut and smiled. 'More to cuddle.'

'What's that?' Dexter's face hardened as she noticed the file with the CIA insignia sitting on the passenger seat. 'Something from Ronnie?'

'My file.'

There was no point keeping it from her.

'What file?'

'About what happened . . . in Fallujah, the kidnapping. All that.' He was done reliving it. Done reading about it. Done talking about it. 'Nothing in there you don't already know.'

'Then why'd Ronnie give it to you?'

'Someone leaked it.'

'Leaked it? Where?'

'It turned up in a trove of documents dumped on the internet by those fuckwits at Wikileaks.'

Bailey hated Julian Assange and his Wikileaks organisation. Sure, governments around the world got up to no good from time to time. But you don't dump millions of pages of sensitive material online for anyone to sift through. Innocent people die. Like the dozens of CIA informants in China who were murdered after Wikileaks published their names in US State Department files about Beijing's alleged violations of human rights. Assange and his mates were reckless arseholes.

'The phone call from Mustafa al-Baghdadi.' Bailey was speaking in a hurried voice. 'Ronnie thinks it might be linked to something in my file.'

'If there's nothing in it, why would Mustafa care?' Dexter said.

'That's what I'm trying to find out.'

Bailey turned and started walking towards the house.

'Bailey?' Dexter grabbed his hand, stopping him. 'Are you okay?'

'I'm fine.'

The nightmares were back. He wasn't fine.

'Remember, you can talk to me. Or go to one of your AA meetings?' As much as Dexter loved him, she was done with the booze. 'You said they were helping.'

'Caught up with my sponsor yesterday. You don't need to worry about me.'

'That's great, Bailey. You know you can talk to me too?'

'I know.'

He knew what the next question would be.

'By the way, who's the sponsor? You haven't mentioned them before.'

There was no simple way to answer this one other than to tell her the truth.

'A woman called Annie Brooks.'

Dexter looked at him like she was waiting for him to finish the sentence. 'How do I know that name?'

'She used to be on TV.'

'The newsreader?'

'That's the one.'

'Right,' Dexter said. 'You two used to know each other, right?'

'We were both stationed in Beirut a long time ago.' Bailey pointed at the house. 'Time to go in, don't you think?'

'Yeah, yeah, of course.' Dexter started walking and then stopped again. 'What's she like?'

'Come off it, Sharon.' Bailey could see the change in her face. 'Don't tell me you're jealous. It's not your style.'

'Of course not.'

He wasn't about to mention the fact that he'd kissed Annie Brooks in Centennial Park the night before. Annie had been low. It was nothing. Just a kiss. An interrupted one at that. He'd stopped it. Really it was half a kiss, if there was such a thing.

'So let's move on then, shall we?' Bailey was desperate to talk about something else.

'Okay.' Dexter started walking towards the house again. 'I'm glad you're still doing the AA stuff.'

Hallelujah.

'What else can you tell me about what you found at the house?' Bailey said.

'Off the record?'

'Sure.'

'Explosives. Pressure cookers. Looks like they were making bombs in the backyard.'

'Bloody hell.' Bailey was surprised that she shared that part. Maybe it was an attempt to make Bailey understand how serious the situation had become so he'd share anything he knew. 'Do you think there are bombs out there?'

'We've seized three.' Dexter went quiet for a moment before speaking again. 'There's evidence suggesting that another two may be out on the street.'

'With Tariq?'

'No one's going that far, yet.'

'What do we tell the Haneefs?'

'Nothing,' she said, catching his eye. 'And leave the talking to me.'

Dexter opened the screen and banged on the door with the ball of her fist.

Within seconds, they heard footsteps tapping the tiles inside. The door was opened by an unfamiliar man dressed in a cream-coloured *thobe*.

'Hello. Can I help you?'

Omar appeared over his shoulder. 'Is it Tariq? Have you found him?' He looked even more tired than he had the day before. And more desperate.

'No, mate,' Bailey said. 'We haven't.'

'Can we come in?'

The man standing in front of Omar held out his hand towards Bailey. 'I am Hassan Saleh, a friend of the family.'

'John Bailey. And this is –'

'Detective Chief Inspector Sharon Dexter.' She stepped in front of Bailey, holding out her hand.

'Detective Dexter, hello. Please.' He gestured for them to follow him into the lounge. 'I am here to help the family during this difficult time.'

'What's happened? Where's Tariq?' Noora got up off the sofa, eyes red, looking just as tired as her husband.

'I'm sorry, Noora,' Bailey said. 'We haven't found him yet.'

'But you know something, why else would you be here?' Omar said. 'Tell us, please.'

'It's probably best if you sit down.'

Dexter touched Noora on the arm and they sat together on the sofa.

'You too, mate.' Bailey sat on the two-seater opposite, patting the cushion beside him.

Hassan Saleh stood in the corner, watching on.

'What's happened?' Omar didn't move. 'Has Tariq been hurt?'

Bailey looked over at Dexter, waiting for her to respond.

'If you could just sit down, Omar. I'll tell –'

'Is he dead? Is my son dead? Just tell me what you know!'

'We think he's still alive, Omar.' Bailey ignored the blunt stare coming his way from Dexter. He knew she wanted to run things, but Omar was getting more wound up by the second.

'You think? How do you think?'

Bailey went to speak again but Dexter cut him off. 'Because we found the house where he was staying and a witness who said he was there.

'We also found evidence of terrorist activities,' Dexter said. 'We are worried about him. Worried that he might be about to do something stupid.'

'Terrorism? Not my son,' Noora said, shaking her head. 'That's not Tariq. He wouldn't. Not my boy.'

It never is, thought Bailey. Right up until the moment they pull the trigger, detonate the bomb, drive the car into a crowd of innocent people. The transition from beloved son to violent killer could happen in a millisecond.

'Have you heard from him?' Dexter said.

'Of course we haven't heard from him!' Omar said. 'If we had, he would be sitting here with us!'

'I'm sorry, Omar,' Dexter said. 'We need to ask these questions if we're going to find Tariq.'

Omar's cheeks and forehead had turned red and he started pacing his lounge room, clenching his fists, shaking his head.

'Just, just get out.' He walked over to the front door and opened it. 'Get out of my house and go find my son.'

'I know this is hard, mate,' Bailey said. 'Detective Dexter's just doing her job.'

'It's okay,' Dexter said. 'I've got to get moving anyway.'

She stood up, her jacket popping open to reveal the Glock pistol holstered to her side. Police weapons had progressed since the Smith and Wesson revolvers that were standard issue back in the eighties. Bailey didn't know much about the new ones. But he could tell you a few stories about those old six-shooters, not least the one about the day a bent copper called Bob Brickhouse had rested the cool barrel against his forehead and threatened to pull the trigger.

'Bailey?'

Dexter was standing over him, trying to get his attention.

He looked over at Noora, gently sobbing on the sofa, and then at Omar, standing by the open front door waiting for them to leave.

'I was just saying.' Dexter tapped him on the shin with her foot. 'We're leaving.'

Dexter was in a hurry and Bailey knew why. She had two terrorist suspects in custody, waiting to be questioned. Police interrogation rooms were no place for journalists. Bailey was staying put. He had more questions for Omar and he wanted to know more about Hassan Saleh. Why he was there.

'I might just hang about for a bit longer,' he said. 'You go on ahead, I've got my own transport.'

Dexter leaned forward so that only Bailey could hear. 'You find out anything more, I want to know.'

The sound of Dexter's car had disappeared up the street before Bailey decided to speak.

'She's a good cop, you know. One of the best.'

'Then why hasn't she found our son?' Omar said.

'We're all trying, mate.'

Bailey wanted to say that it's especially hard to find people when they don't want to be found, although he didn't want to risk upsetting the Haneefs any more than they already had.

'Trying? Really?' Noora's cheeks were flushed. 'How hard are you trying?'

'Noora,' Omar said. 'Noora, don't –'

'The police aren't interested in finding our son, Mr Bailey,' she said. 'Why do you think Omar came to you in the first place? The police don't care about us out here.'

'Noora, Noora, stop.' Omar touched his wife on the shoulder and she brushed his hand away.

'No, Omar! Terrorism is a plague on all of our society – we're not to blame. The police treat us all like criminals. They won't help us, they won't. They . . .'

Noora stormed out of the room without finishing her sentence, sobbing and shaking her head. Hassan Saleh followed after her.

'I'm sorry.' Omar suddenly seemed like the calm one. 'I really do think you should go.'

'Just a couple more questions, please, Omar?'

Omar stood in silence for a moment, contemplating what to do. 'Give me a minute.'

Bailey could hear Omar trying to comfort his wife in the kitchen, telling her that everything would be all right. They were lies, for now. Reassuring, nonetheless.

Noticing the photographs on the sideboard, Bailey walked over to get a better look. There must have been a dozen photos in gold and silver frames. Most of the pictures were of the family together, charting the passing years for the children and their parents. Friends too. At home. At a mosque. In a park. Family and community was the beating heart of this house.

'They struggle with trust, you know.'

Bailey hadn't heard Hassan Saleh return from the kitchen.

'There are many disenchanted people out here. Distrusting of authorities.'

Bailey turned around, noticing the prayer beads turning in his hand.

'Omar and I go back,' Bailey said. 'He knows he can trust me.'

'I'm sure you're a good man, Mr Bailey.' Hassan stepped closer, taking the photograph from Bailey's hand and replacing it on the sideboard. 'Now prove it. Help find his son.'

'That's exactly what we're trying to do.'

'Good. Good.' Hassan patted Bailey on the shoulder, taking a step towards the door. 'Now Omar has asked me to show you out.'

Bailey brushed his hand away. 'You're the family's spokesman now?'

'It's time for you to leave.'

Bailey stopped at the door, his mind drifting back to the photographs on the sideboard. 'Just one question before I do.'

'What is it?'

'Where's Omar's daughter? Where's Sara?'

'At university.'

Bailey couldn't quite explain why he'd asked the question but something about Sara was bothering him. Her brother had been missing for more than a week and she was attending class – getting on with her life – like normal. Bailey wasn't sure what else someone her age should be doing, but it didn't seem right. Not to him, anyway.

'We're trying to keep things as normal as possible for her.' Hassan leaned past Bailey, opening the door. 'This is a difficult time.'

'Omar knows how to reach me.'

Bailey had his phone out before he reached the car.

A six-word message for Dexter.

You need to find Sara Haneef

CHAPTER 24

The hot temperatures were hanging around this autumn and the western suburbs had been bearing the brunt of it.

It was even hotter in Bailey's car because the air-conditioning didn't work. He wound down the window, chasing a cool breeze. Any breeze. It barely made a difference. The humidity was clinging to his skin like honey and the traffic was moving so slowly that the already heavy air was being weighed down by fumes, making it difficult to breathe.

Bailey was tapping his fingers on the steering wheel, trying to process the facts and everything in between.

Tariq had been missing for a week. His parents said they hadn't heard from him and it was becoming clear that they had trust issues with the police. Tariq's school friends were also none the wiser. The house raid. The explosive materials. The possibility of two bombs on the street. Bailey's phone conversation with Mustafa.

Bailey was even more confused about Tariq than when he'd left home that morning on the way to Roselands. His brain wasn't working properly. He needed to eat something. He pulled the car over and stopped outside a kebab shop on Old Canterbury Road. He was halfway through winding up the car window when he was interrupted by the vibrating of his phone. He looked down at the screen. Dexter.

Bailey answered the call with a question. 'How'd you go with the guys you arrested at the house?'

'That's why I'm calling,' Dexter said, sharply. 'Ever heard of a guy called Sammy Raymond?'

Sounded familiar, but Bailey couldn't pin it. 'Should I have?'

'Probably. Your newspaper has done enough stories about him over the years.'

Sammy Raymond. Sammy Raymond. Sammy . . .

Bailey remembered. Raymond was believed to have fought alongside Islamic Nation in Syria. He came back to Australia, via Turkey, a few years back. One of hundreds of foreign fighters who'd returned home, most of whom couldn't be locked up by authorities because there was no concrete evidence that they'd ever picked up a weapon in the Middle East.

'I know who he is. Why're you asking?'

'The guys are talking, ready to cut a deal. They say Sammy Raymond is behind what's happening, that he's the contact with Mustafa al-Baghdadi.'

'Bloody hell.' Dexter had been busy. 'What about Tariq?'

'The kid knows everything, but he's not part of it –'

'Part of what?'

'How about you just listen for a minute, while I tell you what's what?'

'Sorry.'

'I'll start with the guys from the house. The Salma brothers. George and Alex are in custody. Their kid brother, Benji, was the one who got killed. They've done it all. Drugs, theft, standover stuff. Now terrorism.

'Sammy had been working for the Salmas on one of their father's construction sites. That's how he got them involved. He

155

sourced the materials, they made the bombs. They were planning to hit targets all over the city. Until it went to custard this morning.'

'Permission to speak?'

Dexter sighed into the phone. 'Yes, Bailey.'

'You still haven't told me how Tariq's connected.'

'The Salmas said they were told to pick him up and keep him locked away until this was all over. Orders from Sammy Raymond. They said that's all they know. They don't know the targets. They don't know any other names.'

'How could they not know?' It sounded to Bailey like the Salmas were either getting in quickly for a plea deal, or they were passing on misinformation to confuse the cops. 'And you believe them?'

'They say that they were given their part to play without knowing the rest. It's how Sammy has kept it under the radar, how he has stopped people from talking. There's got to be more people involved, we just don't know who.'

Bailey thought of someone.

'What about Sara Haneef?'

'I saw your message. What makes you think she's involved?'

Bailey didn't know how to answer the question. A hunch. A gut feeling. It wasn't enough.

'Bailey?'

'To be honest, I don't know. I just don't get how she can keep going to her classes at university knowing that her brother's out there, missing.'

'Yeah. I agree with you.'

Bailey felt relieved, like he wasn't crazy.

'At the moment, any lead will do. She and I are due for another chat, although she's not answering her phone, so I sent a car to the university to bring her in. I also dropped her name with the Salma brothers. Neither of them flinched.'

'So, what do you know about the targets?'

'Nothing.'

'And what do I do with this information?'

Bailey wanted to know what he could write about. At some point, people needed to know, especially if there were bombs out there.

'Nothing about the explosives. You can publish Sammy Raymond's photograph and say that counter-terrorism police are wanting to speak with him. We just hit his house and, not surprisingly, he's not there. A public ID is a good option at the moment. Same goes for Tariq Haneef – a person of interest.'

'And the Salmas?'

'Being questioned by police. Keep it loose. You can name them, including the dead one. I've emailed you their photographs.'

Bailey wasn't expecting that much. He had a story, all right. He'd need half the front page. 'Still on the record, anything more from the house?'

'We've seized laptop computers, a bunch of phones and a tablet. Who knows what else we'll find. We've got people scraping them right now. That's all I've got.' Dexter stopped talking, waiting to see if Bailey had any further questions. 'Okay. Got to go.'

She hung up.

Bailey thumbed through his phone until he found the next name that he needed to call.

Gerald.

'Mate. Are you in the office?'

'Yes.'

With the upheaval in management and redundancies being worked through, Bailey wasn't surprised.

'Got a front page for you.' Bailey got straight to it. 'The terrorist threat. It's real. I've got names of suspects, details.'

'When can you get it done?' Gerald's voice sharpened.

'I'm sending photographs and IDs.' Bailey climbed out of his car balancing his computer in one hand and phone in the other, closing the door with his knee. 'I'm going to write the story now. You'll have it within the hour.'

'When can we publish?' Gerald said.

'The second it lands.'

Bailey ordered himself a lamb kebab and found a table at the back of the restaurant where he sat down and started crafting his story.

The article was on *The Journal*'s web page by the time Bailey was parking his car outside his house in Paddington. It was almost 9 pm and just as he was killing the lights a call came through. An unknown number. He answered it.

'Bailey.'

No answer.

'Hello?'

After a few more beeps he could hear someone on the other end of the phone.

'Big day, John Bailey.'

Mustafa al-Baghdadi. The last person in the world he wanted to talk to. And the first.

'What do you want?'

'What do I want?'

Bailey flipped his phone over and scrolled through until he found the app that let him record conversations.

'Are you going to repeat everything I say?'

'That police detective friend of yours must be thinking that she's had a good day today, would she not?'

Bailey's throat tightened, struck by a sudden pang of fear.

'Detective Chief Inspector Sharon Dexter. The head of the Joint Counter Terrorism Team,' Mustafa continued.

'What the fuck are you talking about?'

Bailey could hear the rhythm of Mustafa's calm breathing down the line. 'Killing one of my soldiers. There are many more, you know. So many I've lost count.'

'You seem well informed for someone who's supposed to be hiding in a cave.'

'Benji Salma. Shot dead by police in western Sydney. His two brothers are in custody. I have people everywhere. An army of warriors. Tens of thousands, all over the world.'

Bailey looked over his shoulder, up and down the street. He couldn't help feeling he was being watched.

'Petty criminals, I hear. Dumb as doornails, ripe for being brainwashed by a psychopath like you.'

Bailey was trying to get a rise out of him.

'You never did want to learn about me, did you?' Mustafa said. 'You're as ignorant as everybody else.'

'You might be right, I don't know much. But one thing I do know – you're losing your war.'

'That's where you're wrong.' Mustafa's voice tightened, defensively.

'Yeah?' Bailey was getting angry now, remembering what Mustafa's men had done to him during the months he was moved from one hot, filthy room to the next, starved and beaten. 'I know that you've lost all the territory you had in Iraq, most of it in Syria too. Afghanistan's not going to happen. I know there's a growing list of people who want to see you dead. Muslims all over the world think you're a sadistic madman who's betrayed his own religion.'

'Enough!'

'You tell me, Mustafa?' Bailey was in the man's head and he wanted to stay there. 'What's the end game?'

Mustafa went quiet on the other end of the phone. Bailey could tell that he was still there by the heavy breathing down the line. He could hear other sounds, too. Traffic, a faint beeping noise. He couldn't pinpoint exactly what they were. They could be anything. Anywhere.

'You're no journalist, John Bailey,' Mustafa said, his voice calm again. 'You're just like the others.'

'Like who?'

'The Americans. The CIA. Your friend, Ronald Johnson. I've read all about it. The things you told them about me.'

'I still don't know what you're talking about.' Bailey kept fishing. 'What did you read?'

'Eye for an eye, John Bailey.'

The phone went dead.

Eye for an eye?

Bailey had no idea what Mustafa was playing at. Was it a threat?

He clicked play on the recording on his phone to make sure that he'd got it all. He had. Now he had to figure out what to do with it.

CHAPTER 25

'Ronnie!'

Bailey almost tripped over the dead fern by the front door as he hurried down the hallway.

'Are you here? Ronnie!'

A cloud of smoke was hovering above Ronnie's head in the lounge room where he was seated on the sofa watching American college football on the television.

'I wish you wouldn't smoke those things inside, mate. They're stinking up the place.'

'Hold on a second, bubba.' Ronnie held up his hand without looking at Bailey. 'Big play for the Sooners coming up.'

'Are you serious?'

Bailey knew nothing about American football. Ronnie had been sleeping in his spare room long enough for Bailey to know that the Oklahoma Sooners had won this year's Sugar Bowl. Ronnie was an OU alumnus and he'd played on the team back in the day. He must have watched the game five times already.

'Boom!' Ronnie slapped his hands together, sending a spray of ash onto the coffee table. 'He might have attitude, but that kid can throw a ball.'

'Are you done?' Bailey said.

Ronnie watched the Sooners players backslapping their quarter-back as they celebrated another touchdown and then he switched off the television, turning his head to Bailey. 'What've you got?'

'Mustafa called again.'

Ronnie got up off the couch and stubbed his cigar in an empty coffee cup. 'When?'

'A few minutes ago. I recorded it.' Bailey was holding up his phone, proudly. For a technology luddite like him, the recording felt like a coup.

'Old dog has a new trick.'

'Funny.'

'What are you planning to do with it?'

'I want to talk to Gerald and I want to talk to Sharon.'

'You know I'll do better than the locals,' Ronnie said.

'I'm hoping you will.' Bailey had always planned to give Ronnie a copy. 'I owe it to Sharon. Mustafa knows more than I do about a raid that I just watched go down in Wiley Park. And there's more on the recording than just our conversation.'

'Like what?'

'Sounds, outside noise. I don't know,' Bailey said. 'That's for you people to work out.'

'Forgive me for asking,' Ronnie said. 'But what has Gerald got to do with this?'

Gerald was Bailey's best friend. His boss. Someone who knew Omar and the one person Bailey turned to for advice. Gerald had everything to do with this.

'You're forgiven.' Bailey was already walking towards the door. 'We're going to the paper. I'll play you the recording on the way.'

There must have been a half-dozen lawyers sitting on the sofas and chairs in Gerald's office when Bailey opened the door, without knocking. He wasn't interested in counting the suits, he just wanted them gone.

'All right, you lot. Out!' Bailey was pointing over his shoulder at the open doorway behind him. 'Work to be done here. Journalism.'

'Bailey? You can't –'

'I'm serious, Gerald. We need to talk. And they can do the sums on my redundancy in their own time.' He was pointing at the lawyers without looking. 'While I'm still here, I've got stuff to do. And we need to talk.'

Gerald looked over at Ronnie like he was pleading with the big Oklahoman to grab Bailey by the arm and escort him outside to talk sense into him.

'It's serious,' Ronnie said. 'You need to hear this.'

'Okay, okay.' Gerald sighed, turning to the men and women in the room. 'Just give us a few minutes, would you please?'

Bailey watched them all file past him in their flashy ties and pinstriped shirts, pant-suits and pumps. Now he knew where all *The Journal*'s money was going.

'What is it, Bailey?' Gerald said.

Bailey waited for the door to click closed before he got started. 'Listen to this.'

He put the phone face up on the wood of Gerald's old mahogany desk, and clicked play.

'Is that who I –'

'Yes.' Bailey held up his hand. 'Listen.'

They were all standing with their palms flat on the desk, leaning forward, chasing the sound. The recording lasted almost two minutes. When it stopped, the room remained silent. The only noticeable sounds were the car horns in the traffic fourteen floors below.

'Eye for an eye,' Gerald said. 'What the hell's he talking about?'

'I don't know. Sounds like he's blaming me for something. I don't know what.'

'Bailey.' Gerald had a sudden look of panic on his face. 'Where's Miranda?'

Bailey grabbed his phone off the desk, fumbling with it until he found her name.

She picked up. Relief.

'Miranda!' Bailey was almost yelling.

'Dad, what's wrong?'

'Where are you?'

'Peter and I were at the movies. We're on the way home. Why? What's wrong?'

For the first time, Bailey was relieved to know that Doctor Peter Andrews was living with his daughter. But he didn't have a plan. He'd just wanted to hear her voice.

'I need you to go . . . to go . . .'

'Mate.' Gerald touched him on the arm. 'Send her to my place.'

Bailey thought about it for a second. Gerald was the closest thing to a brother that he had. He was Miranda's godfather. He lived in a big house in Mosman with a security fence and a long driveway. Nancy had put so many cameras around the place it was like Fort Knox.

'Go home, pack a bag. I need you and the doc to go to Gerald's house tonight.'

'Dad? What's going on?'

There was panic in her voice.

'I can't talk about it right now. It's just a precaution. I'll tell you more later. Promise. Right now, I just need you to do this, sweetheart. Please.'

'Okay, Dad.'

'Text me when you get there. And sweetheart?'

She was silent on the end of the phone, waiting for her father to speak.

'I love you.'

'I love you too, Dad.'

Bailey hung up. 'Thanks for that, mate.'

Gerald nodded. 'You know I'd do anything for her.'

Bailey looked at his watch. 10.04 pm. 'It's late. Better wake Nancy and tell her she's about to have some visitors.'

'That outside noise near the end of the recording,' Ronnie said, getting back to the task at hand. 'The beeps. A whooshing sound. It sounds like traffic, maybe a crossing.'

'Can't imagine there are any traffic lights in Al-Qa'im,' Bailey said.

'What?' Gerald said.

'I've been there.' Ronnie ignored Gerald. 'There aren't.'

'What're you guys talking about? You mean Al-Qa'im along the Euphrates on the border with Syria?'

Gerald was good with geography. When he and Bailey worked together in Iraq, Gerald was always in charge of the maps.

'Yes, mate,' Bailey said. 'Ronnie traced the phone Mustafa was using to a shop there. It's one of the last places that Islamic Nation still controls in Iraq.'

'So, where do you think he is now?' Gerald said.

Ronnie stepped back from the table, checking his phone, his mind already on his next move. 'Send me the recording, bubba. I'm going to get it to my people and see what we can turn up.'

He paused at the door. 'And Bailey?'

'Yes, mate?'

'Are you sure you need to share it with the locals?'

'Positive.'

Giving the recording to Dexter meant that another team would be analysing the sounds, trying to pinpoint Mustafa's location. Bailey would have thought the more people on this, the better. Ronnie didn't think like that. He knew how to keep secrets and he didn't like sharing them.

And there was another reason why Bailey wanted Dexter to know about the recording. If Mustafa was threatening to hurt someone close to Bailey, that meant her.

'What was that all about?' Gerald said.

'Just Ronnie being Ronnie.'

At least Ronnie had been sharing with Bailey. The CIA file was still weighing on his mind. The file had read like old news to Bailey, apart from one key detail. The cash. The million-dollar ransom paid by private Australian citizen Gerald Summers. Now that Bailey knew the truth, he needed to tell Gerald.

'Mate . . . mate, there's one more thing.'

Bailey didn't quite know how to say it.

'What is it, Bailey?'

'I know about the ransom payment.'

'What payment?'

'Gerald, don't.' Bailey was finding this hard enough without Gerald pleading ignorance. 'One million US. Cash. I know it came from you.'

'Who told you?' Gerald said, failing to conceal his annoyance.

'The CIA has a file on me. I read it.'

Gerald turned away, staring at the hotel rooms stacked on top of each other across the street. Looking for a light on. A distraction.

'Well.' Gerald stumbled. 'You would have done the same for me.'

Bailey couldn't help but laugh at that. 'Where the hell am I going to get a million dollars?'

'You made it out,' Gerald said, not seeing the funny side. 'That's all that mattered.'

Bailey's eyes welled and he didn't know what to say next. Luckily, he didn't need to say anything because his phone vibrated on the table, interrupting the thorny silence.

He looked down at the screen. A message from Dexter.

Still going with the Salmas

Let me know if you've got anything

He'd tried to call Dexter during the car ride to Sussex Street, but she hadn't answered. Now he knew why. Bailey didn't want to send her the recording without speaking to her first.

I need to speak to you in person

Got something for you. It's linked

Which station are you at? I'll come there

'Bailey?'

'I need to go meet Sharon.'

'Okay, mate. And don't worry about Miranda, I won't let anything happen to her. I'll wrap this up and head home.'

Bailey's phone vibrated again. Dexter.

Bankstown

Message me when outside

Don't come in

'Thanks.' Bailey stopped at the door, turning around. 'I mean it, Gerald. Thanks. For everything.'

'It's what we do, right?'

Bailey shrugged. 'Right.'

The lawyers were all standing around in the hall outside Gerald's office, waiting to be let back in. They reminded Bailey of a bunch of seagulls waiting for scraps, or vultures looking for more.

'Don't change the locks just yet,' Bailey said.

CHAPTER 26

It was almost eleven o'clock by the time Bailey arrived at Bankstown police station. He parked his car next to the train tracks, then fired off a message to Dexter.

I'm here

Carpark across the road

Bailey had no idea how long Dexter would be. Interrogations took time.

He'd only been back in Sydney for a couple of days and his neck and back were still carrying the tension from the long flight. He was tired too. His eyebrows felt like sandbags.

It was finally cooling down outside and he climbed out of the car for some fresh air.

Bailey stretched his arms towards the night sky, swivelling his body, his back cracking with the movement. It didn't change a thing. The tension was still there. So was the exhaustion.

Smoke was hovering above a barbeque outside the station entrance, where an old man was packing up his sausage stand. The bangers smelled good. Bailey was so distracted by writing his article a few hours ago that he'd hardly eaten any of the kebab that was supposed to have been his dinner.

'Any of those left?' Bailey said to the guy scraping the grill.

'Five bucks, mate,' he said. 'Can't guarantee the temperature and I've run out of sauce.'

'Surely that qualifies for a discount?'

'That is the discount.' The old man dropped a tired, shrivelled sausage into a bun with a pair of tongs that looked like they hadn't ever seen a scrubbing brush. 'Take it or leave it.'

'I'll take it.'

Bailey walked back to his car and sat on the edge of the bonnet. His phone vibrated.

Miranda had taken a selfie of her, the doc and Nancy.

Arrived safely.

He responded with a kiss.

Still no word from Dexter.

The sausage was lukewarm and full of fat, but it did the trick. His heart might not be thanking him, but his stomach was content.

Bailey lay back on the bonnet and looked at the sky. It was difficult to see the stars through the smog of the city, but there was no hiding the moon. It was a bright waxing crescent. He closed his eyes and his mind turned to Omar. His old fixer from Baghdad might be angry, but Bailey owed it to him to find his son. In fact, he owed Omar much more than that.

Omar was the guy who drove Bailey around Baghdad in his beaten-up Brazilian Volkswagen. In the early nineties, those cars were everywhere in Iraq. Like Holdens in Australia or Fords in America. The thing about Omar's Brazilian was that it had been modified to include an important hiding place. There was a rectangular box under the back seat that was just big enough for a grown man to hide inside when they were passing through checkpoints, or dangerous neighbourhoods, like the Shi'ite slums of Sadr City. Omar used to call it 'the bucket'.

Omar would stash bottles of water and dried fruits in the bucket because they never knew how long Bailey would need to be in there. Mostly, it was minutes, although there were occasions when Bailey had spent hours in there, emerging a sweaty mess, his muscles locked in spasm. He'd lost count of the times the car had been searched while he was hiding in the bucket. It may have been uncomfortable, but it was safe. He'd never been found. Not once.

Bailey's phone vibrated. Dexter.

Down in ten

Bailey had always made sure that Omar had extra dinars to help get them out of a bind. Banknotes were the first and last resort in Iraq at that time, especially with cops. Baghdad police were the worst. Omar and Bailey had a saying back then – 'pay it, don't say it' – because talking always got you into trouble. Omar was careful to carry only enough dinars to pay the small bribes demanded by Saddam's policemen. Larger sums, and American dollars, only aroused suspicion and could get you arrested. When people got arrested in Saddam's Iraq, they didn't come home.

There were criminal gangs in Baghdad that were even more frightening than the police. They were the ones that specialised in kidnapping foreigners and selling them back to their families, employers or governments. Highly organised and prone to extreme violence, they had a business model that worked.

It was almost inevitable that one day a gang would come for Bailey. Luckily, when that day came, Omar had seen them coming.

'Get in the bucket!'

Omar had spotted a fake roadblock up ahead and he wasn't taking any chances.

Bailey had less than thirty seconds to get under the back seat and curl up so he wouldn't make a sound. He closed the lid just as the car was slowing to a halt.

'What's the problem?'

Bailey heard Omar ask the question in Arabic.

'Get out!'

Bailey's Arabic wasn't very good back then, although he knew enough words to know that these guys were on the hunt for a westerner. Eventually, the voices stopped and all Bailey could hear were the sounds of Omar being beaten to a pulp. He knew that much because he saw the aftermath.

When the punches stopped, the rear doors opened, along with the boot of the car. The gang climbed in the back, yanking at seats, ripping off the door of the glove box and tearing at the upholstery with knives.

The thing about the bucket was that it locked from the inside, with the fabric of the cushions reinforced by a metal plate. There was no way these guys were getting it open, even if they'd tried.

When the gang finally gave up on the inside of the car, Bailey heard someone lay into Omar one more time before they packed up their roadblock and left.

Bailey waited for the street to go quiet before he unlocked the bucket and flipped the lid.

Omar was lying, unconscious, barely breathing, in the dirt beside the car. Bailey lifted him onto the back seat and made it to hospital just in time.

That was more than twenty-five years ago. Bailey remembered it like yesterday.

He owed Omar, all right. He owed him his life.

'Bailey . . . Bailey . . . Bailey.'

Dexter was patting Bailey on the shoulder.

'Bailey!'

For a guy who didn't sleep, he was proving difficult to wake. She whacked him harder.

'What?' He sat up, shaking his head. 'Sorry. Nodded off.'

He slid off the bonnet until his feet touched the ground, rubbing his eyes with the backs of his hands. 'Get anything more out of them? Sara Haneef turn up?'

Dexter shook her head. 'No and no. The Salmas are either good at playing dumb or they know nothing about Sara Haneef. I've got them in different cells, telling the same story. They might be telling the truth. Maybe this has nothing at all to do with the sister.'

'Then why's she gone AWOL?' Bailey said.

'I don't know, Bailey. I really need to get back to work.' Dexter was pointing at the police building across the street. 'What else did you want to talk about?'

Bailey didn't know where to start. How does someone ease into a conversation about getting phone calls from the world's most wanted terrorist?

'Seriously, Bailey.' Dexter let out a long breath, clearly tired. 'You said you had something, what is it?'

'Mustafa al-Baghdadi.'

'What about him?'

'He contacted me again.'

Dexter went quiet and turned her back on Bailey, watching a train speed through the station without stopping.

'This time I made a recording.' Bailey was still feeling guilty about not bringing her in the loop earlier about Mustafa, especially now that he suspected that he might be involved. He opened the back door of the Corolla. 'Hop in, I'll play it to –'

'Bailey.' Dexter turned back around, her eyes catching his across the night. 'I know about the phone call.'

'What?' He let go of the door, stepping towards her. 'What do you mean? How?'

She went quiet again, leaving him to answer his own question. It wasn't difficult.

'You're fucking kidding me. You're bugging my fucking phone?'

Dexter folded her arms. 'You can't be that surprised. As I told you before, this is bloody serious. Time is everything if we're going to stop this thing in its tracks . . . and it was for your own safety.'

'Don't give me that bullshit.'

After all the years chasing down stories, Bailey was now part of the story. The guy being tailed. The source of information for cops like Dexter.

What had been done was done. He couldn't change it now. Neither could Dexter.

'C'mon, Bailey. A known terrorist leader. When you stop and think about it, you'll see I didn't have much of a choice.'

'You made a choice all right,' he said, coolly.

Dexter leaned back on the car. 'Think what you like. I'm not going there right now. It's been a long bloody day.'

Bailey was angry but part of him understood why she'd done it. She was the most senior counter-terrorism cop in the state, it was a no-brainer. He just didn't like being used. Especially by the woman who shared his bed.

A train squeaked to a halt on the platform just beyond the fence. Background noise that reminded Bailey what they really should have been talking about.

'So, what'd you make of it?'

'What?'

'The recording,' he said. 'Notice the background noise? Might help with Mustafa's location.'

'We're already looking at that.'

'And?'

'It's been three hours.'

Dexter was talking while staring at her office across the street and it was grating on Bailey. 'Are we done here, are we? Nothing else?'

She fixed him with a squinting stare. 'Don't get all sensitive with me. We come at this from very different places, Bailey. Different jobs.'

'So nothing?'

'I want to know how Mustafa al-Baghdadi knows so much about the raid in Roselands. He's talking like he's got a whole bloody team of terrorists out here. That's what's got me worried.' She pointed at the neon police sign across the street. 'And that's why I need to get back up there.'

A group of people appeared at the exit to the train station, laughing and talking loudly about the bar they were going to next. One guy was swaying as he walked, fiddling with his phone, telling the others that he was booking them an Uber.

'One more thing,' Dexter remembered something. 'Where's Miranda?'

'I sent her to Gerald's house with the doc. They're staying the night. He and Nancy have good security. Electric gate. Cameras.'

'I'll send a uniform around, get them to park out front. At least until we work out how you're involved. If that last phone call was a threat aimed at you, your family,' Dexter said.

'You think it was?'

'Eye for an eye,' she said, quoting Mustafa. 'We all know the saying. Just not what it means coming out of his mouth. Where's Anthea?'

It was weird hearing Dexter say his ex-wife's name.

'In Italy with the banker.'

Ordinarily, Bailey's nickname for his ex-wife's husband would have sparked a smile from Dexter. Her face barely moved. It was like a wall had risen up out of the ground between them.

'What about you?'

'I'm a big girl,' Dexter said, dismissively. 'And I really need to get back to work.'

'Will you let me know what turns up?'

Between Ronnie and Dexter, Bailey was hoping that they'd get something of value off the recording.

'I'll do what I can.'

Or whatever the hell she wanted.

CHAPTER 27

It sounded like an earthquake.

Vibrating glass, inches from his head. White flickering light.

Bailey opened his eyes. His bloody phone.

He reached across and grabbed it from the coffee table beside the couch, where he'd fallen asleep listening to the Rolling Stones.

'So, you do know how to answer your damn phone.'

A grumpy voice barked down the line.

Bailey was resting the phone on his ear, eyes closed, his head flat on the couch.

'Bailey?'

The voice was familiar.

He hadn't registered who it was because he was only just coming to, struggling to read the little digits on his watch: 6.10 am.

'Bailey, you there?'

It was Father Joe.

'It's six o'clock in the bloody morning, mate.'

'Calm down, sleepyhead,' Joe said. 'You know I'm an early riser. You asked me for help and I'm giving it to you. I didn't realise this was a nine to five arrangement.'

'Sorry, Joe.' The old priest was right. 'What've you got?'

'That kid you're looking for, I think I've found him.'

Bailey jolted upright, shaking his head. 'You what?'

'Tariq,' Joe said. 'I think I've found him.'

'Where?'

'Turned up at one of the overnight shelters in Parramatta. I'd put the call out and I've just had one of my volunteers on the phone. She saw your story in the paper, says the kid just walked in looking for a feed a couple of hours ago. Scared shitless. Looks like he's been roughed up a bit. Doesn't want to go to the cops.'

'Where is he now?'

'I'm at the gym in Redfern for the morning session,' Joe said. 'I told her to bring him here.'

'I'm on my way.'

Bailey almost fell over when he stood up from the couch. The record player was still spinning but Mick Jagger had stopped singing hours ago. He pulled back the needle and rested it on the stand, rubbing his eyes again, trying to get them to focus.

He needed a shower to properly wake up and he needed to call Dexter. Whatever was going on between them, they needed to talk. She needed to know about his conversation with Father Joe, unless the cop monitoring Bailey's phone was calling her right now. Bailey had no idea how fast that stuff happened, or whether the phone call from Joe would have sounded the alarm. Either way, the police needed to be careful. If the kid saw flashing lights and a convoy of cop cars, he'd probably run for it.

The drive to Father Joe's gym took him around fifteen minutes. He was a few hundred metres away, looking for somewhere to park the car, when he noticed the flashing lights up the street. Exactly the scene that he'd wanted to avoid. Something was wrong.

Two ambulances were parked out the front of the gym and someone was sitting in the gutter being treated by a paramedic.

There was also a small group of people standing on the footpath, including a couple of cops in uniforms.

Bailey double-parked out the front of the gym just as one of the ambulances was driving away. He flicked on his hazard lights, hopping out. There was no sign of Dexter but he'd spoken to her on the phone and knew that she wouldn't be far away. Bailey couldn't see Joe, either. But he recognised the person sitting in the gutter. Jake. The young boxer who was hitting the bag with Joe a couple of days ago. A paramedic in a blue uniform was wiping blood off his cheek and examining a cut above his eye.

'Hold still, mate.'

'I told you, lady. I'm not going to hospital.'

'Jake.' Bailey sat on the kerb beside him. 'Where's Joe, mate? What happened?'

'I'm sorry.' Jake was shaking his head. 'I tried to stop them, tried to help.'

'Give us a minute, would you?' the paramedic said to Bailey. 'Jake, I need you to stay still for me, please. Cut's not too deep, a couple of steri-strips will do it. I can treat you here.'

Bailey ignored her. 'It's okay, Jake. Where's Joe?'

Jake pointed his finger up the street where the other ambulance had just driven off. 'They're taking him to hospital.'

'Seriously, mate.' The paramedic was getting annoyed. 'Just give me a few minutes here with Jake and then you can ask all the questions you like.'

Bailey stood up, his attention suddenly elsewhere. 'Back in a moment.'

Joe had mentioned a woman on the phone and Bailey had noticed a middle-aged lady talking to a couple of cops over by the entrance to the gym. He sidled up near them so he could hear what she was saying.

'Yes, yes, that's right. I brought the boy here about ten minutes ago.'

'Then what happened?' An overweight cop with a moustache was asking the questions. 'And every little detail will help here, Michelle.'

'Well, Joe met us out here and asked one of the other boys to take Tariq inside the boxing gym so that we could have a private conversation.'

'Who took him inside?'

'That boy over there.' She was pointing at Jake. 'He's the one they punched. He's a brave boy, he tried to stop them.'

'So, tell us again – this boy, you said his name was Tariq?'

'Yes, that's right. Tariq. He was scared, scared of everything. He said he was in trouble and didn't know what to do.'

'Can we help you with something, mate?' The cop with the moustache noticed Bailey eavesdropping on their conversation.

'Yeah, sorry. Joe's a mate. I was on my way to visit him this morning. Is he okay?'

'Who're you?'

'John Bailey.'

Bailey stepped past Michelle and held out his hand to the cop, who reluctantly shook it.

'Okay, Mr Bailey. I'm just going to ask you to wait over there, take a seat.' He was pointing at the wooden bench beside the bus stand. 'We'll come and talk to you in a moment.'

Bailey didn't move. 'Where's Tariq?' he asked Michelle.

'They took him,' she said.

'Okay, mate. You're not listening.' It was the other cop this time. He was a younger version of the fat guy with the moustache, only with glasses and a beard. 'Can you please go over there and let us do our job?'

179

'Bailey!' Dexter appeared from behind him. 'What happened?'

'You know this guy?' It was the older cop with the moustache again.

'Sorry, Alan,' Dexter said. 'Bailey and I go back.'

We go forward too, thought Bailey. Although he wasn't about to tell these guys that he was sleeping with their boss.

'I'm just trying to find out what happened,' Bailey said. 'As I told you on the phone, Tariq was getting dropped here. Looks like that happened as planned, then I'm a bit unclear.'

'Detective Dexter,' Alan stepped past Bailey. 'What we have so far is that the kid goes inside the gym while Michelle here talks to the old priest out front.

'Then a white van pulls up and a couple of guys jump out. The old man tries to block them from going inside and they punch him to the ground. Next, the kid over there,' he said, pointing at Jake. 'The kid takes a few swings at the guys who made it inside, gets belted himself, then they drag the other kid, Tariq, into the van and they disappear.'

'Fuck it!' Bailey said to himself. They had been minutes away from getting Tariq and now he was gone again.

'Thanks, Alan,' Dexter said. 'Let's pull the vision from any cameras we've got in the street and try to get a plate on the van.'

'Already on that,' the cop with the moustache pronounced, proudly.

'Well done.'

'Sharon.' Bailey gestured for Dexter to take a walk. Away from the others. He waited until they were out of earshot before he started talking. 'I'm going to head to the hospital to see Joe. I feel bloody terrible about this, the bloke's in his eighties.'

'Do what you need to. Police job now.' She was speaking with one eye on Jake and the paramedic. 'We'll find the van. If these guys are half as dumb as the ones we picked up yesterday, they'll be parked at the closest KFC getting stuck into a bucket of the dirty bird.'

Bailey liked the analogy, and her confidence. But he wasn't so sure.

'That kid, Jake,' Bailey said. 'He spoke to Tariq. Maybe he knows something.'

'We'll check it out.'

'Hey, lady!' Bailey called out to the paramedic. 'Which hospital will I find the old man at?'

'Vinnies, where all the emergencies go. He's got a head injury, you may not get in to see him.'

Bailey thanked her with a nod. The hospital might not want to let him inside, but he'd find a way. He always did.

CHAPTER 28

The sandstone wall on the eastern side of the old Darlinghurst jail was one of the saddest places in Sydney. It wasn't because of the sorry lives of the convicts who'd been forced to build it, or even the petty criminals who had died in the hangman's noose.

Today's sadness was in the faces of the living.

The Wall, as it was known, had been the city's most conspicuous gay beat for more than fifty years. Mostly young men and boys would loiter along this strip of sandstone waiting for their regulars, or some lonely man to pull over and take them for a ride.

Back in the 1980s, when Bailey was a cub reporter, he would write about gay bashings at The Wall and the cops who never did anything about it. Hate crimes weren't a priority back then because most cops thought that anyone who bashed a 'poofter' was doing the world a favour.

Violent bigots didn't get away with bashing gay men anymore. Other than that, not much had changed at The Wall. The sad faces of lost boys were still plying an old trade.

'Hey, buddy. Looking for someone?'

A bloke with a hoodie called out to Bailey just as he was closing the door of the Corolla.

'No, mate. I'm good.'

The guy wasn't convinced and he stepped forward, pulling

back his hoodie so that Bailey could get a look at his face. 'Are you sure?'

'Yeah. I'm sure.'

Bailey put a bunch of coins in the meter and waited for the ticket, trying to ignore the guy who'd sidled up beside him.

'You're handsome. You know that, Mister Mister?'

The sun was coming up and the bloke looked like he should have been getting ready for school, not propositioning Bailey.

'I'm a cop, kid,' Bailey lied. 'Time to go home.'

'Yeah, yeah.' He smiled. 'Cops are some of my best clients. And you don't look like any cop I know.'

Bailey grabbed his parking ticket and slid it onto the dashboard inside.

He started walking off up the street and then stopped. 'Hey kid!'

'I knew you'd change your mind.'

'What's your name?'

'Jimmy.'

Bailey reached into his pocket and handed him a fifty. 'Go home, Jimmy. Give this shit away.'

'Home?' Jimmy folded the fifty-dollar note, shoving it in his pocket.

'Yeah, Jimmy. Home.'

'Why would I go home?' He shrugged his shoulders with a sad smile. 'I'll just be doing the same thing for my mum's old man. At least here I get paid.'

'Sorry, kid.' Bailey didn't know what else to say.

Jimmy turned his back on Bailey and started walking away. 'Thanks for the pineapple.' He waved without turning around.

Bailey was still thinking about Jimmy when he walked into the reception at St Vincent's Hospital. Paedophiles were rotten to the core, and so were the people who protected them, turned a blind eye. For the few paedophiles who got caught, the punishment never fitted the crime. How could it? Sex abusers destroyed lives. Kids like Jimmy never recovered, the best they could do was just hang on. It's what happens when innocence is stolen.

'Can I help you?'

A bleary-eyed guy in a blue uniform was looking up at Bailey from the reception desk.

'I'm just checking in on someone.'

'What's his name?'

'Joe Henley,' Bailey said. 'Father Joe Henley. He's an old priest, got roughed up in Redfern. I need to see him.'

'Give me a sec.'

The nurse was tapping away at a keyboard with the light from his computer screen bouncing off his glasses.

'He's still being assessed, I'm afraid. You can't see him yet.'

'What shape's he in?' Bailey was determined to at least get some information.

'Are you family?'

'Not really.'

'Then you're going to have to take a seat and wait. Sorry.'

Before Bailey even had time to respond, the nurse had moved on. 'Can I help you?' He was looking over Bailey's shoulder at a woman holding a toddler with a nasty cough.

Bailey stepped out of the way and found a stiff plastic chair in the waiting area.

Ten minutes later, he was back on his feet again.

'Any update?' he said to the nurse.

'Like I told you before, you're just going to have to wait.'

Emergency rooms were busy places and the nurse had a job to do. Process patients and prioritise the ones in trouble. He'd probably already dealt with a dozen impatient people during his night shift. It didn't seem to bother him.

'Okay, mate.' Bailey knew he was pushing his luck, so he sat back down.

Over the next thirty minutes, he watched people get called up, then ushered through an automatic door and down a hallway, where they were met by busy nurses with clipboards. Every time the door opened he stood up, searching for any sign of Joe. Nothing.

It was time to move to Plan B. Unauthorised entry. It wasn't long before an opportunity arrived.

The guy behind the desk called out to the woman who had the toddler with the cough. The doctor would see her now. She got up and headed down the hall. Bailey followed. She was so focused on her son's latest coughing fit that she missed Bailey, who was right behind her, pretending he was part of the family.

The kid didn't sound good and the nurse on the other side of the door thought the same. She rushed the mother and child away.

Like any half-decent reporter, Bailey was good at getting into places where he wasn't supposed to be. The trick was to look confident and busy. He smiled at the hospital staff, walking in and out of rooms, as he made his way into the main triage area. If Joe was waiting to be assessed, this was where he'd be. It wasn't long before he found him.

'I know you're just doing your job, young lady.' Bailey could hear the sound of Joe's voice behind a curtain. 'I've got things to do.'

The confidence in Joe's voice was like an adrenalin shot for Bailey. Relief.

'I'm sorry,' a woman responded. 'You've had a big knock to the head and the doctor needs to assess you. As soon as you've got the all-clear, you'll be fine to leave.'

'Any chance that might happen soon?'

'I can check a few things for you while we wait. That'll speed things up. But at your age, we really need to take a proper look, which is why you're just going to have to be patient and wait for the doctor.'

Bailey peeled back the curtain. He couldn't see Father Joe's face, because he was hidden behind the nurse who'd been laying down the law.

'Okay, tough guy,' Bailey said. 'I think you need to let this nice lady do her job.'

The nurse swung around, surprised. 'Who're you?'

'I'm the closest thing to family he's got. I'm here to check up on him, report back to the cardinal and . . .' Bailey stopped talking when he caught sight of Joe's face. There was a bandage wrapped around his head with a bloodstain seeping through the fabric. His lip was swollen and his right eye was half-closed. 'Bloody hell, Joe. Those bastards didn't miss.'

'Don't worry, mate.' Joe held up his hands and made two fists, so that Bailey could see the red splotches on his knuckles. 'Landed a few of my own.'

Bailey laughed and the nurse gave him a look like she thought the old man must have been joking.

'You got in a fight?' she said. 'Aren't you a priest?'

'You can't always turn the other cheek, love.' Joe winked at her. 'The lord works in mysterious ways.'

The nurse laughed, shaking her head. 'Bizarre. An eighty-year-old man who thinks he's Rocky Balboa.'

'Eighty-one,' Joe said. 'And compliment accepted.'

The nurse took Joe's blood pressure and, after a few more tests, she unwrapped the bandage, revealing an inch-long cut on his forehead.

'That's going to need a few stitches,' she said. 'I'll give it a clean first. Back in a moment.'

As soon as she left the room, Bailey stepped closer to Joe. 'You seriously okay, mate?'

'All good, son. Don't worry about me.'

'Who did this?'

'You tell me. I don't know what this kid's done, but they didn't mess around.'

'Can you remember what happened?'

Joe tried to sit up, his mouth half open in a flat line as he tried to conceal the pain.

'A few minutes after the young bloke arrived, two muscled-up Middle Eastern fellas turned up. Like they had been following him. Maybe they'd been searching the shelters too. Who knows?'

Joe gestured for Bailey to lean in, so that he could lower his voice.

'What's all this about, Bailey?'

He owed him an explanation.

'Terrorism, Joe.' Bailey looked over his shoulder, making sure there was no one else around. 'Tariq's caught up in a plot that might just be about to go bang. What else can you tell me?'

'Nothing. It all happened so fast. The two guys appeared out of nowhere. The rest is a painful history.'

Bailey looked at his watch: 7.58 am. He needed to get moving.

'I'll check in on you later, old boy.'

'I'm fine, Bailey. I'll be out of here in time to pack up the gym after the morning session.' Joe paused, distracted by his own thoughts. 'Those kids better not have taken the morning off.'

Bailey patted the old man on the arm and peeled back the curtain, readying to leave.

'Bailey?' Joe called after him. 'Talk to Jake. He and Tariq had a few minutes together inside, he might know something.'

The nurse appeared through the curtain with a trolley that had a bowl of water and some implements. It looked like Joe was about to get a few stitches.

'Rest up,' Bailey said. 'And do what this nice lady tells you, will you?'

'Of course.'

CHAPTER 29

The air was three degrees hotter and it felt five times heavier by the time Bailey was walking up Redfern Street for the second time this morning. The traffic was inching its way in every direction and the engine fumes were itching his throat. He'd parked the Corolla four blocks away and his brow was needing a wipe by the time he made it to the gym.

'Need a hand, kid?'

Jake was trying to unhook a heavy bag from the ceiling when Bailey walked through the door.

It was 8.36 am. Jake would need to be at school soon. Bailey needed to make a friend. Fast.

'I'm fine.'

He wasn't fine. Jake was shuffling, awkwardly, on his toes. He couldn't quite lift the bag high enough to get the metal ring to slip over the top of a hook that was fixed to the roof.

'Seriously, let me help.'

Bailey had a couple of inches on Jake and he grabbed the other side of the bag, holding it steady.

Click.

The full weight of the heavy bag dropped into the palms of Bailey's hands. He felt his back and stomach tighten as he tried to keep hold of the bag without falling over.

189

'I'll take that,' Jake said.

The bag must have weighed at least half as much as Jake, yet the kid elegantly balanced it on his shoulder, dumping it with the rest of the equipment in the corner of the room.

Jake hadn't told Bailey to piss off yet, which was a good sign, especially after what Dexter had told him when he had called her during the car ride from the hospital.

'He's a little shit,' she'd said. 'Wouldn't tell me a thing. I even threatened to take him in for questioning. He didn't care.'

Maybe Jake just didn't like cops.

Bailey helped him stack the last of the dumbbells and pads without saying a word. Building trust.

'Where's everyone else?' Bailey said when they were done.

'They all did a runner,' Jake replied. 'Funny how cops can clear a room around here.'

'How's the eye?'

The paramedic looked like she'd done a neat job with the cut above Jake's eye, although his cheek had already started to change colour and swell.

'Fine,' Jake said. 'You been to see Father Joe?'

'Yeah. How'd you know?'

'That cop told me. Said you and her were mates.'

'He's going to be fine, Jake.'

'It takes a special kind of prick to bash an old priest.'

There was emotion in Jake's voice.

'Seriously, Jake. He's okay. He even tried to convince the nurse that he could check himself out.'

Jake laughed. 'Sounds about right.'

'You know, Jake, Joe was a big help to me when I was a young bloke.'

'He told me.'

'Different weight division to you, mate.' Bailey smiled, patting his stomach. 'And I wasn't nearly as talented. No way I was hitting a bag like that.'

'Father Joe's a good coach. I'm getting there,' Jake said, proudly. 'But, mate . . . you don't look like you grew up on struggle street. No offence.'

'I've probably had it easy. Always had a home. What about you? You got a home?'

Jake ignored the question and picked up his gym bag, checking that his red gloves were inside before zipping it closed.

'What about that bloke they took – Tariq? Your cop friend reckons they'll find him pretty quick.'

Jake had a peculiar habit of talking without ever looking Bailey in the face. Eye contact can get you into trouble on the street. Bailey wondered if the street was all the kid knew.

'They haven't found him. Not yet, anyway.'

'They'd want to hurry.'

'What makes you say that?'

'He reckons someone wants to kill him.'

'He told you that?'

Jake fumbled with the zip on the side pocket of his bag and withdrew a key attached to a ring with a small metal boxing glove on it. 'I've got to lock up and get to school.'

'If you know something, Jake, you need to tell me,' Bailey said. 'Tariq's in danger. Did he tell you anything else, anything at all?'

The young boxer looked Bailey in the eyes for the first time. He reached into his pocket, withdrawing a piece of paper that was neatly folded into a square, and handed it to Bailey.

'What is it?'

Jake shook his head. 'Don't know. Haven't opened it. He jammed it in my hand just as those two blokes flew through the door. I stuffed it in my pocket then started swinging. Forgot it was there. Otherwise I would've given it to the cops.'

Bailey smiled. 'Would you?'

Jake shrugged. 'Why wouldn't I?'

Bailey patted him on the shoulder. 'You've done good, Jake.'

The square of paper was burning a hole in Bailey's hand but he didn't want to open it in front of Jake. He knew what was inside. He could feel the hard piece of plastic through the paper.

They locked up the gym and stepped outside onto the pavement.

'You take care of yourself, Jake. Keep boxing.'

Jake slung his gym bag over his shoulder. 'Reckon Father Joe will be back for training this afternoon?'

'God help the poor hospital staff if he's not.'

The smell of fresh bread wafting from the bakery on the corner opposite Redfern Park was too good to resist. It was only a few doors up from where Bailey was standing outside the gym and he was headed in that direction. It was early for a meat pie but he'd been awake for so long that his body clock was telling him that it was lunchtime.

While he waited for his pie and coffee, Bailey pulled the square of paper from his pocket, carefully unfolding it. He was right about what was inside.

A memory card.

Bailey may have been a technology luddite, but he knew that much. His best guess was that it contained a video of Tariq Haneef, sitting beneath a black flag, delivering a message to the world on behalf of Islamic Nation.

He grabbed his phone, examining the ports on the side, wondering if there was a hole big enough for a card like this one. There wasn't.

'Coffee's up!'

Dexter or Ronnie would know. He'd call them from the car. He shoved the card in his pocket and headed back to where he'd parked the Corolla.

He was four bites into his pie by the time he got there.

Balancing his coffee and what was left of his pie on the roof, he dug his car keys out of his pocket, jiggling the key in the lock. The door wouldn't open.

'Bloody thing.'

A few years back, someone had broken into his car with a screwdriver, making a mess of the lock. He'd never bothered to get it fixed. Miraculously, it had started working again, if you jiggled it right. It just wasn't happening today.

Bailey gave up and started walking around the car so he could unlock the door from the passenger side.

Boom!

A bright light flashed inside the car, followed by a whooshing sound.

The explosion blew out the windows, sending Bailey flying through the air, crashing to the pavement more than ten metres away. The force of the blast had spun him around. He didn't know which way he was facing. He couldn't move. He couldn't see. His body was numb. There was a loud ringing in his ears. The sound of a fire crackling. The smell of burning rubber.

Bailey could feel the heat wafting from the burning wreckage of the Corolla.

He closed his eyes. Then nothing.

CHAPTER 30

AFULA, ISRAEL 1992

'My baby! My baby! My baby! Please! Please!'

A woman was screaming in Hebrew, running towards the flaming bus.

People were sitting upright in the passenger seats, black shadows against the flames that were swirling inside the bus like a giant rectangular furnace.

A policeman caught the woman in his arms and held her as she kicked and punched him, screaming for him to let her go.

The acrid smell of burning rubber and flesh was stinging Bailey's nostrils as he stared at the flames, not knowing what to do.

He'd never seen a burning vehicle so close before. Never smelled burning flesh.

Tears sprang to his eyes, trying to protect them from the fumes.

He reached for his camera, unclipping it from the bag on his shoulder, and lifted it in front of his face.

Snap. Snap. Snap.

He was taking pictures faster than his brain could process what was happening.

Out of the corner of his eye he caught sight of a young boy running towards the bus. Through the lens of the camera the kid looked like he was only a few feet tall. He was screaming for his father.

'Papa! Papa! Papa!'

Bailey dropped the camera, letting the strap around his neck catch its fall, and started running towards the bus.

The boy was metres away from the burning wreckage when Bailey scooped him up in his arms. He turned and started running the other way just as another blast erupted from behind, knocking them to the ground. Bailey lay there, holding the boy in his arms, shielding him from the explosion and the rush of heat that washed across his back, hoping that the flames wouldn't pull them into the furnace.

'It's okay. It's okay. It's okay.' He kept repeating to the boy, over and over again. 'It's okay.'

'Mate. Mate.' Someone was touching his shoulder. 'Are you all right?'

Bailey didn't recognise the voice.

'Where's the boy? Is he okay?'

Bailey took a deep breath, his nostrils stinging from the burning rubber.

'What boy, mate? Was there a child with you?'

Bailey opened his eyes, expecting to see the boy beside him in the dirt.

He wasn't in Israel, he was lying on a concrete footpath in Redfern.

A hubcap was lying on the ground beside him and Bailey could see flames burning inside a car. He wiggled his fingertips, made a fist with his hands.

Next he moved his toes, then his feet. His back felt like it had been punched with a hot iron and he could taste blood in his mouth.

'What boy?' The same voice again. 'What boy are you talking about?'

Bailey lifted his head, rolling over, trying to balance himself by putting an elbow on the pavement.

'I think you should just lie there, mate. Wait for the ambos.'

Bailey swallowed, trying to get some moisture into his mouth.

He sat up on both elbows, flipping himself over onto his side.

'Fuck me.'

A man in a white singlet was kneeling next to him.

'Anyone else?' Bailey said, coughing his words. 'Anyone else hurt?'

'I don't know,' the man said. 'I could only see you, mate. Are you all right?'

'Where are we?'

'You're in Redfern.'

An ambulance siren was getting louder in the distance and Bailey could also hear the loud wailing of a fire engine.

He held up his hand. 'Help me up, would you?'

'I think you should stay there, mate. You may have hurt your neck.'

Bailey sat up, moving his head from side to side, kicking out his legs and rotating his shoulders. Everything seemed to be in working order. The only pain was coming from the middle of his back.

'Seriously, mate. I'm good.' Bailey held up his arm again. 'I need to get up.'

The guy in the singlet pulled Bailey up off the ground with one arm, while supporting Bailey's back with his other one.

'Aaargh!' Bailey winced.

'Sorry. You've got a burn there, mate,' he said. 'Doesn't look good.'

'Yeah, thanks.'

Bailey touched his cheek and jaw, noticing some blood on his fingertips.

'You were talking about a boy. Was there a child with you?'

'No. Must've been dreaming, something that happened a long time ago.'

The guy had a confused look on his face. 'Your head must have hit the ground pretty hard.'

'It hit something.'

Bailey was struggling to remember what he was doing in Redfern. The last thing he recalled was seeing Joe in hospital.

The fire engine and ambulances arrived at the same time, followed by at least four police cars.

'Over here!' The guy in the singlet was signalling to a paramedic.

A man in a blue uniform came rushing over.

'This guy was launched into the air by the explosion. I saw it. He was standing next to the car.'

'Are you okay to walk?' the paramedic said.

'Yeah, mate. I'm fine.'

Bailey held out his hand to the guy in the singlet. 'Thanks for your help.'

'No worries. Take care of yourself.'

'Hey.' The paramedic was talking to the guy in the singlet. 'The cops will want to talk to you about what you saw. Head over that way.'

The man walked towards the uniformed police, who were stopping traffic in the street and ordering people back from Bailey's car, which was still on fire.

Within a couple of minutes the firefighters had extinguished the flames and the Corolla was transformed into a smoking grey shell, covered in foam.

'Can I get you to take off your shirt?'

Bailey unbuttoned his flannelette shirt and let the paramedic slip it off his shoulders.

'I hope this doesn't have sentimental value.' The guy was holding up Bailey's shirt and pointing to the holes burnt through the fabric.

'Straight from a Hollywood movie, that one.'

'Thought I recognised you. Star Wars, right?'

Bailey liked this bloke already. He had a sense of humour. He probably had to, considering what he did for a crust. He'd probably seen enough motorcycle fatalities to fill a high school yearbook.

Sitting inside the back of the ambulance, Bailey watched the firefighters inspecting what was left of the Corolla, making sure the flames were out.

'You've got second-degree burns here, I'm afraid.'

The stinging in Bailey's back was getting more painful with every minute that passed. He wasn't going to hospital. He'd been there once already today.

'Second degree?' Bailey said. 'Reckon you can clean it up and send me on my way from here?'

'Maybe. Let's see how we go.'

The guy in the white singlet was walking back towards Bailey, a phone in his hand. 'This yours, mate?'

Bailey inspected the phone. Cracked screen, scratches all over. It lit up when he touched it, still working. 'Thanks.'

He called Dexter.

'Sharon.' Bailey coughed into the phone. 'Sorry, where are you?'

'Bankstown. Are they sirens in the background?' Her voice changed. 'Where are you?'

'Redfern. Long story – aarrgh! Careful!'

Bailey was talking to the paramedic examining his burn.

'Sorry, mate.'

'Are you okay?' Dexter said.

'I'm fine but the Corolla's no longer with us.'

'That car explosion? That was you?'

News travelled fast in the force.

'I think we found one of your pressure cookers.'

Dexter was quiet on the other end of the phone and Bailey could almost hear her mind ticking over, processing what Bailey had just told her.

'Are you sure it was a bomb?'

'Look, the Corolla may have missed a few scheduled services over the years, but I've seen enough car bombs to know what it looks like when one goes off.'

The paramedic stepped in front of Bailey with an incredulous look on his face.

'I'm talking to a cop.' Bailey pointed to his back, encouraging him to keep working.

'Who's that?' Dexter said.

'I've got a little burn on my back, just getting it looked at.'

'Jesus, Bailey,' she said.

Bailey was distracted by what was happening on the road in front of him. A fireman was having another go with his hose at the front of the Corolla. That car may have been a pile of junk, but it had sentimental value for Bailey. What a way to go.

'Bailey, are you still there?'

His ears were still ringing from the blast and he was struggling to concentrate.

'Yeah, I'm here.'

'Seriously, are you okay?' It wasn't the policewoman talking. 'You don't sound okay.'

'I'm good. Fine.'

He was lying. He was still struggling to remember. It had happened to him once before after a head-knock on the rugby field. A mild concussion, they'd told him. It had taken him hours to remember the game. Eventually, it all came back. Every detail.

Including the try that he'd scored under the sticks after he caught a beautiful flick-pass from his brother that sent him through a gap the size of a road train. Mike had been a great rugby player. A great bloke. Bailey was banking on his memory returning. If only his brother could do the same.

'Once you're done there, I think you should go home.' Dexter was still talking. 'Actually, go to Gerald's. I've still got a police car stationed out front.'

'Yeah,' Bailey said, acknowledging the suggestion while not knowing quite what he'd do.

'The cops are going to need a statement from you at the scene.' Dexter was sounding like a detective again. 'Don't be a prat about it, just give it to them. We can follow up later.'

'Are you suggesting I'm uncooperative?'

'You're a special man, John Bailey. That's all.'

Whatever the hell that meant.

'When they ask questions, I'll answer them.'

Bailey hung up.

The paramedic had cleaned Bailey's burn and wrapped it with plastic bandages, fastening them with tape across his stomach that was so tight that he felt like he was wearing a girdle. Bloody uncomfortable. Every movement hurt.

There wasn't much left of his flannelette shirt but he did up the buttons anyway. There was a charity shop up near Joe's gym. He'd call in there as soon as he was done with the cops and find himself something to wear.

'I'm going to need to ask you some questions.'

Bailey recognised the policemen from earlier that morning. It was the older guy, unhealthy-looking.

'Sure.'

The guy had food stuck in his moustache, which Bailey hoped was the remnants of a doughnut. What a cliché. He decided not to tell him.

'What do you want to know?'

'Let's start by confirming that you're the owner of what's left of that car over there,' the policeman said, pointing at the wreckage.

'Yeah, she's mine.' Bailey managed a smirk. 'Another classic gone to the gods.'

CHAPTER 31

Jake. The boxer.

He was the reason that Bailey had come back to Redfern. He was able to at least tell the cops that much. Fearing a forced admission to hospital, Bailey had just made up the rest.

When he arrived at the gym the place was locked up and the kid was gone, Bailey had told the cops. And that was about the extent of his statement.

'You going to be okay to get home?'

At least the policeman had shown some kind of duty of care.

'I'll be fine. Going to take a little walk and then grab a taxi.'

The cop may have been satisfied, but Bailey wasn't.

Walking up the street, he was thinking so hard that his head was hurting. Or maybe that was the concussion. He was getting angry about the black hole in his memory.

He remembered visiting Joe at hospital. Next thing he knew he was lying on the footpath, ten metres from his burning car.

He went back further.

The early phone call from Joe. The race to get to Redfern. Being told that Tariq had been grabbed and thrown into a white van by a couple of Middle Eastern looking guys. Joe getting beaten up for trying to stop them.

Bailey had been minutes away from disrupting whatever plot

Mustafa was directing from wherever the hell he was hiding. Now Tariq was missing again and Bailey was no closer to finding out why. The only thing he knew for certain was that someone had put a bomb inside his car. Someone had tried to kill him. Bailey could only guess that whoever did it was working for the leader of Islamic Nation.

He called Ronnie. After two rings, he answered.

'Bubba.'

'Where are you?'

'Not far.' Never a straight answer. 'Why?'

'Hear about that car bomb in Redfern?'

'Not yet.'

'Well, there was a car bomb in Redfern. Target was me.'

'Any dead?'

Ronnie had spent enough time in the Middle East to know that when a car bomb went off, people usually died.

'No. And I'm fine. Just a sore head, thanks for asking.'

'You wouldn't be on the other end of the phone if you weren't.'

Ronnie had a point and neither of them was the sentimental type.

'What have you got, bubba?'

'Missed Tariq by only minutes here this morning. He was picked up by some guys in a van. Sharon's chasing the plate, says it's only a matter of time. The rest I'm sure you read about in the paper.'

Bailey knew that Ronnie would have seen the photographs and names printed in Bailey's exclusive story for *The Journal*.

'You did well there, bubba. Must have a good source in the police.'

Bailey ignored the swipe. 'What've you got for me?'

'Nothing yet. We're still working on your phone call with Mustafa.'

A sudden pain shot through Bailey's head from one ear to the other.

'Bubba, you still there?'

'Yeah. Sorry.' He was struggling to focus his eyes. 'Sounds like it's a waiting game all round then. I'm going to the paper. Let me know if anything turns up on that recording with Mustafa.'

'Don't go far, bubba,' Ronnie said. 'For some reason, all roads are leading back to you.'

'Like I need reminding.'

Bailey had a good reason to trust Ronnie this time around. This wasn't the Middle East, when Ronnie would feed Bailey misinformation to protect American interests. This time they had a common enemy and Bailey was a key source of information. Thanks to Mustafa al-Baghdadi, Bailey had become a central player in the global fight against terrorism. He didn't like it.

A woman in a blue sleeping bag was half-blocking the entrance to the charity shop. She was out cold, sleeping on sheets of cardboard with a Blue Heeler curled up, loyally, beside her. Bailey slipped five bucks into her cup, stepping over her legs, and walked inside.

The shop's second-hand clothes rack was stacked with so many flannelette shirts that Bailey was spoilt for choice. Had he still owned a car he would have bought the lot and shoved them in the boot. The shirts stank of dust but at three dollars apiece, they were a steal.

The guy behind the counter didn't bat an eyelid when he saw Bailey's bruised face and the holes in his shirt. He probably thought he was just another homeless person browsing on the downtrodden high street. Like the woman sleeping on the pile of cardboard.

Not much shocked people anymore. Things that used to be confronting had become the norm. People had stopped asking questions. Stopped caring. It's what happens when people on decent wages can't afford to buy houses, or pay energy bills, anymore.

'If you get any blood on anything, you buy it.'

Bailey was at a loss to explain the number of miserable people who worked in the charity game. Angry at the world. At everyone.

'I'm not going to try these on, mate.'

He handed the guy behind the counter fifteen dollars and took his five shirts out the door. Minutes later he was changing into a red and black chequered number in the back seat of a taxi, headed for *The Journal*.

The sharp pain from his burn was throbbing and every movement, every touch, made it worse. He was leaning forward so that his back wouldn't touch the seat.

His phone started vibrating. He could just make out Gerald's name through the cracked screen.

'Morning, mate.'

'Where are you?'

'On the way to Sussex Street, in a taxi. The Corolla's gone.'

'Gone?'

'Someone put a bomb in it.'

Gerald laughed down the end of the phone. 'C'mon Bailey, we've got enough going on here without you pissing around.'

'I'm serious. That car explosion in Redfern –'

'That was you?' Gerald suddenly sounded concerned. Rachel Symonds would have heard about the explosion on the police scanners and told the boss. Cars don't blow up in Sydney all that often. It was a story.

'Yep.'

'Bloody hell. Are you injured?'

'Apart from a headache and a steaming crater in my back, I'm fine.'

205

'Should you be at hospital?'

'Treated at the scene, mate. I'm all good.'

'Will you write about it?'

That was a difficult question for Bailey to answer. It was going to be hard to write about something that he couldn't remember.

'Don't think I can. If I was the target, I'm knee-deep in this. The only time I want to see my name in a newspaper is a byline at the top of a yarn.'

'Fair enough, mate. Rachel will sort it out. Tell her what you can. She'll write the copy.'

'I'll get some notes together.'

'How long before you get here?'

'Ten minutes, give or take.'

'I'll meet you downstairs. Apparently, Omar's turned up for another chat about Tariq. Maybe he knows something. I'm on my way down to see him,' Gerald said. 'And Bailey?'

'Yeah?'

'The redundancies are happening. The numbers are big, for you and for me. I'm taking it, you should too. We can talk about it when you get here.'

Bailey ended the call without responding.

He was too young to put his feet up and contemplate the past. The last person that John Bailey wanted to spend more time alone with was himself. He'd done that before and it had ended with him suffering a mental breakdown, waking up in a pool of his own vomit with enough alcohol in his system to stock the bar at Flemington on Cup Day.

With Gerald's help, Bailey had made it back to the top of his game. Or as close as the modern media would let him. He wasn't done with being a reporter. No lawyer was going to turf him out the window, golden parachute or not.

*

They were five blocks from *The Journal* when the traffic ground to a halt. The taxi driver was muttering Hindi swearwords under his breath and remonstrating with a guy in a ute who was trying to cut across the lanes in front of them.

'We're at a standstill and this idiot thinks he knows a better way.' The driver was shaking his head.

'Mind if I get out here?' Bailey said. 'I can walk the last bit.'

'Suit yourself.' He clearly didn't like it. 'I'll just sit here, in the gridlock on the street you brought me down, shall I?'

He had a point. The meter was reading just over twenty dollars so Bailey handed him thirty. 'Sorry, mate, someone's waiting for me. Keep the change.'

Bailey got out of the taxi – the extra cash assuaging his guilt – and headed north up Sussex Street. There was nothing on the road coming south and the traffic pointing north wasn't moving at all. There must have been an accident up ahead.

A block away from *The Journal,* he caught sight of the flashing lights of a police vehicle. He looked up at the buildings around him. The police car was stopped out the front of the paper.

Bailey was still on edge after the car bomb and the flashing lights were making him nervous.

He kept walking. His legs moving faster with each step.

His phone was vibrating in his pocket. Dexter. He'd call her back.

He crossed the street, weaving his way around the stationary cars, trying to find out what was going on.

It was probably just a broken-down vehicle.

A breakdown in one of the centre lanes would make it difficult for the traffic to keep moving and even harder for a tow truck to get to where it was needed.

Bailey made it onto the pavement. He could see a crowd of people up ahead. He recognised some of the faces from the paper.

His phone was vibrating again. Dexter. Again. Now wasn't the time.

A lone policeman was standing in the traffic, blocking cars from going anywhere. 'You're just going to have to wait!' He was yelling at an impatient truck driver who was gesturing with his arm out the window.

Bailey was close to the paper now, pushing past some of the gawkers.

He spotted Penelope. Her head in her hands, being comforted by someone from the office that Bailey didn't know.

'Pen! Pen!' Bailey called out to her. 'What's going on?'

The second Penelope saw Bailey she burst into tears.

'Can somebody tell me what's going on?' Bailey asked the bloke from accounts.

'It's bad, mate. I don't know.'

'You don't know what?' Bailey said. 'What's happened? Will someone fucking tell me what's going on?'

Bailey gave up trying to get answers from the others and kept pushing through the bodies blocking his path. When he got to the front he was stopped by a line of blue and white police tape put there to seal off the scene. He counted a half-dozen officers in uniforms. Two ambulances were parked on the kerb – a paramedic inside one of them, treating a female police officer with a cut on her shoulder.

The police were standing in a cordon, blocking the rest of the view. Bailey ducked down, peering around their bodies, through their legs. All he could see was a brown leather shoe dangling over the side of a stretcher that was being wheeled towards the ambulances. He knew that shoe. Italian leather. Expensive. Worn by someone who enjoyed the finer things in life, but never boasted about them.

Gerald.

Bailey busted through the tape, sidestepping the police, running so fast they missed the sound of his boots slapping the pavement. He made it to the stretcher that was carrying the body of his friend.

'What's happened? Gerald? Gerald?' He was looking for a response. 'Is he alive?'

One of the cops tried to grab Bailey under his arm. He shrugged him off.

'Gerald!'

'Get this guy out of here!' The paramedic pulling the stretcher beckoned to the police officer who had his hand on Bailey's shoulder, trying to drag him away.

'Somebody tell me what's going on!'

Blood-soaked bandages were wrapped around Gerald's neck and one of the paramedics was holding them tightly, keeping the pressure.

'Sir, you need to come with me.'

Bailey shrugged off the policeman's hand again.

'Gerald!' Bailey was gently tapping his leg. 'Mate, are you okay?'

No response. Gerald's face was expressionless and grey.

'Sir!' The policeman had two hands on Bailey's arms now. 'You really need to step back.'

'Is he dead?' Bailey stopped resisting, moving out of the way so that the paramedics could do their job. 'Can someone please tell me? Is he dead?'

They were at the back of the ambulance. The woman holding Gerald's neck climbed in first, guiding the front of the stretcher, tilting it upwards, giving Bailey a bird's-eye view of his mate. Gerald's bloody chest, rising and falling, ever so slightly. A sign of life. His mouth wide open, eyes closed, like little shields protecting him from death's door.

'He's lost a lot of blood,' she called back. 'We need to get him to hospital.'

The two other paramedics climbed into the back of the van.

'Let's go!'

'Where are you taking him?' Bailey asked.

'North Shore!' the woman's voice called back just as the doors slammed shut.

The siren blared to life and the ambulance negotiated its way off the footpath and sped off towards the bridge. Royal North Shore Hospital was just over the other side of the harbour. The doctors would have him within ten minutes.

Bailey felt the policeman's grip loosen on his arm. 'I'm sorry, mate. Presume that guy's a friend of yours.'

'Gerald Summers.'

'Sorry?'

'His name. The guy in the ambulance is the editor of that newspaper up there.' Bailey was pointing at *The Journal*'s signage on the edge of the building. 'Gerald Summers.'

'He's your mate, then?'

'Something like that,' Bailey said. 'What the hell happened here?'

The cop looked like he hadn't been wearing the uniform for long. One hook on his shoulder, a rattled expression on his face, and a nametag that read 'Constable Jones'.

'A guy with a knife went after Mr Summers, slashed the shoulder of one of ours too.'

They were standing on the sloping driveway of the underground carpark and Bailey could see exactly where the attack had taken place because of the pool of blood. There was so much of it that it had formed a little red stream, like a bloody teardrop.

Staring at the blood, Bailey felt an overflow of panic inside. Bailey had lost one brother when he was barely a man. He couldn't lose another.

Gerald was the sensible guy who'd always been there for him, who'd helped to rebuild Bailey's broken self, more times than he could remember. The guy who'd watched over his daughter when Bailey was off covering some war. Who had never judged him for falling down, for being human. Gerald understood the frailty of life and the loyalty of friendship. He couldn't die. Not now.

'Sir, I'm sorry but we need to close off this area.' Constable Jones was tapping him on the shoulder.

'Okay, okay,' Bailey said, waving his hand without looking around. 'Just give me a minute.'

Bailey wiped his eyes. When he turned around he noticed the crowd of people looking at him like he was some sideshow. Mouths open, heads shaking, wondering about the violence that had sullied their city. The postcard paradise of fireworks and water views brought to heel by fear.

A little prick was filming him with his phone.

Bailey charged towards the crowd. 'You!' He was pointing at the teenager with the phone. The cheeky bastard still hadn't stopped filming.

Bailey pushed aside the tape and lunged at him, grabbing his phone.

'What the fuck are you doing?' Bailey had him by the scruff of his shirt. 'Making your little fucking videos. What are you going to do with it? Tell me! What are you going to do?'

The boy stared at him, blankly, like he'd done nothing wrong.

'Answer me, kid!' Bailey screamed at him.

'I . . . I . . . don't know.'

'You don't know?'

'Share it, I guess.'

Bailey let go of the kid's shirt and rammed his finger into his chest. 'You want to be a star, is that it? Get people you don't even know to like you? This is real life, not a fucking game.'

'I'm sorry,' the boy said, sounding like he meant it. 'I'm sorry.'

Bailey handed him his phone and just as he was calming down he noticed another guy pointing his phone at Bailey. He was so close that Bailey was able to grab it out of his hand. He smashed it on the ground, stamping his heel into the screen, just to make sure.

'Hey! You can't do that!'

'I just did.'

The guy was older, pushing thirty. Old enough to know better. He stepped towards Bailey and took a swing, connecting with Bailey's left cheek.

Bailey tackled him to the ground, pinning him on his back with his forearm across his neck. 'You pathetic fucking voyeur. Get a life.'

Within seconds the police were pulling the two men apart, rolling them over onto their stomachs, their arms pulled behind their backs.

Some cop had his knee pressed into the burn on Bailey's back so that he could slip handcuffs on his wrists. There was nothing Bailey could do about it.

Lying on the concrete, Bailey stared at the pool of blood. Gerald's blood. Wondering if he was going to survive.

Eye for an eye.

CHAPTER 32

DEXTER

Police were used to deploying quickly. But nothing made cops move faster than an attack on one of their own.

And this time, luck was on their side.

The PolAir 4 was already in the sky above Sydney Harbour when the call went out that a female police officer had been stabbed, and a man badly wounded, in the heart of the city.

The police helicopter had a top speed of more than 220 kilometres per hour. When it locked on a vehicle below, the target didn't stand a chance of getting away. Especially in broad daylight.

The injured police officer had called in the licence plate on the van while she was bleeding and waiting for an ambulance. It was the same van involved in the abduction of Tariq Haneef earlier that morning.

Fifteen minutes later, the PolAir 4 had located the van on Anzac Bridge, heading west.

By the time it was speeding along the City West Link past Iron Cove Creek at Five Dock, the helicopter was hovering above, directing police cars on the ground.

'Where's the BearCat?' Dexter yelled into the radio receiver.

Nugget was sitting beside her, behind the wheel of their unmarked turbo Holden, siren blazing, lights flashing. There was another cop car up ahead and two behind. Dexter wasn't taking any risks, she'd called in resources from wherever she could find them.

They had taken off from Bankstown Police Station the minute they'd heard about the stabbings outside *The Journal*. Dexter had been trying to get through to Bailey, but he wasn't answering his phone. She hoped to god that it wasn't him.

Dexter tried to put the possibility out of her mind. With the van heading west, they were on track to meet these guys head-on within minutes at the Bunnings junction on Parramatta Road.

'The BearCat!' Dexter yelled into the receiver again. 'I need an exact location on the BearCat!'

'Just passing Glebe on Parramatta Road,' a voice crackled back.

Dexter turned to Nugget. 'It's too far away. Looks like it's us.'

She leaned into the back seat, grabbing a vest for herself and one for Nugget.

'I'm stashing this here.' She pointed at the space next to his legs. 'It goes on before you get out of the vehicle. Got it?'

'This isn't my first rodeo, boss.'

Nugget was speaking without looking at Dexter. Travelling at more than one hundred kilometres an hour, it was probably a good thing.

The voice in the helicopter told them the van was three hundred metres out from the junction.

Dexter could see the Bunnings tower up ahead. They might just make it.

She was back on the radio telling the cop behind them in the Landcruiser to pass and hammer it for the junction. To take out the van, if they saw an opportunity.

'Stay back,' she told Nugget.

Dexter recognised the driver of the four-wheel drive as it overtook them. A young buck from Ashfield station. She hoped to hell that he could drive. There were three cops inside, all of them in vests. The guy in the back was slapping the seat telling them to go for it.

As they arrived at the junction, Dexter saw the roof of the van pop over the hill on her left. Just in time.

'There they are.'

The van was travelling in the far left lane. Cars were backed up at the red light meaning the van wouldn't get an easy run across Parramatta Road. The driver had no option other than to take a hard left onto the slip road, and head back towards the city.

The driver of the Landcruiser spotted the move. He sped across the intersection, ramming into the side of the van, bouncing it sideways and up onto the kerb. The force of the collision dented the van driver's door and punctured a tyre. These guys weren't going anywhere.

Within seconds, four police vehicles were parked across the road, blocking the traffic, surrounding the van. Police knew the terrorist suspects inside were at least armed with knives because of the attack back in the city. But they couldn't rule out firearms. Not yet.

'Here.'

Dexter handed Nugget the vest, and he slipped it on while climbing out of the car. They'd parked across two lanes about twenty metres from the van. Nugget scooted around the back of the car beside Dexter. They'd use the vehicle as a shield in case the guys in the van started shooting.

'There! There! There!'

Dexter was waving her arms at the other cops, directing two of them to stop traffic on both sides of the road. The rest were deployed into defensive positions that could switch to offence at any moment.

Within seconds, Parramatta Road was a parking lot and Dexter could see occupants inside nearby cars cowering below the window line, wondering if they were about to get caught in a shoot-out in the middle of a major road. Drivers further away were opening their doors and stepping out onto the bitumen, their heads poking above the traffic like meerkats in long grass.

'Get back in your vehicles!'

Dexter already had her Glock out and it was trained on the van. The guy in the front seat hadn't moved. He looked like he may have been knocked out by the Landcruiser.

'Looks like they're down one already,' she said.

The side door of the van slid open. The first person to climb out was the kid. Tariq. He had his hands in the air and a look of sheer terror on his face. He was standing in the door of the van, one foot on the pavement, a tattooed forearm wrapped around his neck.

'Get out!' Dexter yelled across the roof of the car.

Tariq was shaking his head, talking to the guy with the arm across his throat, his face concealed behind the door of the van.

'Let me go. Please.' Dexter couldn't hear Tariq but she could read the words on his lips. 'Please. Please.'

'Let the kid go!' Nugget called out. 'Hands where I can see them!'

Dexter counted six guns pointed at the van. The guy holding Tariq would only take them on if he had a death wish. That wasn't out of the question.

The driver was still out cold, halving the trouble.

The next few minutes were crucial. It was Detective Chief Inspector Sharon Dexter's play, she was the senior officer.

The helicopter was still hovering in the sky above. Its job now was to keep the television cameras away. Whatever happened on the ground, the police hierarchy wouldn't want the commercial networks filming them on a job where they couldn't guarantee the outcome. The politics of law enforcement.

The traffic was building all around. If this thing went south, the likelihood of a stray bullet hitting an innocent bystander was high. Dexter didn't like it. They had to make a move.

'Stay here, Nugget. Keep talking to him.'

Head down, Dexter was moving towards the front of the car where she'd get a different angle, if this guy came out shooting.

'This is your last chance,' Nugget yelled at the van, keeping the gunman's attention on him. 'Let the kid go and come out with your hands up!'

They were coming out.

Dexter had a clear look at the guy holding Tariq. It was Sammy Raymond. His tattooed arm tight across the kid's neck, a gun pointed at his temple.

'We're leaving!' Raymond screamed.

'Don't do anything stupid here, Sammy,' Nugget called back. 'Let the kid go.'

Raymond wasn't much taller than Tariq, so the kid was making a good shield. Sammy stepped onto the road, back to the van, walking sideways. Looking around, sizing up his options.

'A car! Get me a car!' He ordered. 'Do you want this kid to die?'

Tariq had water on his cheeks. A look of horror on his face.

'You know that's not happening, Sammy.'

'Just put down the gun!' Nugget called back.

Bang! Bang! Bang!

Raymond fired three rounds at Nugget's position at the back end of the car, the bullets embedding in the metal.

'Nugget!'

Nugget ducked onto one knee, looking across at Dexter, who was kneeling beside the bonnet of the car. 'Got a better idea?'

'Let's at least try not to piss him off again.'

You don't antagonise a guy when he's holding a gun to a kid's head, thought Dexter. You give him hope. Show him a way out. Then do your best to slam it shut.

Nugget poked his head up again. 'Okay, Sammy. We'll work on that car! But you've got to let the kid go!'

'He's coming with me!'

Raymond fired his weapon again. Two more rounds. A typical Glock pistol held fifteen bullets. Raymond had ten shots left.

'Sammy!' Nugget yelled, trying to get Raymond to focus on the back of the car without getting shot. 'Don't do anything stupid here, he's just a kid!'

Dexter moved further around the car. She had a side-on view of Raymond and the gunman hadn't clocked her.

Bang! Bang!

Raymond fired at Nugget's position again. Two more bullets buried in the car.

Tariq spotted Dexter beside the headlights at the front of the car, their eyes meeting. She nodded, reassuring him that there was a way out. He was terrified. Wearing a pair of shorts and a baggy t-shirt, he was dressed for a kick at the park, not a gunfight with a terrorist.

Tariq's eyes looked up at Raymond and then he took his chance, ramming his elbow into Raymond's gut, slipping out of his headlock and diving on the ground.

Dexter fired two rounds. One bullet burying itself in Raymond's chest, the other incapacitating his shoulder. His gun arm.

Raymond stumbled back, struggling to raise his weapon.

Bang! Bang! Bang! Bang! Bang! Bang!

The other cops opened up, their bullets making red splotch marks on Raymond's torso. Some hitting the van.

He hit the ground.

Dexter sprinted over to the van, kicking the gun away from Sammy Raymond's dead hand. She knelt on the ground beside Tariq, who was lying face-down, in shock.

'Tariq. It's over, now. You're safe.'

He wasn't responding.

Dexter rolled him over.

There was blood on the side of his face from a wound on the top of his head.

'He's hit!' Dexter yelled. 'The kid's been shot!'

CHAPTER 33

'I see you've got a friend in the force.'

Constable Jones unlocked the cuffs on Bailey's wrists and helped him to his feet. He'd been sitting on the driveway with his back to the crowd, still staring at Gerald's blood.

'Where's the other guy?' Bailey said.

'We're going to keep him a bit longer.' Jones was pointing at the back of the police car parked on the footpath. 'Fucking arsehole with his phone. He's a grown man, should know better.'

'And the kid?' Bailey said. 'I don't particularly want that movie online.'

'Nothing we can do, mate.' He shrugged apologetically. 'If we tried to stop this shit we'd need to triple the size of the force. It's the world we live in.'

'The world's fucked.'

'Detective Dexter said to tell you she'd call you shortly.'

'What do you know about what happened?' Bailey asked Jones.

'Mr Summers came outside to meet someone. The van was parked here in the driveway and a guy jumped out and went straight for him with a knife.'

'And the cop?'

'She was driving past. Pure chance. She jumps out and tackles him to the ground just as he was laying into Mr Summers. The guy then stabs her in the shoulder and jumps into the van he had waiting on the road. She's lucky to be alive. So's your mate.'

'Yeah. Lucky.'

Bailey could feel his shirt sticking to his back. The other cop must have messed up the dressing on his burn when he shoved his knee into him. He didn't blame him, he was only doing his job. But the pain in his back was getting worse, throbbing with each beat of his heart, reminding him about Gerald and all the blood that he'd lost. He'd be at the North Shore by now. Bailey wanted to get there too.

The crowd had started to thin as the voyeurs and pedestrians either returned to work, or got on with their day. There must have been a dozen police officers on the scene. Most of them interviewing witnesses or out on the street directing traffic.

Bailey noticed a familiar face above the crowd. Ronnie Johnson. The big Oklahoman was never far away. He lifted the police tape, saying something to the cop who tried to stop him, and kept walking towards Bailey.

'You okay, bubba?'

Ronnie had an unlit cigar dangling from the corner of his mouth.

'Gerald's in hospital,' Bailey said. 'It's bad. Attacked by some nut job with a knife.'

'I know.' Ronnie put his big hand on the back of Bailey's neck and squeezed. It was the closest they would get to a hug. 'I'm hearing the police stopped a van in the west.'

Bailey's phone was vibrating. Dexter. Maybe she knew something.

'Sharon.'

'Are you okay, Bailey?'

'I'm fine.'

'I know about Gerald. I've checked in with the hospital, he's got a fight on his hands but he's doing okay.'

Bailey was relieved but he didn't want to talk about it. He was closing up, shutting down. It was the only way he knew how to deal.

'Did you get them?'

'We got them, Bailey,' she said.

'Was Tariq with them?'

'Yeah, he was.'

Dexter sounded distracted.

'Where are you?'

'Still here,' she said. 'I'll be here for a while.'

'Are you okay?' Bailey could tell that something was wrong. 'What's Tariq told you about his sister?'

'Tariq's . . . Tariq's not talking, yet.'

'Why not?'

'He got shot, Bailey. A bullet ricocheted off the van.'

'Is he alive?' Bailey said. 'How the bloody hell could that happen?'

Dexter was talking to someone near her, giving orders. 'Tariq's alive, that's all I can tell you.'

Bailey wanted more. 'The others?'

'Sammy Raymond's dead. We've taken a guy called Bilal Suleman into custody. Another shitbag mate of the Salma brothers.' She was talking like a cop again. Cool head. The boss of the JCTT.

'Do you think this was it?' Bailey said.

'What do you mean?'

'The bomb, me . . . and Gerald.' Bailey coughed to get rid of the lump in his throat, pretending it wasn't there. 'Think this was the plan all along?'

'No, Bailey. I don't.'

She told him how they'd searched the van and found a pressure-cooker bomb and a suicide vest. The threat wasn't over until they'd found Sara Haneef. Tariq's sister had never returned home after university the day before. Her phone was switched off. Her parents said they hadn't heard from her, either. She'd vanished.

'Bailey.' Dexter's voice sharpened, like she was about to give him an order. 'I'm organising a safehouse for Miranda.'

'How's that work?'

'It'll take about thirty minutes, maybe an hour. Unmarked cars will pick up her and Peter Andrews from Mosman and take them to the house. You're in the middle of this. She's not safe.' Dexter paused to take a breath. 'And Bailey?'

'Yeah?'

'I think you should go there too.'

'That's not happening,' Bailey said. 'My best mate's on a fucking operating table, Sharon. I'm not hiding in a safehouse. Or any house. I want to catch these bastards, bring them down, just as much as you do.'

'Okay. Okay. Settle down, would you?'

Bailey said nothing. He could feel the distance between them, their two worlds pulling apart.

Dexter changed tack. 'We've already called the Haneefs and told them about Tariq. They're on their way to the hospital.'

'Thanks.'

Bailey could hear someone calling Dexter in the background.

'I've got to go, Bailey. What will you do?'

The only thing he could do.

'Tell your people not to contact Nancy. I'm going to get another update on Gerald's condition and then I'm going to Mosman. I want to be the one to tell her.'

He also wanted to see Miranda before she was taken away by police to a safehouse. Try to explain.

'We'll leave Nancy to you. And one more thing . . .' Her voice changed again. 'Go to my place tonight. I'll be there at some point, I don't know when. You still got your key, right?'

'Yeah, I've still got it.'

Bailey hung up without giving her a proper answer. He wasn't sure about going to Dexter's house. She wasn't asking as his girlfriend. She was asking because she knew that Bailey wasn't safe. Or maybe it was because of his history of turning to the bottle when bad things happened. Whatever her motivation, he had more pressing concerns.

Putting his cracked phone in his pocket, Bailey noticed the plastic bag with his flannelette shirts sitting on the driveway. The red chequered one that he was wearing was wet with blood and whatever else was seeping from the burn. He unbuttoned the shirt and grabbed a fresh one from the bag, changing in the street.

'That doesn't look good.'

Ronnie was holding the bag for Bailey while he got dressed.

'I'm fine.' Bailey turned around so that his back was to the wall. 'Can we just get out of here?'

'Sure thing, bubba.'

The guy that Bailey had been wrestling with earlier was remonstrating with a couple of police officers as Ronnie and Bailey walked past.

'Who's going to pay for my bloody phone?'

'You are, mate.' It was that young cop, Jones. 'Might make you reconsider where you point your camera next time.'

'That's just bullshit.'

'Well, put in a complaint or, better still, take it to the papers.'

Jones winked at Bailey as he noticed him passing by.

Bailey returned a half-smile and gave the other guy the finger. 'Bye. Fuckwit.'

'What was all that about?' Ronnie said.

'Forget about it.'

224

CHAPTER 34

If Nancy had been anywhere near a television, the internet or a radio, she would have known that two people had been slashed with a knife on Sussex Street in broad daylight. A female police officer and a man aged around sixty. Only she couldn't have known that the injured man was her husband, Gerald Summers.

Dexter had made sure that the newspaper editor's identity was kept under wraps until Nancy and their daughters had been told. Standard practice that wasn't always followed. In Gerald's case, the news would stay tight, at least for the first few hours. Gerald was a titan of the trade. Loved by many. Disliked by few. Respected by all. No journalist would dare break this story if they wanted a future in the industry.

By the time Ronnie and Bailey were pulling up out the front of the house, Gerald was already in surgery. Bailey knew that because he'd managed to speak to someone at the hospital. No guarantees, they'd said, but they were expecting Gerald to pull through.

Bailey had wanted to be the one to tell Nancy. He owed it to Gerald. When his old mate woke up he wanted to be able to tell him that he had looked after his wife, that he'd done things the right way.

Nancy had always treated Bailey like Gerald's naughty brother, even once banning her husband from drinking with him. Bailey was part of the family, the lovable rogue. It had been that way for decades. Gerald had loved him and, despite all his faults, Nancy had loved him too.

In the end, he didn't need to say a word.

The sad, lonely figure of John Bailey at Nancy's front door delivered the message loud and clear.

'What's happened, John?' There was no hiding the look of horror on Nancy's face. 'Where's Gerald?'

'There's been an incident.' Bailey was trying, desperately, to keep himself together. 'Gerald's been injured. He's in hospital. But he's okay, Nancy.'

'What?'

Bailey was standing in the open doorway with Ronnie Johnson behind him.

'He was attacked with a knife, Nancy.' During the car ride over, Bailey had decided that he wasn't going to sugarcoat it. There was no point. 'Terrorists.'

'My husband was attacked by a terrorist?'

Nancy was a tough woman. Smart, too. A former journalist who, born in a different year, in another age, could have been the one running the newspaper.

'On Sussex Street, Nancy. Out the front of the paper. He has a wound on his neck and he's lost a lot of blood. I've spoken to the hospital, they say he's going to be okay.' Bailey wanted to believe it. 'A police officer saved his life, Nancy. She disrupted the attack and got stabbed herself –'

'Is she okay?'

'She'll be fine.'

'Dad? What's going on?' Miranda appeared behind Nancy with Doctor Peter Andrews beside her. 'What's happened?'

'Hello, sweetheart.' Bailey felt a wave of guilt wash over him.

It could have been Miranda. *Eye for an eye.* 'Gerald was attacked with a knife. He's in hospital.'

Miranda's face turned pale. 'What?'

Nancy plucked a coat from the rack on the wall and grabbed her purse from the table by the door. 'Which hospital?'

'Royal North Shore,' Bailey said.

'Bubba.' Ronnie's big hand rested on his shoulder. 'I'll drive Nancy. You need to stay here, wait for the cars for Miranda.'

'What cars?' Miranda said.

Nancy kissed Bailey on the cheek, squeezing his arm and whispering into his ear. 'Thanks, John. I'll see you at the hospital.'

Classic Nancy. Strong and dignified on the outside while Bailey knew full well that her mind must have been racing through every possible scenario that awaited her at the hospital.

'Dad? What's going on?'

Bailey closed the door before breaking the news to Miranda and the doc that they had to pack their things and move to a safehouse.

'Why aren't you coming with us?'

She had him there.

'The police want my help with the investigation.'

It wasn't a total lie. As a reporter with more than thirty years of experience, Bailey was good at finding things. He was also the one getting the phone calls from the world's most wanted terrorist. The one who had been approached by the Haneefs. While Dexter and that stumpy cop with the fat neck probably wouldn't say that they 'wanted' or 'needed' Bailey's help, they'd sure as hell take it.

'Dad, what's this all about?' She let go of his hand. 'You're scaring me.'

Miranda was a grown-up, she deserved answers.

Bailey told her about the bomb in Redfern and the fact that she wouldn't be seeing the Corolla anytime soon. About the raid in Roselands and the terrorists – one killed, one arrested – out the front of Bunnings on Parramatta Road. 'This goes back a long way. Gerald and I somehow got caught up in it and became targets.' He wasn't about to tell her about Mustafa al-Baghdadi.

'Miranda.' The doc had been standing there, watching and listening, without saying anything. 'I think we just need to do what the police are telling us to.'

'Okay. Okay.' She backed off, sensing that her father had had enough.

'Thanks.' Bailey winked at Peter.

'Dad?' Miranda grabbed hold of his shirt. 'Is that blood?'

'I'm okay. Just a little burn from the car bomb in Redfern.'

Bailey felt ridiculous talking about a bomb that had been made just for him.

'Peter, come here.'

Peter did as he was told. 'John, would you like me to take a look?'

'Yes, Peter, he would.' Bailey's daughter answered for him.

Miranda led them to the bathroom so that Peter could examine the dressing on Bailey's burn.

'This doesn't look good, John.'

'Doesn't feel too good, either, if I'm being straight with you.'

Miranda rummaged through the bathroom cabinets, handing her boyfriend fresh gauze, bandages, and a bottle of antiseptic. Nancy had everything.

'I'll go pack our things while you fix Dad.'

Peter stopped the blood and pus from leaking down Bailey's back and gave him a fresh, stingy spray of antiseptic. Knowing that Bailey had a burn, Peter had grabbed the cling wrap from the kitchen on the way in. He wound the plastic around Bailey's middle, reinforcing it with a bandage and tape.

'You'll need to get that replaced within twelve hours,' Peter said.

'Thanks, mate.' Bailey slipped his shirt back on. 'And doc?'

'Yes?'

'You're a good man.' Bailey placed his hand on Peter's shoulder, looking him in the eye. 'Get her a nice ring, would you? She'd like that.'

'Of course. I . . . I . . .' Bailey had caught him by surprise. 'I'll do my best there. And . . . thank you.'

Miranda walked back in just as the two men were shaking hands.

'What's going on?'

The doorbell rang.

'Coast's clear, sweetheart.' Bailey kissed his daughter on the forehead. 'Reckon that might be the cops at the door. I'd better let them in.'

At least something good had happened today.

CHAPTER 35

Royal North Shore Hospital was only a short drive from Gerald's house in Mosman and Bailey was halfway there before he realised that he had no idea when he would see his daughter again.

Miranda and the doc had been picked up in an unmarked police car with windows so dark that they couldn't wave to Bailey as they were driven away to a house somewhere on the Central Coast. Away from the city. Away from Bailey. Out of harm's way.

The police had confiscated both of their phones and Bailey had been assured that he'd be able to talk to his daughter on a secure line once they were settled at the safehouse. Nobody could tell him when that might be.

The humiliation of knowing that he was the reason why Miranda had to go into hiding was grating on him and so was the pungent smell of body odour that had blanketed the inside of the taxi like an odious fog. Either the last passengers in the car had just stepped off a rugby field, or the driver was an A-grade shower dodger.

'Mate, unlock my window, would you?' Bailey said to the driver.

The guy in the front seat grunted an unintelligible response and Bailey got what he wanted. The rush of air was like manna from heaven.

With his head halfway out the window as the taxi shot up Falcon Street, Bailey took in sights that transported him back to his old life as a beat reporter in Sydney. Lees Fortuna Court was still there, the same white and green neon sign out front. He'd once spent five hours sitting on the tiled steps of the old Chinese restaurant waiting for a billionaire television boss to emerge from a long lunch so that he could question him about his tax affairs.

About one hundred metres up the road they passed The Crows Nest Hotel, where Bailey and Dexter used to meet back in the mid-1980s to exchange information about the corrupt cops running drugs and prostitutes up at the Cross. These meetings were always done in secret. No one could ever know that Dexter was Bailey's source. There were too many rotten coppers out there who knew how to make troublesome people disappear.

Bailey and Dexter would load-up the jukebox with Rolling Stones tracks and pick a quiet corner where they would talk for hours, drinking schooners of draught beer together. The rookie cop and the cub reporter, both out to make their mark, long before they were lovers.

The taxi swung off the Pacific Highway and up the long driveway to the Royal North Shore Hospital. Ronnie Johnson was standing outside the emergency department, puffing on a cigar, when Bailey climbed out of the car.

'How's he doing?' Bailey said.

'Still in the operating theatre, bubba.' Ronnie was speaking with the cigar between his teeth. 'Doctors say it's going well.'

'Where's Nancy?' Bailey was anxious and wanted to get inside.

'She's inside in the waiting area.' Ronnie knelt and stubbed his cigar into the pavement. 'Let's go. I'll take you up.'

Bailey followed Ronnie through the glass doors and watched him pat a security guy on the shoulder and whisper something before they were let through a set of doors that looked like a staff entry.

'What was all that about?' Bailey said as they were walking along the nylon floor past little rooms with patients lying in beds with beeping equipment beside them.

'Told him I was waiting for you. Plenty of cops upstairs, Gerald's getting the VIP treatment.'

'He's an important fellow,' Bailey said, remembering he had a sense of humour.

Nancy was sitting in a plastic chair with two police officers nearby. She stood up the moment she saw Ronnie and Bailey.

'Have you heard, John?' Nancy said. 'The doctors say that he's going to be fine.'

'Ronnie told me,' Bailey said. 'It's great news, Nancy.'

'We might be able to see him later this afternoon. He's lost a lot of blood but the nurse told me that he's out of danger.'

'That's good, Nancy. Really.'

Bailey's relief was tempered by the fact that his daughter was on her way to a safehouse and Mustafa al-Baghdadi was still out there, like a chess king, directing his psychopathic pawns, plotting his next move. One that might involve Sara Haneef.

For the next few hours they sat on the hospital's stiff, uncomfortable plastic chairs, being drip-fed information about Gerald's condition. His two daughters, Kate and Merryn, had turned up and were sitting either side of their mother, each holding a hand.

Around five hours after Gerald had been attacked, Doctor Sandra Wong appeared to tell them that they'd finished operating.

'The knife narrowly missed the carotid artery in his neck,' she said. 'But the cut was deep and we had to repair the muscle damage inside before we could stitch his neck. It'll be a little bit longer before you can see him. But he's okay.'

A 'little while' turned into an hour, and then two, before Doctor Wong was back. 'Your husband is awake.' She was speaking directly to Nancy, now. 'I'm going to recommend that you and your daughters go in first. He's obviously very tired and fragile after the operation.'

Nancy's eyes wandered from Bailey to Ronnie, then back to Doctor Wong. 'No. I want all of us to go in together. These two gentlemen are like brothers to my husband.'

Doctor Wong went to say something, then stopped herself. She'd only known Nancy for a matter of hours and she could tell that she was the type of woman who was used to getting her way.

'Okay. Let's keep it brief though.'

Bailey was the last person to walk into Gerald's room and he watched as his old friend's pale, exhausted face managed a half-smile for the three most important women in his life. He lifted his right hand up off the bed, reaching for his wife, his hand shaking, until Nancy took it in hers, and held it to her cheek as she sat on the edge of the bed beside him.

'Oh, Gerald,' she said. 'You gave us all a nasty shock.'

Forty-odd years of marriage was flexing its muscles for the room. The love between Gerald and his wife clear for everyone to see.

Bailey and Ronnie stayed back as Gerald's daughters, both of them crying, gently hugged their father and told him they loved him.

'Mr Summers will struggle with his speech for a little while,' Doctor Wong said. 'Maybe a day or two. Until the swelling goes down.'

'Thank god for that.' Bailey tapped Gerald's foot at the end of the bed. 'Means you won't be able to boss me around, hey old boy?'

Gerald forced a smile and beckoned for Bailey to come closer, gesturing with his other hand until Bailey was right beside him. He was trying to say something.

Bailey leaned in. 'Take it easy, mate,' he whispered. 'You heard the doc.'

Gerald had a worried, irritated look on his face and he reached for Bailey to get even closer so that his ear was inches from Gerald's mouth.

'It's not . . .' Gerald paused, his lips smacking together. He was speaking so softly that Bailey could barely hear. 'It's . . . not your fault.'

Bailey sat up. He was the only one who had heard him. The words did nothing to assuage his guilt. His best friend had bandages wrapped around his neck and dried blood and dark bruising on his skin. It *was* his fault. And with no leads other than a recorded phone call with Mustafa al-Baghdadi, he had no idea how he was going to make things right.

'I've got to go,' Bailey said, stepping back off the bed. 'I'll be back, Gerald. You rest up, old boy.'

'You hang in there, Gerald.' Ronnie patted Gerald's leg and pointed to Bailey. 'And don't you worry, I've got bubba's back. You've given me an even bigger reason to step out of retirement.'

If Gerald had heard Ronnie, his joke didn't register on his face. He was still looking at Bailey as he said his goodbyes to Nancy and the girls.

'Where to, bubba?' Ronnie said as they walked back down the corridor towards the exit.

Bailey wanted to get straight back to work. Find Sara Haneef. Get more out of Dexter. But his mind wasn't working right. He still had a pulsating headache from the explosion in Redfern and he was hit by a sudden pang of exhaustion. He needed to shut his eyes for a while, get some rest.

'Give me a ride to Sharon's house?'

'Sure.'

Dexter wasn't answering her phone. Bailey imagined that she was locked in an interrogation room, ripping into Bilal Suleman or the Salma brothers, trying to find out all she could about Mustafa al-Baghdadi and his global terror network. Information that Bailey was also desperate to learn. Dexter couldn't avoid him if he was sleeping in her bed.

CHAPTER 36

'My people are still working on that recording,' Ronnie said when he pulled up out the front of Dexter's house in Leichhardt. 'I'll come back to you when I've got something.'

It suited Bailey just fine. He wanted to be alone.

He still couldn't remember half of what had happened in Redfern. The burn in his back was aching and the throbbing in his head was getting worse by the second. He couldn't concentrate. He could barely focus his eyes. He needed something to make the pain go away. He needed sleep.

He pulled out his keys and unlocked the front door, clocking the Corolla key dangling from the ring. Bloody useless now. A metallic memento of a car that nobody but him liked.

His phone started ringing just as he stepped inside and he squinted his eyes so that he could focus on the screen.

Annie Brooks.

He knew why she was calling and he didn't answer. The attack on Gerald Summers had been all over the news the past few hours.

She tried again. He let it ring out.

He still hadn't moved from the front door. Contemplating his next step.

A message came through.

You're an amazing man, John Bailey

Control the things you can control

Where are you? I can come see you

Bailey switched off his phone.

He walked into the kitchen and opened the cupboard under the sink. He remembered stashing a bottle of whisky there once. Caked in dust, it was two-thirds full of brown.

He pulled a glass from the cupboard and started pouring.

One finger. Two fingers. Three.

He threw it back, slamming the glass on the benchtop.

He poured again. Three more fingers that he was determined to get down.

He stood there. Breathing in and out, making sure the whisky stayed down. Waiting until he was ready to go again.

Another inch of brown, the warm burn in his throat, triggering a smile in his brain. A counter to all that sadness. The throbbing pain in his head.

Again.

Crack!

He slammed the crystal tumbler so hard on the stone bench that it shattered into small, rocky fragments.

Fuck the glass.

Grabbing the bottle by the neck, he tilted back his head and poured a few more fingers straight down the hatch.

He paused for a moment, then went again. And again. Falling to his knees, his stomach. Then he passed out on the floor.

It was dark when Bailey opened his eyes again, woken by a key rattling in the door. His head resting in a pool of dribble on the cold stone floor.

The door clicked open. Footsteps. Dexter.

He was leaning on his elbows, trying to get up, when she appeared in the kitchen.

The sight of him, clambering on his knees on the floor. The bottle of whisky beside him. The shattered glass.

'Oh, Bailey.'

He had made it to his feet, leaning on the bench, pretending nothing was wrong.

'Hey.'

'Bailey, are you okay?'

He looked down at his watch. Eight o'clock. He'd been lying on the floor for at least three hours. Maybe more.

His throat was so dry he could barely speak. He turned away from Dexter and reached for a glass in the cupboard, wincing at the pain as the movement stretched the damaged skin on his back. He filled the glass from the tap, skolling the water.

'Are you okay?' Dexter tried again 'How bad's that burn?'

'I'll survive.' He filled up the glass again, drinking only half of it this time. 'Is Tariq conscious? Is he talking? What about the other guy . . . Bilal Suleman? Have you found Sara Haneef? Is this thing over yet?'

'How's Gerald?'

'He's good. Operation went well, he's out of the woods.'

He turned around and she was standing right in front of him.

'You can talk to me, you know?'

She touched the bruise on his cheek, running her fingers down his face.

'I know.' He stepped back, sipping the glass of water even though he wasn't thirsty anymore. 'What'd you find out?'

'Bailey, let's talk. Let's talk about what happened today.'

'No. I want to talk about Tariq. I want to talk about the bastards who did this.'

'Bailey –'

He put down the glass, shaking his head. 'No, Sharon.'

'Do you really want to talk about this now?'

'Yeah, I do.'

Dexter let out a long breath, staring into the bloodshot eyes of the man in her kitchen. Stubborn as a bull.

She gave in.

'They're still operating on Tariq. Even if he pulls through, we won't be able to speak to him for a while.'

'The others?'

'No sign of Sara yet, but we're still looking. Suleman's not talking but we've already confirmed that it was Sammy Raymond who attacked Gerald.'

Bailey looked away at the mention of Gerald's name. He wasn't done blaming himself. Dexter could see it.

'Bailey?'

'Why are you here?' Bailey was frustrated that it wasn't over. 'Seriously, why are you?'

'What are you talking about? I came here to –'

'Why aren't you back out there, looking for Sara?'

'What the fuck, Bailey? Don't you think we're doing that? I haven't slept in two days.'

He could see the hurt in her eyes and hear it in her voice. Anger too.

'I wanted to see you,' she said.

'Fuck.' Bailey sighed, knowing he was being an arsehole. 'I'm sorry, Sharon.'

'It's okay. I know Gerald means a lot to you. You can't blame yourself for all this, Bailey. Gerald's safe and Miranda's safe too.'

A lone tear had slipped from his eye down his cheek. Dexter caught it with the tip of her finger on the stubble on his chin. She leaned forward and kissed the wet trail it left behind.

'I'm sorry, I really am,' she whispered in his ear. 'Remember the people who love you.'

Bailey cupped her face in his hands and kissed her. He knew that he needed to let someone in, even if it was only for a while.

CHAPTER 37

This time it was loud banging on the front door that woke him.

Bailey sat up, rubbing his eyes. The clock beside the bed told him it was 3.08 am.

Dexter's side of the bed was empty. He switched on the lamp.

'Sharon?'

Someone banged on the door again, even louder this time.

Bailey rolled out of bed, slipping on his jeans, and walked into the hallway. There was no sign of Dexter. She'd probably gone back to work.

Thud! Thud! Thud!

'Okay, okay!' Bailey called out. 'I'm coming!'

Bailey opened the door and Ronnie was standing under the sensor light, smoke billowing from his cigar, a wide grin on his face.

'Mustafa's in London.'

'What?'

'The sounds on the recording. The faint beeps. The bell. The rattling noises. A crossing. A train station. A rail overpass.'

'How can you be so sure?'

'I don't know, bubba.' He blew a puff of smoke at his shoulder. 'Other people analyse this stuff. I'm just telling you what we found.'

London.

241

'Can I come in?' Ronnie stubbed his cigar into the square plant by the door, leaving it in the dirt. 'There's something else, bubba. Let me explain inside.'

Bailey nodded, turning around. He wasn't wearing a shirt, exposing the plastic wrapped around his middle and the bandages on his back. It wasn't bleeding anymore, but it was as painful as hell.

'How's the burn?'

'Shit.'

They walked into the kitchen. Bailey poured himself a glass of water, trying to ignore the bottle of whisky on the counter. The shame.

Ronnie was either too distracted to notice the bottle, or too cool to acknowledge it. 'Where's Dexter?'

'Must have gone back to work.' Bailey drained half the glass of water then placed it on the counter.

'She knows about London. Her people found out before we did.'

'What? When?' Bailey said.

'Yesterday, last night. Does it matter?'

Yesterday. If she knew, why didn't she tell him? It mattered.

'Sharon was here,' Bailey said. 'She stayed the night, at least part of it. I'm going to give her the benefit of the doubt. If she knew, she would have told me.'

'Would she? Her team's been working with MI5 and counter-terrorism police in London ever since your last phone call from Mustafa.'

Bailey's heart started thumping. 'You really think –'

'It's not important, bubba. She probably had her reasons. She's a cop, remember? Anyway, there's something else.'

Maybe Dexter had got the call about London in the middle of the night and had decided not to wake Bailey? After all, he'd been in a bad way when she'd found him in the kitchen. Maybe she'd decided to let him sleep it off? If that was the reason then Bailey would understand, although he wouldn't like it.

'Are you with me, bubba?' Ronnie said, clicking his fingers. 'You want to hear this.'

'What?'

'We discovered something; something connected to you.'

Bailey had forgotten what a full-blown hangover was like. His head was pounding, he couldn't think straight, and he was full of regret.

'Get it out, Ronnie.'

'That house in Mosul – the one you described when we debriefed you in Baghdad after your release.'

'Go on.'

'The things you'd told us helped us locate the house. We've been monitoring it for years. It's an Islamic Nation safehouse. At least, it was. We hit it a few months back, believing Mustafa and his family were inside. Missile strike.'

'Clearly, Mustafa wasn't there.'

'No. But his wife and young son were both killed. He noticed the look on Bailey's face. 'I've been out of the loop. Only got confirmation a few hours ago. I don't know how long we've known.'

'Mustafa's wife, and son? Bloody hell. He fucking blames me.' Bailey leaned over the counter, talking to the stone. 'This is about revenge?'

'Something like that.'

'I can't believe this. This is bullshit. Me? Me?' Bailey was shaking. 'Omar. Tariq. Gerald. The murder out the front of Chatham House. The bomb in Redfern. It all leads back to me.'

Redfern.

Redfern, before the bomb. Jake. The memory card. It was coming back. Maybe the whisky had unlocked something in his brain. Maybe the side-effects of his concussion were wearing off.

'What's wrong?'

Bailey fumbled a hand in the pocket of his jeans. The same old jeans he always wore. The square of paper. It was there.

'This!' Bailey said. 'Tariq gave it to a kid in Redfern . . . the bomb . . . I hit my head, couldn't remember. I don't know what's on it.'

Bailey had barely finished talking before Ronnie was kneeling in front of Dexter's television, running his fingers around the edges, front and back.

'Give it to me.' Ronnie held out his hand. 'We can play it on here.'

Ronnie switched on the television and slipped the card into an inch-long slit at the base of the screen. He grabbed the remote, finding the correct source, and jacked up the volume.

They were staring at a frozen image of Tariq Haneef, sitting in a chair beneath the black flag commonly used by the Islamic Nation group. He was wearing a suicide vest.

'Ronnie, hit play.'

'All right, Tariq.' Someone was talking to the kid from the other side of the camera. 'I just had to wipe the fucking card. This is the last time. Otherwise that bomb might just go bang a little earlier than we'd planned. And you'll be wearing it. Got it?'

Tariq was nodding, a terrified look on his face.

'My name is Tariq Haneef and I'm fifteen years old. If you're watching this video then it means that we're all dead. Sara. Ayesha. And me. We've done our duty and followed the path of the prophet. Jihad is only the beginning. This holy war has no ending. I call on the Governments of Australia and the United Kingdom to stop supporting the American wars in Iraq and Syria. Withdraw your forces today. If you don't, the bloodshed will go on. There are . . . there are many more people . . . people like us. Ready to do Allah's work.'

The image froze just as Tariq slumped forward on his chair, crying into his hands.

'Mustafa's planning more attacks,' Ronnie said, pointing at the screen. 'Sydney. London, somewhere in the UK. This confirms it.'

'Who the hell's Ayesha?'

'I don't know, bubba. It's the first time I've heard that name. Tariq was speaking like he knew her,' Ronnie said. 'His sister's still out there too. This thing isn't over. Not by a long shot.'

Bailey's mind was racing through the scenarios. Tariq didn't look like a killer. He didn't sound like one, either. He looked like a frightened kid. Did Tariq discover some kind of plan that involved his sister? Is that why he went on the run? Why he was kidnapped? Thinking back over his conversations with Dexter, Bailey counted five pressure-cooker bombs and one suicide vest. One of the pressure-cooker bombs had been used to blow up Bailey's car and police had recovered the rest. But what were they supposed to have been used for? Is there another bomb out there? Where's Sara Haneef!

'Do you know how to upload that thing from there?' Bailey said.

'Not without my computer,' Ronnie said.

'Then I'm going to need to play it over the phone, for Sharon.'

Dexter may have forgotten how to share information but Bailey couldn't keep this from her. Nobody had mentioned the name 'Ayesha' before. She needed to know.

CHAPTER 38

DEXTER

A policeman was standing outside the operating theatre where doctors were working on Tariq Haneef, trying to keep him alive.

The bullet that had ricocheted off the van had embedded in Tariq's skull, piercing the fleshy tissue on the outside of his brain.

Doctors were faced with two major challenges. Getting the swelling down to remove the pressure on Tariq's brain, and removing the bullet without causing any further damage.

Medical staff were optimistic, although operating tables were unpredictable places.

Dexter had secured special permission for the family to wait in a secured area up the hall from the operating theatre where doctors were working on Tariq. Just in case someone wanted Tariq, or his parents, dead because they knew too much.

'Is there any more news?' Noora said, hopefully, to a woman in blue scrubs.

'Not yet. Sorry.'

Noora had been asking anyone who walked past for updates.

Dexter was sitting four seats away, careful to keep her distance because Noora was blaming the police for the bullet that was currently lodged inside her son's head.

'Noora, they'll tell us when they have information.' Dexter could tell Noora's constant questioning was beginning to irritate the staff. 'I know this is difficult. The nurses and doctors are doing their best.'

Noora glared back at her. 'What do you know?'

There was no point engaging. Dexter had said her piece.

Hassan Saleh, the family friend from the Haneefs' local mosque, was pacing up and down, flipping prayer beads in his fingers. He stopped beside Dexter. 'Detective, this is a very difficult time. I hope you understand.'

To point out the bloody obvious.

Hassan Saleh's wise counsel was half the reason why Noora was so upset. He was in Noora's ear telling her that he couldn't understand why police had to fire their weapons. Maybe he'd have a different view if he'd seen Sammy Raymond holding a gun to Tariq's head.

Dexter looked down at her hands and noticed a speck of dried blood under her thumbnail. She picked and scratched it away, not wanting a physical reminder about what had happened on Parramatta Road.

Sammy Raymond might be dead, but the city and its people were being choked by fear. The Police Commissioner had called her demanding a personal briefing about the investigation. Police had been called in on their days off to get more uniforms on the streets. Reassure a rattled public. The pressure was piling on Dexter's shoulders like sandbags. She was so tired that her eyes were trembling. But she had to keep going. She wouldn't rest until this was done.

'Detective?' Hassan Saleh was still standing beside her, wondering where she'd gone.

She was about to say something when her pocket started vibrating. It was Bailey. She looked at her watch: 3.25 am.

She walked up the hall, away from the others.

'Bailey, are you okay?'

'Where are you?' he said.

'At the hospital,' she whispered. 'They're operating on Tariq. It's touch and go.'

Noora was staring at Dexter, trying to listen in. Dexter moved further up the hall so that there was no danger of them hearing her side of the conversation.

She stopped talking, waiting for Bailey to continue. He'd called her in the middle of the night. He must have something.

'What's happened?'

'Are you alone?' He sounded cagey. 'I mean, can anyone hear you? I want to play you a video down the line. You need to see it. I'll need to switch the call to video.'

'Hang on.'

Dexter grabbed a headset from her pocket, plugging it into the phone, while accepting the video request.

Bailey's dishevelled head appeared on the screen.

'That kid, Jake, handed me a memory card back in Redfern before my car got blown up. I only just remembered. Must have been that bump on the head, everything that happened. I don't know.' Short-term memory loss wasn't easy to explain. 'Anyway . . . I remember now. The video's from the house in Roselands. It's Tariq and –'

'Just play it, Bailey.'

'Okay.'

He swung the phone around and Dexter could see Ronnie standing beside the television at her place. He hit play.

When the video finished, Bailey's head filled the screen again. 'Does the name Ayesha mean anything to you?'

No. It didn't. But she was going to ask Noora the same question.

'Who's at the hospital? Is Omar there?'

'He went home to get some fresh clothes.' She was already walking back down the hall. 'It's just Noora and that Hassan Saleh guy.'

'How long ago did Omar leave?'

'Fifteen minutes, give or take.'

Dexter knew what Bailey was thinking and it made her nervous. 'It's not a good idea, Bailey.'

'What isn't?'

'Going to the Haneefs' house.'

'How'd you guess?'

'I'm a cop, Bailey. And you're not. Remember that, okay?'

'I know what I'm doing.' Bailey swung his camera phone to Ronnie. 'Anyway, I've got this bloke with me.'

Ronnie gave her a thumbs up in the background.

'That doesn't fill me with confidence. I've got to go.'

Dexter ended the call and walked back down the hall towards Noora and the guy with the prayer beads.

'Noora.' Dexter sat down beside her. 'I need to ask you a question and it's very important.'

Hassan Saleh was standing in front of Noora, out of Dexter's eyeline.

'Don't look at him, look at me.' Dexter waited until Noora's eyes were trained on her. 'Who's Ayesha?'

'What?' Noora said. 'What does Ayesha have to do with this?'

'Then you know her.'

'She's my –'

'Noora,' Hassan Saleh said, 'are we sure the police have our best interests here?'

Dexter stood up. Hassan Saleh was not a tall man and she was eye to eye with him.

'What do you know?'

249

'Nothing.'

Sharon Dexter had been a police officer for three decades. She was good at reading people. Hassan Saleh's eyes were lying to her. His eyes said that he knew 'everything'.

'Hassan.' Dexter stepped closer, one hand hovering next to the gun strapped to her side. 'Give me your phone.'

'No.'

'I'm going to ask you one more time.' She unclipped the button on the holster. 'Give me your phone.'

Hassan Saleh wasn't used to being told what to do, especially by a woman. Dexter could feel it. She also knew that this was a pissing contest that she'd win. Hassan Saleh knew it too. He withdrew his phone from his jacket pocket.

'Unlock it and place it on the ground.'

'This is ridiculous.'

'Do it. Now.'

She took a step back so that she had time to act if he did anything stupid.

He eyeballed her for a few seconds before he eventually did as he was told.

'Now, walk over there and sit in that chair.' Dexter was pointing at an armchair across the hall.

He hesitated for a moment, then walked across the room, shaking his head, and sat down.

Dexter followed him, unclipping the handcuffs from her belt, locking his hands together so that he was fixed to the arm of the chair.

'What is this?' he said. 'I have done nothing wrong. Noora, tell her!'

'Shut up.'

Noora was watching on, mouth open.

Dexter picked up Saleh's phone, swiping the screen so that she could see the most recent apps that he'd been using. One of them was an encrypted messaging service. She opened it. Saleh had sent a message fifteen minutes ago to a number without a name.

Your father is on his way back to the house
They know nothing
Be brave, soldier of the Prophet

CHAPTER 39

A white flashing light lit up the inside of the car as the traffic cameras caught Ronnie Johnson breaking the law. It was the fourth time it had happened.

'Who's paying for these, by the way?'

Bailey knew that it wouldn't be the last red light they'd run. Sydney had enough cameras at traffic lights to rival a Paris fashion show.

'Diplomatic immunity, bubba. I try not to abuse the privilege.'

Bailey laughed. 'You've had an interesting life, mate.'

'You can talk.'

The tyres squealed around the next corner, throwing Bailey up against the door and he winced as his burn bounced against the seat.

'How's the back?'

'Don't ask.'

Best not asking about his hangover, either. The old John Bailey would have knocked the edge off with a two-finger pour of whisky by now. His trusted hangover cure. He needed to ride this one out. One slip-up was enough.

His phone vibrated and Dexter's name was flashing on the screen.

'Bailey.' Dexter spoke first. 'Are you there yet?'

'A few minutes away.'

Dexter went silent on the other end of the phone. She knew something, Bailey could tell.

'What is it, Sharon? What else have you got?'

'You need to wait outside.'

'That's not going to happen,' Bailey said.

'You're not a bloody cop, Bailey.' There was a sharpness in her voice that Bailey had been hearing a lot these past few days. 'You need to let us do our job.'

'If you know something, tell me.'

Bailey could hear someone sobbing in the background.

'Ayesha is Tariq's and Sara's cousin. I'm trying to get more out of Noora, she's bloody hysterical. She doesn't seem to know much. Hassan Saleh, on the other hand, is knee-deep in this. He's been communicating with Sara.'

Hassan Saleh.

That slimy piece of shit. Bailey knew it, from the moment he first met him. Friend of the family, my arse.

'What about Omar? Do you think he's involved?'

'No idea.'

They were two streets away from the Haneefs' house and Ronnie slowed down and killed the lights.

'We're here, got to go.'

'Bailey, my team's on the way. I mean it about waiting outside.'

Bailey hung up without giving her an answer.

'What'd she say?'

'Ayesha's the cousin. Omar may be involved. She wants us to wait outside.'

'That's not going to happen.'

Ronnie opened his jacket so that Bailey could see the Glock dangling beside his chest.

'We've got this, bubba.'

Ronnie parked the car a few doors up from the house. If Omar really was involved, they couldn't risk him seeing them coming.

'You knock on the front door,' Ronnie said. 'I'm going around back.'

Bailey walked up the front steps, slightly nervous about being separated from the guy with the gun.

Bailey wanted to keep believing that Omar was a victim in all this. Now he wasn't so sure.

The clock ticked past 4 am. A light breeze was rustling a pile of leaves clustered on the porch. Otherwise, not a sound.

Knock. Knock. Knock.

Bailey's knuckles on the door were amplified by the stillness of night.

A stick cracked behind him, causing Bailey to spin around. Nothing. Probably just a stray cat, or a fox, searching for food scraps.

There was a light on inside. A shadow moving towards him. Footsteps.

Omar opened the door.

'It's the middle of the night. What do you want?'

It was a different Omar from the one who'd kissed his cheeks in the foyer of *The Journal*, begging for help, three days ago. A cloud of suspicion was already hovering over him. The resentful greeting at the door only confirmed it. Strike one.

'Can I come in?'

'I'm sorry but no, you can't.' Omar was blocking the doorway. 'I need to get back to the hospital. They're still operating on Tariq. I want to be there when he wakes up.'

'This won't take long. I need to talk to you about something.'

Omar breathed out hard, shaking his head. 'I asked you for help, instead you brought in that detective woman. Now my son has a bullet in his head.'

'Steady on, Omar.'

'I'm not talking to you anymore.'

Bailey had one foot inside the house in case Omar tried to slam the door. 'Five minutes, that's all I'm asking.'

Omar held his position blocking the door for a few more seconds, then stepped aside, reluctantly, allowing Bailey to walk past him and inside.

'Let's go in here.'

They went into the living room where two bags, stuffed with clothes, were sitting on the floor.

They sat down on opposite sofas, separated only by the bags and a Persian rug.

'What do you want to talk about? Have the police heard any news about Sara?'

'Not yet, Omar. I want to ask about your niece.' Bailey studied his face, looking for a reaction. 'I want to talk about Ayesha.'

'She can't be involved in this,' he said, defensively. 'She's not even here.'

'When did you last see her?'

Omar was rubbing the tops of his knees with his hands. 'Ayesha? Not for months. We talk often. She lived with us for many years.'

'When?'

'I don't have time for this now.' Omar stood up, taking a step towards his bags. 'Why are we even talking about Ayesha?'

Bailey stayed put on the sofa. He didn't want to give too much away. It was the best chance he had of determining whether or not Omar was innocent.

'When did she live here, and why?'

Omar sighed, sitting back down. 'She was my brother's only child. Her mother died giving birth to her and . . . my brother . . . he got caught up with some bad people in Iraq. He was killed.

255

I don't know where, or when, or even why. But Ayesha came to us as a child. We raised her like a daughter.'

'Why didn't I know about this?'

Omar sat back, folding his arms. 'We haven't seen each other in years. Why would you?'

Bailey stood up and walked over to the photographs on the sideboard. He picked up a frame with a picture of two girls in it, arm in arm. They looked like sisters.

'This her?'

'They were inseparable.' Omar was standing beside him. 'She's a clever girl, studying medicine, like my Sara.'

'Where's Ayesha now?'

'London. She won a scholarship to study there for –'

They were interrupted by a noise in the kitchen.

'Is someone else here, Omar?'

'A cat,' Omar said, dismissively. 'Must have been a cat.'

'Didn't know you had a cat, mate.'

'Not ours, the neighbour's. It comes and goes as it pleases, stupid thing.'

The peculiar smile gave him away. Strike two.

Bailey replaced the photograph on the sideboard and headed for the kitchen.

'I really have to get back to the hospital.' Omar followed him, trying to get his attention.

The back door was open, its hinge squeaking in the wind. Someone was out there. Bailey heard a squeal and then a man's voice.

Ronnie Johnson appeared through the door with one of his big arms wrapped around Sara Haneef. 'Look who I found, bubba.'

'Sara?'

Bailey had never expected to find Sara Haneef here.

Omar raced around the kitchen table towards Ronnie.

'Let go of my daughter!'

Ronnie reached into his jacket, withdrawing his Glock. Omar came to an abrupt halt, almost falling over, the gun barrel inches from his head.

'I think you need to sit down.'

Ronnie used his weapon to direct Omar to a chair on the other side of the kitchen table.

'Okay. Okay.' Bailey had his arms up, signalling for everyone to calm down even though his own mind was racing. 'How about we all sit down at the table?'

'Good idea, bubba.'

Ronnie closed the back door, locking it. He walked Sara to the other side of the table and made her sit down beside her father.

Bailey and Ronnie sat opposite.

Clunk.

Ronnie put his gun on the table, inches from his hand. He nodded at Bailey, happy for him to lead the conversation.

Bailey looked at his watch: 4.14 am.

'The police will be here soon,' Bailey said, catching Omar's eye. 'They will arrest you both. If you want my help, you need to talk now.'

Omar bashed his fist on the table. 'We haven't done anything wrong!'

'If you have nothing to hide,' Bailey said, 'then tell us what's going on. Now's your chance.'

'I'm not hiding from anything.' Sara's voice was eerily calm. 'It's you who's hiding. Hiding behind the –'

'Sara. Sara, no!' Omar grabbed her hand. 'Don't talk.'

'I'm not afraid, Dad. I knew what I was doing.'

'Just shut up, shut up. Stop talking. Please.' Omar's face was red and beads of sweat were building on his brow. 'I just want you to stop talking. Listen to your father!'

'We know about Hassan Saleh,' Bailey said, turning to Sara. 'He put you in touch with Sammy Raymond, right? And Tariq found out what you were involved in, that's why he ran.'

Bailey had been piecing things together in his head.

'What's he talking about, Sara?' Omar said, shifting in his chair so that he could see his daughter's face.

Sara had a look of absolute calm.

'Sara?' Bailey said. 'Your brother is fighting for his life in hospital.'

'Tariq's not involved in this,' she said.

Finally, a straight answer.

'He's just a kid. So are you. This is your chance to make things right,' Bailey said. 'Let's make sure no one else gets hurt.'

A car stopped out the front of the house, its lights beaming through the window of the lounge room and into the kitchen. The police.

'People are getting hurt every day,' Sara said, coldly. 'Every hour. Every minute.'

'Sara. Please, no. No, Sara.' Omar reached for his daughter's hand but she ignored him. 'This can't be true.'

'Sara, look at me,' Bailey said. They were running out of time. 'I need you to tell us about Ayesha.'

She just sat there, silently.

'Sara?'

'There's nothing you can do.' Sara was speaking with dead-eyed calm. 'It's too late.'

There was a loud banging on the front door. 'Police! Open up!'

'Wait,' Ronnie said to Omar. 'Stay there.'

'Too late for what?' Bailey said. 'Where is Ayesha?'

More knocking on the door. Louder.

'Too late for what, Sara?'

'Police! Open up! Now!'

'Answer the man, Sara,' Ronnie said, picking up his gun.

'Your gun doesn't scare me.'

There was a louder banging on the door, like someone was trying to kick it in.

Crack!

The sound of splintering wood prompted Ronnie to slip the Glock inside his jacket.

'Sara.' Bailey leaned across the table. 'Too late for what?'

'To join Ayesha in paradise.'

Two policemen walked through the door behind Omar. One of them was the short and stocky guy Bailey had seen outside the Salmas' house in Roselands. He looked like he'd just got out of bed.

'Detective Don Benson.'

The short guy introduced himself from across the kitchen.

Bailey pushed back his chair, standing up. 'John Bailey.'

'I know who you are,' Benson said. 'What I don't know is what the hell you think you're doing here.'

Bailey didn't like the tone. The implied accusation that he was making things worse.

'And who's this?'

Benson was looking at the big Oklahoman, probably wondering about the bulge in his jacket.

'Ronnie Johnson.'

Benson's eyes fluttered as his brain told him something. Probably that he'd heard the name before and been warned not to fuck with him.

'What are you guys doing here?' Benson composed himself and went again. 'Answer the question.'

'We're trying to find out who tried to kill me,' Bailey said, 'and who's responsible for the knife attack on Gerald Summers and one of your colleagues yesterday morning.'

'We know the answer to those questions.'

'No.' Bailey tapped the table with his fingers. 'Not Sammy Raymond. Not Hassan Saleh. There's another person running this. Isn't there, Sara?'

Sara looked up and smiled.

Mustafa al-Baghdadi.

'Say it!' Bailey thumped the table. 'Say his name, Sara!'

'Why?' Sara said. 'Why, if you already know?'

'Bubba, time to go.' Ronnie was looking at his phone.

'No. No. You're both staying right here.'

Ronnie stepped towards Benson.

'I know you know who I am.' Ronnie was a foot taller than Benson and he was talking to the top of his grey, bushy eyebrows. 'So you know that we're walking out that door.'

Benson puffed out his chest, holding his ground. It was pointless.

'Bubba, get your things. We're leaving.'

Bailey didn't have any 'things', but he guessed it was Ronnie's way of telling him to start moving towards the front door.

'Don't go far,' Benson called after them. 'We may need to talk to you.'

Bailey walked past Omar, who was leaning against the wall, shaking, his face the colour of ash. 'I'm sorry, mate.'

Omar looked away, trying to hide his shame.

'Just do what the cops say, tell them everything.'

Bailey wanted to believe that his old driver from Baghdad had no clue about his daughter's involvement when he first came to *The Journal* three days ago, asking for help to find Tariq. Bailey wanted to believe that Omar was as shocked as everyone else. But Omar's obfuscation during the last fifteen minutes had made it clear he knew something. A father's first instinct was to protect his children. No matter what. By honouring that instinct, Omar was about to pay a hell of a price.

Bailey stopped at the sideboard in the living room. He picked up the photograph of Sara and Ayesha, slipping it out of the frame and folding it into his pocket.

Ronnie tapped him on the shoulder. 'Let's go.'

Back in the car, Ronnie's phone was buzzing again, the light from the screen highlighting the wrinkles in his cheeks and the fierce concentration in his eyes.

'Where to from here?' Bailey said.

'London.'

CHAPTER 40

Developments were being drip-fed in short messages on Ronnie's phone.

The Brits had been hearing 'chatter' about another attack, but had no leads about the type of threat they were facing.

Ayesha Haneef was a start. Another brainwashed soldier of suburbia. Finding her was going to be a challenge. Especially if she didn't want to be found.

'They want your help, Bailey,' Ronnie said.

'Who's *they*?'

'British Intelligence. They need someone who knows Mustafa. And there's every chance that he might call you again.'

'No thanks,' Bailey said. They were talking in the car, heading east, on the way back to the city from Wiley Park. 'I don't work for spooks.'

Ronnie reached across Bailey's lap and grabbed a fresh cigar from the glove box, sticking it in the centre of his mouth. He sparked it, directing the smoke at the window just as he was opening it.

'Don't be so naive, bubba,' he said, eventually. 'We're all on the same side.'

'And what side is that, Ronnie?'

'The side that takes down a mass murderer. The guy who ripped out your fingernails and threw a wet rag on your face, followed by a bucket of water. Whose men played Russian Roulette on your temple. The guy who –'

'Enough!' Bailey slammed his fist on the dash. 'You've made your point.'

'We need to give ourselves every chance to get this son of a bitch. Stop the attacks. The killings. That means you,' Ronnie said. 'Let's make this right.'

'Just stop talking for a minute, would you?' Bailey was staring out the window, head spinning, trying to process. 'I just need a fucking minute.'

Maybe Ronnie was right. Maybe Mustafa al-Baghdadi was the exception to Bailey's rule. The psychopath who was responsible for the attempt on Gerald's life, who put a bomb under his car, the reason why his daughter was hiding in a safehouse. And all the rest.

He knew Ronnie was preying on Bailey's justice streak. Problem was that he was right. They needed to get this lunatic off the street. Shut him down.

'Okay. I'll do it. But, Ronnie?' He turned his head, waiting to catch Ronnie's eye. 'I'm not taking orders from anyone. You, or your friends in Her Majesty's Secret Circus.'

Ronnie made an odd chortling sound. 'Never expected you would.'

Before Bailey was going anywhere, he needed to know that his daughter was safe.

He called Dexter.

'Bloody hell, Bailey,' she answered, abruptly. 'I told you not to go inside.'

'Yeah, the big guy was with me, he's not good at following instructions.'

Bailey looked across at Ronnie, who smiled through a puff of smoke.

'Don't be cute.'

'Sorry if we put you in a difficult position,' Bailey said. 'Time was tight. We had no idea Sara would be there.'

He wanted to say that she should have been grateful because, without their help, Sara probably would have still been on the run. Still a threat.

Dexter sighed into the phone. 'You were lucky, Bailey. You guys missed something.'

'Hang on, Sharon, I'm going to put you on speaker so Ronnie can hear.'

'Sara had weapons. Guns.'

'Bullshit.' Ronnie called across the seat to Bailey's phone. 'There was nothing on her when I found her.'

'We found a bag with a Glock and an assault rifle stashed in the bushes out the back of the house,' Dexter said. 'Anyway, what matters is that we stopped her from shooting up Martin Place at lunchtime today.'

'What?' Bailey said.

'I've been through the messages on Hassan Saleh's phone. He changed the target to Martin Place after what happened yesterday.'

'What was the first target?'

'The public transport system,' Dexter said. 'A bus, a train. We don't know. The communications about that are vague. When we found the bombs, things changed.'

'What I don't get,' Bailey said, 'is why Sara went back home.'

'I think Saleh made a mistake by telling her that Omar was going back there to get fresh clothes for the family. Maybe she wanted to see her father one last time? Maybe she wanted to know about Tariq? Only she can tell us that.'

At least Sara hadn't been armed with a bomb. Dexter told them that, according to Saleh's phone, the last of the explosives were seized in Raymond's van. Suleman – the driver – had already told that to police. Now she had a second source. The terrorist threat to Sydney could well be over, but Dexter wasn't about to make that bold declaration just yet. Not until Ayesha had been found.

'Sharon,' Bailey took the phone off speaker-mode, 'apparently British authorities want me in London.'

'You should go.'

She already knew.

'And this is you advising me as my partner or as the head of the Joint Counter Terrorism Team?'

'I don't have time for this, Bailey.' Dexter sounded cold. 'If you don't want to be a part of stopping this, that's up to you.'

'Haven't made up my mind,' Bailey said. 'This isn't black and white for me.'

'It should be.'

Bailey was done with the dance. 'I need a favour from you.'

'Which is?'

'I need to speak to Miranda. I need to know she's okay.'

'I can do that. Give me an hour.'

Dexter hung up.

Ronnie had been puffing away on his cigar, waiting for the call to end.

'What's the play, bubba?'

'I'm not going anywhere until I speak to my daughter,' Bailey said. 'And I want to see Gerald.'

Ronnie looked at his watch. 'Plane leaves in four hours. We've got time. Let's hope the old boy's up for an early visit.'

CHAPTER 41

Nancy was fast asleep in the reclining armchair beside Gerald's bed when Bailey and Ronnie walked past the bleary-eyed policeman guarding the door and into the room.

'Hey . . . Hey, Gerald, you awake?' Bailey was tapping Gerald's foot through the blanket, whispering so that he wouldn't wake Nancy. 'It's me, old boy. You awake?'

Bailey heard a grunting sound. He tried again, shaking his friend's foot some more. 'Gerald, I need to tell you something.'

Gerald had been sleeping in an upright position. Bailey could see his face in the light that was reflecting through the open door. His eyes opened.

'Mate, how are you feeling?'

Gerald tried to say something and started coughing. He pointed to a glass of water on the table beside his bed.

Bailey handed it to him and Gerald took a sip, coughing again to clear his throat, before taking another longer gulp.

'What the . . .' His voice was raspy, although slightly clearer than it had been the night before. The swelling in his neck must have been going down like the doctor had said it would. 'What are you guys doing here? Isn't it the middle of the bloody night?'

'More like very early in the morning.'

'Where's Miranda?'

Typical Gerald. And one of the reasons why Bailey loved him.

'She's in a safehouse somewhere up the coast,' Bailey said. 'I'll be talking to her when the sun's up.'

'Glad to hear it.'

Ronnie appeared on the other side of the bed, checking out the room. 'This is a bit different from that flashy house of yours overlooking the water.'

'You stink of cigars, Ronnie. Don't get too close. Nancy wakes up and you're both toast.'

Bailey laughed. 'Don't we know it.'

'So, what's happened? Please tell me that you've found the kid and this thing's over.'

Ronnie looked over at Bailey, waiting for him to be the one to run Gerald through everything that had happened since the attack.

'What happens now?' Gerald said when Bailey had finished.

'We're going to London,' Ronnie chimed in. 'Believe it or not, this guy's going to help me catch the world's most wanted terrorist.'

Gerald's laughter quickly turned into a coughing fit and Bailey handed him the cup of water again.

'He's joking, right?' Gerald directed his question at Bailey without looking at the big Oklahoman to his left. 'Please tell me he's bloody joking.'

'He's not.'

'Ronnie, thanks for the visit.' Gerald held up his hand so that Ronnie could shake it. 'Now, get out.'

Ronnie laughed. 'Don't worry, Gerald. I'll be keeping an eye on him.'

Gerald waited for Ronnie to walk out the door before he gestured for Bailey to come closer so that he could talk quietly in his ear.

'Are you sure about this?'

'Not really,' Bailey said. 'But it's got to end somehow.'

'Don't go being a hero,' Gerald said.

'Heroes don't come dressed like me, mate.' Bailey tugged on his second-hand shirt. 'Anyway, they want me there to help profile Mustafa, or something.'

'It's the *something* that worries me.' Gerald shifted in the bed so that he could sit higher, eye to eye with Bailey. 'The guy tried to kill you, Bailey. And me.'

'Yeah, well. He's had his chance.'

Gerald pointed his finger at Bailey like a school teacher. 'Have you seriously thought this through?'

'Not really.' At least Bailey was honest. 'Decision's made though. I've got a flight to catch.' Bailey paused, preparing for the important bit that made what he was about to do all the more real. And stupid. 'Anything happens to me, you'll take care of Miranda, right?'

'Like she was my own.'

Gerald Summers. Bailey's brother from another.

Bailey bent down and put his arms around his mate, whispering in his ear. 'Back soon, old boy. There's going to be a wedding.'

Gerald waited for Bailey to let go before he answered. 'The doc popped the question?'

'He's about to. Miranda will want to tell you herself, so don't let on.'

'Big news, mate.'

'Yeah. I'd better put in that insurance claim on the Corolla. Might at least pay for one of her shoes.'

'Call me when you get to London.'

'Will do, old boy.'

'Bailey,' Gerald stopped Bailey at the door, 'send in the redneck. I want to talk to him again before you guys leave.'

Ronnie's head appeared at the door. He'd probably heard every word.

'Shut the door.'

CHAPTER 42

Guys like Ronnie Johnson and John Bailey knew how to pack in a hurry. They'd taken enough last-minute plane rides to enough places to know exactly what they needed.

Bare essentials only, stuffed in carry-on bags so that they could make a quick exit at the other end when the plane touched down.

For Bailey, that meant passport, bankcards, notebook, pens, toiletries, and changes of underwear and socks. If the weather was anything like last week, it was going to be bloody cold, so he packed his old leather jacket, a spare pair of jeans – identical to the ones that he was wearing – and the three remaining flannelette shirts that he'd picked up from the charity shop in Redfern.

By 6.05 am, the two men were standing on the footpath out front of Bailey's house waiting for a taxi to take them to Kingsford Smith International Airport.

After the hospital visit and the time it had taken them to pack, they had two and a half hours before their plane was due to depart. With an unavoidable stopover, the trip would take them thirty-one hours.

'That was my contact in British intelligence,' Ronnie said. 'They'll be waiting for us at the other end.'

'Can't wait,' Bailey said. 'Any news on Mustafa?'

'Not much. All those sounds together from the recording gave up a hundred different locations in and around London.'

'London's a big place, mate,' Bailey said. 'How the hell are the police going to find him?'

'They're hoping he calls you again.'

'I should have listened to Gerald,' Bailey said, feeling like a piece of cheese in a mousetrap. 'By the way, Ronnie, what did he say to you back in the hospital?'

'Said he'd break all my fishing rods and have me deported if anything happened to you.'

Bailey smiled as a yellow cab pulled up beside them. 'That's our boy.'

At the airport, there were people with guns everywhere. Two army trucks were parked out the front of the international terminal and Bailey counted more than a dozen soldiers walking along the footpath, staring at people, their luggage, their demeanour, searching for that extra bead of sweat above a pair of eyes that looked away too soon.

Bailey didn't even bother to try to count the number of Australian Federal Police who were doing the same thing inside the glass doors of the terminal.

It took a lot to shake this city. A gun battle, a car bomb and a knife attack by terrorists in broad daylight had done it. Authorities had raised the terrorist threat level to its highest marker – imminent – and it wouldn't be brought back down until Dexter and her team were one hundred per cent sure that it was over.

Despite all the extra security, checking in was as painless as check-ins can be. Somehow, planes were taking off on time and Bailey and Ronnie had managed a serve of bacon and eggs before boarding their flight. The eggs were dried and the bacon was dripping with fat, but it was just what Bailey needed to push back on the hangover that was reminding him that he was back to *day one*.

He had dodged another call from Annie Brooks while shovelling his breakfast – he'd sent her a message telling her that he was fine and that he was headed for London – but Bailey couldn't ignore the next call that came through just as the plane doors were closing.

Dexter.

'There's been a complication with Tariq,' she said.

'You're going to have to turn that off please, sir.'

The flight attendant had stopped in the aisle and he was staring at Bailey.

'I'll just be a minute, Marcus,' Bailey said, acknowledging the name tag pinned to his vest.

'It needs to go off now, sir.' Marcus wasn't having any of it. There were rules on planes and he was there to enforce them.

'It's an important phone call.' Ronnie was sitting in the middle seat, closer to Marcus. 'Cut him some slack.'

'He needs to switch it off. Now.'

'While I've got you, Marcus.' Ronnie raised his hand, trying to divert his attention. 'Do you know if my lactose-free meal has been ordered?'

'We'll go through the meal options later.'

'I'd really like to get an answer now. If I get near any dairy, things could get ugly. Like Clark Kent and kryptonite.'

'Sir?' Marcus was leaning over Ronnie's head now, trying to get Bailey's attention.

'Quick, Sharon,' Bailey said. 'We're about to take off. Is Tariq going to make it?'

'Don't know. Something about the swelling on his brain,' Dexter said. 'Anyway, there's something else. We've had people trawling through the devices we found at the house where the Salma brothers were holding Tariq.'

'And?'

'We'd found a smartphone, badly damaged. The sim's been crushed and our techs are trying to get the data off it. Could take a while. It was Tariq's, but we think that it may have once belonged to Sara. A hand-me-down.'

'Why do you think that?'

'The serial number's registered in her name.'

'Sir.' Marcus was trying to stay calm.

Ronnie tapped Marcus on the arm. 'I would seriously like to know if my lactose-free meal has been reserved.'

'Look, we'll sort out the meals once we take off.' Marcus leaned across the seats, tapping Bailey on the shoulder. 'Sir! I'm going to ask you for the last time to get off your phone!'

'Just one more second.' Bailey held up his hand. 'How'd you go with Sara?'

'Nothing. She's a closed shop at the moment. We're trying.'

'Get. Off. Your. Phone!' Marcus had raised his voice so loudly that he startled some of the other passengers.

Bailey had turned towards the window, cupping the phone to his ear so that he could hear Dexter's voice above the commotion.

'Our best chance is Tariq.'

'Sir!' Marcus had lost it. 'I'm about to escort you off the plane.'

'And Bailey?' Dexter said. 'The Brits have both counter-terrorism and MI5 on this. They don't always play nice. You find out anything, you tell me. Okay?'

Dexter had just been unusually helpful with the flow of information. Now he knew the real reason for the call. She wanted him feeding her information from the inside when he got to London so that she had a way of cross-checking the intelligence flow to her team. Everyone was using him. Even his own damn girlfriend.

'I'm sure you'll know anything before I do.' Bailey said, sharply, without giving her the answer she wanted. 'Let's hope Tariq wakes up.'

He hung up and held the phone out so that Marcus could see him power down the screen.

'Thank you.' The flight attendant patted his vest, looking around at the other passengers, trying to compose himself.

'Sorry about that,' Bailey said. 'It was the missus. She had a whole checklist to run through. Wanted to make sure that I'd put the bins out and fed the dog. You know how it is.'

Marcus gave Bailey a look that told him that he had no idea what he was talking about, and didn't care. 'And, sir,' Marcus turned to Ronnie, 'we'll discuss your meal plan shortly.'

They watched the flight attendant walk away, still patting his clothes.

'If the lactose-free option is terrible,' Ronnie said to Bailey, 'I'm eating yours.'

'You'll need to take your complaints to Marcus.'

CHAPTER 43

The stinging, burning pain from Bailey's back was making sleep impossible. Each movement was agony, stretching and splitting his damaged skin.

At least he was managing to steer clear of the drinks trolley. A feat that was made more difficult by the fat guy sitting in the aisle averaging two beers an hour, reminding Bailey how he'd used to travel.

Two hours into the flight, Ronnie popped a pill, leaving Bailey alone with his thoughts.

Inevitably, his thoughts turned to what had happened to Gerald. The car bomb. Father Joe. The fact that his daughter was living in a safehouse.

'Don't worry about me, Dad,' she had told him when she'd rung him that morning from her temporary home. 'You just make it back in one piece.'

That was Miranda. Warm heart. Practically minded. In many ways, tougher than he'd ever been. Resilient. Maybe she was all those things because of the shithouse father he'd been. Maybe that was just how she was built. He wanted to believe the latter.

Thinking back over the terrorist threat in Sydney, Bailey knew that it wouldn't be the last time that bastards like Hassan Saleh, Sammy Raymond, Bilal Suleman, Sara Haneef and the Salma brothers would try to attack innocent people. The whole crazy, repetitive cycle was so frustratingly obvious yet no one knew how to stop it. One bad decision after another was alienating more people, creating more outcasts.

Bailey was angry. He was angry at Tariq for not going to the police when he'd learned that his sister was a wannabe jihadi. He was angry at Omar and Noora for missing the signs. At Hassan Saleh for infecting young minds with extremist ideology. And at Mustafa al-Baghdadi, the lunatic pulling the strings from wherever the hell he was hiding.

Bailey was angry at the authorities in New South Wales for failing the Islamic community in western Sydney. For making them the enemy. It was the most basic failure that no one wanted to talk about. Not politicians, not police, not welfare groups, not even the Muslim communities themselves. People were either too afraid to speak up, or too weak to lead.

Was life so bad in Australia that hundreds of young men should want to travel to Syria and Iraq to die on battlefields in the name of fundamentalism? Were Australian authorities so despised that good people felt compelled to cover the tracks of those who went?

Something in Australia had gone rotten, and nobody with any influence or power had the sense, or courage, to ask why.

When police like Sharon Dexter tried to speak to families about a relative, or an associate, who might be fighting in Syria or Iraq, doors slammed in their faces. The lack of trust between police and Islamic communities in Sydney's west was an even bigger problem today, because foreign fighters were coming home and bringing their bomb-making skills with them. Adding weapons to their cause.

Like the bomb that blew up Bailey's Corolla.

After being defeated on the battlefields of Iraq and Syria, Mustafa al-Baghdadi was desperate to keep his movement alive, turning people into warriors wherever he could. It was chaos theory, driven by hatred. The forever war.

But there was something else driving the Islamic Nation leader.

If Ronnie was right about Mustafa's wife and son being killed in the house in Mosul, then Bailey had given Mustafa one more reason to kill. Revenge.

The anger was building inside him and Bailey felt like he was about to explode.

Sleep-deprived, emotionally spent, his mind was racing so fast that he was struggling to breathe. He was having some kind of panic attack.

The air in his throat was bashing up against a wall in his neck, blocking it from getting into his lungs.

He couldn't breathe.

Rocking back and forth, Bailey was trying to stay calm. He grabbed Ronnie's wrist on the armrest in between them, jolting him awake.

'Bubba?'

The muscles in Bailey's throat had seized up. He felt like he was choking.

'Bailey!' Ronnie slapped Bailey on his cheek, grabbing him by the chin so that Bailey would look at him.

'Bubba! Look at me!'

Bailey did as he was told, finding comfort in a familiar stare. His lungs opened. He started breathing in short, sharp bursts, until his lungs relaxed enough to take a full hit of air.

'Are you okay, bubba?'

Bailey leaned forward, resting his elbows on the tray table, dropping his head into his hands.

'I need to get off this fucking plane.'

CHAPTER 44

LONDON

Hundreds of people were in queues in front of the UK immigration desks. The lines were moving slowly. Everything at Heathrow Airport took time. Everyone needed to wait their turn. With more than two hundred thousand passengers passing through these terminals every day, it was no wonder. Passengers were just numbers. Bailey and Ronnie – together – made two. But this morning they were two passengers that someone was very eager to meet.

'Ronnie Johnson and John Bailey?'

A guy in a suit approached them just as they were joining the back of the long, snaking queue for non-European passport holders.

'Yeah, that's us,' Ronnie said.

'Tony Dorset.'

He held out his hand and Ronnie and Bailey took turns in shaking it.

'MI5, presumably?' Ronnie said.

Tony nodded, annoyed that he was so obvious.

'Where's Ann?'

'She sent me.'

Bailey guessed that Ann was Ronnie's MI5 contact.

'Let's go somewhere we can talk,' Tony said. 'Follow me.'

Dorset led them past the immigration counters and down a corridor with a nylon floor and a series of grey doors. It reminded Bailey of a prison ward.

Ronnie had given Bailey one of his sleeping tablets for the second leg of the flight – Hong Kong to Heathrow – and he'd finally managed to get some sleep. His back was aching but at least his mind was rested. He could think again.

He had called Dexter as soon as they were off the plane. She didn't answer. A few minutes later a text message landed.

Tariq's awake

Talking to him

Let me know what you learn from Brits

Bailey felt like her inside man. He didn't like it.

Let me know what he says

Nothing from this end

Just arrived

'In here.' Dorset opened one of the grey doors, ushering Bailey and Ronnie inside. 'Have a seat.'

Now wasn't the time to think about the situation with Dexter.

'Have you found the girl?' Ronnie said before they'd even sat down.

'No.'

'Then make it quick,' Ronnie said. 'You know why we're here. We don't have time to fuck around.'

Watching Ronnie Johnson get all business-like was like watching a croupier break a deck. Clinical and in complete control.

There was something about Tony Dorset that was bothering Bailey, and he could tell that he was already under Ronnie's skin. The bloke just didn't seem right. Sharp suit. Oxbridge accent. Cocky swagger. Or maybe it was because he had ushered them into the type of room that would be used to interrogate drug runners and criminals trying to slip into the UK.

'You're quite a seasoned reporter, Mr Bailey.' Dorset smiled. 'You've probably seen just as much action as your friend here, the legendary Ronnie Johnson.'

'What are we doing here, Dorset?' Ronnie said.

'No small talk?' Dorset leaned back in his chair, folding his arms. 'Heard that about you.'

'Yeah? What else have you heard?'

'You've been around, is all. South America, China, the Middle East, you've –'

'Careful, pal.' Ronnie rested his chin on his knuckles, elbows on the table. 'You're a bit too talkative for someone who's supposed to know how to keep secrets.'

'Settle down,' Dorset said. 'I'm just trying to get acquainted.'

'I don't need a new friend,' Ronnie said.

'Look, mate,' Bailey said, 'I'm sure you don't need any new friends, either. You've got plenty already, and doubtless they all rave about you. But we've been travelling for over thirty hours, so can you just cut to the chase? What do you need from us?'

'I'll rephrase that for you,' Ronnie said. 'You have exactly five minutes with us and then we're gone.'

'You may not have noticed, Ronnie . . . you're not in the United States.'

'You really want to dance with me, Tony?'

Ronnie eyeballed Dorset like he wanted to follow through with a headbutt.

The seconds ticked over in silence.

'Four and a half minutes,' Ronnie said.

'Okay, then.' Dorset turned to Bailey and smiled, then tapped the desk. 'Mustafa al-Baghdadi.'

'What about him?'

'We want to know why he's been calling you.'

'Call it a crush,' Bailey said. 'I have that effect on people. It's a gift.'

'You guys really need to do your research,' Ronnie said. 'Get Ann on the phone. This is a waste of time.'

'We know about Baghdad. The kidnapping. The year in captivity. And –'

'Ten months.' Bailey corrected him. Every minute mattered.

'Ten months, then. And we know about Mosul.' Dorset tapped the table again, ignoring Ronnie's glare. 'But there's no written record, no transcript, about that first phone call you made in Sydney. Why didn't you tell anybody you were making that call to begin with?'

Bailey didn't like what Dorset was insinuating. 'I'm not a cop, remember. I'm a journalist.'

'That's exactly what I'm worried about.' Dorset continued his annoying habit of tapping the table. 'We need to be able to trust you.'

'I want to find this prick more than anyone.' Bailey didn't bother to hide his annoyance. 'What is this bullshit?' He turned to Ronnie, hoping he'd intervene.

'What's the play here, Dorset?' Ronnie said. 'Time isn't exactly on our side. And you still haven't found Ayesha Haneef.'

'We're getting close on that front,' Dorset said.

'Close, how?' Bailey said.

'We've been speaking to her friends. We know where she lives. We know what mosque she visits –'

'Which is?'

'Are you asking me as a journalist or someone who is willing to cooperate to find Ayesha and Mustafa al-Baghdadi?'

'I'm here, aren't I?' Bailey said. 'If I have a question about a story, then I'll tell you. But it's pretty fucking clear that I came here to help. So why don't you cut the patronising bullshit.'

'Or we walk out of here,' Ronnie added.

'It doesn't work that way.'

'Yes. It does.' Ronnie's chair squeaked on the floor as he stood up. 'Sounds like we're done. I've got my people here too. They know what you know. So if this is how you're wanting to play it then this conversation's over.'

Dorset kept his eyes on Bailey, purposely avoiding Ronnie's stare. 'Ripple Road mosque in Barking, East London. Ayesha Haneef has been part of a prayer group that we've been monitoring. The guy who killed Patricia Jones out the front of Chatham House was part of the same group. We've already made some arrests.'

Patricia Jones.

It was the first time that Bailey had heard anyone say her name. The woman that he'd watched get butchered on the street at St James's Square.

'But you've lost Ayesha?' Ronnie sat back down.

'Let me finish.' Dorset was like a different person. 'The key suspect we've arrested is a guy called Umar Masood. He's been running a prayer group in the evenings. Kids as young as eleven, twelve years old. Watching Islamic Nation videos. Even role-playing attacks. One of the children we've spoken to has confirmed seeing Ayesha there several times. And we've made another link, one that ties this thing together.'

'Which is?' Bailey said.

'Umar Masood has been talking to someone in Sydney.' Dorset was tapping the table again. 'Someone who has also been running a prayer group for young Muslims. His name is –'

'Hassan Saleh.' Bailey finished the sentence for him.

'And you have no idea where Ayesha is right now?' Ronnie said.

'No.'

'So what's the play?' Ronnie said.

Dorset reached into his coat pocket and pulled out a phone, sliding it across the table towards Bailey. 'We want you to use this instead of yours. It's your number, all your details and contacts are on the SIM inside. In case Mustafa calls again.'

Bailey looked at Ronnie for advice. He nodded.

'What do I do with this one?' Bailey was holding up his phone with the cracked screen, the one that the New South Wales Police had been listening in on. He wondered whether they'd now lost that privilege.

'You turn it off and you leave it off. Looks like you could do with an upgrade, anyway.'

'Wasn't what I had in mind.'

Bailey switched off his phone and then powered up the new one. The screen lit up and he took a moment to check all his contacts and messages to see that Dorset hadn't been bending the truth.

'It's all there. Impressive, and bloody disturbing.' Bailey put the phone in his pocket.

Dorset stood up, looking at his watch. 'It's still early, just gone half five. We've booked you guys hotel rooms at the DoubleTree at Millbank. I'll take you there. Take a couple of hours to sort yourselves out, then I'll send a car to bring you to Thames House to meet the team.'

'Yeah, I'll play that one by ear,' Ronnie said. 'I've got some things to do, people to see.'

'Of course you do,' Dorset said. 'But I want Bailey with us.'

'I'm okay with that.' Ronnie turned to Bailey. 'I won't be far away. Bubba?'

'Yeah, fine,' Bailey said.

They were all on their feet now, following Dorset out of the room.

'Every call that comes in on that phone, we'll be listening in,' Dorset said.

'Great,' Bailey said. 'Guess I'd better stay off the hotlines.'

CHAPTER 45

Just like Sydney Airport, there were guns everywhere. Men and women in blue uniforms armed with high-powered weapons slowly pacing the airport terminals. There were even more police walking the terminals than when Bailey and Gerald had been here the week before, when the terror alert level was raised after Patricia Jones was murdered. The automatic weapons reminded Bailey of the days after September 11, when British authorities sent soldiers and tanks to Heathrow Airport as a show of force.

Tony Dorset had a car waiting for them in a no-stopping zone outside the airport, where cabs were beeping their horns and jostling for space.

'Shouldn't take too long to get to the hotel at Millbank. This time of the morning, forty minutes tops,' Dorset said. 'Get showered. Get some breakfast. Ben will come back for you at eight-thirty. Could be a long day.'

Ben was the driver. 'One of my best agents,' Dorset said. Ben was an athletic-looking black guy with a thick neck and a shaved head. He didn't talk much.

Bailey looked at his watch. If Dorset was right, they'd be arriving at their hotel around 6.25 am. The shower and breakfast was a no-brainer. After a long flight, what Bailey really needed was a walk to stretch his legs. His body clock was still out of kilter and he was keen to get ahead of the usual wall of jet lag. Exercise helped.

Ronnie and Bailey threw their bags in the back and it wasn't long before they were speeding along the A4, with Ben steering the car in and out of the traffic, taking advantage of his licence to speed.

Bailey rested his head against the window, watching row after row of white single-storey houses flash by as they raced through Hounslow. The Brits had built houses like these ones close and tight after the war. No quarter-acre blocks with four bedrooms and three-car garages like the suburbs in Sydney. Londoners lived on top of each other. Townhouses, apartments and sprawling council estates. The high density living meant people mostly travelled together in packed buses and trains. The wealthy, the poor, and the people in the middle. All targets for crazed people with axes to grind.

'Go.'

A call had come through on Dorset's phone and he had his head balanced up against the passenger-side window, listening intently to what was being said.

'Wait a minute.'

Dorset pulled out his notepad, scribbling something that neither Bailey nor Ronnie, seated in the back seat, could see.

'Say that again?' Dorset waited another ten seconds before he spoke again. 'Got it.'

He slipped his phone inside his jacket and twisted his head around. 'The Aussies have got some intel off Tariq Haneef's phone.'

'And?' Ronnie said.

'Some kind of coded language buried in a conversation on an encrypted messaging service. They think it's an old conversation between Sara Haneef and Ayesha. Looks like they were using made-up names, but the comments reflect two very angry young girls –'

'What about the codes?' Ronnie said.

'I'm getting to that,' Dorset sounded irritated by Ronnie's interruptions. 'Here's the first one: one-four-one-L-B-eight-one-five-two-zero-zero-four.'

Bailey was scribbling the letters and numbers into his notebook as they were relayed by Dorset.

'And the second. B-L-H-B-seven-one-five-two-zero-zero-four.'

'Your people got any idea what the hell they mean?'

'Not yet,' Dorset said. 'Might be nothing . . . or everything. Ring any bells for either of you?'

Ronnie looked across at Bailey, who was shaking his head.

'No.'

Bailey stared at the fresh ink on the paper in front of him, wondering why the hell he was getting this information from Tony Dorset instead of from Dexter. So much for information sharing being a two-way street.

'Here we are.'

A rare word from Ben the driver as they pulled into the turning circle at the DoubleTree.

'See you soon, gentlemen,' Dorset said. 'And Ronnie?'

'Yes, Tony?'

'Your guys crack those codes first – you do the right thing.'

'If you're extending the same courtesy.'

'I am.'

Great, thought Bailey. A pissing contest between two spooks. As if the excursion to London needed to get even more complicated.

With time zones changing three times during the last twenty-four hours, Bailey had somehow managed to eat four breakfasts since Sydney. The last thing he felt like doing was sitting down to a hotel buffet. After taking a quick shower and dumping his bag in his room, he resisted the smell of bacon in the restaurant, opting instead for an apple and a walk along the Thames.

It was 6.45 am when Bailey stepped outside the hotel and the traffic was already heavy along Millbank. Black cabs. Buses. Cars. People dressed in wet weather gear weaving through the slow-moving traffic on scooters and bicycles, the usual clobber for a grey London commute.

A misty rain was falling, marking little dots of moisture on Bailey's leather jacket and adding weight to his thick sandy greying hair. Zipping his jacket to protect himself from the wet and cold, he headed east towards Lambeth Bridge, crossing the Thames and skirting the edge on the other side, down the stairs and onto the Queen's Walk. He had to step around a guy in an old weathered coat who was feeding a piece of bread to an eager seagull perched on the rail.

Walking alone, wondering whether Mustafa al-Baghdadi really was in London, Bailey was on edge. He was studying his surroundings, taking in every detail. Did Mustafa know that Bailey was in the city too? Hopefully not. How could he?

The sun had already started its rise, yet it wasn't light enough for the lamp posts to rest, their yellow lights slicing through the drizzle and bouncing off the hazardous sheen on the path.

The rain wasn't heavy enough to dissuade the morning joggers. There was a long line of people pounding the pavement, most of them dressed in long tights and waterproof jackets.

Across the water, the normally majestic buildings at Westminster were hidden behind tonnes of scaffolding, part of a restoration project with a price tag big enough to bankrupt a smaller nation. Even the clock tower was distorted by nets and awnings, undoubtedly leaving tourists feeling ripped off. How could anyone say they'd experienced London if they hadn't seen Big Ben?

The exercise and the cool morning air was helping Bailey's brain to reopen its doors and shake off the fog of air travel. His thoughts turned again to Ayesha Haneef.

He knew that Ayesha was tight with Sara. Like sisters, Omar had said. Bailey also knew that Ayesha's father and mother had died many years ago in Iraq and that Omar had raised her like a daughter. He knew that she was a bright girl, having won a scholarship to study medicine. And he knew that she had been attending a prayer group at an East London mosque where a man had been trying to radicalise young people and turn them into murderers.

That was about all that he knew about Ayesha Haneef.

It was all the things that Bailey didn't know about her that worried him.

Dexter had told Bailey that Sara had changed her target once the bombs had been found. That the communications on Hassan Saleh's phone suggested that Sara, armed with guns, had switched to an attack at Martin Place. But what was the original plan? And how did it involve Ayesha?

After climbing the steps at Westminster Bridge, Bailey paused at the top to contemplate which way he'd go. Deciding to keep heading east along the river, he crossed the street, walking back down the steps on the other side. The London Eye was only a few hundred metres further along the Queen's Walk and it was enormous, stretching higher than any tourist photograph could show. There must have been a magnificent view up there. When that thing was full, and spinning, it would make one hell of a target for a terrorist. Bailey hated that his brain went there. But it was true.

His thoughts returned to Ayesha.

If a bomb had been made for Sara, then it was possible that a bomb had been made for Ayesha too. That was an assumption he was willing to make.

Any attack, either organised, or inspired, by Islamic Nation, always involved the killing of innocent people. Ayesha's potential targets were many.

As Bailey passed under a capsule dangling from the arch of the big Ferris wheel, he grabbed his notebook from his pocket, opening the page to where he'd scribbled the codes that Dorset had shared with them in the car. He stared at the two lines of letters and numbers, hoping they'd ring a bell.

141LB8152004

BLHB7152004

Nothing.

Bailey wasn't expecting to hear from either Dexter or Dorset if, or when, they'd cracked the codes. Bailey was only there to fill in the gaps, when they appeared. He also knew Ronnie Johnson well enough to not expect a steady flow of information from him either, despite his assurances. Cops and spooks only cared about one thing – the job. Bailey could identify with that.

He stopped walking, stepping to the side of the path, leaning on the stone wall beside the river, still staring at the scribbled letters and numbers, wondering what the hell they meant.

He started with the first line. It had more numbers than the second and broke them into groups, trying to make sense.

Was there a time reference in there? 1.41 pm? 2.10 pm? 8.15 am? 8.15 pm? 8.04 am or pm? The options raced through his head.

Or a date? January 14 was one possibility, but that was months ago. The next numbers – 815 or 8152 – were too high. But 2004?

He looked at his watch, checking that he was right. The 20th of April was today.

He looked at the second code. The numbers 2004 were the last four digits in that code too.

Had Sara and Ayesha originally been planning attacks on the same date? It was possible. But it was also all guesswork. Bailey struggled to remember the pin number for his bank cards. He was no code-cracker.

He stepped back on the path and collided with a jogger, barrelling along at a cracking pace. Bailey dropped his shoulder at the last minute – an old reflex action from his days playing rugby – causing the guy to almost fall over.

'Watch out, mate!'

The guy's headphones fell from his ears and he stepped to Bailey, shoving him in the chest with the ball of his hand. Bailey fell back against the stone wall and tried to hide the sharp pain that shot up his spine from his burn. The guy looked twenty years younger and a good deal stronger.

'Easy, tiger.' Bailey dropped a foot behind, staggering his stance, just like Joe had taught him, wondering whether the guy was about to take a swing. 'It was an accident.'

'Well, be more careful. Muppet.'

The guy put his headphones back in and took off.

Bailey was relieved. Despite all the boxing sessions in Joe's gym, he'd always been better with words than he had been with his fists.

It was 7.45 am when he made it to Waterloo Bridge, where he'd planned to loop back around to the other side of the Thames and head back to his hotel.

Something made him stop.

A tall red bus had stopped down the road from the bridge to pick up the people waiting in line. With the last new passengers on board, the bus headed towards him, Bailey's eyes capturing the bold yellow writing on the black billboard on its curved red noggin: 176.

Bailey had his notebook in his hand just as the bus passed by, studying the letters and numbers of the first code again, trying to make sense of them.

He started at the beginning: 141.

He took a punt and typed 'London 141' into the search engine on his phone, his fat fingers making it a frustrating exercise. When he finally got it right the result flashed onto the screen. He froze.

141 Towards London Bridge

With the notepad in one hand and his phone in the other, he started joining the dots. If '141' was the bus route then 'LB' could stand for London Bridge.

He pressed his finger on the screen again. The bus route started at Tottenhall Road and ended at London Bridge Station. The bus came every fifteen minutes.

He looked at the notepad again.

141LB8152004

141 was the route. LB was the place.

'Holy shit,' he said to no one.

The target was London Bridge at 8.15 am on the 20th of April. Rush hour. Today.

He did the same with the second code, punching the start of it into the search engine. The letters B-L-H-B. Nothing came up other than a web page about abbreviations.

He didn't have time to mess around. If he was right about the first code then he'd just need to run with it or, at least, get a second opinion.

He hit Ronnie's name on his phone.

'Pick up! Pick up!'

'Bubba.'

'I think I know what she's doing – the target, the time, the place.' Bailey was speaking quickly, struggling to get his words out.

'Slow down, bubba. What are you saying?'

'Listen, Ronnie!' Bailey yelled, diverting his gaze from the startled man walking by. 'One of those codes that Dorset shared with us. The fucking letters and numbers, Ronnie! I think I've worked it out. It's a bus. Ayesha's going to hit a bus on London Bridge in –'

He looked at his watch.

'– in bloody twenty-five minutes!'

'How can you be so sure?' Ronnie said. 'Walk me through it.'

'I'm not so bloody sure.' Bailey sighed, knowing that if they were going to stop this thing then he needed to explain it. Slowly. 'But if I'm right, we don't have much time. The one-four-one is a bus route. The letters "LB" stand for London Bridge. The eight, one and five is a time, maybe eight-fifteen this morning, and the last four digits are today's date.'

'What about the second code?'

'No fucking idea, mate. Maybe that was Sara's plan, who knows?' Bailey took a breath. 'Sara's in custody. Ayesha's not.'

Ronnie was silent on the other end of the phone.

'Ronnie!'

'Where are you?' he said, coolly.

'Waterloo Bridge.'

'Stay there. I'll come get you.'

'Where are you?'

'Oxford Circus.'

'No,' Bailey said. 'There's no time.'

'What the hell do you think you're going to do, then?'

'I'm going to find Ayesha.'

Bailey ended the call.

For a guy with a history of being in the wrong place at the wrong time, this one took the cake. Ronnie was miles away and, with MI5 listening in, this information would only just be reaching Tony Dorset and his team at Thames House, which put them two miles and ten minutes behind Bailey. He had to do something. He didn't have a choice.

If Ayesha was going to cross London Bridge at 8.15 am, then she was probably already on the bus. And she had to be heading south, making London Bridge Station on the other side of the bridge the final stop. It would make no sense for Ayesha to be travelling in the opposite direction because the bus would have only just begun its route and there would be far fewer passengers on board. Fewer people to kill.

Bailey went back to the bus route, studying the stops that she would pass by to get there.

With a rough plan in his head, he turned back to the road and, seeing what he needed, held out his hand. Seconds later a black cab stopped beside him.

'Where to, guv?' A man with a beard and a north London accent thicker than oil twisted his head in the front seat. 'In a hurry, I take it?'

'Bank Station.'

Rummaging in the inside pocket of his leather jacket, Bailey found the photograph that he'd stolen from the sideboard at Omar's house. The photograph of Sara and Ayesha.

He studied Ayesha's smiling face, wondering what was going on inside her head when the photograph was taken. They were dressed in school clothes. It couldn't have been too long ago. Time enough for these girls to be turned into killers.

CHAPTER 46

Six roads intersected at Bank Station.

Bailey directed the driver to get him to the north side onto Princes Street. The route of the 141. He paid the fare and raced across the two lanes of traffic to Bus Stop B, where a short line of people were standing, waiting for a bus.

7.58 am.

He'd made it with a few minutes to spare. Unless the bus had come early.

The giant grey stone wall of the Bank of England was casting a permanent shadow across the narrow footpath, where there was just enough room for pedestrians to pass by the people queuing for the bus. Bailey joined the end of the line, trying to catch his breath.

'Are you waiting for the one-four-one?' he asked the woman standing in front of him.

'Yes,' she said, politely. 'Any minute now.'

His next move was a gamble that he'd rather not be making. If he was right about what was about to go down, he didn't have a choice.

A bus came around the corner, heading in their direction. The 43.

The woman in front of Bailey turned around. 'You can get this one. Same stops.'

'Thanks.'

Bailey didn't know how to explain to her that he was happy to wait because it wouldn't make sense, so he followed her to the open door of the bus, before stepping away at the last second.

He stared inside the bus windows, studying faces. No sign of Ayesha.

The 141 was due any second. If Ayesha was planning an attack on London Bridge at 8.15 am, then she'd be on the bus. Bailey hoped that he was wrong.

Moments later, the 141 turned the corner, travelling like it was in slow motion until it squeaked to a halt beside him.

He held up his Oyster card, waited for the beep, and continued down the aisle behind a fat guy with a baseball cap that was covering the tops of his ears.

The double-decker bus was nearly full. Standing room only. Bailey grabbed hold of a handle that was dangling from the roof, balancing himself as the bus started moving. The windows had clouded with the fog of many breaths and passengers were pushing their way up the staircase halfway along, searching for seats.

Bailey moved with the crowd further down the aisle, studying the faces of people sitting and standing as he went. People clutching tightly to handbags and briefcases, listening to music or something else through earphones, reading books or thumbing through their smartphones.

He wanted to stay downstairs because, if Ayesha Haneef had brought a bomb onto the bus, that's where she'd be, where the trajectory of the blast would go upwards and outwards, causing maximum impact. Bailey had seen enough wreckages to know that much.

His pocket vibrated. Dexter.

'Yep?' Bailey was speaking softly, trying not to bring attention to himself.

'Bailey!'

'Sharon, can you hear me?' he said, slightly louder.

'Bailey, are you there?'

Dexter's words were coming out quickly, almost shouting.

'Yeah, I'm here.'

'Where the hell are you, Bailey?' she yelled through the phone.

He didn't answer.

Bailey had a good view up both sides of the bus from where he was standing near the rear doors. He was mentally checking off each row of seats, face by face, as he listened to his phone. A bald guy in an overcoat. Check. A guy in a rugby jersey. Check. Two girls in school uniforms. Check. A middle-aged woman in a black puffy jacket. Check.

'Bailey!' Dexter tried again. 'I've spoken to Ronnie. The police are on their way. Please tell me you're not on that bus!'

'It's okay,' Bailey said.

'What?'

'Sharon, it's okay.' Bailey was speaking quietly, calmly. 'I've found her.'

He hung up.

Ayesha Haneef was sitting two seats from the back doors, across from the stairs, staring out the window. Bailey could see the reflection of her eyes in the clouded glass, wondering if she was staring back into the bus through the reflection, or at the world going by outside. A city of more than eight million people. People going about their day. Living.

Bailey was wondering what was going through the eighteen-year-old brain inside her head. Wondering whether she had a bomb. Wondering whether she would use it.

The woman sitting beside Ayesha was checking her makeup with a small mirror. She touched Ayesha on the arm, apologising for bumping her as she rummaged through her handbag, looking for something else to improve her face on the way to work. Ayesha gave her a half-smile, as if not to worry, and then went back to staring out the window.

Bailey still had his phone in his hand and he fired off a brief message to Ronnie.

She's here

The bus stopped again. King William Street.

The guy with the baseball cap was complaining that no one was moving down the back of the bus. After a few loud sighs, he started pushing down the aisle. Bailey had no other choice but to follow him, because more passengers were cramming on behind him and a girl was bumping her shoulder bag into the burn on his back. Every step he took, another bump. Another shot of pain.

When the momentum stopped, Bailey found himself standing next to the woman doing her makeup, which meant that he was less than a metre from Ayesha Haneef.

The bus started moving again.

The next stop was Monument Station and people were already gunning for the door.

'Excuse me, excuse me, excuse me.'

Somehow, Bailey managed to hold his position over Ayesha's shoulder. He needed to stay close.

Unlike the image in the photograph in his pocket, Ayesha wasn't wearing a hijab. She looked like any other young woman on her way to university, her long brown hair tucked under a navy coat. Bailey was staring at the back of her head when it occurred to him that he hadn't given much thought to what he would do if he found her.

All Bailey knew was that he had to find her.

And he had.

'I'm the next stop.'

The lady sitting beside Ayesha stood up, offering her seat to Bailey.

'Thanks.'

Bailey sat down.

Ayesha was still staring out the window. Sitting beside her reminded Bailey that he had a daughter too. Miranda. He should have tried to speak to her before he got on the bloody bus. Suddenly, all he wanted to hear was his daughter's voice. One last phone call, just in case. He would tell her that he loved her. That he was glad that she was marrying a good guy like Peter Andrews. He would make Miranda put the doc on the phone so that he could tell him to take care of her if anything happened to him. But there was no time. A missed opportunity. Another reason to make it off the bus in one piece. At least Gerald would be there for her if this went bad.

The bus stopped, doors opened. More people got off, more people got on.

The doors closed. Once again, they were moving.

London Bridge was only a few hundred metres away. Bailey looked down and noticed a bag next to Ayesha's feet. He couldn't see her hands because she had a scarf resting on her lap.

The bus stopped in the traffic ahead of the bridge and Bailey sat, wondering what to do.

Maybe she didn't have a bomb at all. Maybe she wasn't going to go through with it.

'What's in the bag, Ayesha?'

Ayesha jolted at the mention of her name and turned to look at him. 'What?'

'What's in the bag?'

She hesitated for a few seconds, like her brain was searching through the faces it had on file.

'Who're you?'

The bus stopped suddenly and the driver sounded his horn.

'John Bailey.' Their eyes met. 'I'm here to stop you from doing something stupid.'

'It's too late.'

Bailey grabbed the scarf from her lap. Her hands were gripped around a small box, her thumbs pushing down on something. It looked like a remote control from a 1980s computer game, with a wire running into the bag at her feet. Her thumbs were holding down a button. A trigger.

He lunged onto her side of the seat, wrapping his hands around hers, holding them as tightly as his fists could clench. He didn't know what else to do. If the pressure was pushing down, then she couldn't let go. She couldn't detonate the bomb.

'Let go! Let go of my hand!' Ayesha was screaming at him, drawing the attention of other passengers. 'Let me go!'

'Are you okay, miss?' A man leaned in. 'Is this guy bothering you?'

'Yes, yes he is!'

'Listen, buddy –'

It was the guy in the baseball cap and he looked like he was about to rip Bailey out of his seat.

'She's got a bomb!' Bailey yelled at the top of his voice. He didn't have a choice.

The guy caught sight of the wires, the bag, Bailey's hands wrapped around Ayesha's, and he stumbled backwards, falling onto the two schoolgirls sitting across the aisle.

'What's going on? What is it?'

Different voices were asking the same questions from all around.

'There's a bomb!' The guy with the cap was scrambling to get off the girls. 'There's a bomb on the bus! She's got a bomb!'

Within seconds, people were out of their seats, pushing towards the front of the bus, some of them screaming to get off.

'There's a bomb! There's a bomb!'

Bailey could see out the front window. The bus was moving onto the bridge, the driver oblivious to the chaos behind him. Seconds later there was water to Bailey's left. Boats moving along the river. Water taxis. A barge. A rowing boat with eight guys pulling on oars and a small guy at the back, giving the orders. An ordinary day on the Thames.

'Stop the bus! Stop the bus!'

'Let go of me!' Ayesha was elbowing Bailey, trying to push him away. 'Let go!'

Bailey used his bodyweight to pin her up against the glass, while keeping his hands clenched tightly around hers. Ayesha was a slight girl and Bailey was much stronger, with at least one thumb that was in good working order. He had lost partial movement in the other the day it was bashed with a hammer by a madman. That whole incident didn't seem so bad now that he was sitting on a bus with a wannabe suicide bomber and a backpack that was probably filled with nails, ball bearings and other pieces of metal designed to maim and kill.

'Move! Move!'

Word had reached the top level of the bus and passengers were piling down the stairs.

'Smash the window!' A call came from the back of the bus.

Crack!

The bus suddenly stopped.

The driver was standing at the front, looking down the aisle, trying to decipher what the hell was going on.

'A bomb! A bomb! Let us off!'

People were screaming at him to open the doors. Seconds later, he did.

'Let me go!'

Ayesha was still wriggling and trying to push Bailey away. It was no use. He had her pinned against the glass.

Passengers were heaving towards the doors, leaping onto the road and running as fast as they could in all directions away from the bus.

A young girl was on the floor of the bus, trampled by the stampede for the doors. She had blood coming from her cheek and she was being helped to her feet near the back doors by the bus driver, who directed her onto the road and told her to run for it. They were the last people on board, other than Bailey and Ayesha. The driver was about to follow her out the door when he stopped and stepped closer to where Bailey and Ayesha were seated together.

Bailey guessed that this guy was probably thinking that if a bomb was going to go off, it would have done so already. He didn't know that Bailey's hands were wrapped around some kind of a trigger until he got closer and looked down.

'Good god.'

'Time to go,' Bailey said.

'Are you going to be all right, mate?'

'Who knows?' Bailey shrugged. 'No point all of us being here. You should get off.'

The driver stood there, staring at them. Bailey could see that he didn't want to leave them on the bus – his bus – alone. That he felt some kind of responsibility for his passengers. Bailey could see the torment in his eyes. An ordinary man who wanted to do the right thing.

'I've got three kids and I . . . I –'

'There's nothing you can do here, mate.' Bailey was trying to make the decision easy for him. 'Seriously, time to go.'

The driver gave Bailey a helpless smile. Like the smile that the priest gave Bailey at his brother's funeral. A look that said everything would be all right when Bailey knew that it wouldn't. That from that day onwards, life would never be the same.

'Good luck.'

The driver jumped out the back door and onto the road. Bailey watched him jog along the bridge, knocking on car windows and gesturing for people to move away from the bus.

Bailey turned to Ayesha. 'Looks like it's just you and me, kid.'

CHAPTER 47

It didn't take long for the authorities to clear the bridge. Five minutes. Seven. Eight, tops.

Bailey was only guessing, because he wasn't in any position to turn his wrist and get a look at the face of the old watch that his father had given him back when Bailey was a young reporter chasing stories – and not part of them.

There must have been about fifty metres of clear space in front of the bus before a line of abandoned cars blocked the road. Bailey wondered if he would get an insurance payout for the bomb that had destroyed his Corolla. Cheeky bastards probably wouldn't cough it up.

Bailey didn't know the situation at the back of the bus – he wasn't game to look over his shoulder – but he guessed it was the same. The only people who'd get close to the bus now were the poor bloody cops who were paid to do it. Dorset's people should be there now. Ronnie too. London's counter-terrorism police – SO15 – had probably arrived first. Police with training to take down a terrorist, which would have been mildly reassuring for Bailey had he not been sitting beside her.

He could hear a helicopter hovering above. From up there the big red double-decker bus must have been cutting a solitary scene on London Bridge. It wouldn't be long before London's loneliest bus would be beamed around the world via smartphones and television cameras. If this thing went bad, Miranda would have a lasting image of her father that no daughter should ever see.

Bailey really should have thought this thing through.

The temperature was cool outside, but Bailey was so hot that he could feel beads of perspiration on his forehead, and sweat building under his armpits. The bandage covering his injured back had split and his salty sweat was stinging his burn. His leather jacket was suffocating him, adding to the obvious discomfort of sitting on a bus beside a girl with a bomb.

'Are we just going to sit here forever?'

Bailey still had Ayesha pinned up against the window, afraid that if he released any pressure she'd wrestle his hands away from the trigger.

'Ayesha?'

She stared out the window, ignoring him.

'Because I can, you know. I've sat in shittier places for a lot longer.'

Ayesha turned to him. 'Who are you and why're you doing this?'

'Good question,' Bailey said. 'I'm a friend of your uncle's.'

'Are you a cop?'

'I'm a journalist, but I'm not here about that.'

'You came all the way from Australia?' She was speaking with a confidence that Bailey found disturbing. 'To find me?'

'Yeah.'

And Mustafa.

'That was pretty stupid, wasn't it?'

Bailey laughed to himself. Yeah, it was stupid. Cracking the code about a bomb attack on a bus and thinking that he could be the one to stop it. Real stupid.

'What's so funny?'

Bailey looked into her eyes, searching for a signal that Ayesha had a sense of humour. That there was just a confused kid in there. A kid who had gotten caught up with some bad people and had been tricked into doing something crazy. But the eyes that met his were as cold as the water of the Thames twenty feet below.

'Nothing,' Bailey said. 'There's nothing funny about what's happening here. It's just sad. A tragedy. A waste.'

'Then leave.'

Bailey looked down at his hands clasped around her hands. 'I'm not sure that's a good idea, for either of us.'

'I don't fear death.'

Neither did I – once – thought Bailey. That was until he remembered that he had a daughter who needed him and people who loved him.

'Well, you should,' he said.

'Why?'

'I don't believe in God, your god, or any other god, but I can tell you one thing –'

'I'm not interested.'

'It's some sick joke that your god's playing on you if you think he's got something special in store for someone who kills a bunch of innocent people.'

'Don't speak about things you know nothing about.'

'I know the Koran says that suicide's a sin.'

'Believe what you like,' she said, her voice sharpening.

'I'm not the believer.'

Bailey had given up on religion the day a doctor had told him they were turning off his brother's life support in hospital. The things he'd seen as a journalist in times of war and peace had only reinforced his feelings. He'd read all the books and concluded that if there really was a God then he was one sick bastard.

'I also know the Koran forbids the killing of innocent people.'

'You know nothing.'

'Whoever kills a soul unless for a soul or for corruption done in the land, it is as if he has slain mankind entirely . . .' Bailey paused, trying to remember the rest. 'And whoever saves one, it is as if he has saved mankind entirely.'

Ayesha turned to him with piercing green eyes. 'Don't quote *my* book.'

'All the books tell us the same thing, one way or the other,' Bailey said. 'They say that killing someone's a sin.'

'So why do your politicians claim to be killing for God?'

Bailey stared into her eyes again, wondering how to penetrate the mind of someone who had been reprogrammed – dehumanised – so young. Wondering how to hijack her hate.

'I don't think I've got all the answers here, Ayesha.'

'But knowing a few verses from the Koran, you think you can teach me why I'm wrong?'

'I'm no teacher,' Bailey said. 'And I'm not trying to tell you that you're wrong. I'm trying to tell you that you could be wrong. And that's a hell of a gamble for a young woman to take.'

She turned away, again.

For the next few minutes they sat in silence, their hands still locked together, clasped around a trigger.

'And what about all the innocent people you kill, including Muslims?' Bailey said, eventually. 'You didn't answer that question.'

'They're not innocent,' Ayesha said. 'Only those taking part in the jihad are innocent.'

Through the front windows of the bus, Bailey could see heavily armed police fanning across the road, taking cover behind the parked cars. Ronnie Johnson was further back, chewing on an unlit cigar, talking to Tony Dorset and pointing at the bus. The bus driver was there too, presumably telling them about Bailey, Ayesha and the bomb.

'Where'd you learn to hate like this,' Bailey said, 'if you don't mind me asking?'

'I'm fighting for a bigger cause. Bigger than all this, something that will right the wrongs . . . for the future.'

'Violence never solved anything.'

'Don't be such a hypocrite. The last century, the one before . . . the only way people get to stand up and be heard is by fighting. If that means people die, so be it.'

'I don't think you really believe that.'

'You don't know anything about me.'

'I know that your parents both died in Iraq and that you were raised by your uncle and aunt in Sydney. People who love you. I know that you're young enough to still have a life. Sara too.'

'What about Sara?' she said, tersely.

'She's okay. We caught her before she did something stupid.' Bailey paused, considering his lie. 'She turned herself in. She knew it was wrong. She wants a second chance.'

'You're lying.'

'Am I?' Bailey said. 'And what about Tariq? He was almost killed. Is that okay?'

'I never meant for Tariq to find out.' Ayesha turned towards the window. 'People like us, we're different. We've always been different. We're told that every day.'

'What do you mean?' Bailey noticed a change in her voice, like she wanted to explain herself. He didn't want to push it.

'We're all dumped in the same places, told the same things, pushed into the same jobs.'

'Your uncle has worked hard to build a life for you all. Aren't you studying medicine? That speaks of opportunity, surely.'

'I'm the one in a million. I can't support a system like this. You think my uncle likes driving a taxi and getting called a "sand nigger"? Do you think he likes getting told to fuck off back to where he came from? Don't talk to me about my family.'

'Racism is everywhere.'

'Yeah, but in places like Australia there's a special kind of racism. It's dressed up as something else. Border protection, citizenship tests, what it means to be an Australian citizen. People talk like the Australian way of life is being threatened by hijabs and halal meat.'

'Nobody likes politicians.'

'Then why do they keep getting elected?' Ayesha paused again, shaking her head. 'There are millions of people like me sick of being persecuted and told they're different, inferior. In places like Britain and Australia we keep getting told to respect British or Australian society, even prime ministers have said that. Like we don't understand.

'It's time they stopped to understand us, to understand British and Australian Muslims. Countries built on multiculturalism can't pick and choose.'

'You're a smart girl, Ayesha,' Bailey said. 'Too smart to do this.'

'Well . . . there's no way out, now.'

'Yes. There is.'

Bailey could see Ronnie Johnson walking towards the bus. He'd taken off his jacket so that all he was wearing was his shirt and a pair of jeans. He was walking with his hands in the air. When he was a few metres from the front of the bus he lifted up his shirt, flashing a gut that was painfully thinner than Bailey's, while turning on his heels to show Ayesha that he was unarmed.

'Who's that?' Ayesha said.

'He's a guy who's going to help get us out of here.'

*

'How're you doing, bubba?'

Ronnie was standing beside the back door of the bus, poking his head inside with a forced smile on his face.

'Ronnie Johnson,' Bailey said. 'Meet Ayesha Haneef.'

Ronnie held up his shirt again.

'Enough of that, thanks, mate,' Bailey said with a wink.

Ronnie put one foot onto the step of the bus. 'Mind if I get on here, Ayesha?'

She looked at Bailey like Ronnie must be joking.

'I think that's a yes, mate,' Bailey said.

Ronnie still had half a cigar wedged in the corner of his mouth and Bailey could see that he was biting down hard on the stub. He might be a seasoned professional, but Ronnie was nervous.

'Ayesha and I were just talking here about how it's not too late for this to have a happy ending.'

Ronnie peered over the railing so that he could get a look at the bomb for himself. 'I see.'

Ayesha's eyes were bouncing from Bailey to Ronnie, and back to the bomb at her feet.

'How are you, Ayesha?' Ronnie's thick southern accent made him sound like he was greeting someone he'd known for years.

Ayesha was watching him without saying a word.

'Ayesha, are you okay?' Ronnie tried again.

'I guess,' she said. 'Considering.'

'What say you, Ayesha?' Bailey said. 'Are we ready to go?'

Ayesha let out a long sigh, closing her eyes. When she opened them, they were filled with tears that overflowed down her cheeks. She started sobbing, her chin falling into her chest.

'It's okay.'

Bailey wanted to put an arm around her to comfort her, let her know that she was still just a kid, that kids made stupid mistakes and that they came back from them. Got second chances. But he couldn't put his arm around her because his fingers were still locked on her hands and the button that was connected to the bomb.

Eventually, she looked up at Bailey. 'I'm sorry.'

'Let's get you off this bus.' Bailey turned to the big Oklahoman. 'Ronnie?'

'Yes, bubba?'

'I'm going to need your help.'

'How exactly are you planning on doing this?'

'Don't worry about that part. Just head off back there and find me a roll of gaffer tape.'

Ronnie hesitated, like he was workshopping Bailey's plan in his mind. 'Okay, bubba.' He stepped off the bus and walked back towards the police cordon with his hands in the air.

'Ayesha, I need you to do exactly what I say, okay?' Bailey was speaking in a gentle tone that he'd usually reserved for his daughter. 'You need to trust me.'

'Okay.'

Bailey had always believed that it was almost impossible for people to lie with their eyes. Right now, Ayesha's teary eyes were telling him that she didn't want to die.

'I need to get a look at the trigger beneath your fingers.'

She nodded.

'My guess is that the bomb's live, and that the second the button's released, it goes bang, right?'

Ayesha nodded again. This time her eyes were saying she was sorry.

She slid her right hand slightly over so that Bailey could see that her index finger was holding down a black button, about half as wide as a one-pound coin.

'I need to get my finger onto that button so that I can keep it down when you release it.'

'Okay.' Ayesha's voice was shaky.

Their hands had been clasped together for so long that they were greased with sweat.

Bailey gently slid his good thumb over the top of Ayesha's fingers, before slipping it down and onto the button.

'There.' Bailey felt his finger hit the metal. 'Now I need you to, gently and slowly, remove your finger so that I can take over the pressure.'

She did as she was told and within seconds she was sitting beside Bailey with two free hands.

'Time for you to go.'

Bailey's thumb was holding down the button with such force that his hand was shaking. He had no idea how much pressure was required and he wasn't taking any chances.

Ayesha stood up, carefully climbing over the backpack and past Bailey's knees.

She stopped at the door, turning around. 'It should be me staying here.'

'This is the only way,' Bailey said, knowing it was the truth. 'I'm not sure I would have been as trusting of you as you were of me.'

Ayesha held his gaze for a few more seconds, like she had suddenly realised the person that she had almost become, before stepping off the bus and onto the road.

'Ayesha!' Bailey called after her.

She stopped next to the open door of the bus. 'Yeah?'

'You're going to need to lose the jacket to show the cops that the bomb is still here with me. And put your hands in the air. Walk slowly.'

'Mr Bailey,' Ayesha called back to him, 'I'm sorry.'

'It's all part of growing up.'

Ayesha left her jacket on the step of the bus. She was still a child, eighteen years old, idealistic. Her misguided rebellion had materialised into a homemade bomb that was sitting at Bailey's feet, with his good thumb trembling on the trigger.

Through the bus window, Bailey could see Ronnie talking with Tony Dorset from MI5. They looked like they were having an argument. The fact that Ronnie made it back to the bus soon after with a roll of silver gaffer tape in his hand meant that the American had won.

'What did he want?'

'The stupid prick had all these other ideas he wanted to go over with his team before deciding which option was the best.' Ronnie was shaking his head. 'He was probably about to bring out a fucking whiteboard.'

'And?'

'You want the summary?'

Bailey looked down at his hand. 'That'd probably be best.'

'I told him there was a bomb in your lap and you'd appreciate a quick decision.' Ronnie held up the tape and rested a knee on the seat beside Bailey. 'And here we are.'

Bailey slid his thumb to his right so that Ronnie could see the size of the button they needed to lock down with the tape.

'So, I fix the tape to the edge of the button and you reckon that's going to hold it down?'

Ronnie used his shirt to wipe away Bailey's sweat from the metal and also from Bailey's skin.

'You're not going to do anything, mate,' Bailey said. 'Just tear me off a few strips, stick them to the railing and I'll do the rest.'

'I'm staying.'

'Bullshit, you are.' Bailey raised his voice. 'There's no point both of us dying if this thing goes tits-up.'

'Yeah, but it won't go wrong if I'm here with you.'

'It's not up for discussion. Tear the tape and get the fuck off the bus.'

'Sorry, bubba,' Ronnie said. 'We almost lost one good pal this week. He's probably watching this on television from his hospital bed. I promised him I'd look out for you. I'm not going anywhere.'

The mention of Gerald sent needles through Bailey's spine.

Ronnie was right, the best chance that Bailey had of making it off the bus alive was with Ronnie's help. Bailey didn't want to die. He had a wedding to go to. A daughter to walk down the aisle. Gerald. Miranda. Dexter. They were probably all watching. The sound of the helicopter overhead confirmed it.

'You're a stubborn bastard, you know that?' Bailey said.

'Coming from you?'

'Let's just get this done.'

Ronnie started tearing off strips of tape, sticking them to the metal railing in front of the seat, until he had all the tape that he needed. One by one, he fastened the strips of gaffer tape to the edge of the button, each strip covering more of the trigger.

'I reckon that's enough.'

'Wait.'

Ronnie made a few more strips, fixing each one, carefully, on the button. With Bailey's thumb taking up half the space, the tape could only catch a few millimetres of plastic.

'Not enough pressure and this thing goes boom.'

'Okay.'

Ronnie was on his knees, pressing the corners of the tape, testing its strength.

'This is where we hold hands and pray.'

'That's how this mess began,' Bailey said, dryly. 'Here goes.'

He hesitated, knowing that there was no coming back if they'd got this wrong. A few more seconds. One more breath.

Bailey let go.

'Shit.' He sat back in his seat, his hand still shaking and aching from the pressure.

Ronnie grabbed the roll of tape and wrapped it around and around the remote so that there was no danger of the button moving.

'What do we do with that?' Bailey said, stepping over the backpack.

'Leave it here.'

'Good for me. Let's get the hell off this bus.'

The two men stepped onto the road and started walking, hands in the air, towards the police and ambulances further along London Bridge.

Behind the police cordon, crowds of people were lining the Thames on either side of the bridge, like they were waiting for the royal barge at the Queen's Diamond Jubilee.

'Shirts up, fellas!' a cop called out.

There were so many guns pointed at them that Bailey didn't even try to count them.

'Better do what they say,' Ronnie said.

'You think?' Bailey lifted his shirt, offering a view of his pudgy middle. 'I hope they don't get this on camera.'

CHAPTER 48

A guy holding a sign that read 'British bombs for hire' was arguing with a policeman on the steps of Thames House when the four-wheel drive carrying Bailey and Ronnie skidded to a stop beside the footpath out front.

'Here we are, chaps.'

Tony Dorset had been riding in the front seat and he'd barely said a word to the two men in the back during the short drive from London Bridge to Lambeth.

Bailey had spent the car-ride staring out the window, waiting for his heart rate to normalise and for the fog of fear to lift. Like the rest of London, it would take time.

Dorset climbed out of the car first and then opened the back door.

'Let's go, gentlemen.'

Bailey didn't want to get out of the car. He wanted to stay in the back seat and tell the driver to take him to Heathrow so that he could head to Sydney to see his daughter. See Gerald. Break bread with Dexter. After his near-death experience, the precious things in his life were flashing in his head like the Sydney Harbour Bridge on New Year's Eve. But Bailey knew that he wasn't going anywhere. Not today. Not tomorrow. Not anytime soon. He was stuck in London for as long as they wanted him there.

In a few minutes time he would be taken into a room where he'd be hit with a million questions by British spooks about what had just gone down on London Bridge and anything he could tell them about Mustafa al-Baghdadi.

'I'll try to keep this as brief as possible,' Dorset said.

A reassurance that reminded Bailey of the day his dentist told him that root canal was routine treatment. Five hours later, he had been dribbling soup down his chin with a gaping hole in his mouth and five more appointments in his calendar.

'Sure you will.'

'Come on, bubba.' Ronnie nudged Bailey with his elbow. 'I won't let this get out of hand.'

Bailey and Ronnie followed Dorset across the pavement and up the steps towards the entrance. The argument between the cop and the guy holding the one-man protest looked like it was getting heated. By the time they made it to the top of the steps under the big grey arch, they could hear the two men going for it.

'You're telling me I need to make a reservation to protest a week in advance?'

'That's exactly what I'm telling you.' The policeman was clearly losing his patience. 'It's the law!'

'Not my law.'

'I've explained the rules. If you don't leave now, I'll arrest you.'

Bailey felt sorry for the guy with the sign. What happened to free speech? Since when was staging a protest like booking a table in a restaurant?

'I'm not going anywhere.'

The protester sat down on the cold stone steps, defiantly, his legs partially blocking the door.

'Move,' Dorset said.

The bloke didn't move an inch. 'You can piss off too.'

'I don't have time for this shit.' Dorset turned to the policeman. 'Get rid of him.'

'That's what I'm trying to do, sir.'

Dorset stepped over the protester's legs, almost tripping as he pushed open the door, and waved his hand for Bailey and Ronnie to do the same.

'Let's go.'

'Got to stand up for what you believe,' Bailey said to the protester as he stepped over his legs. 'Good on you, mate.'

'Indeed.' The man smiled, folding his arms.

Bailey and Ronnie followed Dorset through the front door to the security desk, where a woman in uniform was waiting for them. There was also a screening machine that reminded Bailey about the bomb in Ayesha's backpack. The bomb disposal unit had been preparing to conduct a controlled explosion just as they were leaving London Bridge. Bailey thought he would have heard a loud bang by now, considering they were only a mile away.

'Arms up, please.'

Ronnie offered himself for a pat-down first, his big arms stretching wide. He was so tall that the woman searching him looked like she was tugging on a clothes line.

'Okay, you're done.'

The body-scanner didn't make a sound when Ronnie walked through.

Bailey's turn.

'Arms up, please.'

'Easy, love.' He touched the woman's hand as she started running her fingers under his jacket. 'I've got a little burn on my back, be gentle.'

She gave him a vacant stare and her hand brushed the bandage, sending a stinging pain up his spine. She made no attempt to be gentle. Maybe she was worried about being thorough in front of the boss.

Dorset noticed Bailey squirm. 'We'll get that looked at in a bit.'

They followed Dorset into an elevator and then out again on a different floor. Bailey hadn't bothered to watch the numbers tick over. He was feeling lightheaded from the pain that had returned with a vengeance in his back.

Dorset led them down a wide corridor with green carpet and portraits of people Bailey didn't recognise, and into a large boardroom. There must have been a dozen people sitting around a table filled with documents, maps, photographs and newspaper clippings. There was a whiteboard at the other end of the room with Mustafa al-Baghdadi's name written on it. Arrows linking him to other names. The Haneef girls and people that Bailey had never heard of before. Bailey's name was up there too, circled in red.

A short, stocky woman with a neat hairdo and glasses was standing by the window. By the look on her face, she was expecting them.

'Ronnie Johnson.'

She made her way around the large table with a big smile on her face, her hand outstretched for the big Oklahoman.

'Long time, Ann.'

The room went silent and the heads around the table all turned towards the door, where Ronnie and Ann were now shaking hands.

'Ann Pritchard,' Ronnie said, 'meet John Bailey.'

Pritchard looked like she'd been in the spy game even longer than Ronnie. Her extra chin and rounding middle suggested that these days she did most of her spying from behind a desk. Ronnie respected her, that much was clear. Bailey could sense the history in their two-armed greeting.

'Pleasure to meet you, Mr Bailey.' Pritchard offered her hand to Bailey and he shook it. 'Terrible thing you've just been through.'

'Thanks,' Bailey said. 'I've had better London commutes.'

Bailey's joke sank without a trace and Pritchard was clapping her hands, commanding the attention of the room. 'Okay, everyone. Out! Get some caffeine, call your husbands, wives, mistresses . . . whatever. Nobody goes home tonight. Back here in ten.'

She waited for everyone to clear out before she started talking again.

'I saw your speech at Chatham House last week. Damn tragedy what happened outside. I enjoyed the talk though. Insightful.'

'Thanks.'

Bailey's speech at St James's Square felt like it had happened last year, not last week. And he could have done without the trip down memory lane.

'Gentlemen, do we need anything?' Pritchard asked. 'Water? Tea? Coffee?'

'Let's just cut to it,' Ronnie said. 'It's been a hell of a few days.'

'Understood,' Pritchard said. 'Tony, let's get some water in here.'

Dorset looked like he was about to say something but he decided against it and walked out the door.

'Gentlemen, please sit.'

Bailey grabbed a seat facing the window. The view was something else. The red bridge stretching across the Thames, Lambeth Palace, and further along, the big wheel of the London Eye and the tip of the Shard. London Bridge was a bend and a half away, out of view. Not out of mind.

Pritchard obviously wasn't one for small talk because they sat in silence while they waited for Dorset to return. It didn't take long. He came back with four bottles of water, handing one first to his boss, then to the men in the room, before he sat down smack in the middle of Bailey's view of the big wheel.

Cracking the plastic cap, Bailey took a long pull of his water, emptying half the bottle. He was dehydrated from sweating on the bus and the two long plane rides to London.

He sat forward so that his back wouldn't touch the leather chair. He was tired but the pain was keeping him alert. The Brits would have a long list of questions. Bailey was determined to go first.

'What did you do with Ayesha?'

'She's in custody, being questioned,' Pritchard said.

'Have you spoken to her?' Bailey was pointing his finger at Pritchard. 'Down at the bridge, did you speak to her?'

'No.'

'Then who's questioning her?'

'What is this?' Dorset said. 'The girl was about to –'

Pritchard raised her hand and Dorset stopped talking. 'Ayesha Haneef has a lot of explaining to do. We've got her at a secure location.'

'Remember, she's just a kid.'

'Barely,' Dorset said. 'She just tried to kill a lot of innocent people.'

'Yeah, only she didn't. Did she?' Bailey had decided that Dorset was a shithead. 'And like I said, she's just a kid.'

Ronnie cleared his throat and tapped his fingers on the table, like he was trying to break the rhythm of the conversation that was bouncing from one side of the room to the other. 'What do you need from us, Ann?'

'C'mon, Ronnie, you know why you're here.'

Bailey took another sip of his water. He'd said his piece and now he was happy for Ronnie to do the talking.

'Not much has changed with you, has it?' Pritchard laughed through her nose, adjusting her glasses. 'Do we have a problem?'

'Your country. Your rules,' Ronnie said. 'I'll tell you when I have a problem.'

'I know you will.'

'Meaning?'

'No games, Ronnie.' Pritchard dropped the smile. 'This is too sensitive, too dangerous.'

'Here's what we know – the facts,' Ronnie said. 'An eighteen-year-old girl carries a bomb onto a bus. You knew she was here. You knew who she'd been spending time with. You missed it. The only reason why that bus didn't go bang on London Bridge is because of the fella sitting next to me – who wouldn't know half the shit we know – no offence, bubba.'

'None taken.'

'Anyhow, as fuck-ups go,' Ronnie kept at them, 'this one's up there.'

'Hang on a minute!' Dorset's face had turned the colour of beetroot. 'We know we missed a few things here.'

'You think?'

'That's enough, Ronnie,' Pritchard said. 'This isn't helping anyone.'

Bailey shifted uncomfortably in his chair, trying to remove his leather jacket. Each movement was causing the bandage to dig into his burn. 'How long's this going to take?'

'We need to come to an agreement about Mustafa al-Baghdadi,' Pritchard said. 'We need to coordinate.'

'Any idea how he got in the country?' Ronnie said.

Bailey could see the anger in Pritchard's eyes. 'I don't see the point in walking you through our intelligence failures because, as you know, we're not alone. You Americans have had your fair share. We dodged a bullet today. We made a big mistake. But this isn't over, you and I both know that.'

Pritchard turned her eyes on Bailey, pointing at him with her index finger. 'We agree with the assessment that Mustafa al-Baghdadi's in London. And right now, you're the best chance we have of finding him.'

'Because of the phone calls?' Bailey said. 'You think he's going to call me again?'

'We don't know anything for sure. You'll need to stay in London until we've got him. We can't let you go home with a threat like this hanging over our country.'

Bailey looked at Ronnie, hoping that he would tell these guys to get lost, that there was a time limit on this. That in a few days Ronnie would have a special CIA plane on the tarmac at Heathrow waiting to shuttle Bailey out of the United Kingdom and back to Australia. But he could tell that Ronnie had an agenda here too. Mustafa was the world's most wanted terrorist. The Americans were desperate to catch or kill him too. Ronnie might be Bailey's friend but that hadn't stopped him using him before. Dangling him like bait. Bailey felt like he was staring at a bunch of fishermen and he didn't like it.

There was a knock at the door.

'Come in!' Pritchard called out without getting out of her chair.

A man's head appeared through the door. 'Ma'am, I've got Commander Daniels on the line. Says it's urgent.'

Ann gestured for the man to come in and hand her the phone.

'Robert,' she said.

She spent the next thirty seconds listening into the receiver before, eventually, she handed the phone back to the guy who had brought it in and waited for him to leave.

'Anything you'd like to share with us?' Ronnie said.

'The second code. The Met's Counter Terrorism Command has been working with our Australian counterparts on it.'

'And?' Bailey said, knowing that she was talking about Dexter's team.

'The target was Sydney Harbour Bridge,' Pritchard said. 'Some bus route called a B-Line, or something. The girls had timed their attacks to happen at the same time at opposite sides of the world. But, as you know, after her brother was found, Sara Haneef had altered her plan to hit Martin Place instead. And then, of course, she was arrested too.'

Bailey grabbed his notepad from his pocket, thumbing through the pages to find where he'd scribbled the codes. He found it.

BLHB7152004

The B-Line was a two-storey bus that left the city packed each evening to ferry commuters up to the northern beaches. Ten stops in thirty kilometres. A lot of people would have died.

Two iconic bridges. Two devastating attacks. One timed to go off during London's early morning rush hour, the other at exactly the same moment at 7.15 pm on the Sydney Harbour Bridge at the tail end of the day, and the start of prime time on television.

'The Australians are coming to London,' Pritchard added. 'To assist with the investigation and the questioning of Ayesha Haneef.'

Bailey wondered if that meant Dexter, but he didn't ask. He'd find out soon enough. 'I reckon we're done here.'

The sound of voices was building in the corridor. The ten minutes that Pritchard had given her staff was up.

'Okay.' Pritchard stood up, signalling that the meeting was over. 'You obviously need some medical attention and some rest. Big day.'

'You think?'

'A car will take you to your hotel,' she said. 'A doctor will look at you there.'

Ronnie was already on his feet with Bailey's jacket in his hand.

It took Bailey a bit longer to stand up, even though his mind was already out the door.

CHAPTER 49

Six days and nothing. No phone calls. No messages. No proclamations or rallying cries on social media. Nothing.

Mustafa al-Baghdadi had gone quiet.

If Mustafa was in London, then he wasn't about to risk blowing his whereabouts by making another phone call to Bailey.

Gerald had been calling Bailey at both ends of the day, chasing updates about the hunt for Mustafa and whether or not Ayesha Haneef was talking. The doctors were keeping Gerald in hospital for another week and it was driving him bonkers. The two men had a lot to talk about.

Top of the list was their jobs at *The Journal*. Gerald and Bailey had made their decisions. They were getting out.

The Journal's lawyers hadn't even tried to talk them out of it. They'd obviously need to stage-manage the departure of the editor, but they just required a signature from Bailey. His redundancy payout was big, although it wasn't about the money. Social media had poisoned the fourth estate. News wasn't *news* anymore. Whatever it had become, it had to be delivered in a hurry. It had to be sensational. Right or wrong, it didn't matter. Facts weren't being checked anymore. The news business was broken and no one seemed to know how to fix it.

And without Gerald running the shop, leaving was a no-brainer.

Dexter had been in London for four days and she was staying in a hotel up the river on the other side of Scotland Yard. She'd been so busy that Bailey had barely spoken to her. The only times they'd seen each other was in the so-called 'war room' at Thames House, where MI5, the Metropolitan Police and Dexter's team were working together to find Mustafa al-Baghdadi and stop any other acts of terrorism.

As an Australian citizen, Dexter was also leading the interrogation of Ayesha Haneef.

'How's she doing?'

Bailey had cornered Dexter at Thames House. He knew that Ayesha was in a world of trouble, but he wanted to know that she was all right.

'She's okay,' Dexter had said. 'The Brits are in no rush to lay charges. Right now, I'm just building trust, hoping she might be able to tell us something that will lead us to Mustafa al-Baghdadi.'

'So she's talking?'

'Yes. There's a deal on the table that'll reduce her jail time, so she's got a reason.'

Their conversation had been interrupted and everything else that Bailey had learned about Ayesha had been gleaned from the daily briefings that Dexter had been giving the 'war room'.

Ayesha had told Dexter that she had been instructed by the Islamic Nation group to carry out the attack on London Bridge and she gave up the address of the house in Crouch End where two men with English accents had given her the backpack with the bomb in it. That house had been promptly raided by British police and, not surprisingly, found to be empty.

Dexter had also painted a picture of Ayesha and her cousin, Sara, as two girls who'd used to listen to Coldplay and watch Star Wars movies. Their lives had changed when they started attending

Hassan Saleh's prayer group at Wiley Park, where he'd told them stories about America's silent war on Islam and showed them videos of US soldiers urinating on dead bodies in Afghanistan and torturing prisoners at Abu Ghraib. Within six months, Sara and Ayesha had both been brainwashed and radicalised. After Ayesha had moved to London, Saleh had sent her to the Ripple Road mosque in East London to meet Umar Masood, another recruiter for the Islamic Nation group.

For Bailey, being stuck at Thames House was tedious. But he had been given access to a flow of information that an investigative reporter could only dream about.

The New South Wales Police had laid formal terrorism charges against Sara Haneef. Along with a raft of terror-related offences, the Salma brothers, Hassan Saleh and Bilal Suleman had been charged with the attempted murders of Gerald Summers and Karen Copeland, the policewoman Sammy Raymond had slashed in the shoulder with a knife. And they'd also been pinged for the bomb that had blown up Bailey's car and the kidnapping of Tariq Haneef.

Tariq was recovering well in hospital and he was also talking to police. The poor kid had seen some messages – exchanges between Sara and Ayesha – on his phone. He'd wanted to confront Sara at one of Hassan Saleh's prayer group sessions. When his sister hadn't turned up, Tariq had made the mistake of confiding in Hassan Saleh about his concerns, thinking that the religious preacher might help him – talk some sense into his sister – only to find himself being hoodwinked and thrown into the back of a van by the Salma brothers.

Bailey had called Omar to check on him after everything that had happened. But his old driver from Baghdad was like an empty shell on the other end of the line, with Bailey's questions met by long, echoey silences. The phone call had ended with Omar telling Bailey that it would be best if he never called him again. Bailey had tried to reassure him that life would get better again, but he knew it was a lie. Omar would always be the father and uncle of the girls who'd tried to blow up buses.

When Bailey wasn't at Thames House sharing everything he knew about Mustafa al-Baghdadi, he was sitting in his hotel room. Tony Dorset didn't want him going out unless it was absolutely necessary. When he did leave his hotel room, he was stalked by British agents. After Patricia Jones had been killed at St James's Square, and the near-miss on London Bridge, British authorities couldn't afford any more mistakes. Armed police were everywhere and the British Army had been called in to guard the government buildings around Westminster and, of course, Buckingham Palace.

Ronnie was off somewhere being Ronnie. Even though he was sleeping in the hotel room next door, Bailey had barely seen him.

Bailey was starting to lose the plot.

There weren't any black cabs waiting in the turning circle at the DoubleTree when Bailey stepped outside, so he thought he'd chance it on the street.

While he was waiting, he dug out his phone from his pocket. He owed someone a phone call and it'd been preying on his mind.

She answered after two rings.

'Annie, it's Bailey.'

'Hello, stranger.'

'Yeah, sorry about that. A bit going on here.'

She went quiet on the other end of the phone, probably waiting for Bailey to explain what he meant.

'Where's here?' she said, eventually.

'London.'

'Are you okay?'

Bailey thought about giving her a detailed answer but he didn't know where to begin.

'I'm good. Considering.'

'Considering what?' She sounded confused. 'What are you doing in London?'

He had to tell her something. 'I'm helping British authorities with a terrorism investigation.'

Annie knew Bailey well enough to know what had happened to him in Iraq. His links to Mustafa al-Baghdadi.

'What about the drink?'

'Haven't touched it here.' He needed to tell her the truth, especially after she'd come clean with him about her recent dance with her vodka devil. 'Had a slip-up in Sydney. Woke up hating myself. I'm good now.'

'You sure?'

He wanted to change the subject. 'How about you?'

'I'm fine, Bailey. But I'm worried about you.'

Annie was a smart woman. She'd obviously been reading the papers and joining the dots.

'Mr Bailey! Mr Bailey!'

A young bloke in a suit was calling out to Bailey. He was about twenty metres away along Millbank.

'Annie, I've got to go. I'll call you when I'm back in Sydney.'

'Make sure you do.'

Bailey hung up just as the young man caught up to him, puffing like he'd just finished a marathon.

'Mr Bailey, where're you going?'

'I'm heading out for a while, mate,' Bailey said, holding out an arm towards the street.

'You can't do that, not without telling us. You know the arrangement.'

Bailey stopped walking. 'It's Ben, right?' He remembered him from the day they'd landed at Heathrow.

'Yeah, that's right.'

'Look, Ben . . . I'm going nuts in there. I need some fresh air. I need to stare at something other than the walls of a conference room or that shoebox I'm living in.'

'Dorset says you can't go anywhere alone.'

'Yeah, well. Dorset's not here, is he?'

'C'mon, Mr Bailey, I'm just doing my job here.'

A black car skidded to a stop on the road beside them, interrupting their conversation. Dexter was behind the wheel. She flicked on her hazard lights, opening the door.

'Off for a walk?' she said, stepping onto the footpath.

'Something like that,' Bailey said. 'Checking up on me now too, are we?'

Dexter turned to Ben. 'Give us a minute, would you?'

She waited for Ben to walk out of earshot before she started. 'Bailey, this has got to stop.'

'I don't know what you're talking about.'

Dexter shook her head, making a puffing noise in her nose. 'Don't be a prick, John. You know exactly what I'm talking about. The cold shoulder. Other than quizzing me about Ayesha, you've barely even acknowledged we're in the same room when I've seen you at MI5.'

'You've been busy.'

'Don't be coy.'

'Yeah, well . . . what's happened has happened.'

Bailey had wanted to repair the damage that had been done to their relationship, but there was something blocking the way.

331

He was still pissed at her for withholding information from him when he'd thought that they'd had an understanding. More than an understanding. A deal. And he didn't like feeling used.

'Bailey, I'm a police officer. With a job to do, rules to follow.' It was like she'd been reading his mind. 'For Christ's sake, I'm the head of the bloody Joint Counter Terrorism Team.'

'I know how important you are.'

'Fuck you, Bailey.' She turned towards the river, spinning her neck back around with a squint. 'That was a cheap shot.'

'Yeah, well, if it hadn't been for Tony Dorset, I would never have known about those encrypted messages between Sara and Ayesha. I never would have made it onto that bus.'

Now, that was a cheap shot. Bailey knew it. He couldn't pin that on Dexter. It wasn't right. He could see the humiliation in her eyes.

'I'm sorry.' He tried to save himself, reaching out, touching her elbow. 'Something's broken here. I don't know how to fix it.'

'This is bigger than you, Bailey.' Dexter was backing down too. 'Bigger than me. Bigger than us.'

'I know. That was a low blow.'

Bailey was done being an arsehole. Dexter was right, she did have a job to do. An important one. Dexter had always sought justice the right way, by working hard, doing things by the book. Bailey couldn't mark her down for not sharing sensitive information with a reporter. Even the one who'd been sleeping beside her. It was arrogant for him to have thought otherwise. Unfair.

Tiny drops of rain had splattered on Dexter's cheekbones, making them glisten. She managed a smile, a web of lines wrapping the edges of her tired eyes. She looked beautiful in the afternoon light, reminding Bailey about the other person in there.

'What're you doing now? Want to grab a bite?'

'I can't, Bailey. I want to, but I can't.'

'Work?'

'I'm going back to talk to Ayesha.'

'Fair enough. Later then. You know where to find me.'

'I really am sorry, y'know.' She put her hand on his cheek. 'Bailey, there's something I need to know.'

'Shoot.'

'Do you love me? I mean . . .' She paused, looking for a way to rephrase the question. 'I mean, after all this is done. Can we? Do you? I just need the truth.'

Yeah. He loved her. He just didn't know how to say it.

Dexter withdrew her hand. 'I'll take that as a no.'

She turned to walk away, but he grabbed her, pulling her close so that she could feel his breath on her face.

'I don't love anyone else.'

He put his arms around her, holding her in the street so that they could both forget, even for just a few seconds, where they were, and why.

'You're bloody hopeless,' Dexter said, stepping out of his embrace.

'And hopeful.'

She smiled. It was good enough. For now. 'I've got to go. Wait up for me . . . maybe a late dinner tonight?'

'Sounds good.'

Bailey watched her drive away as Ben sidled up beside him, a cheeky smirk on his face.

'So you and the cop, eh?'

'It's complicated.'

'Always is.'

Bailey turned to face him after Dexter's car disappeared up the road. 'Do you like rugby?'

'Yeah, I do. Used to play a bit.'

'Didn't we all,' Bailey said. 'Local derby between Harlequins and Saracens. Kicks off in an hour at Twickenham.'

'The Stoop,' Ben said, knowingly.

'Guess you won't mind coming with me, then?'

'Do I have a choice, Mr Bailey?'

'No, you don't,' Bailey said. 'And, Ben, one more thing before we go.'

'What is it?'

'Stop bloody calling me "Mister" Bailey.'

CHAPTER 50

The Stoop was an old stadium with seats painted the same maroon, blue and green as the Harlequins' playing jersey. The grass was immaculate, but the stadium was in serious need of a refurbishment. It didn't bother Bailey, he'd watch a game of rugby anywhere, anytime.

They'd made it in time for kick-off and, just as the ball was sailing into the air off the boot of the Harlequins' New Zealand import, Bailey was sitting down with a hog bap in his hand.

People with accents from New Zealand, Australia, Ireland and Scotland were mixing in with the locals, belting out songs and yelling at players on the field. *Tackle harder! Run faster! Smash him, bro!* Rugby might be having its problems back in Australia, but hearing the crowd reminded Bailey that it was a global game. And he loved it.

There was nothing like watching rugby *live*. Hearing the thud of the tackles, broad shoulders crashing together in scrum-time collisions, scrum halves directing the traffic and fly halves calling the moves. Bailey loved the camaraderie of the contest.

Today the Saracens were on the back foot and their players were screaming for someone to take down the Quins' little winger who'd been cutting up the field every time he got the ball.

Ten minutes in and the Quins were 12-nil up on the scoreboard. They were running the ball from everywhere, and the Saracens players didn't seem to have any answers.

Rugby was like a chess game. It could turn at any moment. One poor kick, intercepted pass or missed tackle, and the Saracens would be back in it.

Bailey was getting into it, egging the visiting team on.

And then his phone started vibrating. Dexter.

He answered just as the Saracens number two jumper plucked the ball from the air and his forward pack crowded behind him, forming a perfect rolling maul, the ball transferring to the back, tucked under the arm of a wily hooker who, seconds later, fell over the line to claim the Saracens' first points of the game.

Yeah!

The crowd erupted in cheers.

'Sharon! Are you there?' Bailey yelled into the phone, his hands cupped around the receiver. 'Sharon!'

When the roar of the crowd subsided, Bailey could just make out Dexter's voice on the other end of the phone.

'Where the hell are you, Bailey?'

'I'm watching a rugby game down at Twickenham.'

'You're what?'

'Don't panic. I've got young Ben here watching over me.'

'Twickenham Stadium?'

'The Stoop,' Bailey said.

'Ayesha wants to talk to you.'

'What about?'

'I can barely bloody hear you over the noise of the crowd.' Dexter was sounding annoyed. 'I'm coming to pick you up, I'll text you when I'm close. Meet me out the front.'

'Okay.'

Bailey looked at his watch. Beer was off the table but he probably had time for another hog bap. It'd be a crime not to.

'There she is.'

Dexter was double-parked about fifty metres up the road from the stadium, leaning on her car and looking at her watch.

'Hello there, stranger,' Bailey said. 'Twice in one day, I'm starting to feel blessed.'

She walked up close to Bailey. 'Are you sure being out like this is a good idea?'

'I've been locked in a bloody room for days,' Bailey said, slightly annoyed. 'I needed to get out.'

'Well, you're about to get locked in another one. Ayesha's waiting for us.'

Bailey turned to Ben. 'You get your car, I'll travel with Sharon.'

'Sure,' Ben said. 'But you'll need to wait for me.'

Dexter nodded her head. 'Meet you here?'

'Yeah, give me five.'

Ben turned around and jogged off towards the carpark.

It was getting cold outside so Dexter and Bailey climbed in the car to wait for him.

'So, what's this about?' Bailey said.

'She wouldn't tell me. Something about Mustafa al-Baghdadi, I'm hoping,' Dexter said. 'It's not the first time she's asked for you. What you did on that bus – apart from being stupid – it left an impression on her. She trusts you.'

'Yeah, well. As I keep trying to tell people, she's just a kid.'

Dexter checked her rear-view mirror to see if Ben was close. 'What's this idiot doing?'

Bailey turned and clocked an old four-wheel drive speeding on the wrong side of the road towards them.

'What the –'

At the last minute the four-wheel drive swerved and rammed into the side of their car, throwing Bailey out of his seat and up onto the dashboard, bashing his head on the windscreen, before he bounced off the door and back onto his seat.

He opened his eyes. Something warm and wet was running down his forehead.

Dexter had her seatbelt on so she hadn't been thrown like Bailey, but there was blood coming from her nose and she was holding the back of her neck.

'Are you okay?'

Bailey felt Dexter's hand on his shoulder.

'Bailey? Are you okay?'

He was dizzy but he didn't feel like he'd broken anything. 'Yeah, I think so.'

The four-wheel drive's bonnet had crinkled like a potato chip and smoke was billowing out the sides. it had rammed into Bailey's side of the car, which meant that he couldn't open his door. Two men wearing face masks were walking around the front of the car, pistols in hand, towards Dexter's door.

Bailey's senses were coming back. 'Hit the lock!'

Dexter locked the door just as the two men appeared at her side of the car. One of them pulled a crowbar from his jacket and used it to punch through the window, then reached inside and unlocked the door. He grabbed hold of Dexter and started pulling her out of the car.

'Let her go! Let her go!'

Bailey had a hold of her left arm in a tug-of-war with the two men outside, while Dexter bashed at them with her fists. As an Australian cop on British soil, Dexter wasn't carrying a gun. All she could do was fight. The bastards were strong and Bailey was being dragged across the gear-stick and onto the driver's seat as they tried to wrench Dexter out the door.

One of the men let go of Dexter and pushed past her to get to Bailey. He pointed his pistol like he was about to shoot Bailey in the head. Only he didn't, switching grips so that he was holding his gun like a hammer, bashing it into Bailey's cheek.

Once.

Twice.

By the third blow, Bailey was out cold.

Bang! Bang! Bang!

The sound of gunshots brought Bailey back.

His head was aching and he was lying across the centre console of the car, his cheek resting on the driver's seat in a pool of his own blood.

He looked up and saw Ben standing in the middle of the street pointing his gun at a blue van speeding off down the road. A few rounds from Ben's gun smashed its back window. It wasn't enough to stop them. The van disappeared around a corner.

Bailey was clambering out of the car, trying to steady himself, looking for any sign of Dexter. There was glass from the shattered window all over the footpath. A splatter of blood. Dexter was gone.

'Your car! Where's your car?' Bailey yelled at Ben.

Ben turned around and Bailey could see that he was talking on his phone. Calling it in. Calling for back-up. Calling for a helicopter to track the blue van with a rear window that had been blown out by gunfire.

'Where's your bloody car?'

Ben put his phone away and jogged over to Bailey.

'I never made it back to the car. I saw the four-wheel drive speeding along the street . . . the men in masks . . . I didn't have time. I just bolted.' Ben was trying to catch his breath. 'When I got here they were shoving Dexter into the back of the van. They were coming back for you when they saw me with my gun out.' Ben pointed at the footpath beside Bailey. 'I was right here. I tried to stop them. I did. I'm sorry.'

Bailey was up off his knees, wiping the blood from his eyes with his shirtsleeve.

He dug his phone from his pocket, searching for the only name he could trust.

'Ronnie,' Bailey yelled into the receiver. 'Dexter's been taken.'

CHAPTER 51

The boardroom at Thames House was packed with people.

For John Bailey, it felt like the loneliest place in the world.

Documents and laptop computers were spread across the table and counter-terrorism police and MI5 agents were busily sharing intelligence and handing each other photographs and sheets of paper filled with information about terrorist suspects.

Bailey knew that trying to find Dexter was like searching for a lost coin in long grass. A job that needed more luck than skill.

'I want you to chase down every source you have, every rat hole that an Islamic Nation cell could be hiding in.' Tony Dorset was addressing the room, standing in front of the whiteboard with Mustafa al-Baghdadi's name and photograph on it. 'Three thousand active terrorist investigations. Twenty-three thousand persons of interest. We're looking for anyone with a suspected link to Mustafa al-Baghdadi.'

Bailey felt like he was sitting in a war room listening to a general talk about dropping bombs without knowing specific targets. It was useless. But Dorset wanted him there because, whether Bailey liked it or not, he knew more about Mustafa than anyone.

'If anyone fits the profile. If anyone has ever had any allegiance, suggested or otherwise, to Islamic Nation, then speak up!' Dorset told the room. 'Talk to me or talk to John Bailey. The clock's ticking on this, we don't know what the next play might be, we only know that it's coming.'

Ronnie Johnson appeared at the door with Ann Pritchard leading the way. They came straight over to Bailey.

'I'm sorry, Bailey,' Pritchard said. 'We'll find her.'

'Yeah, you better.'

'Anything more from the Met?' Dorset had joined them. London's Metropolitan Police had sent hundreds of cops to addresses all over the city looking for any sign of the blue van or the masked men who'd been at the wheel.

'They found the van,' Pritchard said. 'Set on fire in St John's Wood. Police are going through CCTV to see what they can find. Anything here, yet?'

'We're working on it.'

Pritchard and Dorset excused themselves to the corner of the room so that Dorset could update his boss on everything else, leaving Ronnie and Bailey standing together.

'We'll find her, bubba,' Ronnie said, resting one of his big hands on Bailey's shoulder.

'What makes you so sure?'

'I've got my people working on it too.'

'Yeah, well. I've seen how these things ...' Bailey stopped himself from finishing the sentence. 'And we've been in here for hours, already. Where the bloody hell have you been?'

'Working. We've got our own eyes and ears all over this city. It's why I'm telling you that we'll find her. This isn't Raqqa or Mosul. In this city, these guys are amateurs. Fanatics. They won't be able to hide in a concrete jungle for too long without getting noticed.'

'Mustafa's avoided you all so far.'

'Trust me, bubba.'

Over the next six hours, Bailey worked as hard as anyone in the room, answering random questions and studying photographs and files of people he'd never heard of before. There were empty pizza boxes and coffee cups piled in the corner along with plastic bags with half-eaten curry takeaways. The room was starting to smell like a sweaty kitchen in a cheap Brick Lane restaurant.

Ronnie was off chasing his own leads from whatever American assets he had thrown together in London. He'd promised to check back in with Bailey if anything moved.

Bailey looked at his watch. It was 1 am.

'You should go get cleaned up, get some rest.' Tony Dorset was standing beside Bailey with a plastic ID card in his hand. 'I cut you a security pass, means you can come and go.'

'I'm fine, mate.'

'You're not fine, Bailey, you've still got dried blood on the side of your neck and your clothes are a mess. I'm not saying don't come back. I'm just saying at least go get yourself cleaned up. We'll keep going here, don't worry.'

Bailey touched his neck and he could feel the crusted blood on his skin. He thought he'd wiped it away with the wet towel they'd given him hours earlier. His shirt was torn and stained with blood and dirt. Maybe Dorset was right. Bailey didn't feel like he was contributing much at the moment, anyway.

'Okay.' He took the security pass and lifted the lanyard over his neck. 'Thanks for this.'

He was halfway down the corridor when a voice called out to him.

'Mr Bailey!'

It was Ben. Bailey stopped and waited for him at the lifts.

'I'm sorry about what happened back there. I know that she was . . . is –'

'Forget it.' Bailey patted him on the shoulder. 'Wasn't your fault, kid. Just do me a favour: find her.'

'I'm not going home till we do.'

CHAPTER 52

The warm water needles of the shower felt good.

Bailey made a thick lather of soap with his hands and scrubbed his neck and face, watching the brown water circle down the drain at his feet. Dried blood turning to liquid.

Drying himself in front of the bathroom mirror, Bailey caught sight of the discolouration on the right side of his face where the guy in the mask had bashed him with the butt of his pistol. There were red and purple bruises on his chest and stomach too. The adrenalin had long gone and the pain was kicking in.

He swivelled his body and lifted his arm so that he could inspect his back. At least the burn was healing. A crusty scab had formed where the blistering skin had been.

Bailey leaned across the wash basin, patting his face with the towel, staring at the middle-aged man in the glass. A man he barely recognised. Greying hair, drooping eyes, weathered skin. A man who'd become a danger to anyone who got close to him. Gerald. Father Joe. Miranda. Now Dexter had been taken and he felt powerless to find her.

Whack!

His fist crashed into the mirror, splintering the glass like a spider's web.

Specks of blood were growing like miniature balloons on his knuckles. One by one, they popped, leaving a bloody trail down his fingers as they trickled into the white porcelain sink.

Bailey turned on the tap to wash away the blood and grabbed a small towel, wrapping it around his fist.

He looked at himself again, the face in the mirror distorted by splintered glass.

Bailey knew this guy. The damaged alcoholic loner who didn't sleep. He knew this guy, all right, and he loathed him.

Thud. Thud. Thud.

Bailey woke to the sound of someone bashing on the door of his hotel room.

Thud! Thud!

The knocks were getting louder.

He was lying down, flat on his back, naked on the bed. He looked at the clock on the bedside table. It was 3.07 am. He sat up, rubbing his eyes.

Thud! Thud! Thud!

An empty glass and four small bottles of whisky were sitting on the table next to the television. The brown liquid still inside. Bailey had just sat there, staring at them, wondering what kind of man hit the bottle after his girlfriend had been kidnapped.

Turns out that it wasn't him.

'Bailey, you in there?'

He recognised the voice, and the accent. He slid off the bed, onto the balls of his feet.

Ronnie was chewing on an unlit cigar when Bailey opened the door.

'Sorry, mate. Must've fallen asleep.'

'There's been a development. Get dressed.'

Bailey hadn't realised that he was naked in the open doorway. He didn't care. 'What is it?'

Ronnie handed him his phone.

'Oh my god.'

He was staring at a picture of Sharon Dexter, seated with her arms tied to a chair, a gag splitting her lips in a false smile. She was a tough woman. But there was no hiding the fear in her eyes. The helplessness. Bailey felt like he was going to vomit.

'Tell me you've got more than this,' Bailey said. 'Tell me you've got a fucking lead here, mate.'

'I do,' Ronnie said. 'Get something on.'

Bailey grabbed a pair of boxer shorts, socks and a flannelette shirt from his bag, quickly putting them on, along with the jeans that were lying, crumpled, on the floor next to his boots. He was dressed in under two minutes.

'Let's go.'

They walked past Ronnie's room next door and up the hallway to another room five doors away. Inside, a man and a woman were hunched over in front of computer screens. They looked up when the two men walked in, before turning their attention back to the screens.

'Got an address, yet?'

'We're close.' The woman sounded confident.

'Everyone, this is John Bailey,' Ronnie said. 'Bailey, this is everyone.'

This must have been the team that Ronnie had assembled when they'd arrived in London. Bailey hadn't even known that they were there, which was probably the idea.

The photograph of Dexter was up on the monitors on the table.

'What're we looking at?' Bailey said.

'This.' The woman was pointing at the window blind behind Dexter. 'We think we've found something. Watch this.'

She clicked the mouse a few times so that she could zoom in on the background. There was a small gap in the blind behind Dexter and, as she enlarged and enhanced the image, they could see outside onto the street.

All Bailey could see was a wall of red. 'What's that?'

'A bus,' the woman said.

'What does it tell us?' Bailey said.

'It's not the bus we're interested in.' She opened another image that showed the bus window, zooming in again. It was reflecting what looked like a house, or a shop, on the corner of the street opposite. There were objects stacked on the footpath that looked like white goods – washing machines, dishwashers – and a few people walking by.

Bailey couldn't believe his eyes. 'All this from the reflection in the window?'

'One thing I can tell you about the people holding Sharon Dexter is that they've got a bloody good camera,' she said. 'High-res. We've ripped a lot of detail.'

'I think I've found something.'

Bailey had forgotten about the guy sitting at the other side of the table, hidden behind his computer monitor.

'What is it, Raj?' Ronnie said.

'Almost, almost.' He was talking to himself. 'C'mon, baby, c'mon. Got it!'

They squeezed around the table so that they could all peer over Raj's shoulder.

He had two windows open on his screen. On the left, he had a program that looked like Google Earth and on the right, the grainy image of the house reflecting in the bus window. He adjusted the grainy image so that it was transparent, then dragged it across the screen and rested it on top of the other picture. A few more clicks and he was done.

'Holy shit,' Bailey said.

'And look there.' The woman was pointing at the white sign with black and red writing plastered to the brick wall of the house, or shop, on the corner.

First Avenue. W10.

'Great work, Raj,' she said.

'Where is it?' Ronnie said.

'The bus was travelling along Harrow Road.' Raj navigated the screen, giving them a view of the street where the bus must have been driving by. 'If I spin the aspect so that we're looking back at the house, we can be almost certain that the photograph was taken on the first floor of this building.'

Bailey was mesmerised by what had just happened. From a small crack in a window blind, they'd used the reflection in the window of a bus to identify the house where Dexter was sitting in a room tied to a chair.

'Harrow Road. West London. What are we talking . . . Ladbroke Grove? Kensal Town?' Bailey used to live around the corner at Maida Vale.

'Kensal Town.'

'What're we waiting for?' Bailey said.

'Kim,' Ronnie addressed the woman, taking control again. 'How many people can we mobilise?'

'The two of us and you makes three,' she said. 'At three in the morning, that's it. We'll tap the local CCTV cameras so we'll have eyes on the area when we're in the van. But as for the numbers . . . what about the Brits?'

Ronnie looked over at Bailey, who'd gone quiet. He was staring at the image of Dexter with the gag in her mouth. 'We'll get her back, bubba.'

'Ronnie, the Brits?' Kim asked again.

'I'll call Pritchard when we're on the way. I don't want them racing in and shooting up the place.'

'Mustafa al-Baghdadi's a pretty big target, shouldn't we –'

'Think I don't know that?' Ronnie cut her off. 'Smaller the team, the better. We need to presume there are bombs in that house. We don't know what else. And believe me . . . I want Mustafa more than anyone. He's the reason I'm not baiting my hook at my favourite fishing spot in Sydney. So don't tell me things I already know.'

'Okay, okay.' Kim held up her hands. 'Your way, then.'

Raj lifted a large duffel bag onto the bed, unzipping it. Inside was a stash of weapons – pistols, rifles, boxes of ammunition and kevlar vests. After double-checking the contents, he tossed in two laptops, zipped up the bag and slung it over his shoulder. 'Good to go.'

'I'm coming with you,' Bailey said to Ronnie.

'That's not a good idea.'

'I'm not giving you a choice.' Bailey knew that everyone – the Americans, the Brits – were all pumped up about the prospect of arresting, or killing, Mustafa al-Baghdadi. The only thing that mattered to Bailey was the woman in the chair. 'Sharon's in that room because of me. I'm coming.'

Kim was shaking her head. 'It's too dangerous.'

Ronnie was leading the mission. His call. 'Okay, bubba, but you're staying in the van.'

CHAPTER 53

It was just after 4 am and there was hardly anything on the road.

Bailey was sitting in the front passenger seat, watching the night, trying not to think about the absurdity of a guy like him riding in a van with a group of CIA agents armed to the teeth.

Within minutes they were passing Buckingham Palace, cutting through Green Park and on to Paddington, where they hit Harrow Road just after Maida Vale.

Streets that would soon be bustling with commuter traffic were virtually empty, apart from the garbage collectors and delivery vans trying to get a jump on the day.

Bailey could have named a dozen pubs within walking distance of the house where Dexter was possibly being held. These streets were his old stomping ground when he was *The Journal*'s Europe correspondent. The place where he used to stumble home. Where he broke down.

They parked the van outside a garage in a side street, about three hundred metres from the house. Close enough to move in, but not so close that they might be seen.

The trip from Millbank had taken them less than twenty minutes.

Inside the van looked like the control room at a TV station. Walls of monitors, computers and swivel chairs with headphones

351

hanging off the back. Raj was busily tapping away on his keyboard, trying to get the CCTV cameras up, while Kim and Ronnie plotted their next move.

'We go on foot from here.' Ronnie unzipped the bag and started handing out equipment. 'Rifles and pistols. Vests on.'

Bailey was watching them prepare in silence. He doubted that any of them had managed to get any sleep for almost twenty-four hours. It didn't show. Maybe it was the pills that he'd watched Kim dole out back at the hotel. Dexedrine, most likely. Something to turn up the senses and eliminate the threat of tiredness.

Ronnie checked the magazine in his Glock, tucking it into a holster on his waist. 'Any joy with the cameras, Raj?'

'Almost.' Seconds later, four small squares showing street scenes appeared on the screen in front of Raj. 'Here we go.'

Ronnie put a hand on Raj's shoulder, leaning in to get a better look. 'What am I seeing here?'

'These are the nearest cameras to the house on the corner of First Avenue. And that one . . .' Raj's finger touched one of the squares. 'That's the closest. It shows the back of the house. There's some kind of garage and rear access behind that wall.'

'That's our way in.'

Ronnie pulled a small box out of the bag and opened it, handing tiny pods to the other two. They followed Ronnie's lead, putting them in their ears.

'What do I do?' Bailey said.

'Stay here with Raj.'

Bailey wanted to argue. He needed to help. He couldn't shake the image of Dexter's terrified face from his mind. But the last thing he wanted to do was get in the way. What the hell did he know about raiding a house? The only place he'd ever broken into was his home in Paddington after he'd locked himself out.

'We're going to need to stay close.' Ronnie was talking to Kim. 'Remember, people are still tucked up asleep. Every sound will carry.' Ronnie was still fiddling with his earpiece as he spoke. 'We'll do a comms check when we're out of the van. Any questions?'

Everyone shook their heads.

Ronnie slid open the door and stepped onto the concrete, Kim in tow.

A car pulled in behind the van. Bailey poked his head out the door in time to see Tony Dorset climb out of a black BMW four-wheel drive. He headed straight for Ronnie and Kim, who were standing on the footpath in their vests, each holding an M4 carbine rifle, ready to go.

'What the fuck is this, Ronnie?'

Four more four-wheel drives pulled up, blocking off the street.

'This is exactly what I wanted to avoid,' Ronnie whispered loudly, pointing at all the cars. 'You try to blast your way in there and this thing's over before it begins.'

'Need I remind you that these are British streets. And we've had a little more experience with terrorism here than you guys.'

Bailey was out of the van, standing behind Ronnie.

'And what the fuck is he doing here?' Dorset was pointing at Bailey.

'He's staying with the van,' Ronnie said. 'Anyway, if you've got a better idea, then go ahead. You've got exactly thirty seconds.'

Bailey was confused about what was going on. One minute, Ronnie was running the show. The next, he was preparing to take orders from Tony Dorset.

Ronnie got distracted and touched his ear. 'Can you repeat that, Raj? Raj? I've got static, I can't hear you. Raj?'

They were so close to the van that Raj just stuck his head out the door. 'There's someone coming,' he whispered. 'A guy on the footpath. Sweatpants and a hoodie.'

'How far?'

Raj's head disappeared again as he checked the monitor. Then he was back. 'Fifty metres, maybe less.'

'Get in the van,' Ronnie said to Bailey. 'Everyone, out of sight.'

Bailey did what he was told and Ronnie climbed in beside him. The door of the van was still open and they could see the corner of Harrow Road through the side-mirror. Kim stayed outside, crouching behind the bonnet of one of the four-wheel drives.

The guy in the hoodie stopped at the corner, head down, like he was holding a phone, looking for directions. He turned and started walking along the footpath beside the vehicles.

'Okay,' Ronnie whispered. 'It's probably nothing, but we can't take the risk. Kim, you need to grab this guy.'

Kim stepped forward onto the footpath. She wasn't carrying her rifle, probably to avoid scaring him. 'Sir, can I have a quick word?'

The guy turned and started walking onto the road in between the cars.

'Sir?'

'Something's not right,' Ronnie whispered.

'Sir, if you'd just stop for a moment.' Kim followed the man's path onto the road, unclipping the Glock from the holster in her armpit. 'Sir, you need to stop, right now.'

Bailey couldn't see Kim anymore.

'Bomb! He's got a bomb!' The panic in Kim's voice was amplified by the still of night.

'Take him out!' Ronnie yelled.

Bang! Bang! Bang!

BOOM!

A light flashed outside and the force of the blast flipped the van onto its side, sending Bailey and Ronnie and Raj all bouncing into each other.

Bailey's ears were ringing and his vision was blurry from the flash. He started moving his limbs, one at a time, checking that nothing was broken. He could hear screaming outside the van and the crinkling, flickering sound of fire.

'Ronnie? Raj?' Bailey called out. 'Are you guys all right?'

The computers in the van were buzzing with static and the screens were riddled with cracks.

'We've got to get out,' Ronnie said. 'Raj, are you okay? Answer me, Raj?'

Raj was out cold. Blood was running down his face from a cut somewhere on his head.

'Raj?' Ronnie leaned in to listen to his breathing. 'He's alive.'

Ronnie turned Raj onto his side, feeling around his head to find out where the bleeding was coming from. 'It's just a scrape.'

'What the fuck just happened?' Bailey said.

Ronnie ignored the question and climbed over the front seat, pushing open the driver's door, like he was opening the hatch of a submarine. 'Bailey! Come on! We'll come back for Raj.'

Outside, there was a smoking crater in the road at least three or four metres wide. Three of the four-wheel drives had been flipped by the force of the blast. Metal was twisted, cars were on fire, two of them with black silhouettes of people inside. Dead. There were so many bodies on the ground and inside the burning vehicles that it was impossible to count them. The smell took Bailey back to Beirut and his first ever car bomb. The one that took out a president and ten others. It was the day he met Ronnie Johnson.

Bailey climbed down the side of the van onto the road and started looking around for survivors. There was a guy on his knees, clambering away from one of the burning vehicles. Bailey ran over to him, helping him to his feet, wondering how on earth he was still alive. He sat the guy down, away from the burning cars, and went looking for other survivors.

Ronnie was standing over the bodies of two of Dorset's team. They'd been crushed by the cascade of cars that piled into each other from the force of the bomb.

'Ronnie!' Kim was more than ten metres away, her vest torn and dented by shrapnel from the bomb, limping towards them, checking her arms and torso for any sign of injuries. She had been blown clear by the bomb. God knows how she'd survived.

'Are you okay?' Ronnie said.

'I'm not sure . . . I don't think anything's broken.'

Kim had pockmarks of blood on her cheek and chin. Ronnie ran his hands over her neck, arms and shoulders. 'You're one lucky woman,' he said. 'What the fuck happened?'

'I pulled my gun when he wouldn't answer . . . he had something in his hand . . . with wires coming from it.' Kim was speaking in short bursts, trying to catch her breath. 'A gun in his other hand . . . he just unloaded on me . . . I fired back as I leapt behind the car . . . trying to find some cover.'

'Ronnie!' Tony Dorset's head appeared at the front of a four-wheel drive that was lying on its side in front of them. He was trying to kick out what remained of the shattered windscreen so that he could get out. 'Give me a hand, would you?'

'Get back.' Ronnie climbed up onto the car, kicking at the windscreen until it folded in.

Dorset and two other men climbed out. One of them was Ben.

'You okay, kid?' Bailey said.

'I think so,' Ben said.

Dorset was straight onto his phone, calling for ambulances, firefighters and every cop in the area to get there. When he was done, he turned to Ronnie. 'We need to lockdown these streets, no one goes near the house.'

'They knew we were coming,' Ronnie said.

'What're you saying?'

'It took my team less than an hour to find the house after that image was posted. They wanted us here. This was a trap.'

Dorset was shaking his head. 'What the fuck have we walked into?'

'We need to move,' Ronnie said. 'We can't waste time.'

'No. We need to wait,' Dorset said.

'For what?' Bailey said. 'Dexter could still be in that house. Wait for what?'

'I've got another team on the way,' Dorset said.

Bailey didn't like it. 'How far?'

'Ten, fifteen minutes. No more.'

'No. No.' Bailey was shaking his head. He turned to Ronnie. 'Fuck this, mate. We've got to get to Sharon.'

Mustafa had probably rigged the place with explosives, or stationed some of his loyal lunatics inside with weapons. Or both. Every minute mattered.

'There's no "we" here, Bailey,' Dorset said. 'You're not going anywhere.'

'Don't you see what's going on here, Dorset?' Ronnie said. 'This attack was directed at you and your guys. If you send a special ops team charging through the front door then that house is likely to go boom.'

Dorset put up his hand 'Hang on, Ronnie . . . give me a minute to think.'

They didn't have a minute.

'We need a small team at this,' Ronnie said. 'Anything more, they'll see us coming.'

Ambulances had arrived and the street was being transformed into a triage centre, with people like Raj being treated in an area littered with smoking debris. The only uninjured people left were standing around Dorset, waiting for him to make a call.

'Okay.' Dorset relented. 'But you're not doing it alone. I'm in good shape, so's Ben. That makes four.'

'I'm coming too,' Bailey said.

'Don't be stupid,' Dorset said. 'You're staying here.'

Ronnie pulled Dorset aside, speaking quietly so that nobody else could hear. Then he climbed into the back of the overturned van, returning with a Glock in his hand. He held out the weapon to Bailey. 'Know how to use one of these, bubba?'

'No.'

'That's the safety.' Ronnie pointed to a small switch on the side of the gun, shifting it back and forth with his thumb. 'When the safety's pointing this way, it can't go bang. And the bullets come out this end.'

'Got it.' Bailey took the Glock and shoved it in the back of his jeans, like he'd seen people do in the movies. That was about all that he knew about guns.

'He's your responsibility,' Dorset said, pointing his finger at Ronnie.

'No problem.' Ronnie winked at Bailey. 'We've done this before.'

'Not quite,' Bailey said.

'At least you get a gun this time, bubba.'

They were standing outside the three-storey building on the corner of First Avenue, searching for signs of life inside.

Police had blocked off a large section of Harrow Road that ran from Elgin Avenue all the way to Queen's Park Library up on Fourth Avenue. The few uniformed officers who had arrived were going door-to-door evacuating people from the houses and apartments. Trying to explain to them why they needed to leave.

Bailey could see a woman in a pink dressing-gown looking down at the street from her flat above a hairdresser, woken by the loud bang that'd shaken the dust off her walls. The gunshots. Sirens. Screams. Her pale face illuminated by a street lamp detailing an expression of horror. Confusion. Fear. Wondering what had become of her street. Her city. Her home.

'How do you want to do this, Ronnie?' Dorset said.

They had all agreed that the house was most likely rigged with explosives, so they shouldn't attempt to go through any doors or windows. Front or back.

'Up there.' Ronnie was pointing at the skylight at the back of the house. 'We'll go in through the roof.'

'Dorset. Kim. You come with me,' Ronnie said. 'Ben, you head around the front of the house on Harrow Road in case anyone tries to make it out the front door. Rules of engagement, Dorset?'

'One warning, then shoot to kill.'

'Good,' Ronnie said, without hesitating.

Bailey felt the metal of the gun digging into the small of his back, pressing into his crusting burn. He wondered whether he could follow through on those rules. He doubted it. 'What do I do?'

'You'll be our eyes on the back of the house.'

Bailey nodded his head. 'I can do that.'

Ronnie wasn't finished. 'Anyone comes out that doesn't look like Sharon, or any of us – shoot them.'

CHAPTER 54

DEXTER

The explosion had felt like an earthquake, rattling windows, shaking floorboards, smashing plates and glasses in the kitchen.

Dexter knew it was a bomb because she'd seen the guy slip his arms through a suicide vest.

She'd also been forced to listen to him explain why he was happy to die. A one-way conversation because Dexter had been gagged so tightly that the cloth was stretching the corners of her mouth, slicing her skin.

All she could do was listen.

'We're under attack,' he'd said. 'The West is the root cause of all suffering in the Muslim world. Afghanistan, Iraq, Syria, Yemen . . . these are defensive wars. We're not instigating these battles. Our jihad is a response to the ongoing assault on Islam.'

Dexter had been raised by her father to question everything, but she had no way of trying to reach inside this young man's head to change his mind. Cleanly shaven and dressed to fit in, he spoke with such certainty about something so finite. Brainwash complete. The only way he was going to find out the truth was by dying. The jihadi's curse. No way back if you're wrong.

Dexter had counted three men in the house. Most of the time they spoke to each other in Arabic. When they spoke in English, they didn't care about using names in front of her. Thomas. Aydin. Qasim. Probably because she'd been kidnapped to die.

Dexter had no idea where she was. All she knew was that she was in some kind of split-level townhouse with white, crumbling walls, cracked floorboards, stained carpet and the type of furniture you'd find in a charity shop. She was being kept in a lounge room that adjoined a kitchen on the first floor. There was a television, a small wooden table and five chairs, including the one that she was sitting in. Otherwise, nothing. No pictures on walls. No coffee table. No books. No sound system. No family photographs. Nothing indicating that this place was anything more than a halfway house for terrorists.

They had untied her arms and legs only twice so that she could use the toilet on the lower floor, where she'd managed to see two suicide vests on a table in another room, as well as several bricks of C4 explosives, wire cables and too many rifles and pistols to count.

She had no idea what time it was when they took the photograph of her and uploaded it to the internet. But she knew that the second the image went live, something had been set in motion.

The men had knelt and prayed together, before hugging one another, like they were saying their last goodbyes.

Next came the weapons.

The two other men helped Aydin dress like it was his wedding day. The suicide vest was strapped to his torso, a black hoodie slipped over the top. A handgun in one pocket and the trigger for the bomb in the other. Then Aydin went out the door. A walking weapon.

Within minutes of the explosion up the street, Qasim came back up the stairs and sat in the same armchair opposite Dexter that Aydin had been preaching from earlier. He had a Kalashnikov rifle lying across his knees and a bomb strapped to his chest.

The second vest was for him.

And then Thomas appeared. A pistol in one hand and a laptop in the other. He knelt down in front of Dexter, opening the computer so that the screen was facing her. Seconds later the screen came to life and a man was staring back at her.

'Do you know who I am?'

Dexter froze. She knew exactly who he was. She'd seen enough photographs of this face to know that the person staring at her through a computer screen was Mustafa al-Baghdadi.

'Just nod.'

Dexter slowly nodded her head, unable to speak because of the gag in her mouth.

Mustafa looked nothing like the terrorist leader she'd seen in videos and grainy photographs. His beard was gone, his head shaven and he was wearing a hoodie.

'I can see you judging me.' He was stroking the stubble on his cheek, leaning closer to the camera. 'I'm freeing you, don't you see?'

Dexter felt the bile stinging her throat. She wanted to reach through the screen and slam his head against the table in front of him.

'Let me show you something.'

Mustafa clicked a button on his keyboard and the screen split into four video streams, the terrorist leader top right. The three other feeds showed different camera angles of burning vehicles, at least two of them flipped onto their sides.

'It's beautiful, isn't it?'

Dexter could see people staggering on the road in the darkness, the flames occasionally flickering light on their faces.

'Can you see him?' Mustafa squinted, looking away from the camera lens, studying his screen. 'I think I see him. Can you?'

Dexter looked harder and glimpsed Bailey, his unmistakable mop of hair, square shoulders. That crappy old leather jacket he always wore. He was standing beside two other men. One of them was tall. Ronnie Johnson. Maybe.

And then she saw the bodies. One. Two. Four. There must have been more. A convoy of police vehicles. The rescue mission. Aydin's target.

Dexter bit down hard on the gag, rocking against her restraints in the chair.

'You know, where you're sitting now is just how it was with your friend, John Bailey. He was stubborn, like you. He didn't want to listen. He didn't want to know. Has he told you much about his time with my men in Iraq?'

She didn't flinch. She didn't want to give Mustafa the satisfaction of discovering that she knew all about Bailey's ten months in captivity. The torture.

'You think you're winning.' Mustafa was shaking his head, an unhinged smile on his face. 'No. No, you're not winning. We're at war, don't you see? Islam existed without any warring doctrine for more than a decade until the Prophet's *hijrah* from Mecca to Medina to escape persecution. From that day, we've always been at war. We always will be at war. The Prophet made it so. People being attacked are expected to fight back in defence. Are they not? We're not the aggressor.'

Dexter had already been forced to listen to the guy with the bomb strapped to his chest, now she was copping a sermon from the man who'd planted the sickness in his head.

'The United Nations, the World Bank . . . they're just tools of modern colonialism. Western governments are trying to destroy us. You stand for nothing. You know no God. Jihad only requires soldiers. There are one billion Muslims. The soldiers are many.'

Dexter was staring at the video feeds of the bomb attack up the street, knowing that it must have been close. The blast had happened only minutes after Aydin had left the house.

The split-screen disappeared again and all she could see was Mustafa.

'My soldiers are ready to die for their beliefs, are you?'

The screen went black.

Thomas calmly picked up the laptop from the carpet and went downstairs, leaving Qasim sitting in the chair in front of her.

His English wasn't as good as the others. He just sat there, beads of sweat forming on his brow. His eyes were empty and cold. He must have been barely twenty years old.

You don't have to do this, Dexter wanted to tell him. *You're just a kid. Kids make mistakes. There's still time.*

The other guy was probably rigging the C4 to every entry point he could think of, preparing for when the cops stormed the house.

Dexter couldn't stand the thought of what was about to unfold, wondering how many people had died up the street. How many more would die trying to save her.

Hope was all she had left.

Click.

Qasim sat up, startled by the foreign sound, trying to figure out where it had come from.

Click.

It sounded like a door creaking on its hinges.

Qasim got out of his chair and walked across the room behind Dexter. She couldn't turn around, but she could hear him pushing back the blind so that he could peer out the window at the street. When he reappeared, he raised his index finger to his lips. A warning for her to keep quiet. Not that she could make much noise, gagged and strapped to a chair.

Click.

The sound was coming from the kitchen.

Qasim raised his Kalashnikov and walked, slowly, towards the open door. The kitchen was only five metres away, but it was taking him forever. He was moving slowly to prevent his shoes from squeaking on the frayed and flattened carpet.

The kitchen light had been switched off. It was still dark outside, so the only light was from the dust-stained yellow globe hanging above Dexter's head in the lounge room.

Qasim was at the door now, pointing his rifle at the dirty dishes piled in the sink and the microwave that had heated up their dinner. He switched on the light.

Dexter saw the shadow before Qasim did – a flicker of movement from the skylight in the kitchen roof. Qasim looked up, his Kalashnikov travelling slower than his eyes.

Bang! Bang!

He fell to the floor, his weapon clunking onto the lino beside him.

Lying flat on his back, his right hand was still moving, feeling for the detonator that had slipped from his palm and was dangling at the end of a wire inches from his fingers.

He's got a bomb! Shoot him again! Again! Dexter was trying to scream, bouncing up and down in her chair.

Bang! Bang! Bang!

Qasim went limp after three more bullets were embedded in his body – two in his chest, one in his head. Whoever was up there had killed people before.

Ronnie Johnson dropped through the skylight, landing on the floor with a loud thud. He had his Glock in both hands, swinging it around the room, searching for another target.

He kicked away the rifle from beside Qasim and, briefly, got down on one knee so that he could feel for a pulse in his neck.

'Any others?'

Dexter nodded, gesturing with her head towards the staircase to her left.

'How many? One? Two?'

Dexter nodded, then shook her head.

'One?'

She nodded again.

Ronnie was pointing his gun at the top of the staircase.

'We got one more in here!' He yelled.

A woman that Dexter didn't recognise dropped onto the floor beside Ronnie. He tapped the air with his fingers and within seconds she'd fanned across the other side of the room, giving them two positions to take down anyone who came up the staircase.

The woman was standing beside Dexter. With her gun in one hand pointed at the stairs, she withdrew a knife from her belt and sliced through the gag wrapped around Dexter's head.

Dexter coughed, spitting a ball of cloth onto the floor.

'There's . . . there's . . .' She swallowed to help with her speech. 'There's another guy, heavily armed. And they've got enough C4 to take down the entire block.'

A few more seconds and the woman had cut through the rest of Dexter's restraints.

Dexter had been in that position for so many hours that it took her two goes to get up out of the chair. The woman handed her the Glock she had been using and then knelt, grabbing the compact Sig Sauer she'd strapped to her ankle.

'I've fired six rounds, which means you've got nine left. Take this.' She handed Dexter a spare magazine. 'In case you need it.'

'Thanks.' Dexter took the weapon and the extra bullets, and followed the woman closer to the staircase, waiting for Ronnie's call.

'You good?' Ronnie whispered.

Dexter nodded.

Ronnie turned his head back to the kitchen. 'Stay up there, Dorset! Weapons and explosives in here, keep an eye on the back door.'

There was a noise on the stairs and Dexter could just make out the top of Thomas's blond head, the flashes from his gun.

Bang! Bang!

One of the bullets hit Dexter in the shoulder and she fell back against the wall.

'Get down!'

Kim pushed Dexter further out of the way and started firing.

Bang! Bang! Bang!

Next they heard the sounds of footsteps racing down the stairs and a window being smashed.

'Kim, stay with Dexter.' Ronnie moved towards the top of the stairs, the gun in his hand leading the way. There was a splash of blood on the wall. Kim had hit him. A flesh wound. Bad enough to make him run for it, not enough to kill him.

Struggling for breath, Dexter was slumped on the carpet, back to the wall, using her fingers to find the hole in her shoulder, trying to assess where it had hit. Whether there was an exit wound.

'Just breathe.' Kim was kneeling beside her. 'We'll get you out of here.'

The bullet was just wide of her heart and Dexter could feel the warm blood rushing across her breast, down her stomach.

She could feel Kim's hand on her now, pushing down hard on the wound. 'You've got to breathe.'

Dexter let her head rest against the wall. The skin of her forehead felt like dead weights on her eyes, so she closed them.

'No. No. Eyes open, Sharon.' Kim was tapping her on the cheek. 'Stay with me. Keep breathing. Stay with me.'

'He's gone!'

Ronnie came running back up the stairs, yelling at the open skylight in the roof.

'Dorset! Gunman's on the move!'

Bailey had counted ten gunshots from inside the house and he was hoping to hell that Dexter hadn't been hit by any of them.

He was kneeling behind a car across the road from the house on First Avenue. It was a beaten-up old sedan that reminded him of the Corolla – God rest its soul. Pieces of gravel on the footpath were digging into his knees. He needed to stay low, out of sight, like he'd said he would. Bailey was in the exact spot where Ronnie had told him to position himself before he'd climbed up the high dividing wall of the terraced house and onto the roof with Dorset and Kim.

Although it was dark, the moonlight and street lamps gave Bailey a good view of everything he needed to see. The back door, windows and the skylight position on the roof, where Tony Dorset was kneeling, looking down into the house, talking to someone.

Dorset was still looking down when a guy smashed a window on the floor below and leapt out, landing heavily on the corrugated iron roof of the cheap extension at the back of the house. In the dim light it looked like he was carrying a gun. Bailey kept his position at the rear of the car, following him as he moved. The man was limping, but it didn't stop him from jumping – albeit awkwardly – onto the brick retaining wall.

'Stop! Drop the gun!' Dorset called out from his position on the roof. He had a rifle pointed at the guy on the wall and he looked like he was about to shoot.

Bang! Bang!

Dorset missed. The guy jumped off the wall and onto the footpath, losing his balance and falling onto one knee. He stood up, his back to the wall, shielding himself from any more bullets from Dorset's rifle. He was less than fifteen metres from Bailey, nervously looking from side to side, wondering which way to run. Bailey couldn't let him get away. He'd asked to be involved, and now he needed to do something.

'Mate!' Bailey called out from his position across the road. 'Drop your gun, would you!'

Bang! Bang! Bang! Bang!

The bullets sprayed the car, covering Bailey with shattered glass and making him fall onto his backside.

'Fuck me,' he said to no one. He really was bad at this.

The guy started walking towards the car that was shielding Bailey, dragging his left foot along the road, firing his weapon. More bullets pelted into the car, like hailstones hitting a tin roof in a storm. The bloke must have figured that Bailey was a cop, not some washed-up journo who'd never held a gun before, let alone fired one.

Bailey had no choice but to fire back. He pointed the gun across the boot of the car, squeezing the trigger.

Bang!

The metal jolted in his hand and he could feel the recoil in his shoulder joint, tensing his neck.

He peered over the car. He'd missed and the guy was getting closer.

Bang! Bang!

Two more bullet holes punched into the car.

Bailey flung his arm up onto the paintwork and squeezed the trigger again.

Bang!

He kept squeezing until all he could hear was the clicking sounds of an empty chamber. He tossed the gun onto the ground. It was useless now.

The footsteps were still coming, rounding the back of the car, confirming that Bailey had missed again. What the fuck did he know about firing guns, anyway? This was a bad idea.

The guy was coming for him.

Bailey bent down so that he could see which direction the guy's feet were moving around the car. At least he was travelling slowly, one foot scraping the road.

He was only a few metres away. Five more steps and he'd be standing right beside him.

Bailey had to move.

He took off for the front of the car, bending low so that the guy would need to shoot through metal panels to hit him. He raised his head, peering through the windows. Nothing. The guy must have been bending down, or hunched over. Bailey could hear his feet moving, scraping the pavement, metres away. Only the shell of a bullet-riddled car between them.

Bailey had made it to the rear of the car again, hoping the other guy was at the front. He wasn't. He appeared out of nowhere, right in front of him, gun pointing at Bailey's head.

Bailey stared into the little black hole, the world slowing down. He was fucked. He closed his eyes.

Bang!

Bailey felt nothing.

He opened one eye just in time to see the second bullet smack into the guy's shoulder, knocking him backwards, forcing him to lower the arm holding his pistol. He tried to raise his hand again. He couldn't. It wasn't working right.

Bailey started running, circling around the other side of the car, clinging to the metal panels for cover. The gunman was staggering after him, switching his gun into his other hand, firing randomly.

Bang! Bang!

One bullet hit the car and Bailey heard the other one zing past his head and into the wall behind him.

Bang! Bang! Bang!

The gunman dropped to the road, his head making a loud cracking sound as his skull crashed into the bitumen.

'Bailey! Are you hit?'

It was Ben.

Bailey stood up. He could see Ben standing over the dead body of the guy who'd tried to kill him.

'He's dead!' Ben called out to his boss on the roof.

Bailey looked up at the house, where the lone figure of Tony Dorset was standing, his rifle trained on the dead terrorist on the road, like he was ready to kill him all over again.

CHAPTER 55

'Where is she?'

Before Dorset could answer, Bailey spotted Ronnie climbing through the window at the back of the house with a body slung over his shoulder.

Dexter.

'We need an ambulance here!'

Ben was already on his radio calling one in as Ronnie ran along the back wall, balancing Dexter's slight frame like she weighed no more than a child.

'Front door, every fucking door, is rigged to blow!' Ronnie yelled. 'No one goes inside!'

By the time Ronnie had reached the edge of the wall, Dorset was down on the footpath beside Ben, ready to receive her. Bailey was there too. They each grabbed limbs, lowering her to the pavement.

'Sharon. Sharon. Sharon!' Bailey was studying her face, trying to see if she was alive.

Nothing.

'Bullet wound in the shoulder!' Ronnie called down from the wall.

Dorset placed two fingers on her neck. 'She's alive, Bailey. We need to get her to a hospital.'

The flashing blue lights of an ambulance flickered on the wall beside them and seconds later it skidded to a halt.

'Jesus, Sharon.' Bailey had one hand on her cheek, pressing the other on the source of the blood flow. 'Stay with me.'

'Move! Move!'

Two guys with a stretcher bounced out of the ambulance, pushing Dorset and Bailey to the side. Within seconds, they had Dexter lying flat on the stretcher, lifting her through the back doors of the ambulance.

'I'm coming.'

'Sorry, sir.' One of the paramedics tried to block Bailey from climbing in. 'You'll need to meet us there.'

'No,' Bailey shot back. 'I'm coming. I won't get in the way. She's my . . . my . . .'

What were they? Bailey didn't even know how to describe the life they had together. He only knew that he needed her. That he didn't want to lose her.

The guy took a split second to read the expression on Bailey's face before deciding that it wasn't worth the fight. 'Okay.'

The doors slammed shut and Bailey moved to the corner of the van so that the paramedics could do their thing. With scissors, they cut away her clothes and bra, revealing a small, fleshy hole in her upper chest. The dark-red blood was seeping out of a gunshot wound that was surrounded by black and purple skin.

'She's still bleeding heavily.'

One of the paramedics injected Dexter with something and her head rolled to the side so that she was facing Bailey.

He felt useless. Staring at her expressionless face. Mouth open. Strands of hair plastered to her blood-stained cheek.

She opened her eyes.

'Sharon. Sharon. Sharon.' Bailey quickly reacted. 'It's okay. We're getting you to a hospital.'

He found her hand on the side of the stretcher and held it tight, squeezing it as he spoke to her. 'I'm here. I'm not going anywhere. I'm here now.'

And he meant it. After all these years, he was there. In this moment. Watching the woman that he loved fighting for her life, battling for every breath. She wasn't alone.

The corners of her mouth dipped sideways and her eyes narrowed. 'You . . . you . . .'

She was trying to say something.

'Don't, Sharon,' Bailey said. 'Just hang on. Don't try to talk. We'll get through this.'

She ignored Bailey's instructions.

'You've done good . . . Bailey.' She closed her eyes again, her head slumping on the mattress.

'Sharon! Sharon!'

'Mate!' One of the paramedics put his hand on Bailey's arm. 'She's still with us . . . she's lost a lot of blood. She'll be on the operating table in ten. You've got to let us do our job.'

Bailey didn't want to let go of her hand but he knew he had to. He needed to get out of the way, let these guys do everything they could to save her.

He just wished that she could still see him. Hear him. Listen to all the things that he needed to say. The things he'd never said. Like 'I love you'.

CHAPTER 56

It had taken sixteen hours.

Sixteen hours for Mustafa al-Baghdadi's London terrorist network to be obliterated.

Once the bomb squad had cleared the house in Kensal Town, investigators had discovered a treasure trove of information.

Names. Places. Weapons. Plans.

British police had spent the day raiding properties across the city. At least two dozen terrorists had either been killed or arrested. More attacks had been foiled.

The house in Kensal Town was only the beginning.

The number of officers killed in the suicide bombing on the street had risen to eight. Six men and two women. It was the largest single attack on British police in history.

Bailey felt sick thinking about it. Fathers, mothers, sons and daughters who wouldn't be going home tonight. Heroes who'd died fighting against a rotten cause. They would be written about, talked about, their names etched in stone. Nothing would bring them back.

And Mustafa al-Baghdadi was still out there. A ghost.

Sixteen hours.

That was how long Bailey had sat at University College Hospital at Westmoreland Street, his nostrils caked with the sterile smell of antiseptic and cleaning products. His vision distorted by the bright neon lighting of the hospital's hallways. Watching people wheeled in on stretchers. Motorcycle accidents. Stabbings. Police injured in other London raids.

'Mr Bailey.'

Bailey was slumped in his chair and he hadn't noticed the doctor standing in front of him.

He stood up. 'How's she doing, doc?'

'I'm sorry.'

'What d'you mean?'

Dexter had been 'lucky', they'd told him, because the bullet had missed her heart. The operation was about extracting the bullet, patching her up, transfusing some blood.

'I'm sorry, Mr Bailey. She's dead.'

'No.' He was shaking his head. 'No. That can't be right.'

The doctor put his hand on Bailey's elbow. 'Is there someone we can call for you?'

Bailey didn't respond. Not another word. His blank stare telling the doctor all that he needed to know about what Sharon Dexter had meant to John Bailey.

He walked through the hospital doors towards the taxi rank, dizzy with the news that had just been delivered to him by the tired doctor with sad, drooping eyes.

'Where to, guv?'

'I don't know, mate. Away from here.'

Bailey closed the door and rested his head against the window.

The sun had risen and set again by the time the driver was taking him away from the hospital. 'How about a drive along the river then, hey guv?'

'Yeah. Good, idea.'

There was something about London cabbies. Something special. Proud people who knew their city, their passengers.

'Only thing I need to know, guv . . . which way when I hit the Thames? We going east, or west?'

The driver had a thick cockney accent that Bailey could have listened to all night. Reassuring, friendly. Someone Bailey could trust. He didn't know why, but that's what he thought.

'West, mate. Thanks.'

The gentle hum of the engine was vibrating through Bailey's head like a Buddhist mantra. Calming. Almost hypnotic.

'You want to talk about it, guv?'

Bailey could see the driver's eyes in the rear-vision mirror.

'I lost someone.'

Dexter would want him to talk about it. She'd hated how he'd shut down, keep her out. Hide from his problems until they'd boiled over.

'Someone special, eh?'

'Something like that.'

It was after ten o'clock and the streets were empty. Barely a vehicle on the road. The cab driver could be steering the car from side to side across the lanes and he wouldn't hit a thing. Not only that, but the footpaths were empty too.

'Where the hell are all the people?'

'Inside. Off the streets.' The driver's eyes were darting between the road and the guy in the back seat. 'You're my first ride for hours. It's a travesty what's happening to this city. All those terror raids . . . people are too afraid to go out. And then they put out a picture of that fella from Islamic Nation.'

'What?'

'Who'd have thought . . . Controlled half of bloody Iraq and Syria, now he's on the run in old Blighty. Can't make it up, guv.'

'No. You can't.'

They drove on again in silence until Bailey spotted something out the window that was calling for him.

'I'm going to get out here, mate.' Bailey rummaged through his jacket for his wallet, poked a tenner through the glass.

'Take care of yourself.'

Bailey watched the car pull away up the street towards Waterloo Bridge and then turned around and walked in the opposite direction, down a side street and into the little shop with the yellow sign out front.

Bailey looked up at the shelf behind the guy manning the counter until he found what he was looking for.

'Bottle of single-malt, mate.' Bailey was pointing at the dusty bottle of Glenfiddich on the top shelf. 'The big one.'

Bailey walked out of the shop towards Waterloo Bridge, nursing the bottle in his hand in a brown paper bag.

He still hadn't opened it by the time he hit the river. He hadn't decided whether or not he would. He was just going to walk along the Thames towards his hotel. Take his time. Suck in the air. Maybe sit on a bench and take a few swigs from the bottle in his hand, when it called for him. Think about Dexter. The woman that he'd let down.

I don't love anyone else.

What a fucking idiot. A coward. Of course, he loved her.

In her heart, maybe she knew. He'd hang on to that thought. Tell himself that it was true.

Bailey stopped walking, leaning against the wall, looking out over the water, placing the bottle on the ground beside him.

A light drizzle was falling and it was getting cold. Bailey zipped up his jacket, lifting his collar to his ears, resting both elbows on the wall. He watched a water taxi zip along the river, wishing he was on it. Wishing he was being taken somewhere else. Anywhere but here.

After a day like this one, he'd usually be hunched over a keyboard writing a story about what he'd seen. Not this story. Not any story. Not anymore.

Standing in the open air, Bailey didn't know whether to keep walking, or turn back around and go somewhere else. But where?

He looked at his watch. 10.16 pm. This was London. *London*. Streets that would usually be bustling were virtually empty. Buses passed by with only a handful of passengers on board. No young revellers racing to the next nightspot. No couples enjoying a post-dinner walk along the river. Terrorism had done strange things to this city. It was keeping people inside. Away from the danger. Away from the fear.

The rain was seeping through his hair, coating his skin. The night breeze caused him to shiver. Everything about the night felt wrong.

His right hand was still numb from what had happened at Kensal Town. Bailey had never fired a gun before and, almost seventeen hours later, his hand was still tingling from the entire magazine that he'd unloaded at the bloke who'd tried to kill him. Maybe it was his mind playing tricks on him but the strange buzzing sensation just wouldn't go away.

Bailey felt another tingle. A vibration in his pocket. He pulled out his phone and saw Ronnie's name flashing on the screen. By now, Ronnie would have heard about Dexter. Bailey didn't want to talk about it. Not with Ronnie. Not with anyone. Telling the cab driver was enough to have made it real. Now Bailey just wanted to be alone.

He looked down at the brown paper bag on the stone beside him. If there was ever a night when Bailey had deserved a tipple, this was it.

He grabbed the bottle and kept walking, under Hungerford

Bridge, alongside Whitehall Gardens. He stopped again when he spotted the London Eye on the other side of the river. The moonlight was enough to illuminate the white metal beams of the big circle that was suspended in the sky like a giant dream catcher. Too late to catch the nightmare that had befallen Bailey.

A few minutes passed before Bailey realised that there was someone standing beside him. A guy dressed in a black tracksuit, staring out over the river, close enough to start a conversation, but not so close that he needed to.

Bailey started walking again but before he had managed a few paces he heard a scraping sound behind him.

He turned just in time to see the knife shimmering in the light above his head. Bailey stepped back, holding up his hands in defence, deflecting the guy's hand and the blade that was spearing towards his throat.

'What the fuck!'

The guy in the tracksuit wrestled Bailey to the ground, straddling him like a jockey, pushing down on the knife.

The tip of the blade pierced the ball of Bailey's shoulder, delivering a sharp pain as the blade cut deeper, slashing the skin down his arm.

Bailey had both hands locked around the guy's wrist, pushing the knife away from his shoulder and out of his flesh.

Bailey caught a glimpse of the man's face in the struggle. His eyes. Mustafa al-Baghdadi. Beardless and with a shaved head.

'Get the fuck off me!'

Bailey struggled beneath him, trying to drive the knife away from his neck.

'I'm going to kill you,' Mustafa said, his voice rising with each word.

'Help!' Bailey screamed to no one.

'You killed my wife! My son!'

'You're bloody insane!' Bailey said. 'Fucking lunatic. Get off me!'

'I should have hanged you off a bridge in Mosul.'

Mustafa took one hand off the knife, taking a swing, his fist crashing into Bailey's cheekbone, splitting his skin. The shock of the blow made Bailey loosen his grip and the knife speared towards his neck. He only just managed to divert it at the last moment and the blade cut into his shoulder again. Deeper. The warm blood making his shirt stick to his skin.

Mustafa punched him again. This time Bailey was ready and the knife stayed steady, hovering above him, shivering under the pressure of the struggle.

Bailey turned his head to his left, then his right, searching for anything that he could use as a weapon. There was nothing but an old soft drink can and pages from a newspaper, blowing along the path.

With both hands back on the knife, Mustafa was pushing down, the blade edging close to the Adam's apple jutting from Bailey's neck.

Bailey noticed the brown paper bag sitting upright next to the wall. Inches from his hand. A weapon. He grabbed the bottle by the neck and crashed it into the side of Mustafa's head. The glass smashed, spraying the two men with the sweet-smelling liquid and shards of the shattered bottle.

Bailey still had hold of the bottle. All that was left was a row of jagged glass teeth. He rammed it into the side of Mustafa's neck, driving deep. He withdrew the stem and stabbed him again, this time in the side of his stomach. And again. And again.

The knife fell from Mustafa's hand, making a clanging sound on the stone. His eyes wide open with the shock of what had just happened. Still sitting on Bailey, he reached for his neck, trying to stop the blood flow with his hand.

Mustafa was looking down on Bailey, trying to speak. All that he could manage was a popping sound, each word muffled by his own blood choking him, filling his lungs.

Bailey pushed him off and Mustafa fell flat on the floor beside him. He was almost limp, barely moving, although there was life still left in his eyes.

Using the arm of his uninjured shoulder, Bailey sat up so that he could look Mustafa in the face. One last time.

After everything that Mustafa al-Baghdadi had done, all that he'd preached, he'd surrendered to a most basic instinct. Revenge. And he'd lost.

'Bubba!'

Ronnie appeared out of nowhere, dropping to his knees beside Bailey.

'Are you cut? Injured?'

Bailey could feel his shirt, covered in blood and whisky, clinging to his body. He didn't know how deep the knife had cut into his shoulder. It felt like a flesh wound. Like most of the blood was coming from Mustafa.

'A cut . . . I'm not sure. Don't think it's too bad.'

'Is he dead?'

'Fucked if I know, mate.'

Ronnie shuffled on his knees to his right, feeling for a pulse, before reaching for his phone. 'I need an ambulance at Victoria Embankment, by the river next to Horseguards . . . two men injured, one critical.'

Ronnie tore off his jacket and wrapped it tightly around Mustafa's neck. 'You got him good, bubba. How'd you –'

'Bottle of single-malt. Best thing I've ever done with it.'

Sitting up against the wall, Bailey was feeling light-headed. He reached for his shoulder and felt an open flap of skin, the blood soaking his chest and arm.

'Actually, mate, I'm in a bit of trouble here.'

Ronnie slid over to Bailey, inspecting his wound. 'Keep the pressure on, bubba. You'll be okay. Won't be long.'

'How'd you find me, Ronnie?'

They could already hear a siren in the distance, getting closer.

'You didn't take my call. I looked up where you were. That phone Dorset gave you. One of the features.'

The bait.

Bailey should have been pissed, only he wasn't. He was angrier about the fact that Ronnie appeared to be doing everything he could to keep Mustafa from bleeding-out on the footpath beside them. If anyone had deserved to die, it was this guy.

'What are you doing?'

'I want him alive.'

EPILOGUE

The glazed arched roof at Paddington Station was like a big iron rainbow with white light beaming through the glass panels onto the orange and grey tiles below. It was so bright outside that the lights dangling from the roof needn't have been switched on, although Bailey had known London long enough to expect that a thick cloud could blanket the city at any time, and probably would.

He looked up at the old iron clock: 2.59 pm. The train to Portsmouth was due to depart in six minutes.

It had been four days since Bailey had listened to a doctor tell him that the woman that he loved was dead. Dexter's body had been loaded into the cargo-hold of a plane that morning. Bailey wasn't going home to bury her. He still blamed himself for her death and nothing was going to change that. Not the commiserations from friends and colleagues. Not even a hug from his daughter.

In the end, Gerald had been the one who'd told him that it was okay not to come. Gerald knew that his old friend needed some time. And he trusted Bailey not to go off the rails, threatening to hop on a plane and personally come to England if he did. Gerald had done it before.

The New South Wales Police service would look after the funeral arrangements and Gerald said that he would assist in any

384

way that he could, now that he was out of hospital, albeit with a large scar in his neck.

'I think I can match it, by the way,' Bailey had said when they'd spoken on the phone that morning.

'What?'

'That little scar of yours.'

The knife attack from Mustafa had opened up two large gashes in Bailey's shoulder. Luckily, there wasn't much damage to the tendon and doctors were expecting him to get all of his movement back. But right now Bailey's right arm was in a sling, taking the pressure off the eighteen stitches in his shoulder. Gerald only had six.

Gerald had dismissed the quip with a question. 'Where will you go?'

'Got a cousin down Hampshire way.'

'Hampshire?'

'She's got a pub. Says she'll give me a room, I might even help out behind the bar.'

Gerald laughed, awkwardly. 'You, working in a pub?'

'She'd be foolish not to utilise my experience.'

'Just don't sample too much of the merchandise.'

'Doesn't work for me anymore.'

'Good . . .' Gerald said. 'Bailey, one more thing?'

Bailey could hear the change in Gerald's voice and he knew what was coming.

'It wasn't your fault, you know that, right?'

'Yeah, sure,' Bailey said. 'Look after Miranda for me. I told her I'm all-in for the wedding. Just make sure she knows, okay?'

'What are we talking, weeks, months?'

'I'll be back to walk her down the aisle.'

With that, Bailey had hung up.

Word hadn't gotten out that John Bailey had been attacked by Mustafa al-Baghdadi alongside the Thames. It never would. According to British authorities, the incident had never happened. Tony Dorset had arranged for a media release to go out from the Metropolitan Police saying something about a drug deal that had gone wrong. A cover story aiming to blow any attention away from Bailey and let the Brits concoct a tale about how they'd managed to take down the world's most wanted terrorist in a daring raid on a house in North London.

Ronnie Johnson was okay with the Brits claiming the credit because he'd also gotten what he'd wanted. Mustafa al-Baghdadi was alive.

The big Oklahoman had visited Bailey in hospital a few days ago and told him that he wouldn't be seeing him for a while. Bailey hadn't bothered asking why because he knew the answer. Ronnie was about to escort Mustafa al-Baghdadi on a military plane to a CIA black site somewhere like Poland, Romania or Afghanistan.

Bailey didn't like thinking about this side of Ronnie, knowing that he'd crossed a line a long time ago. A line that enabled him to do bad things to bad people for the greater good.

A whistle sounded on the platform as a train snaked its way along the tracks beside him. It was a thing of beauty. The black edges and yellow paintwork surrounding the tinted glass of the driver's carriage made it look like an oversized racing helmet. The guy sitting in the front seat, slowly bringing it to a halt, had one of the best jobs in the world. An adventure every day. Getting out of the city, away from the hustle. His job was as clear as the winter sun in Baghdad. He had a purpose.

Bailey used to be just like him. Now that part of him was gone. *You've done good.*

Dexter's last words had been repeating over and over in his mind.

What now, Sharon? Where to from here?

The doors closed and the whistle sounded again.

Today he was on his way to Hampshire.

He had no idea about the rest.

ACKNOWLEDGEMENTS

Firstly, I'd like to thank everyone at Simon & Schuster Australia for your encouragement and support, particularly Fiona Henderson, and editor, Deonie Fiford, for workshopping ideas and pushing me to make *State of Fear* the best book possible. I'd like to single out my 'reader in chief,' David 'Mac' McInerney, for always being poised with his pen, and my other ever-reliable reader, Gavin Fang, for his friendship and encouragement. Thanks also to Stan Grant for his advice and insights along the way, and to the brave reporters around the world who often put their lives at risk to tell the ghastly truth about Islamic terrorism. And special thanks to my wife, Justine, and our children, Penelope and Arthur, for filling our house with laughter and love.

ABOUT THE AUTHOR

Tim Ayliffe has been a journalist for 25 years and is the Managing Editor of Television and Video for ABC News and the former Executive Producer of *News Breakfast*. His day job in journalism has proven to be the perfect research ground for writing global thrillers. He is the author of the 'John Bailey' series including *The Greater Good*, *State of Fear*, *The Enemy Within* and his most recent novel, *Killer Traitor Spy*. Ayliffe's thrillers have also been optioned for TV. When he's not writing or chasing news stories, Ayliffe watches rugby and surfs. He lives in Sydney.

Also in the John Bailey series

'Ayliffe delivers a taut, nail-biting page-turner, stamping
his mark on the modern day Australian thriller.'
BETTER READING

TIM AYLIFFE
THE GREATER GOOD

A JOHN BAILEY THRILLER

TIM
AYLIFFE

THE
ENEMY
WITHIN

A JOHN BAILEY THRILLER

TIM AYLIFFE

AN OLD WAR HAS A NEW BATTLEGROUND

KILLER TRAITOR SPY

A JOHN BAILEY THRILLER